"*To Catch a Bride* is Anne Gracie at her best, with a dark and irresistible hero, a rare and winsome heroine, and a ravishing romance. Catch a copy now! One of the best historical romances I've read in ages."

—Mary Jo Putney, *New York Times* bestselling author of
Loving a Lost Lord

Praise for
His Captive Lady

"With tenderness, compassion, and a deep understanding of the era, Gracie touches readers on many levels with her remarkable characters and intense exploration of their deepest human needs. Gracie is a great storyteller."

—*Romantic Times*

"Once again, author Anne Gracie has proven what an exceptionally gifted author is all about . . . She gives life to unforgettable characters and brings her readers along for the ride in what has proven to be an exciting, fun, and heartfelt emotional journey. Absolutely one of the best romances I've read this year!" —*CK²S Kwips and Kritiques*

"Anne Gracie has created a deeply emotional, at times heart-wrenching journey for these two people who must learn to trust one another with their deepest feelings and darkest fears." —*Romance Novel TV*

"Anne Gracie at her best, and her best is very good. She has a lyrical writing style reminiscent of Mary Balogh, and the talent to bring readers vibrant characters, potent plots, and sizzling sensuality . . . YUM!" —*Reader to Reader Reviews*

"A winner . . .   mance . . .
Anne Grac   esh Fiction

D0955167

To Catch a Bride

Anne Gracie

BERKLEY SENSATION, NEW YORK

THE BERKLEY PUBLISHING GROUP
Published by the Penguin Group
Penguin Group (USA) Inc.
375 Hudson Street, New York, New York 10014, USA
Penguin Group (Canada), 90 Eglinton Avenue East, Suite 700, Toronto, Ontario M4P 2Y3, Canada
(a division of Pearson Penguin Canada Inc.)
Penguin Books Ltd., 80 Strand, London WC2R 0RL, England
Penguin Group Ireland, 25 St. Stephen's Green, Dublin 2, Ireland (a division of Penguin Books Ltd.)
Penguin Group (Australia), 250 Camberwell Road, Camberwell, Victoria 3124, Australia
(a division of Pearson Australia Group Pty. Ltd.)
Penguin Books India Pvt. Ltd., 11 Community Centre, Panchsheel Park, New Delhi—110 017, India
Penguin Group (NZ), 67 Apollo Drive, Rosedale, North Shore 0632, New Zealand
(a division of Pearson New Zealand Ltd.)
Penguin Books (South Africa) (Pty.) Ltd., 24 Sturdee Avenue, Rosebank, Johannesburg 2196, South Africa

Penguin Books Ltd., Registered Offices: 80 Strand, London WC2R 0RL, England

This is a work of fiction. Names, characters, places, and incidents either are the product of the author's imagination or are used fictitiously, and any resemblance to actual persons, living or dead, business establishments, events, or locales is entirely coincidental. The publisher does not have any control over and does not assume any responsibility for author or third-party websites or their content.

TO CATCH A BRIDE

A Berkley Sensation Book / published by arrangement with the author

PRINTING HISTORY
Berkley Sensation mass-market edition / September 2009

Copyright © 2009 by Anne Gracie.
Cover art by Voth/Bannall.
Cover design by George Long.
Cover hand lettering by Ron Zinn.
Interior text design by Laura K. Corless.

ISBN: 978-0-425-23022-0

BERKLEY® SENSATION
Berkley Sensation Books are published by The Berkley Publishing Group,
a division of Penguin Group (USA) Inc.,
375 Hudson Street, New York, New York 10014.
BERKLEY® SENSATION and the "B" design are trademarks of Penguin Group (USA) Inc.

PRINTED IN THE UNITED STATES OF AMERICA

10 9 8 7 6 5 4 3 2 1

With thanks to Anne McAllister and Marion Lennox
for friendship and generous support,
to the Maytoners, one and all for general wonderfulness,
and to the Word Wenches,
who so warmly welcomed me into their blog.

Prologue

England
December 1817

A whip cracked, shattering the stillness of the icy landscape. The thunder of hooves grew louder as the curricles approached the bend, neck and neck. The road was narrow, the bend was sharp but neither curricle slowed.

The horses raced, straining to get ahead, heads outstretched, breath steaming in the frosty chill.

As they hurtled around the bend the wheels of the claret and silver curricle grazed those of the black and yellow curricle.

"For God's sake, Rafe, show a little care, if not for yourself or me, for my shiny new curricle," Luke Ripton, the driver of the black and yellow vehicle, yelled.

For answer, Rafe Ramsey's whip snaked out over his horses and cracked just above their flanks.

"You're driving like a lunatic, man, more so than usual."

"I've got a wedding to go to." Rafe snapped the reins and urged his horses faster.

"You want to get there alive, don't you?"

Rafe glanced across at his friend. His eyes flashed blue ice.

Seeing that look, Luke had no qualms about easing back to

let his friend's curricle take the lead. He and Rafe raced all the time. Usually it was a joyous madcap experience.

But the mood Rafe was in today . . .

It wasn't directed at himself, Luke knew. Rafe had arrived at their rendezvous that way. Nothing Luke could say could snap him out of it. Rafe had responded to each sally and quip with a cold, barely restrained politeness, as if politeness could bite.

Luke, knowing the signs of old, gave up trying. Rafe was one of his oldest friends and was usually the coolest, calmest fellow he knew. But on rare occasions he descended into these moods and the only thing to do was to let them burn themselves out.

The cause was always the same: Axebridge.

Rafe rarely took his anger out on his friends—anger in Rafe didn't show outwardly, it burned him up from within. The war had been a useful outlet. These days he raced.

Today Luke had pressed Rafe harder than ever, hoping that by the time they got to Harry's wedding, Rafe would have burned away his anger and become his usual charming self again.

Instead Rafe remained wrapped in ice and burning with rage; his eyes held a curious blank expression that told Luke his mind was far away. Luke raced more cautiously, as if he could make up for his friend, who drove like a man possessed.

The entrance to Alverleigh came into sight, the high stone walls of the estate broken by an imposing pair of black wrought-iron gates, supported by two large stone pillars. Today they stood open to admit the earl's guests on the occasion of his half brother Harry's wedding to Lady Helen Freymore.

Rafe's curricle hurtled down the slope toward the gates, the light vehicle swaying and bouncing with every bump and pot-hole.

He was going far too fast for the freezing conditions, Luke thought. "'Ware ice at the bottom of the hill," he shouted.

Rafe made no sign. He seemed oblivious, wrapped up in dark thoughts.

Something, some small animal—a fox perhaps—darted across the road in front of the horses. One horse reared and stumbled, the other jostled it, the curricle swayed wildly, hit a patch of dark ice, and began to skid in a slow, inevitable arc toward the stone walls and the iron gate.

"Save yourself," Luke shouted, certain Rafe was going to

smash into the stone walls or be impaled on iron gates. "Jump!"

Rafe hauled on the brake with one hand and the reins with the other, forcing his frightened horses back under control. The brake sharpened the angle of the skid but didn't slow it; there was no purchase on the ice.

Rafe thrust his team ruthlessly through the gates, hard and fast, and released the brake. The weight of the skidding curricle pulled the horses backward and to the right. They plunged in confusion and terror.

He lashed out with the whip. The horses leapt forward. There was a loud scrape of wood against stone or iron. The curricle lurched, bounced, and tipped sideways, balancing on a single wheel. Another second and it would overturn for sure.

"Jump, you fool, jump!" Luke yelled.

Instead Rafe hurled himself sideways over the edge like a yachtsman, using his weight as a counterbalance. For several endless seconds the curricle teetered on the brink, then lurched back with a loud thump onto both wheels.

He glanced back at Luke, tipped his whip in salute, and raced his sweating horses up the driveway.

Luke arrived as Rafe was instructing the Alverleigh grooms to cool his horses slowly, then give them a good rubdown, a hot mash, and the very best of treatment.

"You maniac," Luke declared, jumping down from his curricle and tossing the reins to a groom. "You were nearly killed."

Rafe's mouth twisted in a mirthless smile. "That would have thrown the cat among the pigeons. The succession plans in ruins."

"Harry and Nell's wedding in ruins, more like!" Luke snapped. "I don't give a hang about the Axebridge succession, either, but you're among friends now, so get a grip on yourself."

Rafe blinked and the hard glitter slowly faded from his eyes. In a much calmer voice he said, "You're quite right, Luke. I wasn't thinking of Harry and Nell."

"You weren't thinking at all," Luke told him bluntly.

Rafe gave his friend a searching look and gave a rueful sigh. "That bad, was I?"

Luke, relieved the worst was past, relaxed. "Worst I've seen in ages. Think we both need a drink."

"Agreed." Rafe unknotted his silk scarf and removed his leather driving gloves. "And since I won, you owe me a monkey."

"I know, blast you," Luke said as they walked toward the front steps of Alverleigh. "Kills me to admit it, but that was a tidy piece of driving back there. Thought you were going to smash into those pillars. Your horses were magnificent."

"Grace and courage under fire," Rafe agreed. "What time is this ceremony? I don't know if I have the stomach for a wedding just now."

"You'd better find it, then," Luke warned him.

Rafe gave him a faint smile. "Don't worry, I will, for Nell and Harry's sake. This marriage, at least, is one to celebrate."

As he spoke, their friend Gabriel Renfrew, brother of the earl and half brother of the groom, strolled lightly down the steps to greet them. "How was your trip?" he asked after the greetings were concluded.

"Bloody hair-raising," Luke told him.

Gabe raised an eyebrow. "All your races are hair-raising. What made this any different?"

Luke jerked his head at Rafe. "He's just come from Axebridge."

Gabe glanced at Rafe. "I see. You've finalized the wedding arrangements, I presume?"

Rafe did not reply. A tiny muscle in his jaw twitched.

"A drink," Gabe decided.

"Several," Luke agreed. "And make them large ones—he needs it."

"Nonsense," Rafe said coolly. "I'm perfectly calm."

"I know, dear boy," Gabe said. "That's the trouble."

A few hours later Rafe sat in the church pew watching his friend Harry pacing like a caged lion, awaiting his bride.

There was a stir at the entrance of the church. Rafe didn't need to turn his head to see who had arrived. Harry's gray eyes, usually so bleak, blazed as he saw his bride. They were so filled with naked emotion that Rafe had to look away.

Rafe heard the quiet certainty and pride in Harry's voice as he promised to love and cherish his lady.

He caught the fleeting intimate smile Gabe exchanged with

Callie, the princess of his heart, as they remembered their own wedding.

To have and to hold . . . To love and to cherish . . .

Until death us do part.

Rafe felt cold to the marrow.

Could he make promises like that? Not to Lady Lavinia. Not after what he'd learned at Axebridge.

But could he ever?

What did it matter? There was no love in Rafe anyway. There never had been.

He wasn't like Gabe, who had taken love lightly and often until he'd fallen deeply and irrevocably for Callie.

He wasn't like Harry, who'd fallen in love twice, the first time so disastrously he hadn't cared whether he lived or died. Now, truly and deeply in love, he stood at the altar, gazing at his bride, a man transformed.

Rafe hadn't understood it then and he didn't now.

He'd never been in love like that, not once in all his twenty-eight years, not even for an hour, and at his age, he wasn't likely to start.

Women, yes, but only on the strictest understanding that the relationship was purely physical. He treated them well and was generous in parting. They didn't seem to mind. None of them had managed to pierce his essential coldness.

In the war the coldness had grown. It was useful, in war, to stay cool and coldly analytical, not to let yourself get carried away by passion. He'd found strength in it, keeping the world at bay, keeping heartache and grief from touching him. People could die of heartache and grief.

He thought he'd reached perfect control, a state where very little could upset him.

And then he'd come home. More accurately, he'd returned to Axebridge.

Rafe's father, the former Earl of Axebridge, had died while he was at war, so Axebridge was no longer the hostile place it had been when Rafe was a child. And since the current earl, his older brother, had produced no children in ten years of marriage, Rafe understood that it fell now to him to marry and secure the succession. For the first time in his life Rafe was needed by his family, and he was prepared to do his duty.

His brother had even found him a suitable bride. Rafe wasn't particularly enamoured of her, but he'd found no one himself, and Lady Lavinia Fettiplace was of excellent family—the best bloodlines and breeding in England. She came with a fine fortune and was even pretty.

He could do it, he'd told himself a hundred times.

Until this morning, when his brother had revealed the terms he and Lady Lavinia had agreed to, without reference to Rafe . . .

Cold rage welled up in him again. Rafe stamped down on it. This was not the place, the time. He was not a small boy anymore. His family could only hurt him if he let them.

*T*he wedding was over, the celebratory dinner consumed, and they'd danced the night away. In the morning the bride and groom had driven off in a joyful cavalcade, Nell incandescent with happiness, little Torie in a basket beside her, and Harry so proud and with a light in his eyes that Rafe had never seen.

The remaining guests left soon afterward, hurrying to get home for Christmas, praying the clear weather would hold. Rafe and Luke, in no particular hurry, were among the last to depart. They'd said their good-byes, and hating to wait around after that, had wandered toward the stables to await their curricles.

"I'm not racing you back," Luke announced as they crunched down the gravel drive. It was a cold, clear morning, the air dry, with just a light breeze. Perfect for a race.

Rafe inclined his head. "As you wish."

"I know you," Luke persisted. "Under that veneer of calm you're still wild about whatever happened."

Rafe shrugged. He could have reassured his friend that his driving would be back to normal now he'd made a decision, but he didn't. Racing wouldn't purge the anger within him this time. The betrayal. But he knew what would.

They waited in front of the stables, stamping their feet in the cold, watching as the stable lads hitched their teams up.

"Want me to come with you to Axebridge?" Luke offered.

"But it's almost Christmas." Rafe was startled. "What about your family?"

"Mother and the girls won't mind." Luke was the only living son in a family of girls. His mother was a widow, and all but the youngest daughter were married now, but they still doted on their brother.

Rafe smiled. "You are such a liar."

"I'll explain," Luke said. "They won't mind when they know it's you. You know how fond Mother is of you—the girls, too."

Rafe shook his head. "No. Go home and celebrate Christmas with your family. Give my best to them all."

"Then come home with me," Luke said. "Spend Christmas with us. They'll think it the best gift of all."

"I've already sent your mother a gift," Rafe told him. As a boy, he'd spent many a happy Christmas with the Ripton family. It was a haven from his own family, a much older brother he hardly knew, and a father who barely acknowledged his younger son's existence.

"You're so stubborn," Luke said, shaking his head. "Very well then, be miserable if you want to. I'll see you at Axebridge in the new year."

"Ahh, yes . . . The house party . . ."

Luke gave Rafe a searching look. "You sound suspiciously vague, Ramsey. Cold feet about getting betrothed to Lady Lavinia after all?" He gave Rafe a searching look. "Or is it all off?"

Rafe shrugged. "The house party is still going ahead as far as I know."

"Well then, I'll see—"

"I won't be there, however," Rafe finished, watching critically as a young stableboy buckled a harness.

"What? Where will you be?"

"Remember who I was seated with at dinner last night?"

Luke wrinkled his brow, trying to recall. "Some old lady, wasn't it? Must say, thought it was a damned poor place to seat you—"

"Lady Cleeve. Very interesting old lady. Told me an interesting story."

Luke stared at him. "What the devil are you talking about? Told you a story?"

Rafe nodded. "Seems she's missing a granddaughter."

"What do you mean missing? Gal run off with someone?"

"No, nothing like that," Rafe said. "The old lady thought the girl had died along with her mother more than twelve years ago. Been grieving ever since. Her son died six years ago, and since then Lady Cleeve has thought herself all alone in the world."

"Very sad," Luke said, "but what has this to do with—"

"A few months ago, Alaric Stretton—you know, that artist fellow who travels the world and writes books about it—turned up on her doorstep after years in some far-flung corner of the world. Seems they're old family friends—he used to visit them in India."

Luke gave him a look as if to say, why are you telling me this?

Rafe continued, "Stretton told her her granddaughter was alive and well and with her father only six years ago. He even produced a sketch of the girl and her father—the one of the little girl is rather touching—he's a damned good artist. So now Lady Cleeve thinks the girl might still be alive. She's desperate to find her."

"Sounds like a load of moonshine to me."

"It might very well be."

"But what's this got to do with you not—" Luke broke off with a stunned expression. "Don't tell me—this is why you're going to skip out on your betrothal house party?"

Rafe just smiled. He'd been tempted just to not turn up to the house party; it was what they deserved, after all. But that wasn't Rafe's way. Instead, this morning, he'd sent a coldly polite note to Lady Lavinia and another to his brother and sister-in-law, giving his regrets.

Luke flung up his hands in exasperation. "To go on a wild-goose chase after some batty old lady's mythical granddaughter? Based on a sketch done by some mad explorer who spends nine years out of every ten in the most godforsaken parts of the world?"

Rafe said nothing. He'd made up his mind.

Luke persisted. "I know you have a soft spot for old ladies, but—"

"Lady Cleeve was a girlhood friend of Granny's," Rafe said simply. "They corresponded all their lives."

"Oh Lord, that's all it would take, then," Luke said, shaking his head in resignation. "So where was this granddaughter last seen?"

"Egypt."

Luke's jaw dropped. "You're going on a wild-goose chase to *Egypt*?"

Again, Rafe smiled.

Their curricles were ready. Luke didn't move. "Rafe Ramsey, you are stark, staring mad."

Rafe shook his head. "Not mad, dear boy. Just . . . angry."

"Well, do what the rest of us do when we're angry," Luke said in exasperation. "Hit someone! Hit your brother, hit me— hit anyone! It's better than haring off to *Egypt*."

Rafe just smiled.

One

Egypt
1818

"There he is, the man I told you of," Ali said, pointing with a small, grubby finger. "They say his name is Rameses. They say he has come from England to buy a girl, and he will pay in gold."

Rameses? The name of a great king? From the dim shadows of the alley Ayisha had no difficulty singling out the foreigner asking questions; he was a head taller than any other man in the marketplace.

Rameses. It was a strange name for an Englishman.

He wasn't like the others who'd come after her in the past.

He was clean for a start.

And beautiful. Not in a pretty-boy way—Ayisha knew all about pretty boys—but with a hard-edged, austere sort of elegance. As if sculpted from marble.

His skin was lightly tanned, but still paler than most people she knew. More like her own color, under her clothes. He wore a light-colored hat to shield his face from the sun, but his clothes were foreign: English and close-fitting, letting no breezes in to cool the body. His dark blue coat was cut tight to reveal a powerful set of shoulders. Beneath it he wore a white shirt with a tie around his neck tied tight in a complicated knot.

Too many clothes, too tight, and the cloth too heavy.

Yet he didn't look sweaty, hot, and crumpled the way Englishmen new to the country usually did. This man looked cool and unruffled. Hard.

She couldn't help but stare at the buff-colored breeches molded to long, hard-muscled, masculine legs and tucked into high, gleaming black boots. They were very . . . revealing.

The men Ayisha saw every day wore loose, flowing robes or baggy pants and loose, long shirts. Their clothes didn't show the shape of the body. Not like this, almost shamelessly: every hard masculine angle revealed. She swallowed.

If they had, she would never have been able to pass herself off as a boy called Azhar all these years.

She watched the flex and pull of muscles as the Englishman strode through the dust and chaos of the marketplace with the lithe power of a lion.

She felt suddenly hotter, even though she stood in the cool shade.

Rameses. The name suited the man.

"He has a drawing of the girl he wants," Ali went on. "A Frankish girl. He showed it to many people in the marketplace yesterday. Gadi saw it. He says it could be your little sister, if you had one."

Ayisha stilled. *Gadi said what?* Gadi could see a resemblance between a sketch of a young Frankish girl and Azhar, the wily young Egyptian street boy?

Her thoughts flew at once to a sketch made more than six years ago by an English visitor who'd stayed with them once. He could draw to make a person come alive. She still remembered the wonder of it, watching his pencil flying over a page, and then, her own thirteen-year-old face staring back at her from a sheet of white paper.

It couldn't possibly be that drawing . . . could it?

No, that Englishman had taken the sketch with him when he left Egypt, heading for China. She'd been too shy to ask him for it.

How could that drawing have fallen into the hands of this Englishman? And even if it had, why would he bring it to Egypt?

Why would he show it around? And offer money for the girl in the picture?

It could be your little sister . . .

That sketch could ruin her life.

She stared across at the tall foreigner, trying to read the answers somehow in his face. Behind her in the spice souk, a spice seller was roasting sesame, coriander, and cumin seeds with nuts to make *dukkah*. Her stomach rumbled at the delicious aroma, but she did not take her eyes off the Englishman. As if he sensed her interest, he changed direction and walked toward the alley where she was hiding.

The crowd split before him like the parting of the waves, and not just because he was tall and foreign. It was something about the man himself. He moved like a pasha, like a sultan, like a king—not swaggering, but with an unconscious air of assurance, of command bred in the bone—and the crowd responded instinctively.

He was a man accustomed to going wherever he wished.

A man accustomed to getting whatever—or whoever—he wanted.

Not this time, she vowed silently. Not her.

"They say he's an English milord," Ali said. "They say he has gold to buy whatever he wants and spends it like water. But why come all this way to buy a girl? Don't they have girls in England?"

Ayisha sniffed. "Yes, of course. A fool and his gold are soon parted." Brave words. They belied the cold shifting in the pit of her stomach.

"Gadi said if you were younger, he would dress you as a girl and sell you to this Rameses and make his fortune." Ali laughed heartily at the joke—the private and the public joke. In all of Cairo, only he and Laila knew Ayisha was a girl.

Ayisha's throat tightened. She had to get that picture, get it and destroy it. Gadi thought she resembled the girl in the drawing . . . Gadi was a stupid young man. He knew nothing. But if he kept making that joke to everyone who would listen . . .

Bile welled up in her throat.

Gadi's uncle had been one of those who had pursued her, all those years before. If he saw the picture now . . . if Gadi made his joke to his uncle . . .

Gadi's uncle was a lot smarter than Gadi. Gadi's uncle knew what she looked like before.

Once people started picturing her as a girl—even as a joke—it would not be long before someone realized . . .

Gadi's uncle was not the only one who'd hunted her, all those years ago.

"Gadi talks a lot of rubbish," she told Ali.

Ali shook his head. "No, Gadi knows much about the world."

Ayisha said nothing. The ten-year-old orphan had a tendency to hero-worship the most unsuitable men.

Why could the boy not choose someone decent to emulate?

Not that there was much choice for a fatherless boy. The back-streets of Cairo were not exactly crowded with decent men. Poverty and slum life didn't typically breed decency. Who knew better than she?

She leaned deeper into the shadows and waited for the Englishman to come nearer. She wanted to see him close up, close enough to look into his eyes. It was risky, but she needed to see for herself what manner of man she was dealing with.

Know thy enemy.

He strode through the milling crowd, indifferent to the noise, the movement, the dirt. She'd never thought of men as beautiful before, but this man had a spare, hard, manly beauty that made her want to stare. And stare.

He was like someone out of one of Mama's tales; beautiful but deadly. Mama always told wonderful, terrible stories, and though some were true, most weren't. The difficulty was in discovering the difference . . .

But Ayisha was no longer a wide-eyed, gullible child, and she was no man's easy prey. Six years on the streets had turned her into a different person. She was skilled, clever, cunning as a fox, as a vixen.

The Englishman paused, pushing his hat back on his forehead and turning his head as if seeking a breeze in the still, dusty air. She was close enough to see his face clearly, the sculpted lines of a hard jaw, a straight, bold nose, a broad forehead.

His skin was smooth and lightly tanned, free of pockmarks and blemishes, just one small, straight, silvery scar next to his mouth. It drew her eyes to his mouth . . . and what a mouth. Firm, chiseled lips, tight and compressed at the moment. She wanted to slide a moistened finger over them . . . see if they softened.

But his eyes drew her most; heavy-lidded eyes, almond-shaped and sleepy-looking.

Sleepy? A cold prickle ran through her. Sleepy as a cobra, his eyes missed nothing. He was looking straight at her.

He could not possibly see her clearly, she reminded herself—not with the sun so bright in his eyes and with Ayisha in the darkest shadows the narrow alleyway afforded. She'd picked this spot with care. The spice souk was the darkest. Sunshine was not good for spices.

Still he did not move, his eyes, no longer sleepy-looking, boring into the shadows, straight at her, as if he could see her, spear her with his gaze. She froze, as still as a mouse facing a python, and as she looked into his eyes, a steely coldness ran down her spine.

They were like no eyes she'd ever seen—a cold, pale blue, like the sky just before dawn, the hour when hope ebbed lowest and souls departed this earth. They held no warmth, no hope, no pity. A man to whom life or death made no difference. No wonder the crowd parted before him.

She pressed herself against the bricks, becoming one with the deepest shadows. He could not possibly see her, but the directness of his gaze was very unnerving.

Nearby, the spice seller began to crush the *dukkah* mixture with salt.

If he made the slightest movement toward her, she'd run. There were a dozen escape routes; she knew this city, every alleyway and souk and drain. She would not be caught. She waited, breathlessly, every muscle tense.

The stench of crushed and roasted spices thickened in her nostrils, threatening to choke her.

His dark brows tightened, his eyes narrowed, and his nostrils flared slightly, as if he scented game. English lords liked to hunt foxes. Papa had told her all about it, had promised that one day he would take her to England, take her hunting.

Papa had also been a teller of tales. She'd believed every word of them, for who could ever doubt Papa in anything?

But Papa had died, and his tales turned out to be less truthful than Mama's made-up stories. Ayisha would never see England, the green and pleasant land of her father's stories.

And even if she did, nothing, no English lord could *ever* make her go fox hunting.

She'd been hunted too often to take sport in such a thing.

This was the first time an English lord had come, however. Was he bored with English foxes that he should come all this way to hunt . . . a girl?

A sudden crash and shouts came from the other side of the market—a squabble at the orange seller's—and the pitiless blue gaze shifted, just for an instant. In a flash Ayisha moved, leaving the dark alley and diving under the covers of a stall.

She watched through a crack between fabrics as he took in the scene at the orange seller's stall, then returned his gaze to the alley. To the exact spot where she had been.

His brows snapped into a faint frown as he scanned the surroundings. He glanced at the stall and his eyes narrowed, as if he knew she was there, crouched under the table, hiding behind some pink-and-orange striped fabric, and he could not, it was not possible, not unless he was a *djinn* or a wizard.

Ayisha didn't believe in such things. The superstitious folk she'd lived among for the last six years might believe in *djinns*, *afrits*, and other evil spirits. Ayisha did not. She was educated—a bit—could read and write in several languages—a bit—and was a Christian, besides. Evil eye, what nonsense.

She crossed herself, just in case.

And then suddenly he moved, continuing on his way, striding through the marketplace, the intense blue eyes under their sleepy lids missing nothing.

Ayisha breathed again.

No, he was not at all like the ones who had come after her before. He was much, much more dangerous.

She waited until he'd reached the far side of the marketplace, turned a corner, and disappeared, then she slipped out from under the stall and found Ali heading purposefully toward the far corner of the square. She grabbed him by the scruff of his neck and hauled him backward.

"Ow, what are—"

"You're not to follow that man," she told him in a stern voice. "He's dangerous."

Ali snorted. "But I can—"

"I mean it, Ali." She gripped his skinny shoulders tightly. "Don't follow him, don't even speak to him—do I make myself clear?"

He squirmed under her gaze. "But, Ash, I want to see that picture, I want to see if it's as much like you as Gadi says."

"It's not."

"How do you know when you've never seen it?"

"I don't need to see it to know it's one of Gadi's stupid tales."

Ali said sulkily, "If I got some of his gold, we could get that house in Alexandria—"

"And how would you get the gold?"

Ali's gaze shifted.

"Ali! You are not to think of stealing from that Englishman!"

Ali hung his head and muttered, "Gadi says the Englishman has so much gold he wouldn't miss it."

"Then let Gadi try to steal it—and remember what I said when people call him Gadi-one-hand." She gave a scornful snort. "That man might look like a sleepy foreigner, but he's dangerous."

Ali scowled and hunched his shoulder. "I could do it if you taught me."

"Well, I won't. Stealing is wrong. And dangerous."

"You do it."

"I don't." She marched him through the narrow lanes and walkways, twisting and turning, not even having to think about which way to go. These streets were her territory.

He said sulkily, "You used to. And you were only a bit older than I am now. Gadi says—"

"Gadi talks too much. I stole when I was young only because it was that or starve. But now I work, and work is honorable. And you—" She touched a fist lightly to his thin brown jaw. "You will never starve, not while Laila and I are alive. *You* have a choice."

"But—"

"Enough!" She shook him by the arm. "It would kill Laila if anything happened to you. You are the apple of her eye—though I cannot imagine why she cares about a wicked, grubby boy who wants to become a thief."

"Aw, Ash." Ali rolled his eyes and tried to look tough instead of pleased.

"Don't aw-Ash me, now go." She gave him a little push toward the back entrance of their home. A delicious smell of baking pastry filled the air. "Help Laila with the pies. And don't eat too many. And stay away from the Englishman."

"Rameses," Ali reminded her. "But I want to see that picture. I want to show you—"

"Not another word about that man or his picture!" she said in exasperation. "Now go."

It didn't take her long to find the Englishman again; apart from being a foreigner, he was the sort of man people noticed.

She found him at the house of Hassan, her father's former garden boy. Even if five different people hadn't already told her that a great foreign pasha had come to speak with Hassan, she would have known he was there. His long, black, shiny boots stood by the front door.

She was half tempted to take them, not to steal but to hide them. Teach the Englishman to come hunting her! Let him try it in bare feet as she was. But there were too many people watching.

She hadn't spoken to Hassan for six years—she hadn't spoken to any of her father's former servants—after what had happened she didn't dare to—but she knew this area well.

Hassan's house was small and old. There would be just two rooms for the whole family. The tall Englishman would be cramped, and it was hot, so they might open the back door. From the rear, she might be able to see.

She disappeared down an alley barely as wide as she was and, unobserved, shimmied silently over a wall and up some stairs onto the roof of the house behind. The houses were so close together she had a perfect view into the tiny courtyard at the rear of Hassan's house, where a woman was cooking something over a small earthenware stove. She made tea and took it in for the guest, leaving the door open.

Ayisha lay on her stomach, cupped her hands over her eyes to shade them from the glare, and tried to see into the house. It was difficult, but eventually her eyes adjusted enough for her to see the Englishman take the picture from inside his coat and show it to Hassan. Hassan looked, nodded, and said something, then shook his head.

She craned to catch a word, anything, but she could hear nothing. It was very frustrating. So many Englishmen talked in loud, booming voices as if everyone in the city would wish to hear them, but this one, curse him, was quietly spoken. His voice and Hassan's came in a low murmur.

Ayisha lay watching, hot, thirsty, and frustrated. Finally the

Englishman stood up, gave Hassan something— probably gold, she thought bitterly—and left, having to bend his head to get out the door.

She climbed back down and raced around to the front, worried she might lose him again. She raced into Hassan's street and skidded to a halt in the dust.

The Englishman looked up and looked at her—right at her. He hadn't finished putting on his long, tight boots, but he stopped tugging on them and stared at her. The cold eyes narrowed and his dark brows came together.

Ayisha cursed and ran in the opposite direction. She would circle around to catch him up later.

He'd noticed her, had stared at her, had frowned.

Stupid, stupid, careless, foolish girl, drawing attention to herself like that. Of course he looked. Anyone would, at some boy who rushed out into the street like a madman, then turned and fled.

Her heart was pounding. He couldn't possibly know who she was, she told herself firmly. No one of her father's world had seen her in the last six years, and anyway, she was living as a boy. If her disguise could be seen through in one swift glance, she would never have survived six years on the streets. No lone female would be tolerated, let alone one dressing herself in men's clothing. It was a sin, a crime. She would have been punished severely according to the law, and then . . . she shuddered at the possibilities.

No, her disguise was good. Nobody knew she was a girl; only Ali, who was like a little brother to her and who slept on a straw mat near her each night. And Laila. She'd discovered the imposture years ago, but she'd kept the secret and helped Ayisha perfect her disguise. Laila understood the need for it.

To everyone else Ayisha was that street boy, Azhar.

And nobody—not even Laila—had any idea who her parents were. That knowledge was more than Ayisha's life was worth.

Rather, it was *exactly* what her life was worth.

She trusted no one with that secret. She did her best to forget it herself. It was only when someone came hunting her that she was forced to remember.

Someone like this Englishman.

But he couldn't possibly have divined her secret, not in one glance, not in two. She'd just been careless, skidding to a halt like that, showing too much interest in him, that's all. It wouldn't normally matter, except those uncanny eyes seemed to see everything.

She would be more careful in the future.

She caught up with him again a short time later. She'd changed her turban, and now instead of a dusty blue cloth, it was white, with a strip of red twisted through it. She always kept an extra tied around her waist. In a crowd, people searching for you looked for your turban; change it and you were a different person.

She shadowed him all day, keeping herself well back, hidden in shadows or doorways, down alleys, behind others. Several times he turned and scanned the surroundings as if he knew somehow she was there. Luckily she was small and shabby and very skilled at being inconspicuous.

He visited most of her father's former servants that day. He was very thorough, damn him—not like the others who'd come before.

Each time he took the leather folder containing her picture from the inside pocket of his coat and showed it to them. Each time they would peer, nod, then shake their head or shrug.

But at no point was there any chance for her to steal the picture. A dense crowd would be best, like the one she'd first seen him in, but he hadn't returned to the busiest part of the city.

All afternoon it had been small houses in narrow lanes or dead-end alleys; bad locations for an out-of-practice thief to revive her old skill, even if he wasn't followed most places by curious onlookers and street beggars, some of whom she knew. And who, therefore, knew her. And would be sure to gossip about Azhar's interest in the picture.

Now the Englishman was standing at the doorway of a man who'd done odd jobs. He was fatter now, but she remembered him. Gamal. She'd never liked him. It would have been polite to invite the foreigner in. All the others had, but Gamal wanted everyone to see his grand visitor, so kept him outside in the sun.

Ayisha couldn't approve his rudeness, but she could take advantage of it. Luckily a small group of curious onlookers had gathered. She edged closer.

"Hah! I knew you were lying when you said you weren't interested," a voice whispered triumphantly at her elbow.

"Ali, what are you doing here?" She cursed silently and hauled the boy back out of earshot. "I told you to help Laila with the pies."

"And so I did," Ali said indignantly. "And now she has sent me to pick greens for tomorrow's pies." He held up a cloth bag.

"I see no greens growing here," she pointed out. "The river is the place, so go. I told you to stay away from this man."

"Aw, Ash, picking greens is woman's work and—"

It was an old argument and Ayisha had no patience with it. "And eating and being disobedient is a boy's? Do you want to grow up like Omar?"

Ali grimaced, not liking the comparison.

Laila's brother Omar bestirred himself as little as possible. It was Laila who earned the money that fed them, baking bread and pastries in the clay oven in the tiny courtyard. She scoured the city surrounds for wood and dried animal dung to burn in the oven, she made fillings for her pies with wild greens and herbs and just a smidgeon of cheese, but she was a born cook and her pies sold as fast as she could cook them.

She was also a born mother, her barenness notwithstanding. She ached at the plight of the street children, would have fed them all if she could, but Omar forbade it. He took every coin that Laila earned. It was his right, as the head of the family.

Every coin that he knew about. Laila and Ayisha had hatched a plan . . .

"Omar is not a man; he is a leech," Ayisha said. "And there is no such thing as women's work, only work. So if Laila asks you to pick greens, you pick greens—understand?"

Ali sighed and nodded, then glanced wistfully to where the Englishman stood in his long black boots, looking tall and handsome and exotic and in every way so much more exciting than an herb. "Can't we just ask to see the picture?"

"No."

"Why not? You want to, I know. Otherwise why are you here?"

"I was passing and stopped out of curiosity," she told him. "But I have work to do and so, my little greens picker, do you. So go." She pushed him lightly in the direction of the river.

Ali left, his steps lagging, a vision of martyrdom, but then, boy-like, he suddenly brightened and bounded off. Ayisha grinned. He was unsquashable, that child, and she loved him for it. She turned back to the Englishman, but he was leaving, his face remote and unreadable.

Gamal remained outside his house and boasted to the small crowd of curious neighbors who came closer now that the Englishman had left. Ayisha sidled up behind them to hear what Gamal had to say.

"He is a great lord from England, my visitor—Rameses, brother to the English king."

Ayisha tried not to snort. As if a royal English prince would be wandering the backstreets of Cairo with one interpreter and no armed guard. Even if the English king allowed it, Mehmet Ali, the pasha, would not.

Gamal drew himself up to his full girth and said, "Indeed, he traveled all the way from the other side of the world just to talk to me. He asks about the Englishman who used to live in the rose-colored villa near the river."

"Is that one not dead?" someone asked.

"Yes," Gamal said, "but property went missing and the Englishman's family wishes to recover it."

Property. A cold trickle ran down Ayisha's spine.

"Did you steal it, Gamal?" someone joked, and everyone laughed, not in a friendly way.

"Why should I, who speaks with English lords, bother with ignorant fellahin?" Gamal gave his neighbors a disdainful look and went inside, closing the door.

The neighbors muttered huffily and began to drift away in small indignant clumps. There was nothing more to be learned and the day was passing, so Ayisha left them to it.

She caught up with the Englishman and his interpreter as they turned off the main road and into a quiet, cobbled alleyway. Ayisha's steps faltered. She knew that street. The third house from the end was well known in certain circles . . .

Zamil's.

Sure enough, they stopped at Zamil's and knocked on a thick, iron-reinforced door.

Anxiety coiled in the pit of her stomach. What business would he have with Zamil?

She loitered in the shadows while the interpreter spoke to someone through a grill. A moment later they were admitted. The heavy door clanked shut behind them.

Every instinct she had shrieked to get as far away from this place as she could. She started to leave, then turned back. She had to know what she was up against. She had to. She dithered for a moment, uncharacteristically indecisive.

"What do you want at Zamil's, young bantam?" growled a deep voice behind her.

She whirled and found a huge man looming over her, his hideously scarred face bristling with a large black mustache. Ayisha recognized him at once. He was known to all who lived on the streets as the Greek, Zamil's Greek, the fastest man with a knife in all of Cairo. And the most vicious.

"Well, speak up! Trying to sneak a look at Zamil's merchandise, eh?" He bent and thrust his face close to Ayisha's, grinning through teeth that were broken and blackened. Several had been filed to points. His breath was fetid.

Fatal to show fear in front of such a man. Ayisha jerked her head casually toward the door. "My master, the English lord, is in there."

"Master!" The Greek sneered. "No customer of Zamil, let alone an English lord, would keep a scrawny, ragged pup like yourself in his service. Get thee gone, whelp—unless—" His eyes ran over her and his smile turned into a leer that made Ayisha sick to her stomach. "Unless you have something to sell."

Her skin crawled, but she pretended not to notice his interest. "Nay, I sell only information, effendi. Who do you think guided the foreign lord to this house? Do you think his tame servant would have knowledge of Zamil's?"

She snorted, then gave the big man a cheeky look. "Perhaps the great Zamil—or his most excellent right-hand man—will reward me for it, eh?"

The Greek stared a moment, then threw back his head in a roar of laughter. "I like thee, bantam," he said and thumped Ayisha on the back.

He bashed a meaty fist on the door and the grill opened. The Greek said, "This cheeky monkey thinks he is old enough to gaze upon Zamil's merchandise. Let him in to join his master." As the door swung open, he said to Ayisha, "Take care of those big eyes, bantam."

"My eyes?" She frowned.

"That they do not pop out of their sockets when they see Zamil's women," he said, and both men roared at the joke.

Ayisha managed a halfhearted grin and sauntered jauntily

through the entrance as if her heart were not thudding like a drum. The door shut with heavy finality behind her, and she stood in another world, a world far removed from the dusty, crumbling city.

She stood in a courtyard, paved with honey-colored stone, framed by carved arches and fluted columns. A fountain tinkled into a pond on which water lilies floated. Jasmine coiled up an elegant wrought-iron screen.

A dozen richly dressed men waited in the courtyard, each with servants in attendance. They talked among themselves, the sort of talking strangers did while waiting for something to happen. In a shadowed doorway a tall Turk stood, giving orders to unseen people within.

She knew what they were waiting for. Her stomach clenched. She wanted to flee, to be on the other side of that big ironbound door. The safe side.

Servants brought refreshments to the waiting men: tea, sherbet, small exquisite dishes of food. She could smell the food, fragrant and delicious. She was hungry; she hadn't eaten all day, but even if they offered her anything—which they would not—she couldn't swallow a morsel. Not in this place.

She spotted the Englishman on the far side of the courtyard. His foreign clothing drew curious and faintly hostile glances, but he stood, apparently unconcerned, looking about him with a cool, unreadable expression.

Keeping her head down, she wandered over, taking care to remain inconspicuous, and took up position behind him, squatting humbly against the wall as the lowliest servant would, waiting for his master.

The Englishman said something to his interpreter who moved toward a man sitting on a raised stand in the other corner of the courtyard, a plump man in flowing silken robes. Zamil.

He was intercepted after three paces by Zamil's men, but after a short conversation, was escorted to Zamil by his minions. A few moments later Zamil waved the Englishman forward.

Ayisha slipped through the crowd to get closer.

He pulled out the folder and showed Zamil the picture. Zamil looked at it and shrugged. The Englishman said something else—Ayisha could not catch it.

She edged nearer, in time to hear Zamil say, "No, a young white virgin fetches a fine price and six years ago . . ." He shrugged. "Who knows where this one is now? One thing is certain, she will be a virgin no more."

He looked at the Englishman's impassive face and chuckled. "But fresh fish is tastier than old fish, no?" He jerked his chin toward the auction stand. "The auctions will start soon if you want to buy."

But the Englishman didn't even glance that way. With a curt farewell he turned and left, striding through the crowd of buyers as if they weren't there. Like the folk in the marketplace, they drew back to let him pass. It was those blazing silver-blue eyes, she thought as she made to follow him out. They were enough to freeze your marrow.

She followed him, but she was slow; nobody made way for a scruffy young boy. The Englishman had already stepped out into the streets when Ayisha heard the crowd behind her stir.

She pressed toward the gate, not wanting to look.

But she could hear.

It was a female slave. Ayisha heard the stir of anticipation, heard the announcement, "A young Circassian woman, a certified virgin . . . , " heard the ripple of appreciation.

Ayisha's stomach jerked in reaction. She stumbled to the exit, wishing she'd got out when the Englishman had.

The man at the door laughed at her ashen face. "So much naked female beauty is too much for a boy, I see. The Greek did warn you. Still, that little Circassian beauty will sweeten our dreams, eh, boy?" He chuckled as he unbolted the door. "And now, every time you look at a woman in a yashmak, you will know exactly what that yashmak is hiding, yes?"

Ayisha pushed past him and ran. She ran and ran until her ribs were aching and her breath came in great sobbing gasps.

Two

She ran until she reached the Nile, that endless, flowing source of life. And of death. Being near the river always brought her some measure of comfort. And a reminder never to let her guard down, because there were always crocodiles . . .

In and out of the water.

She sat on the banks and hugged her knees to her chin, staring out over the water and remembered . . .

Remembered wood splitting under rough blows, locks being wrenched apart. Rough, deep voices. The robbers had come. They always knew when to strike.

The servants had all fled at the first sign of plague.

There was nobody here to stop them. Only Ayisha. With a dead father and a dying mother.

Mama had clutched Ayisha's hand with feeble insistence. "Hide." She pointed under the bed.

Ayisha slid under the bed in one quick movement. She lay as still as a mouse, hardly daring to breathe. Above her Mama breathed slowly in . . . out . . . in . . . out . . .

A pair of large, bare, dirty feet approached her mother's bed cautiously. They halted a few feet away.

Ayisha held her breath. The nails of the man's feet were twisted and horny and ingrained with filth.

"Dead," the owner of the feet said after a moment.

Not Mama, she thought. Not yet. Mama was hiding, too.

"Any sign of the child?" another man asked.

"No, but she'll be here."

Here? She braced herself, sure that any moment he would haul her from her hiding place.

"Keep looking. A white child-virgin will bring us a fine sum in the slave market. More than all of this put together." He shook a fistful of her mother's jewelry so that it jangled.

And Mama had opened her eyes and cursed him . . . with her dying breath . . .

Ayisha shivered, hugged her knees, and stared at the river, the endless, eternal flow. The river had seen everything. Nothing shocked it, nothing worried it . . . Everything passed.

Her pounding heart slowed. The sick feeling passed.

It was pointless to dwell on things she could not change. Her goal was survival. It had been foolish to go to Zamil's. So it made her sick with fear and revulsion. What did she expect?

She stood. It was late, and she'd wasted most of the day following the Englishman instead of earning her keep.

She'd earned only a few coins today. The least she could do was gather fuel for Laila's ever-hungry oven.

She collected dried reeds, twigs and grasses, and dried camel dung. The familiar task soothed her. The first time she'd met Laila, Laila had fed her and Ayisha had paid for her supper with fuel. It had formed a bond between them.

How far she'd come since then, she thought. She was no longer that desperately hungry, frightened child. She was a woman, and she had choices. She just had to make them.

*T*he sun was low in the sky as she trudged home with the fuel. She still paid for her supper with work, but Laila was like family now, like a mother. She'd taken first Ayisha under her wing, and later Ali. She would have taken them into her house if she could, but for Omar.

The two-room hovel and everything in it—including Laila—belonged to Omar, Laila's brother.

Ayisha entered by the rear gate into the tiny backyard and

placed the fuel in a neat pile beside the oven, ready for the morning.

Mmrrrow? Her cat, Tom, greeted her as he always did from the high wall that surrounded the yard. Tom liked to observe the world from on high.

Ayisha smiled as he stretched, then jumped down and wound himself lovingly around her ankles. Ayisha picked him up and cuddled him. He purred loudly and butted her head.

She glanced at the pallet under the bench where Ali slept. It was empty. "Where's Ali?" she asked the cat. "He should be home by now."

She knocked lightly on the back door. She and Ali rarely went inside the house. Omar didn't allow it. If Laila wanted to take in dirty street beggars, it was her foolishness, but they would not come inside his house and he would not pay a penny to feed or clothe them.

So Ayisha and Ali slept at the back, under a bench on a pallet. It was not so bad. In winter when it got chilly, they slept next to the oven, which retained some warmth long after the fire had burned out, and Tom slept at Ayisha's feet, keeping them warm. And in summer, it was cooler outside than in. It was infinitely better than sleeping in the streets.

Laila opened the door. Her lip was split and crusted with dried blood.

"What happened?" Ayisha asked. As if she didn't know.

After fifteen years of marriage Laila's husband had returned her to her brother Omar like an unwanted parcel. Divorced for barrenness. It was the end of all Laila's dreams, for no one wanted a barren woman. Now she had to live with Omar, who was stupid and lazy and selfish.

Ayisha despised him. He treated Laila like the lowest servant, as if her barrenness made her less than human.

Laila shook her head. "It's nothing. But . . . he took all the money for today. It was a good day's takings, too."

Ayisha glanced at the house. "Has he gone?"

"Oh yes, we won't see him again until he's spent it all in the brothels." She gave Ayisha a hopeless look. "We will never get away, never."

"Yes, we will," Ayisha said briskly and began to work free the loose brick at the far corner of the oven. "He doesn't know about this, does he? And even if he has stolen your money, I still have something to add." She pulled the brick free and from the hollow inside pulled out a small leather bag. She added a small fistful of coins to the hoard and replaced it in the hollow. "So we are still better off than yesterday. One step closer to Alexandria."

It was their dream to get enough money together to leave Cairo, telling no one. They would start afresh in Alexandria, and Omar would never find Laila, and no one would come searching for Ayisha. They would be free. They would rent a house and build an oven, as they had before. People in Alexandria would enjoy Laila's pies just as much as in Cairo.

And without Omar to steal the profits, who knew what they could achieve? There might even be enough money to buy Ali an apprenticeship. Keep him off the streets and out of trouble.

"Laila, Laila, are you there?" a woman's voice called. It was the neighbor.

They opened the door in the wall.

"Did you hear? Ali—he is taken! My son told me just now," the neighbor said.

Beside her Laila made a small distressed sound.

"Taken by who? What happened?" Ayisha asked quickly. The neighbor had a tendency to dramatize everything.

"Ali tried to rob a foreigner," the woman explained. "But the man caught him and took him away."

"Oh God!" She knew at once which foreigner and what Ali had been trying to steal. "The little fool."

"They will cut off his hand," Laila whispered, ashen-faced. "He will become a cripple, a beggar."

"If the pasha's men caught him, his fate would be sealed," the neighbor agreed. "But the foreigner took him. Who knows what foreigners do with thieves?"

"It is good news," Ayisha said, sounding more certain than she felt. "He might get a beating, but his hand will be safe. English people don't cut off children's hands," she said, hoping it was true. She turned to the neighbor. "Where did the foreigner take Ali?"

"To the pink villa on the far side of the river. The one with the big sycamore tree."

Ayisha's old home. She hadn't been there since . . . "I know the place," she said. "I will go there and get Ali back."

"But how?" Laila asked. "We have no money to pay and Omar will not—"

"I can get inside without the Englishman knowing. I will find Ali and steal him back."

"But—" Laila cast a glance at the neighbor.

"It will be all right," Ayisha told her. "There is still time before the gates are shut."

Under the pasha's rule, as a simultaneous measure against plague and crime, every quarter in Cairo was closed off by gates at each end of the street at the fall of night. People could move about the city at night only by asking the guards to unlock each gate. An additional law required anyone outside at night to carry a source of light—a torch or a lantern. The measures had cut crime, at least, dramatically. Plague was another matter.

"I will go now to the Englishman's house and wait until darkness falls. Don't worry, Laila, Ali and I will be home after dawn."

From a hook in the courtyard wall she took a coiled length of rope and wrapped it around her waist.

She always carried a knife hidden under her top. Now she tied a thong around her calf and slipped another weapon, a thin dagger, between it and her skin. She hoped it wouldn't come to knives.

Laila hugged her. "Allah keep you safe."

Ayisha nodded. She'd never killed before, but she would kill the Englishman before she'd let him take her.

*T*he trap was set. The boy was asleep. Rafe rose from the chair beside the bed and walked quietly out, closing the door behind him.

He stood at the open French doors, looking out into the velvet night, breathing deeply. A crescent moon gleamed through a gauzy waft of cloud, turning the river below to a ripple of silk. The night air was cool and moist. A faint breeze stirred the leaves of the big old sycamore by the wall, and he fancied he could smell the faint, spicy scent of the desert. Out here, the crowded, dirty, dusty town seemed a world away instead of half a mile.

By daylight Sir Henry Cleeve's former home had a forlorn, shabby elegance: at night it became a place of beauty and enchantment. Cicadas shrilled outside in the lotus trees and the scent of Damascus roses wafted up from the courtyard below.

Almost a pity to have turned it into a trap. Almost. But someone had been following him all day, he could sense it, feel it in the rising hairs on the back of his neck.

And someone had sent that boy to steal the picture.

Interest had been stirred up by the picture and the gold, just as Baxter had said. And interest was a hopeful sign.

Rafe had secured the Cleeve house for just three weeks. He'd got it by a stroke of luck. On his first day in Cairo, he'd made a visit to Johnny Baxter, the cousin of a friend of his.

"Johnny is the man you need in Cairo," his friend Bertie had told him. "Knows everything and everyone."

Johnny Baxter, Bertie told Rafe, had been badly wounded in the Battle of the Nile and had elected to remain in Egypt, to die in sunshine instead of in the stink of a ship's hold.

Not only had Baxter lived, he'd thrived. He survived Napoleon's occupation of Egypt and had managed to keep his head low throughout the turmoil that followed. He loved Egypt and intended to live out his life there.

"Good thing, too," Bertie told Rafe. "Went completely native. Married the woman who first took him in, wounded. She died last year, but it made no difference to Johnny. Still dresses like an Arab, jabbers away in the native lingo, made his fortune there, but no plans to come home. Never know to look at him he was an Englishman, let alone an Eton man—family have disowned him, of course. Embarrasin', havin a chap go native.

"But Johnny's a good egg, all the same. Thick as thieves with all the locals—from street beggars to the sultan or whatever y'call the top native fellow. If anyone can get you on the inside track, Johnny can."

But when Rafe called on Baxter, he discovered something Bertie hadn't mentioned: Baxter habitually shunned the society of Europeans.

He'd refused to see Rafe at first. He didn't receive visitors from England, had left the world of polite morning calls behind him, his servant said.

But Rafe was not fobbed off so easily. His experience in the army had taught him that good local knowledge would save a lot of time and errors.

Rafe sent in his card for the second time, this time with a terse, handwritten message.

Baxter had greeted him in full Arab robes, gave a silent bow, and called in Arabic for coffee to be served. He waited in silence, cross-legged on a low divan, observing Rafe with a shrewd eye. He was about forty, his face weather-beaten and slightly scarred. Powder burns and shrapnel, Rafe decided.

Recognizing the tactics, Rafe made no attempt to fill the silence but sat back, relaxed, and waited. When the coffee arrived, a bitter brew of grainy mud that he frankly thought disgusting, he drank it down without a word.

The silence stretched.

Eventually Rafe yawned and said, "We used to play a game like this when I was at school, only then it was the first one to blink who lost. I usually won. I'm quite competitive, you see."

"And yet you spoke first," Baxter said softly.

Rafe shrugged. "I bore more easily these days. Besides, I'm tired of childish games." He met Baxter's gaze steadily.

After a moment, Baxter inclined his head in acknowledgment, and the atmosphere eased. He ordered more coffee.

Rafe held up his hand. "Not for me, I thank you."

Baxter stiffened. "You don't like my coffee?"

"No, it's appalling," Rafe said calmly.

There was a pause, then Baxter chuckled. "Few men would have dared tell me that, but you're quite right. My cook and his family left unexpectedly yesterday to return to their village— a death in the family—and I've not yet replaced them. Would you believe it? Not one person in my employ can make decent coffee."

He sat back and said in a much friendlier tone, "Now, tell me how you met Cousin Bertie—the only member of my family who speaks to me. You were both in the war, I gather."

They spoke of the war, and Rafe gave him news of his cousin. Then the politenesses over, Rafe explained the errand he was on. "I was advised to seek assistance from the members of the English community here."

"And yet you ignored that advice?"

Rafe shrugged. "It seems to me that if the English community knew anything about the girl, word would have filtered back long ago."

Baxter snorted. "Absolutely right. Most of them here are ignorant snobs. Know nothing about the local people but find them wanting, all the same. I have as little to do with them as possible."

Rafe nodded. "Bertie said you'd be the best man to advise me on the local situation."

Baxter found the whole story of Sir Henry Cleeve's missing daughter fascinating. He agreed with Rafe that since no news of the girl had come from the foreign community, he was better off setting the locals to find her. "Flash that picture around, spend a bit of gold—that'll soon flush any information out."

He told Rafe about the vacant Cleeve house and who to see to rent it. He advised Rafe to get the search over with as quickly as possible. "For plague can become a problem in the hotter months."

"I will," Rafe assured him. "I intend to be back in England well before then."

"Good. I also recommend you visit Zamil, the slave trader. For if the girl is alive and nothing's been heard of her for six years, chances are she's in a harem somewhere. Unspeakable, I know, and better to tell the old lady she's dead, but a young white virgin would fetch a high price, and Zamil deals with only quality goods. Tell him Baxter sent you."

And so he'd gone to Zamil's.

Quality goods. Rafe's jaw clenched. He hoped to God the little girl in the picture had not ended up in a place like that.

And all for nothing; Zamil had proved unhelpful.

Rafe sipped his brandy and waited, the tranquility of the night all the more perfect for the knowledge it would not last.

Showing the picture around and flashing gold had indeed stirred up some interest. Someone was sniffing around, and there had to be a reason for that.

It was extraordinary, that moment of awareness there in the marketplace. The knowledge, the feeling that someone was watching, watching *him*. With intense particularity.

The watcher had stood in the shadows of that narrow alley, and the instant Rafe was distracted, he'd moved. But the prickle between Rafe's shoulder blades continued, throughout the day. He was being followed.

After the market, there was that street urchin who'd come

racing around the house, seen him, turned, and bolted like a rabbit—a dead giveaway. He thought he'd spotted the same youth at Zamil's but he couldn't be sure. And then there was the boy, Ali, who'd tried to steal the picture.

The prickle between Rafe's shoulder blades intensified. Someone was out there in the dark right now, watching.

A thief? An assassin? The person who'd sent a boy to do a man's job? His pulse thrummed with anticipation.

He glanced at Ali sleeping, bound and gagged on the bed in the next room.

The imprisonment of small children—pickpocket or no—didn't sit well with Rafe, particularly such a game little lad.

But the boy was the key to whoever had been following him all day, the first sign that Rafe hadn't come all this way on what he'd been sure was a wild-goose chase. Until now.

A dead giveaway to go for the picture instead of his purse.

Young Ali might be an incompetent pickpocket, but he would have made a fine soldier. He'd admitted nothing except his name, even though Rafe, through an interpreter, had grilled him rather hard. In a shaking voice he'd claimed to have no family, no home, and no master. And he'd insisted—repeatedly—that nobody had asked him to steal the folder with the drawings. Insisted rather too much, Rafe thought. Brave little beggar.

Would the master come for the boy? The coward, sending a child to risk his hand for the sake of a worthless drawing.

Though clearly it wasn't worthless to someone.

Rafe was very glad he'd come to Egypt. He felt more alive than he had in ages. And all day the sun had beat down on him, soaking into his bones. He couldn't get enough of it. He'd felt so cold for so long . . .

He settled down to wait. Such a long time since he'd been on watch . . .

*T*he moon was riding low in the western sky. Rafe drifted in a blue reverie, contemplating with grim outrage the future his older brother had mapped out for him. Driven by his obsession to ensure the succession of the Earls of Axebridge . . .

The scrape of something against the bricks outside brought Rafe to full alertness.

He moved silently into position by the window. The room was open to the night, the carved wooden shutters fastened back. He stood in the shadows and waited.

A shadow slid noiselessly over the balcony. Small and slight. Another boy, dammit. Older than the first one, a youth rather than a boy, but still, not a man. Not the master who Rafe was coming to despise.

Rafe had left a lamp burning low in Ali's room. The boy's shape in the bed was visible through a door deliberately left ajar. Like a wraith the intruder stepped through the open window and glided across the floor toward the boy.

Rafe caught a glint of light on steel. A knife! An assassin? He leapt forward and chopped at the hand holding the knife. A soft exclamation and the knife clattered across the floor. The boy whirled and kicked—straight for Rafe's balls.

Rafe dodged and a hard foot collided only with his upper thigh. It would have crippled him had it connected with its target. The lad had a kick like a mule!

The boy lashed out with a fist and at the same time kicked again for the same target. Rafe might not care about the succession, but he did care about his balls. Rafe, swearing, kicked the lad's feet out from under him and knocked him to the floor.

The boy spotted the knife and made a grab for it. Rafe kicked it under the sofa. He turned and saw the boy making for the window. He dived, knocking him to the floor, landing on top of him.

The boy was still for a moment. Rafe could hear him fighting hoarsely for breath. He'd knocked the wind out of him. Good. He flipped the boy over, but even though he was still gasping like a landed fish, the youth fought back, punching and kicking, and all the time writhing like a damned eel, trying to get a foot free to go for Rafe's family jewels once and for all.

He was small—half starved no doubt—and though he fought like a little demon, his strength was pitiful by comparison with Rafe's. Enough to be a damned nuisance, all the same, Rafe thought, dodging another punch, trying to grab the flailing fists to subdue the boy. He needed to question him, but first he had to tame him.

"I won't hurt you if you surrender," he said in English, then realizing it, repeated it in French.

The boy bared his teeth in what Rafe thought could be a smile. He relaxed slightly and the boy lunged.

"Ow!" The little bugger had *bitten* him. Enough was enough. A quick scientific punch to the boy's jaw knocked him cold. His head fell back and he didn't move.

Rafe grimaced. He must have hit harder than he intended. He'd meant to subdue the little devil, not knock him out.

He sat back on his haunches, kneeling astride the youth's supine body and regarded his young assailant. In the soft light from the other room all he could see was an urchin face smeared with dirt. He looked about fifteen, thin and as raggedly dressed as Ali. His turban had come off in the struggle and his hair was very short, chopped jaggedly in a cut that Rafe decided the boy had done without benefit of mirror or scissors. It wasn't unattractive, he decided. Might even take off—the Urchin Cut. He favored the Windswept, himself.

The youth's features, under all that dirt, were quite delicate . . .

Good God. If he didn't know better . . .

He thought of the lad's lack of muscle. The way he'd succumbed to the merest tap on the jaw.

He stared at the youth's chest. Flat as a pancake.

He shifted his position back, till he was sitting on the lad's legs. He peered at the place where the legs joined the torso. The pants were very baggy, but . . .

There was only one way to tell. He brushed down over the base of his prisoner's stomach and between his legs . . . Nothing. Or rather not nothing, but nothing that would have been there if his youth had been a boy.

He was a girl. And, he thought, staring at the girl's features in the dim light, not just any girl.

Her eyes fluttered open. "Filthy pervert!" she snapped in French and in the same moment that Rafe recalled just where his hand was resting—and removed it—she exploded under him.

If he'd thought she was angry before, it was nothing to the desperation with which she fought him now—bucking and writhing, kicking and biting, punching and scratching.

"Calm down," he panted in English, trying to hold her down without injuring her any further. "I'm not going to hurt you. I've come to help you."

She kept fighting.

He repeated it in French, in case she'd forgotten her English. She spat in his face.

He swore and grabbed at her hands, keeping her hips jammed between his thighs. His thighs imprisoned her effortlessly, but she continued to squirm and buck against him.

"Stop it, you little fool," he said. "Your grandmother sent me."

In French she cast aspersions on his mother's virtue and told him to put that grandmother in an anatomically impossible place. And then she bit his arm. Again.

"You little shrew! Do you want me to punch you again?" He couldn't. He'd never hit a woman in his life—until tonight. And it made him angry.

She bucked and, getting a hand free, tried to scratch his eyes out. He dodged and caught her hand again, but not before he felt blood trickling down his neck.

"This is becoming excessively tedious," he grated. He could easily throttle the little she-cat—and enjoy doing it. But they both knew he had the upper hand in every respect.

She wasn't going to give up. There was only one way to subdue her without hurting her any more than he had. Rafe knew exactly what to do.

In one swift movement he pinned her whole body to the floor, pressed under his; his powerful thighs pressing down her slender, smaller thighs. His big body covered her small one, intimately, not a breath of air between them.

She struggled frantically, but Rafe was bigger, stronger, and heavier; he overlapped her in every way.

He lay on top of her, unmoving, letting his weight do the job, sending a silent message: she was his prisoner.

Her head flailed madly. He caught her face between his hands and held it still. He didn't trust those pearly white teeth anywhere near his skin.

He kept her arms pinned down by his elbows. She struggled vainly and, realizing she was utterly helpless, let fly with a stream of what he imagined was the finest gutter Arabic.

He waited until she ran out of breath and said, "Well, that was a waste, wasn't it? I don't speak Arabic."

She instantly switched to French.

"How delightful," he said conversationally. "So you do understand English." He wished he could see her eyes. The curve of her cheek was quite lovely, and he could see enough to know her skin was streaked with dirt. It felt like silk, though.

She tried to buck him off but all that happened was that his body, already aware of a slender female body in extremely close proximity, responded.

She felt it, too, he could tell. She went instantly still, then called him a filthy pervert, again in French.

He chuckled.

She stiffened. "Have you no shame?" she hissed in French.

"Not really. Frankly I'm just pleased that everything down there seems to be in fine working order after your very determined assault on my masculinity."

"Assault?" she snapped. "You're a fine one to talk." She said it in English.

It was the moment he'd been waiting for. He shifted, moving both their bodies so that they were face-to-face. "Miss Alicia Cleeve, I presume."

Three

She lay in rigid silence for a long moment. He wished he could see her face properly, but the moon had slipped behind the clouds again and though he could make out shapes and angles there was not enough light for any detail.

Rafe simply lay on top of her and waited. The silence stretched. His body throbbed and strained toward the object of its desire. Bizarre. It had no idea what was good for it.

Give her half a chance and she'd cut it off.

Rafe might know nothing about love, but he knew women. Especially physically. They were—usually—all softness and smooth curves.

This one seemed entirely made of elbows. Sharp, jabbing, uncomfortable elbows. And claws. And teeth.

And yet his body was as hard and wanting as he'd ever experienced. It must be all the sun he'd experienced in the last few weeks. All that heat pouring into him. The heat had to go somewhere. And it had.

His body was burning—burning for a dirty little savage who'd just tried to disembowel him.

It was most unlike him. He was famous for his elegance and discrimination. Particularly in women.

Could a certain part of his anatomy be suffering from sunstroke?

"Get off me," she snarled at last. "You're like an elephant, squashing me."

"And you're like a bagful of cats."

Her mouth twitched. Could she possibly have a sense of humor?

"I can't breathe," she insisted. "You're smothering me."

"I imagine that's from spitting out that torrent of abuse. Quite remarkable, abuse in three languages. Did it take a lot of practice?"

That time he was sure she was trying not to smile. She did have a sense of humor. He felt her body soften under his. Rafe relaxed. The skirmish was over. Miss Cleeve had decided to be sensible.

"Having exchanged compliments, I suppose I should introduce myself. Rafe Ramsey, at your service." He released her and started to sit up.

A mistake. The moment she felt him shift off her, she exploded into action. He wrestled her back down beneath him. In three seconds he had her pinned under him again, only not quite so neatly this time. Lord, but the girl was all bones. And piss and vinegar.

"This is extremely tiresome of you, you know. I mean you no harm."

"You'll break my arm," she growled.

"Probably," he agreed. "If you keep struggling like that. It won't be intentional on my part—"

At that moment a ray of moonlight lit her face. Rafe stared at his prisoner. She was . . . lovely. Her eyes were rather fine—blue, or green, or somewhere in between—fringed with dark lashes and set at an intriguing angle. Her nose was small and straight, her lips full and lush. And her skin, under the truly amazing amount of dirt, felt soft and smooth.

"My God," he whispered. "What a rare little beauty."

She jerked her head back and biffed him on the nose, hard.

"Ooof!" It hurt like the very devil. He had to hand it to the little demon. She didn't give up easily. Without letting go of her wrists, he managed to plant an arm over her head and held it pressed to the floor. His nose ached. His eyes watered.

She gave him a smug look.

"Whoever brought Cleopatra to Rome wrapped in a rug knew his business," he told her with feeling.

The rather fine green eyes narrowed to furious cat slits.

Her turban lay near his right hand. He transferred both her wrists to his left hand, shook out the coils of the turban, and used it to bind her hands together. He sat up, caught her kicking feet, and tied them together with the other end.

"Ah," he said as he discovered the knife strapped to her calf. "What a devious young lady you are, Miss Cleeve. But what a useful weapon." He removed it.

"Don't call me that!"

"Call you what? A young lady? It does stretch the point, I agree."

"Miss Cleeve," she said crossly. "I'm not her."

"No? The grubbiest thief in Cairo just happens to speak perfect English?" He used her knife to cut off the leftover turban fabric, and helped her to sit up.

She glowered at him. "I speak many languages."

"So I heard. Most of them from the gutter, I'm guessing, but your English—"

"I picked it up from English sailors in Alexandria."

He laughed. "Frightfully genteel sailors they have in Alexandria, then. Your accent is perfect—"

"So? My French accent is perfect, as is my Russian and my—"

"Undoubtedly, but every syllable of your English reeks of the upper class and not the sort you pick up on the docks of Alexandria, so stop the nonsense. I wasn't born yesterday and I don't like liars."

"Good, I don't like you, either, so let me go and I won't bother you again."

"You're not going anywhere." He hauled her upright. "You're Alicia Cleeve, the only daughter of Sir Henry and Lady Cleeve, and I'm here to take you home to your grandmother."

She glared at him and repeated. "For the last time, Englishman—"

"Ramsey, Rafe Ramsey."

"Englishman," she repeated stubbornly. "I am *not* Alicia

Cleeve, I don't have a grandmother, and I'm already home—or I will be if you will just let me go."

He shrugged. "It's no use, you know. I have a picture of Alicia Cleeve at thirteen and there's no doubt in my mind that it's you. You're older, thinner, and dirtier, and your company manners have probably taken a distinct downhill turn, but other than that, you haven't changed much at all."

She glowered at him in silence. Her gaze roamed around the room. "What have you done to Ali?"

"He's in the next room." Rafe jerked his head. "Sleeping."

"Sleeping?" She snorted and fought against her bonds. "Through all this noise? You've hurt him, haven't you? Or drugged him. If you've hurt him, I'll—"

"I don't hurt children," he snapped. "Or drug them. Now stop that or you'll hurt yourself." In her struggles her head missed the leg of the table by a scant quarter inch. He bent and scooped her up. Lord, but this little spitfire weighed nothing.

"Let me loose. I need to see him," she demanded. She pretended to be unaware of her helpless position, but her body was tense and stiff with fear. Her sharp little chin jutted belligerently.

"You'll stay tied up until I say so." The spark of anger deep within him grew. What the devil had people been about to allow a gently born young English girl—a baronet's daughter, for God's sake—to starve in a foreign land? Whatever she'd experienced had turned her into a wildcat.

"I won't say a word until you prove to me that Ali's all right." Her soft, full lips clamped together in a thin line. She glared at him through slits of green suspicion.

"Fair enough." Rafe carried her into Ali's room. He'd carried women often enough before, and when you held them against your chest they were usually a soft, satisfyingly solid armful. Not one of them had felt like a skinny little alley cat, trapped and ready to explode with fear and rage.

Yet his body was still—despite all that had happened—aroused.

He set her carefully on the bed and retreated a few steps out of the glow of the lamp he'd left burning for the boy, and willed his body to behave itself.

Ali sat up in bed. He gave her a silent, speaking look.

"He's gagged!" she said indignantly. "He can't breathe."

"He can breathe," Rafe said calmly and untied the strip of cloth. "He just can't warn any associates. Not that it matters now."

There was a torrent of angry-sounding Arabic then as she rapped questions at the boy. He mumbled answers with hanged head and guilty grimaces.

"A bath?" she said to Rafe with a scowl. "You made him take a bath?"

Rafe shrugged. "He was dirty." Did she think he'd tuck a dirty, verminous street boy into a bed made up with clean sheets? He was very tempted to offer her one as well.

He'd instructed his valet, Higgins, to draw a bath for the boy, make him scrub himself well, and ensure there were no lice in his hair. But Higgins had reported the interesting fact that the boy's dirt was limited to his face, hands, and feet. Underneath, he seemed surprisingly clean. Though he still made him bathe.

Someone had looked after him quite well. Rafe, looking at the way Miss Cleeve smoothed back Ali's short, spiky hair as she continued her interrogation, was almost certain who. No doubt her dirt-streaked appearance was mainly superficial also. She hadn't smelled the least bit dirty when he was rolling around on the floor with her.

Of course, he realized. The dirt was a disguise.

She smelled . . . he thought back . . . like a dusty little cat. She was clean beneath the dusty exterior. He wondered whether beneath the furious spitting and snarling she might be . . . softer. Sweeter.

It would be fun teaching this little she-cat to purr, he thought. His body ached to try.

But she was his charge, he reminded himself sternly. Lady Cleeve's granddaughter, not a potential mistress. Lady Cleeve's little wildcat. Not his.

Her head whipped around accusingly. "Ali said you fed him something."

"No drugs, and I don't starve children, either," he told her coolly. "He ate what I ate."

With those looks and that spirit she'd take London by storm.

She turned back to Ali and the boy obviously confirmed it, for after a small humph—annoyance that she hadn't caught him out in any dastardly act, he presumed—the exchange continued.

Rafe watched, the language flowing over him like water

through a dry bed of stones. He'd learned a little Arabic from a book on the voyage out here, but their speech was too rapid for him to pick up more than an occasional isolated word. But you could pick up a great deal about people from simple observation.

She scolded the boy the way mothers the world over scold errant children, yet she was far too young to be his mother. In any case he was obviously Arab and she, just as obviously, was not. So—

"You didn't!" Rafe blinked as her voice cut into his thoughts. She stared at him, with an odd expression. "I don't believe it."

"Believe what?" he asked her.

"He claims you told him a bedtime story!"

Rafe looked vague. "What?" He wasn't going to admit a thing.

"'Ali Baba and the Forty Thieves.'"

"I don't speak Arabic—how could I tell him anything, let alone a story?"

"Opennn sesameeee," Ali chimed in with a grin. Wretched brat.

Rafe stood and briskly scooped her into his arms. "Now that you've satisfied yourself that the boy is unharmed, I have questions for you. You, boy," he said severely. "Go to sleep."

"Opennn sesameeee," Ali responded happily.

Rafe kicked the door shut behind him. He carried her across the room. Again the spurt of anger flared deep within him. There was nothing to her, nothing. Nothing but skin and bones and defiant courage. And eyes full of knowledge . . .

Dammit, he was aroused again. He dumped her on the sofa.

She held her bound hands up. "Aren't you going to untie me?"

"No."

"Don't you trust me?" Her face was all shadows and angles.

"Not the least little bit." His nose still ached. So did other parts. He turned away, ostensibly to light a lamp, but also to have a stern word with his unruly body.

He returned, the lamp lit, and found she'd wiggled herself into the far corner of the sofa and was sitting with her knees up to her chest and her bound wrists hooked over them. A small defensive knot.

He put the lamp where it would light her face and keep him

in shadow. She glowered at him, her face streaked with dirt. She looked about fifteen.

According to her grandmother, she was nineteen, almost twenty. He tried to imagine her cleaned up and in a dress. Yes, nineteen would be about right. With the eyes of a woman much older.

"How old are you?"

She planted the small decided chin on her knees and said nothing. The silence lengthened. Rafe said nothing. Silence, he knew from his time in the army, could be both a tool and a weapon.

The lamplight glowed on the silken, sulky mouth, the most feminine part of her. No, not the most feminine. His palm remembered the softness he'd felt between her legs. He folded his arms, doing his best to blot out the memory.

He didn't need this. It was entirely inappropriate. He'd been sent to find this girl, not lust after her.

"None of your business." She watched him suspiciously, hostile, braced for trouble, trying very hard not to let him see how afraid she was.

Rafe frowned. Why was she still afraid? He'd told her several times he was here as her grandmother's agent. He'd come to rescue her. He'd assured her several times he wasn't going to hurt her. And she knew damned well he hadn't hurt Ali even though he'd caught the boy trying to rob him.

But she seemed more nervous than ever. Even as he thought it, the answer came to him; she must have noticed the state he was in. Dammit.

"All appearances to the contrary, you are perfectly safe with me," he said in a firm voice. "I don't hurt women, either." He moved to another chair farther away.

"Tell that to my bruises."

"I'm sorry, but I had no idea you were a woman. If you will come sneaking into people's houses dressed as a criminal bent on assassination . . ." He shrugged.

"So you're not sorry at all, then, are you?"

He gave her a look. "I am a man of my word. Your grandmother wouldn't have sent me if there was any danger of me hurting you."

She snorted. "I don't have a grandmother. Untie me."

"I said I was sorry, not that I was stupid."

She muttered something explosive sounding in Arabic.

"To be sure," He settled back in the chair. "Now, if you've finished maligning my character and antecedents, I will tell you about your grandmother."

"I told you, don't have a grandmother."

"Then I'll tell you about Lady Cleeve, the Dowager Lady Cleeve, grandmother to Miss Alicia Cleeve, to whose portrait you bear an amazing resemblance."

She glared at him over her knees.

He smiled. "That's right, my prickly little captive audience, you have no choice."

She gave a long-suffering sigh and closed her eyes.

"I met your gr—Lady Cleeve at a friend's wedding."

He told her about Lady Cleeve, how he'd met her for the first time at Harry's wedding in December. "At first she was just some old lady sitting beside me at the table. Imagine my surprise when she turned out to be Allie Todd, my grandmother's oldest friend."

The green eyes remained closed but a faint frown wrinkled the smooth brow. She was following the story.

"Granny always called her by her maiden name, Alicia Todd," Rafe explained and the frown disappeared. "I presume you're named Alicia after her."

Her eyes remained still shut but the quality of silence had changed.

He continued, "Granny used to read me bits from her letters. They weren't like normal letters. They were exciting, full of stories about snakes under beds, and tigers eating goats and people—they hunted down the man-eaters riding on elephants."

He could tell she was interested, despite herself. "Those letters made a small boy dream of traveling to India for adventure." He glanced up and she instantly shut her eyes.

He continued, "When Sir John, her husband, died, Lady Cleeve came home to England. That was eight years ago. She found everything had changed, most of her old friends gone, died, mostly."

He added coolly, "My own grandmother was among them." His voice never wavered.

He'd never spoken of his grief before and he wasn't going to start now. He'd been at school at the time, and nobody had thought to tell an unimportant small boy his grandmother had

died. Not until weeks after the funeral, when he was sent to
Axebridge in the school holidays instead of to Granny's, as
usual. And when he'd asked why, his father told him because his
grandmother was dead, of course.

Quite as if Granny hadn't been the only person in the world
who cared about him . . .

But that was in the past. Rafe didn't dwell in the past.

He took a sip of brandy, then continued. "Lady Cleeve planned
to come to Egypt—she hadn't seen your father for some years—
but the war delayed her, and then, just as it became possible and
her arrangements were finally in place, she got word of his
death."

He paused, gathering the words to explain the unexplainable.
"She didn't know about you, didn't know you were alive. I don't
really understand why."

She hugged her knees to her chest and said nothing, her face
set and hostile as if she didn't care about any of this. He couldn't
imagine what her life had been like the past six years, but he
couldn't blame her for being angry and untrusting.

"She'd had a letter some years before from your father, you
see, in which he told her his wife and daughter were dead. It
didn't explain much—I suppose he was incoherent in his grief."
He shook his head. "Lady Cleeve thought he meant *you* were
dead. She told me to tell you she grieved terribly for her little
granddaughter namesake. Before that she always sent you letters
and presents, remember? A golden-haired doll?"

She didn't move a muscle, was determined not to acknowl-
edge a word. Stubborn little creature. He admired her strength
of purpose, even if he didn't understand why she didn't simply
say, "Thank you very much, yes, take me to my grandmother,
please."

He would bend her to his will in the end. She would come
back to England with him; she had no choice.

She was no longer simply an excuse to leave England or a
favor for his grandmother's oldest friend. He could not, would
not leave this courageous little scrap, this woman dressed as a
boy—hiding in dirt and rags and anger—to her fate.

Somehow, in that violent exchange on the floor, this wild
little beauty had got under his skin, as no woman had.

This was now a personal challenge.

"Apparently your father had always been a poor correspondent and after your mother's death, the letters were even more infrequent and bare of any personal references. And then he died."

He waited, but still she said nothing. He continued, "For the past six years your grandmother thought she was alone in the world, no family, only some distant cousins and a few remaining friends."

It didn't compare to how alone her granddaughter had been. The way she sat bunched defensively in the corner of the sofa gave testimony to that.

"A few months ago Lady Cleeve received a visit from Alaric Stretton—perhaps you remember him—the famous traveler and artist? He called on your father several times."

She didn't flicker an eyelash.

"Lady Cleeve had first met him in India years ago. He visited your father a month or two before his death, and he gave Lady Cleeve a couple of keepsakes. These."

He rose and opened the brown leather folder for her to see.

Ayisha stared at the pictures that had caused all this trouble. There was Papa, looking exactly as she remembered him, stern, a little aloof, serious. And there, on the other half of the folder, her own thirteen-year-old face looked back at her, a little anxious, a little dreamy.

She remembered Mr. Stretton well. Tall and lanky and blond, with kind blue eyes. He'd told her stories of his travels to keep her still while he sketched. Stories entranced her.

But she wasn't that girl any longer. Stories could weave a trap . . .

The Englishman continued in that deep voice, quiet yet so compelling. She wished it wasn't. She hadn't meant to listen to any of this, but that voice . . .

"Lady Cleeve realized it was not you who'd died, but another daughter, perhaps a baby. And so she asked me to come out here to search for you. And, here you are, found at last, like a long-lost heroine in a storybook."

Ayisha stared at the picture of her father and her much younger self. Her stomach churned, and her jaw ached from where he'd punched her. She shivered, feeling suddenly cold.

He noticed and fetched a blanket, wrapping it carefully around her shoulders, tucking it in to make sure she was warm.

She hardened herself against him.

He wasn't the sort of man who'd hurt a woman deliberately, but she wouldn't make the mistake of trusting him.

He was dangerous in other ways.

"Your grandmother is lonely, Alicia. It is the dearest wish of her heart to find you and bring you home to Cleeveden."

She wouldn't look at him.

He leaned forward and his voice was like rich dark coffee as he said, "Come with me and you will never go hungry again. Your grandmother will ensure you will never want for anything— ever again. And when she dies, you will inherit her house and her fortune."

She didn't move a muscle. He must not know she cared.

He went on, "She is an old woman who needs you. All she wants is to bring you home and love you."

Ayisha was silent for a long time. *To bring you home and love you . . . you will never want for anything again.*

Oh, he was a sorcerer indeed, with that deep, persuasive voice of his. Had he read her mind, that he'd given voice to the dearest wish of her own heart: to have a home of her own, to be loved. To be part of a family.

"It is a terrible thing to have no family," she whispered finally. "To belong to no one." She remembered those first achingly miserable months of aloneness, before her cat had befriended her.

"I know." The Englishman knelt and began to untie her bound feet. "I'm glad you've decided to be sensible. If we leave for England in the next two days, we should be in England by Easter. It's early this year—in March."

Ayisha bit her lip and stared at the big hands deftly unknotting the fabric that tied her. They were not a gentleman's hands, not a scholar's like Papa's.

Oh, she wanted to, wanted to accept his offer, to go to this grandmother who offered her love and a home, a home in England, that green and pleasant land where Papa had always said he would take her . . . In time for an English Easter. An English spring.

It was a fairy tale he offered her, but she was not the fairy-tale princess of the story.

She looked at his hands: warrior's hands, or a horseman's, nicked and scarred and tanned and strong. Those same hands had punched her on the jaw and bound her hand and foot, she reminded herself. They could probably choke the life out of her without straining. If they knew what she had kept secret all these years, what would they do to her?

She closed her eyes tightly against the lure of those blue, blue eyes. They were frightening, those eyes, the way they never shifted from her, seeming to look straight into her soul, inviting her to trust his words, trust him, give herself over to his care . . .

It was like looking into a deep pool and knowing it would pull you down and drown you, but wanting to jump in anyway.

And the worst thing was, she did want to. She wanted to believe him, to believe that somewhere there was a loving grandmother who wanted her, loved her, offering her a home, a place in the world, safety . . .

But she'd had a home, love, and safety once, and they'd melted away like a puddle in the sun. She and Mama had thought Papa was a god, all protective, all powerful—and yet he'd left them with nothing. Less than nothing. Worse off than before, because they knew how good life could be . . .

"You will never go hungry again," he added, his voice so deep and persuasive, like dark honey laced with opium. "Nobody will harm you ever again. You'll be safe and secure forever."

The words wound themselves insidiously around her heart, tugging, trying to find a way in.

Dangerous, untrustworthy words. Words that, even if she believed them, were not for Ayisha. They were for another girl.

She shook her head, as if to clear it of his spell. "Tell the old lady that Alicia Cleeve is dead." She made a futile little gesture with her bound hands. "Here, there is only Ayisha."

Four

*H*e let you go?" Laila was stunned. "He knocked you out and tied you up, and then he just *let you go*?"

"Yes," Ayisha said. "He said I was to think it over and go back." She'd returned to Laila's house the moment the city gates were unlocked.

"Go back for Ali—he is all right?"

"Yes, I told you." Ayisha had told Laila a dozen times that Ali was all right, but Laila had been up all night fretting and would not be wholly reassured until he was home, safe.

Ayisha squatted to feed the oven fire. Laila was usually up at dawn to start the baking, but today she was fretting instead. So they'd started the baking late.

She found the Englishman's action puzzling, too—more than puzzling—it was disturbing. She didn't understand what game he was playing, but she was sure it was a deep one.

"How will we get Ali free? Is it money the Englishman wants?" Laila asked, with a glance at their hiding place behind the bricks.

"No. He has more money than you and I will ever see in

a lifetime." Ayisha thrust a handful of twigs in the fire.

Laila pulled off pieces of risen dough and rolled them into balls. "He wants you in exchange for Ali?"

"Yes," Ayisha said. The morning air was chilly, so the heat of the oven was a comfort. She washed her hands and face in a bucket of warm water.

"But he had you. He could have kept you." Laila kneaded dough briskly. "So why set you free?"

"He wants me to come back of my own free will," Ayisha said with irony.

"And you really are English?" Laila was still not convinced.

"Half English, yes."

"And your father was a lord? And you can speak English?"

"Yes."

"Say something."

"Laila is my best friend," Ayisha said in English.

Laila pinched her chin affectionately. "And you, little chick, are the daughter of my heart," she responded in the same language. They stared at each other and laughed.

"You speak English?" Ayisha exclaimed.

Laila chuckled. "Not so good as you. I learn when I was girl. I work for English people before I marry. And look at you—all this time, and I never guess you are English girl." She flattened dough balls into rounds.

"I'm not. I was born here."

"Phhht!" Laila waved that notion away. "Your father was an English lord. That make you English. And all this time you have been hiding in fear, dressed as a boy."

Ayisha said, "You know why."

Laila waved the reason away with a floury hand. "Of course I know why. But now it will be different. Let this man, this Englishman, take you to this grandmother in England. Why not?"

"Laila, you know why not."

"Pah! They do not know, so why should you care? The old lady will look after you and you will take good care of her, and after she dies you will be rich and own her house and will want for nothing."

"I cannot do it."

Laila slapped dough balls flat. "What is wrong with you, girl? It is everything you have dreamed of and more."

"I know, but—"

"But nothing. This is the chance you have been waiting for. And if this old woman is indeed your grandmother, you must go to her and take care of her, for she is your blood and you are hers. And this you know is true."

Laila dusted flour off her hands and stroked Ayisha's cheek with the back of her hand. "To have imagined yourself all alone in the world, Ayisha, child—and then to find you have family— it is a gift, a holy gift." Her soft brown eyes were moist with emotion.

"But I—"

"Not you, the old lady. She has lost her husband and her only son and now, when she is in the twilight of her life, alone, lonely, and without hope, here is the beautiful young granddaughter she thought was dead and gone, restored to her. Of course it is a holy gift and you cannot refuse, little one."

"But you and I both know it's not me she wants. You are my family, Laila. You and Ali."

Laila shook her head. She cupped Ayisha's chin and said, "Listen to me, daughter of my heart. What future is there here for you, dressed in men's clothes, hiding all the time from those who come looking? How will you marry? How will you have children?"

"Maybe I don't want to marry."

Laila shook her head, her eyes wise and knowing. "You will, chick. One day you will meet a strong, handsome man and your heart will beat thud-thud-thud." She thumped her fist against her chest. "And your knees will go weak and your woman's loins will warm and—aha, you blush! Perhaps you have already met someone, perhaps this Englishm—"

"No, it is your foolishness that makes me blush," Ayisha retorted. "My woman's loins will warm indeed!" She could feel her cheeks warming, nevertheless. So what if she did find the Englishman appealing to look at? He was handsome, that was all.

Laila chuckled. "Ah, little one, until you have gripped a strong man between your thighs and felt him thrusting like a stallion as he pours his hot seed into your body, do not talk to me of foolishness."

Ayisha stared, her mouth drying at the picture Laila's words conjured in her mind. Laila had always been earthy, but this . . .

"Now you really are blushing, and me, too." Laila gave a deep chuckle and hugged Ayisha. "It's been so long since I have had a man in my bed, I forget my manners."

"Is it truly like that between a man and a woman? So . . ." Ayisha groped for a word. "Magnificent?"

Laila sighed. "With my husband, it was, though I know from other women it is not always like that with their men. But he was mad for me, and I for him, and when he came to me at night, he was like a stallion." Her eyes glowed, remembering.

"But he divorced you." Ayisha could not imagine the pain it must have caused Laila.

The light died from Laila's eyes. "I thought he loved me, and perhaps he did, a little." She made a helpless gesture.

"But not enough. Marriage is about property—and my family is poor, remember?—and about children, and so when I could give him no child, he divorced me and took another wife." She gave a wistful sigh. "She brought him land and gave him sons, so he was probably a stallion with her, too."

Ayisha shook her head. After fifteen years of love and trust in a man, that was Laila's reward. Tossed aside and thrown to the mercy of that slug Omar.

It was what happened when you trusted a man to take care of you. It happened to Mama, it happened to Laila. Ayisha would never make the same mistake. Never.

"Do you think of him often?" Ayisha asked.

Laila shook her head. "No, it is just . . . Sometimes I wake in the night, hot and restless, and I miss . . . a stallion in my bed."

She looked at Ayisha and giggled. "Look at your face! I have shocked you, an old woman like me talking of such things. Come, let us get the baking finished. The morning is passing."

"Five and thirty is not old," Ayisha said.

"It might as well be, living on memories as I must." Laila sighed. "I will sleep alone the rest of my life, for Allah has made me barren, and what man would take a barren woman to wife? But you, Ayisha—you choose to live like this, hiding as a boy."

She let her words sink in, then said, "It is not a future for you, dear child; it is lifelong imprisonment."

She was right, Ayisha knew.

Laila arranged the rounds of dough on baking sheets. "Take the cover off and I'll see if the oven is hot enough." She took up a small jug of water and a sprig of herbs. Ayisha removed the cover of the oven door. Heat gushed out.

Laila flicked water onto the stone base of the oven with the herb bunch. It hissed. "Perfect," she declared. "Pass me the trays."

Ayisha passed the bread trays to Laila, who pushed them deftly into place with a long wooden paddle, then covered the door again.

"Don't let me forget the time," Laila said, her face flushed from the heat of the oven. She started wiping down the bench. "Your father would want this for his only living daughter."

Ayisha grimaced. "My father left me with nothing." Worse than nothing. He had left her to be a target for evil men.

"If you were not meant to go to England, you would not be given this chance. Besides, blood is blood; you have obligations to your father's mother."

"And what if they find out?"

"Piff!" Laila waved an airy hand. "How will they know? They are in England, on the other side of the world."

"There were people here who knew. English people, who are now in England." People who had shown no mercy, no kindness to a nine-year-old child.

"Worry about that if it happens," Laila said. "If your grandmother did not know, how would anyone else? No, you must go to England."

"But what about you and Ali?"

Laila snorted. "Foolish child, have you so soon forgotten who takes care of you? Am I suddenly an old woman who cannot take care of her family? Do not worry about me and Ali. We will do very well, you will see. Now, the bread will be done, I think." She tossed Ayisha the cloth to protect her hands from the heat and picked up the flat wooden paddle.

Ayisha fetched the flat rush baskets they carried the bread in and for the next hour or two they concentrated on baking bread and selling them through the wooden hatch in the wall that looked out into the street. The morning batch always sold quickly: people could not resist the delicious smell that wafted in the air.

When all the bread was sold and half the takings securely hidden in the hollow behind the bricks, Laila made them both a coffee from Omar's special hoard.

They sat in the backyard, sipping the thick, steaming brew, and shared the last, fresh, hot round of bread that Laila always saved for them. Today she spread it with honey for a special treat.

Ayisha sipped the coffee and licked honey off her fingers. Hot bread and honey and coffee was her favorite meal in all the world, but today the coffee seemed too bitter, the bread tasteless, and the honey merely sticky.

Laila didn't understand. To her, the choice was simple: be rich or be hungry; take care of your grandmother and the rest would take care of itself.

But Ayisha already lived a life of deception and it had been hard, harder than Laila realized. She didn't mind deceiving strangers. But when you started to get to know people, to become friends with them, to care about them, such deception became . . . complicated.

And when—if they came to care about you, it became . . . painful.

In this life only Laila and Ali knew she was a woman. Omar had no idea. Even Ali hadn't known at first. Childlike, he'd accepted her as she was. But when he first learned she was a woman, she knew he had felt betrayed.

It would be worse in England. Lying to her grandmother, letting an old lady come to care for her . . . It was one thing to get bread under false pretenses; it was quite another to steal love meant for another, to raise hopes built on lies.

To go to England and make a new life—it was what she'd dreamed of. But at the price of living another lie? It might not be imprisonment, but it would be an ax poised over her head, waiting to fall.

The only way to avoid deception was to tell the Englishman the whole truth. But that would put her entirely in his power, and that she simply could not, would not—dared not—do.

"You look worried, my chicken," Laila observed.

"I don't want to go with him. I don't trust him."

"Did he try to do anything to you?" Laila asked sharply.

Ayisha thought. She'd felt his arousal . . . He could have taken her if he'd wished, though she would have put up a fight with every breath, but . . .

"No," she said. "He treated me with honor. But then, with Lady Cleeve's granddaughter . . . he would."

There was a short silence, then she added, "But I don't want to go back there."

"I can see this," Laila said. "What about Ali?"

Coils of guilt swirled in Ayisha's belly. "Can't you go?"

Laila shrugged. "I will try, of course, you know I will, but if it's you he wants, it will do no good. Is he a stubborn man, do you think? Or persuadable?"

Stubborn? More than stubborn, Ayisha thought. As persuadable as the sphinx. And as easy to understand.

She sipped the bitter brew thoughtfully. She had no choice. Ali was her responsibility.

"I will go." She drank the last of her coffee, hesitated, then upturned the cup upside down on the saucer. Then she handed the cup to Laila. "Tell me."

Laila examined the patterns of the drained grounds in her cup. It was all nonsense, of course, Ayisha thought. She wasn't superstitious; she was educated, a Christian. Still, it was useful to know, just in case . . .

Laila frowned. "There is much happening here, many . . . contradictions. A powerful force will enter your life, and you will—" She broke off.

"What?"

Laila gave a careless shrug and put the cup down, "It's not clear. Sometimes the coffee is like that."

Ayisha didn't believe a word of it. "Tell me."

Laila sighed and took the cup back. "Some difficult—and very painful—choices lie ahead. I see danger. I see heartache. You are pulled in several directions, and the paths ahead are tangled and many. You cannot see which one to take and you will feel lost and afraid."

Ayisha pulled a face. Nothing new then. She was already confused and unsure of what to do.

Laila continued, "There is a man and a question of trust. You must listen to your heart and follow it—even when it seems to be breaking."

Her heart? Every instinct she had told her to get as far away from Rafe Ramsey as possible.

The man was dangerous. In all kinds of ways.

But there was Ali. She'd got him into it, she had to get him out. Laila called Ayisha her daughter of the heart. If that was so, then Ali was the little brother of Ayisha's heart.

Follow her heart? The message was clear. Rescue Ali.

*I*t had been a calculated risk, Rafe said to himself for the tenth time. Set her free, establish the beginnings of trust. He was a man of his word. He'd said he wouldn't hurt Ali and she would see that it was true—if she came back. But if she cared about the boy—and he was sure she did—she wouldn't leave him here. She would return.

If he was any judge of character.

Therein lay the rub. He could judge men, but women—now they were another matter entirely.

What the hell did she mean, Alicia was dead, there was only Ayisha?

Some kind of tortuous female logic, he presumed. Alicia Cleeve is dead indeed, when her own face looked back at her from Alaric Stretton's drawing.

Rafe knew better than to try and unravel that thread of reasoning—if she wanted to be called Ayisha, he'd do it. He'd call her the Queen of Sheba if it got her to come with him to England without fuss and botheration.

But if fuss and botheration was what it took, he'd do it. He had no qualms about dragging her back to England kicking and screaming. And no doubt scratching and biting, he added to himself, gingerly touching the side of his neck where she'd scratched him last night. It still stung a little. The scratch of a she-cat usually did.

His valet, Higgins, had observed the marks this morning with pursed lips, too well trained to show his disapproval openly. He'd shaved Rafe very carefully, avoiding the long scratches, then applied one of his special salves, muttering that in Oriental climes it didn't do to neglect wounds.

Rafe came downstairs. Ali was seated at the dining room table, stuffing his very clean face with toast, lamb sausages, and scrambled eggs. Higgins, who Rafe had appointed to watch over the boy, sat beside him, attempting, if Rafe were any judge, to teach Ali English table manners. He didn't approve of Rafe's order to have the boy served breakfast in the dining room. Such a boy, his demeanor indicated, should be lucky to eat in the scullery.

Higgins stood as Rafe entered.

Ali looked up and waved a fork at Rafe in a friendly fashion, clearly not intending to abandon his breakfast.

Higgins sighed and drew the boy to his feet by the collar. "Say, 'good morning, sir,'" he said and demonstrated a respectful bow.

Ali, who'd grabbed a sausage in his hand as though he might be dragged off any minute, swallowed a giant mouthful of eggy toast and said to Rafe with a happy grin, "Goomorneesor, open sesameeee." He gave an uncannily exact replica of Higgins bow that at the same time mocked it completely, then returned with all speed to empty his plate.

Rafe couldn't help but chuckle. Cheeky little sod. "Thank you, Higgins. *Sabaah el kheer*," he said to Ali. *Good morning* in Arabic.

Ali's eyes widened. He responded with a torrent of rapid Arabic.

Rafe held up his hand. "Slow down," he said. "I only know a little." He filled a plate with scrambled eggs and sausages from the covered dishes on the sideboard. It was odd seeing the array of covered dishes set out on the sideboard exactly as it would have been in England, but this was a house that had been leased to various Englishmen over the last few years, and the handful of servants that came with the house had been trained accordingly. And no doubt if they hadn't, Higgins would have seen to it. A man who knew just how things should be done, Higgins; he was more than a valet.

He bit into a sausage and an explosion of exotic tastes burst onto his tongue. It was nothing like an English sausage—made of lamb, not pork. It was highly spiced and fragrant with herbs, more like the sausages he'd eaten in Portugal and Spain. Delicious.

The important thing was that against all the odds he'd found Miss Cleeve. Alive and well. And not in a harem.

What the devil had possessed him to turn her loose?

If she failed to return this morning, he was back to square one.

A kitchen servant arrived with fresh coffee and poured Rafe a cup. "Higgins, has Miss Cleeve sent any message?"

"I couldn't say, sir. I've been attending to this young savage. Wipe your mouth with the napkin, boy, not your sleeve," Higgins told Ali, handing Ali a clean napkin.

Ali immediately pocketed it.

The doorbell jangled in the hall.

Rafe drained his coffee cup. Excellent, he hadn't lost her after all. "Get the door, will you, Higgins? That will be Miss Cleeve."

Rafe rose as his guest entered, looking around her suspiciously, the very image of a ragged street urchin poised to flee. Her gaze went straight to Ali to check he was alive and unharmed, presumably, then darted to each corner of the room, before returning to Rafe.

What did she think, that he would have half a dozen burly henchmen hidden, waiting to pounce on her? Her wariness sparked the flame of anger within him again: God only knew what she'd endured since her father died. He thought of her portrait at thirteen: the impression of a shy and vulnerable young girl.

Now, six years later, there was not a trusting bone in her body.

He took her hand. "Miss Cleeve, delighted you could rejoin us again." Interesting, he thought. Her face was, if anything, dirtier than last night.

She snatched her hand back. "Don't call me that. I told you, I know nothing of Alicia Cleeve; I am Ayisha." She made her way to Ali and made a rapid inquiry in Arabic.

Rafe pulled out a chair and seated her beside the boy. She sat down absently, concentrating on Ali's responses. The morning sun lit her skin. Rafe took the opportunity for a closer look.

As he thought, the dirt had been carefully applied. Along the chin she'd rubbed in a bit of ash, giving the faintest hint of the darkness of an incipient beard. An artist in dirt, Miss Cleeve.

"Yes?" She gave him a sharp look over her shoulder. Green eyes fringed with lush, dark lashes sparked a warning at him. Miss Cleeve didn't like men standing too close, it seemed.

He was about to step back when he noticed a darker-colored patch on the other side of her jaw.

"Let's just have a look at that," he said and took her chin gently in his hand. She tried to pull away.

"Steady," he said quietly. "I just want to look at the bruise I gave you last night." He turned that side of her face to the light, and there they were, the marks of his fist clear and dark beneath the artistic layer of dust.

"I'm sorry," he said as he released her. "If I'd known you were a woman . . ."

"It doesn't hurt," she said quickly and turned away.

Rafe signaled a servant to bring fresh coffee and as the man hurried off, Rafe placed eggs, toast, and sausages on a plate and set it in front of her.

She looked up. "What's this?"

"Breakfast." She was going to argue the point, he could see. "But—"

"I always feed my guests, and since you've joined us at breakfast time . . ." He sat down.

She frowned at the plate. "Thank you, but I've already broken my fast." She didn't sound at all certain. Best not to push the point; if he tried to insist she would probably refuse.

He shrugged. "What can I say? The obligations of hospitality. A few morsels, and form has been observed. Ah, and here is the coffee." He addressed himself to his coffee and ate another sausage just to make the point. Or perhaps not entirely to make a point. He was very fond of English sausages, but these spicy things were excellent. He didn't look at her.

Ayisha stared at the plate. Two fat sausages, warm and plump and smelling heavenly. How long since she had eaten meat? And eggs, creamy and golden and smelling of butter and a hint of cheese.

But there were obligations once you'd accepted a man's food . . .

"Don't you want that?" Ali asked.

She glanced at his empty plate. "How many of these have you had?" She touched a sausage with her fork.

"Four," Ali said proudly. "They are called *lemsausages* and they are the best thing I have tasted in my life, Ash. If I ate another one I think maybe I would burst. But I have two more in my pocket for later and if you don't want those, I could—"

"No," she said hastily, with a glance at the tall man at the end of the table. He was eating, apparently ignoring them. "It is bad manners to steal food when your host has offered it freely."

Ali's face fell. "Must I give them back?"

She hesitated.

"I have never eaten such wonderful things, Ash," he whispered. "But I would not wish to insult Rameses when he has been so good to me, so if you say I must give them back—"

"Good to you?" she burst out. The Englishman looked up, and she instantly lowered her voice, even though she knew he couldn't understand them. "He kidnapped you and tied you up."

Ali shrugged. "I tried to steal from him. He could have given me to the pasha's men, but he didn't."

"Yes, but—"

"He didn't even beat me, Ash. And he brought me to his own table and shared with me food he himself ate. The best food I have had in all my life. Taste it and see."

Bewitching aromas teased her, making her mouth water. Ayisha looked at the laden plate and glanced at the Englishman. He seemed engrossed in something on the table beside him, so she cut off a small piece of sausage and popped it into her mouth.

The flavors melted in her mouth. It was unbelievably delicious. And once she started she couldn't stop.

"Told you," Ali whispered beside her as she worked her way silently through first one, then the other sausage. "*Lemsausages.*"

She ate the scrambled eggs, too, and the toast, and washed it down with milky European-style coffee. Heavenly.

"See, his food is good and so is he," Ali said as she finished. "And I know you don't believe me, but he did tell me a story last night."

She blotted her lips with her napkin. "How could you know what he was saying? You don't know English and he doesn't speak Arabic."

"I know what I know," Ali said with that stubborn jut to his sharp little jaw she knew so well. "And I like him."

Ayisha frowned. "The bath last night, what happened?" Ali usually put up some resistance to a bath.

"It was in a big tin, with hot water that came up to my ears, and soap that smelled good enough to eat." He grimaced. "It didn't taste so good though."

"He didn't hurt you? Or threaten to hurt you?"

"Who, Higgins? No. He just pointed to me and then the bath, and he stared down his long nose—he looks like a camel—until I got in." Ali shrugged. "Then he took my clothes away and gave me a shirt to sleep in, and in the morning my clothes were clean. See?"

Ayisha rolled her eyes. After the trouble she and Laila usually had to get the little wretch to wash, all it took was someone to point at a tub of water and look down a long nose, was it?

"And nobody hurt you?"

"No, I was frightened at first, but they have been good to me, Ash." He gave her an anxious look, as if she might spoil things by being rude.

She glanced down the long table at the Englishman, only to find he was watching her.

She looked away and a moment later glanced back. Still he was watching her. Why?

A bit of egg, maybe? Her hands itched to check. She crossed them over her chest. She shouldn't care if there were bits of egg all over her face. She wanted to look as unattractive as possible, and food on the face was extremely unattractive. So if there was egg . . . that was good, she told herself.

It was just the way those blue eyes looked at her . . . It was very unnerving. Like a caress.

She felt her cheeks warming, put her chin up, and stared back at him. Not at all like a caress.

He smiled, folded his napkin, and rose, saying, "Now that you've finished your breakfast, Miss Cleeve, let us discuss your future in the sitting room." He rang the bell.

Suddenly the food felt like lead in her stomach. "What about Ali?" she said. "I'm here now, let him go."

"Ali stays," the Englishman said crisply.

"But Laila will be worried about him—he's been gone all night."

He considered that. "Very well. Higgins," he said to the man who'd appeared at the door. "Take the boy home. Take the interpreter with you and reassure this Laila that Miss Ayisha is safe. Will that suffice?" he added, turning back to Ayisha.

She nodded, relieved Ali would no longer be a hostage. She added to Ali, "Tell Laila I am all right and not to worry."

Ali nodded, and with a friendly wave to the Englishman, turned to Higgins, apparently unworried about Ayisha's fate.

"I'll join you in the sitting room in a moment, Miss Cleeve," the Englishman said. "You go on ahead. I just need to have a word with Higgins."

Five

She entered the sitting room alone and was swept instantly back to the past. There was the heavy brass lamp hanging from the ceiling; she remembered it swinging gently, making shadows dance.

There were the fans Papa had rigged up as they had them in India. Even the old Persian carpet, spread over the tiled floor was the same, though a little more faded and worn.

The smell was different; no hint remained of the cigar Papa used to smoke each evening. The room had been painted light green instead of cream, and some of the furniture had changed. Otherwise it was the same.

She gravitated, as always, to the bookshelves. To her amazement, many of her father's books remained, though they were well worn now, their spines cracked, the title lettering faded, read by the various people who'd lived in the house since, people who didn't worship books as Papa had, who took less care of them than he did.

She ran her fingers lightly over some of the titles left behind, caressing books she remembered, a few she'd loved. How long since she'd read a story?

"Old friends?" The deep voice behind her made her jump. She turned and found him standing close, so close she could smell the clean, distinctive scent of him, the fresh tang of cologne and clean, sun-dried linen, and something darker, more masculine underneath. It made her want to just lean into him, lean against that broad, strong chest and . . .

She swallowed and stepped back, putting some distance between herself and the books, herself and his faint, disturbingly appealing scent.

She pretended to misunderstand him. "Friends? No, I was looking at the books and the pretty patterns." She stroked the gold lettering. "Is it real gold?"

"Yes, and I'm quite sure you can read the 'pretty patterns,' too. You had no trouble finding the sitting room."

She shrugged. "It wasn't hard to find."

"No, not for someone who used to live here."

She turned away from the bookshelf. She hadn't realized how much she'd missed books until she saw these ones again.

"I expect this room has stirred up a few memories."

Not trusting herself to answer, she gave an indifferent shrug. Stirred up was right: she had to get calm again, regain control. Protect herself. Rebuff him.

He gestured her toward a chair, but it was one her mother had favored for embroidery so Ayisha chose a light rattan chair instead. The Englishman sat in a large, heavily carved armchair opposite her: her father's favorite seat. Her eyes searched for the stool she used to sit on when Papa gave her lessons, but it was nowhere to be seen.

"Now, Miss Cleeve—"

"My name is Ayisha," she interrupted. "I am not who you think I am and I won't go to England with you." There. It was said.

He leaned back, crossed his long legs, looked at her with those piercing blue eyes, and said, "Why not?"

"Why not?" she repeated. "Because as I said, I am not who you think—"

"Yes, yes, I've heard all that before, but even if you are not really Miss Cleeve, why wouldn't you come with me to England, where wealth and comfort are waiting for you?"

She stared at him, puzzled. "I don't understand."

"You are poor, one step away from starvation, living on the streets—"

"I am not living on the streets!"

"Close enough, from where I sit. You are stealing to make ends m—"

"I do not steal!" she said angrily.

"You broke into a private house, last night, armed with two knives—"

"Because you kidnapped a child."

"I saved a boy from punishment as a thief. I suppose you sent him to steal the picture—"

"I did *not*! I would *never* encourage him to steal. I told him not to go anywhere near you! I strictly forbade him even to follow you and—"

"Nevertheless he tried to steal the picture of you."

She bit her lip.

"I believe the punishment for stealing here is quite harsh. They cut off a hand, don't they? The pasha, Mehmet Ali, runs a very strict, law-abiding country, they tell me."

She swallowed, having no answer for his accusation. She did not send Ali to steal, but it was because of her he'd been tempted.

"So," he continued, "you are living in poverty, in a country not your own—"

"I was born here."

He slammed his fist on the arm of the chair. "Your father was an Englishman—a baronet, dash it—and you know perfectly well you belong in England with your grandmother! You're nineteen, for God's sake!"

She looked away, shaken by his anger, annoyed by it. What did he have to be angry about? She was the one being bullied.

She felt ashamed of herself even as she thought it; he wasn't a bully. It was just that she had no answers for him—none that would not make her life even worse than he was making it out to be.

He continued in a hard, even voice, "Look at you! You're half starved, living a life where you have to disguise yourself as a boy for your own safety, a hairsbreadth from discovery and disaster—and yet when you are offered a home, a fortune, and a safe, comfortable new life, you reject it. Without even giving it a moment's consideration. Why?"

She frowned.

"You still don't understand, do you? An impostor wouldn't hesitate for a moment. A clever little street thief—"

"I don't steal," she said automatically, but he ignored her.

"A clever little street thief opportunist would snap up my offer in a heartbeat. Wouldn't she, Miss Don't-Call-Me-Cleeve?" He sat back in his chair, those blue, blue eyes boring into her.

The silence stretched. "You said there was a fortune," she said at last. "How much?" She tried to look eager and conniving.

He threw back his head and laughed at that. "Don't ever try and earn your living on a stage. You'd never make it as an actress. Too little and far too late, my dear."

He leaned closer. "I watched your face last night, when we were talking. When I told you your grandmother was lonely and wanted a family, you were genuinely moved."

Ayisha made a gesture of repudiation.

His voice deepened. "You tried to hide it, but I saw. You were touched, deeply. Then later, when I mentioned her having a fortune you barely made a flicker of an eyelash: you were just waiting for me to stop talking so you could tell me Alicia was dead, and that here, there was only Ayisha."

"It's true," she told him.

He didn't believe it, she could see. The trouble was, no explanation she could give him would make sense—except the truth. And the truth was too dangerous.

"Very well." He settled back as if waiting to be told a story. "Explain it to me. If I tell your grandmother I found her long-lost granddaughter but didn't bring her home, I'll need a dashed good reason."

She set her jaw. "I told you what to tell her: that Alicia Cleeve is dead."

"But you're not."

She shook her head.

"Enough of this nonsense. Nothing you can say or do will convince me you are not Alicia Cleeve, so let us be done with this pointless fencing. What happened to you after your father died, Alicia?" He waited. And waited.

She turned herself side on, so she didn't have to meet those blue eyes.

He went on. "I was told the servants had deserted the house.

It must have been very frightening for you, being left all alone with your father lying dead in his bed."

Ayisha tried not to think about it.

"Did you get sick, too? I know they found two bodies there—Sir Henry and a woman—some kind of servant, they s—"

She cut him off. "I never get sick." *Some kind of servant.* Mama's epitaph.

"So did you leave because you were frightened of getting sick?"

The silence stretched. And all the while those intense, blue eyes bored into her.

"I told you I don't get sick," she said at last, unable to stand the silence.

He nodded. "I see. But I don't understand why you left. Why not wait until someone came—the local authorities, someone from the British consulate? They would have looked after you."

She struggled to keep her face free of emotion. Memories swirled through her, stirred up by this room, his questions . . . Images she'd tried so hard to lock away. The sight of Papa's body racked and stiff in death. And Mama, so distraught, sick herself, but smoothing his white cotton sheet over and over, in utter despair . . .

She picked up a cushion and started fiddling with the fringe. "I don't know what you're talking about. I wasn't here." She avoided his gaze. She was no good at lying, she knew it. People always caught her out when she tried to tell a direct lie. She could act a lie, that was no problem, but when it came to looking someone in the eye and giving them false words . . . she was hopeless. She felt guilty, so she looked guilty.

It made no difference. He refused to believe her. "But why leave the house? You would have been safer—" He broke off, his gaze sharpening as if he'd just thought of something—or read her thoughts.

He leaned forward. "You didn't feel safe in the house anymore."

Of course she didn't feel safe. Why else would she have left? She gave him a flat look and curled her legs under her on the chair.

"They told me at the consulate the house was deserted and had been robbed at some stage. Was that it? Were you there when the robbers broke in?"

She didn't respond, just picked at the fringe of the cushion, her face set, her eyes downcast, trying with all her might to focus on the cushion.

Instead she saw the large, bare, dirty feet approaching her mother's bed . . . stopping . . . just inches away from her face . . . the nails of the man's feet, twisted, horny, ingrained with filth . . .

Ayisha had lain there for she didn't know how long, not daring to breathe, certain that she was about to be hauled from her hiding place.

As she had done in nightmares ever since that terrible night . . .

"Ayisha, did men come and . . . hurt you?" he asked gently.

Her eyelids prickled with unaccountable tears. She blinked them away. The softness of that deep voice was insidious. It was a deep siren song, coaxing her, tempting her to trust him, to tell him everything, let him look after her. But if she did, she told herself fiercely, the struggle of the last six years would be for nothing.

She said brusquely, "They didn't rape me, if that's what you're thinking." She'd been in no danger of rape that night . . . On the contrary.

Keep looking. She'll be somewhere—she has nowhere else to go. A white child-virgin will bring a fine sum at Zamil's.

She didn't even know what a virgin was then, but she knew they meant her. And that Zamil's was the slave market . . . for very special slaves.

The Englishman persisted. "Then why didn't you go to the British consulate?"

Because she didn't believe she'd be any safer with the men from the consulate than the robbers. English law did not count in Egypt; only the law of the pasha, so for Ayisha the end result would have been much the same. As it could be if this Englishman discovered the truth about her.

She would *not* become a thing.

She shoved the cushion down the side of the chair. "I won't go to England with you, and this conversation is pointless." She untucked her legs and started to get up.

"Lady Cleeve needs you."

"No, she doesn't," she flashed. "She doesn't even know me. But there are people here who do need me, so—"

"Who? Ali? You could take him with you to England. Send him to school—"

She snorted. "And have him treated like a 'dirty native' for the rest of his life? I think not."

"But—"

"Besides, I can just see Ali in a rigid English boarding school. He would loathe it. No, Ali belongs here. And so do I."

"Is that what you're worried about?" he persisted. "That English people won't respect you? Because Ali might encounter those attitudes—though not everyone in England is so blinkered—but it wouldn't be like that for you. You are the daughter of Sir Henry and Lady Cleeve and granddaughter of the Dowag—"

She stiffened at his words. Aye, there lay the crux of it: *the daughter of Lady Cleeve*. Which she was not.

"No. It is out of the question. I have responsibilities here, and nothing you could say will convince me to go. Tell the old lady Alicia Cleeve is dead." It was the truth, after all, she thought.

And now," she said, standing with hands braced on her hips, "Will you release me?"

He raised a single dark brow. "I wasn't aware you were a prisoner."

"Oh," she said. "Good. Then I'll leave." She needed to go, to be free of his disturbing presence, so she could think things through with a clear head.

She stalked to the door, wrenched it open, and paused. "What would you do if I disappeared?"

"Oh, I don't know," he said idly. "Probably send the pasha's men after you."

She blanched. "You wouldn't."

Rafe smiled. "Probably not, but I wouldn't try it, if I were you. In the army my men trusted me because they knew I kept my word. They also realized I was a ruthless bastard who'd do whatever it took to achieve my aims and that it was easier to go along with me than oppose me. I promised Lady Cleeve I'd do my damnedest to find her granddaughter and bring her home. And I will." He let that sink in, then added, "So I'll see you for dinner this evening."

Ayisha stared at him in disbelief. He'd just threatened to send the pasha's men after her and now he casually invited her for dinner?

"No, you won't." She wasn't going to linger an instant longer in this devil's den than she had to.

"You have another engagement? What a pity, they'll miss you."

She frowned. "Who will?"

"Your friend Laila and young Ali."

"What?"

"I invited them for dinner. Just after sunset." He gave that faint, annoying smile again. It invited her to argue and at the same time smugly declared she wouldn't win.

"They won't come." Laila would be dying of curiosity, and Ali would rave about those sausages, but there was no question of Laila coming.

"Oh, I think they will."

"They won't. Virtuous Arab women do not eat in the company of strange men, especially not strange foreign men," she informed him loftily.

She was relieved that Laila would not meet him. Laila would probably agree with him, urge Ayisha to go with him. Laila had a weakness for a good-looking man.

Laila didn't understand the danger he represented. Laila thought a small lie was harmless. She would think the Englishman was harmless. She would only see a handsome man who wanted to take Ayisha to a better life. And a lonely grandmother who needed family to take care of her in her old age.

Laila did not see what a threat this man was to Ayisha—on every level. Laila would not feel as if those blue eyes sliced open her every defense, leaving her naked and vulnerable.

"A pity, I was looking forward to meeting her." He did not seem unduly upset.

He bent and took her hand in his and stood looking down at it, at her small brown paw held in his large, elegantly shaped hand. His hands were strong, she knew, strong enough to hold her safely over the edge of a precipice, but his fingernails were so clean and polished and smooth. Hers were ragged and grubby. Embarrassed, she tried to pull it from his grip.

And then he did an amazing thing; he lifted her hand and pressed his lips firmly against the back of her fingers.

"Adieu, Miss Cleeve." His lips were warm and firm. A tingle ran right up her arm. She stared at her hand in surprise, snatched it back, and gathered her wits.

"Not adieu," she said firmly, "but good-bye, Mr. Ramsey."

She turned the handle of the front door. It was unlocked. She stepped outside, half expecting that at any minute he would snatch her back. She glanced back at him.

He bowed, gracefully. "Adieu," he reiterated with an infuriating half smile.

She walked at a dignified pace to the front gate which, to her surprise, was also unlocked. She closed it carefully behind her, checked that he couldn't see her any longer, then fled.

Six

*I*t had been years since he'd fished for trout, Rafe thought as he watched her stroll with exaggerated casualness down the drive, but this felt just like it. Let the line play out, then reel her in. Let her fight, struggle, swim away. Then reel her back again.

Little Miss Cleeve could fight and argue all she wanted, but Rafe had made up his mind: she was his.

He'd never met such an extraordinary young woman in his life. And if she thought he could just walk away . . .

It took all the self-control he had to let her go: his every instinct was to take her—drag her if necessary, kicking and scratching and biting—away from this appalling life. He could have her on a ship leaving Alexandria by tomorrow if he wanted.

He could still feel her under him on the floor, all bones and spit and desperate courage, risking her life for a ragged little street thief.

She had pride, this girl, and courage, and after eight years at war, Rafe knew the value of both. He would roll her in a carpet and haul her onto a boat if he had to, but he'd prefer her to walk up the gangplank of her own accord, head held high.

He watched her carefully close the gate and saunter out of sight as if she didn't itch to be gone as far away as possible from him.

How had she survived all this time on the streets? As a boy? The loose Arab clothing disguised her shape, and the streetwise swagger was perfect, and the dirt disguised what he was fairly sure was a fine complexion, but to Rafe, everything about her was deeply feminine.

Even if nobody divined her true sex, there were plenty of men who would prey on a pretty boy.

Why didn't she want to go to England? What was she so afraid of?

And what the hell did she mean by *Alicia is dead, here is only Ayisha?*

She'd said she wasn't raped, but something had happened, he was sure of it. There was a world of knowledge in her eyes, and some deep lurking fear.

She didn't have that brutalized expression he'd seen in the eyes of raped women—he'd seen too much of it at war—a dead, dull look in the eyes that could spark to corrosive rage or bitter self-loathing.

But why else would she say she was dead and call herself by another name?

The question ate at him.

The sooner he got her home to England, the better. She could put whatever it was in the past and start a fresh, new life.

But first he had to cut her free from the ties of this life. The woman, Laila, and the boy, Ali.

Laila must have some sort of a hold over Miss Cleeve. Ali bore all the marks of a thief in training, albeit a clumsy one, while Miss Cleeve had silently scaled the high walls surrounding the house and slid noiselessly inside. It wasn't the first time she'd done that, he'd swear.

Laila could be some kind of thief master. He would meet the woman, and soon.

As it happened, he met Ali in the street a short time later. He suspected the boy was lurking out of curiosity, or perhaps in the hope of food.

"Come and take some refreshment," Rafe said through his interpreter.

Ali needed no second invitation. He sat at the table and waited, eyes shining with anticipation.

Higgins, showing a rare understanding of boys, brought out a large plate of sandwiches, some fruit, and a tall glass of milk. While Ali worked his way through the food, Rafe questioned him.

"This Laila, does she make you work for her?"

"Yes, of course. All the time. Work without cease," the boy declared.

"What kind of work?"

Ali looked around in a conspiratorial manner, leaned forward, and said, "Women's work!" He drained the glass and wiped off a milk mustache with his sleeve. Higgins handed him a napkin. Ali thanked him gravely and pocketed it. Higgins sighed.

Rafe had no interest in napkins. "What does women's work mean?"

"Collecting greens and herbs from the river, sweeping, and selling pies and bread in the streets," Ali told him. "The selling is not so bad, because Laila's pies are the best in all Cairo and I get to eat the broken ones, and the sweeping, well, nobody can see me do that. But the greens . . ." He shook his head in a dire manner. "Other boys mock, make fun of me."

Rafe's lips twitched. Perhaps the boy was not exploited after all, not in the way he'd originally suspected. He seemed a bright lad.

He recalled Miss Cleeve's reaction to his suggestion that Ali could come with her to England. Would the boy feel the same? he wondered. The two were clearly fond of each other.

"Do you know I am going to take Ayisha to England?"

Ali munched unconcernedly on a sandwich. "She told me you want this, but she will not go. She is stubborn like a mule. Nobody can make Ash do what she does not want."

"What if you could go with her to England?"

Ali stopped in mid-bite. He put the sandwich down and considered the matter. "To England?"

"Yes."

"Me and Ash together?"

"Yes."

"Why?"

"Because Ayisha has a grandmother in England and she wants her to come and live with her."

Ali nodded and picked up the sandwich again. "Old people need family to take care of them."

"The old lady is very rich. Ayisha will also become rich if she goes."

Ali nodded appreciatively. "That will be good."

"But you could go with Ayisha if you wanted."

Ali gave him a shrewd look. "Laila, too?"

Rafe shook his head. "No, not Laila," he said firmly. Lady Cleeve might be willing to accept a ten-year-old Arab street urchin as the price for getting her granddaughter back, but he was certain she'd draw the line at a middle-aged Arab peasant woman.

Ali shrugged and, having finished all the sandwiches, started munching on an apple. "Then I stay here. Laila, she have no one, only Omar, and he is no good."

"You would prefer to stay?"

Ali gave him a direct look and said simply, "Laila, she take me from the streets, treat me like a son. A son looks after his mother. I stay here. When I am a man, I will have my own house and Laila will live with me there."

Rafe was speechless.

Encumbrances was clearly the wrong word.

He watched the small boy vigorously demolishing the apple, core and all, until all that was left was the woody stem.

Rafe believed in loyalty, valued it, demanded it from those close to him. That loyalty should be rewarded was an axiom he'd never questioned.

Until now. But Ali's direct sincerity had knocked him for six with its simple power. Because loyalty could not be allowed to keep Miss Cleeve from taking her rightful place in society.

He was curious to meet this Laila. She certainly could inspire loyalty.

And then what would he do? Defeat her? Outwit her? Coercion? He would know the right tactics when he met her. He didn't doubt there would be a fight of some sort.

Ali, having eaten everything in sight, stood up, thanked Rafe and Higgins for the meal, and left. A very direct boy. And a remarkable one.

Rafe glanced at the clock in the hall. Still time to write a few letters and then fit in a few visits this afternoon.

He would call on Laila and discover what sort of woman she was. But before that, a visit to the most unsociable man in Cairo.

*A*zhar! Ho, Azhar!"

Ayisha turned to see who was calling her. It was Gadi. He came running up to her, slapped her on the back, and hooked his arm through hers in the usual manner of friends.

Her instincts prickled: *beware.* Gadi had never been her friend. It was Ali who sought Gadi's company, not the other way around.

"So, Azhar, not selling pies today, I see. Let us walk together." His gaze dropped to her chest and stayed there an instant too long.

Ayisha knew at once what he was looking for: evidence she was a female. He would see nothing, she reminded herself, reminded her quickening pulse. Her breasts were bound tightly, and she wore several layers of loose clothing over them.

He looked up and reaffixed his smile. "Where are you off to?"

"To the river, collecting greens," she said, showing him the bag.

Gadi made a rude noise. "Pah! Women's work!" He sent her a crafty, sideways glance. "But you don't mind that, do you?"

"It's quiet and peaceful at the river. Collecting greens gives me time to think."

He snorted. "A real man would find it demeaning to do such work."

She gave a faint smile. "From the look of you, Gadi, you have always eaten well. When your stomach has gone days without food, real man or not, you learn that any work that puts food in your belly is good work."

Gadi frowned. "Are you saying I'm fat?"

She repressed a smile. Gadi was a good-looking thickhead, and his vanity was not a small or a shy thing. "No, Gadi, you are strong and tall. Me, I have gone hungry many a time, so I am but small and puny."

Gadi squeezed her arm. "You are puny," he agreed complacently. Keeping hold of her he turned a look of close attention on her. "My uncle says he knows you."

Ayisha shrugged. "Does he? Maybe. I don't know him." Her voice sounded bored, uninterested. She hoped Gadi hadn't noticed the way her pulse had leapt.

"He says your father owes him something." Gadi watched her face carefully.

Ayisha gave him a look of mild puzzlement. "My father? Maybe. I wouldn't know. I haven't seen my father since I was very small."

"My uncle says your father was a rich Englishman."

Ayisha stared at him a moment, then laughed. "An Englishman? Oh yes, behold me, the rich English boy in my rich English clothes." She walked a few steps with a mocking swagger, then laughed again.

Gadi looked doubtful, but persisted. "You have light skin and strange eyes. You could be English." Under the guise of checking for national traits, Gadi scrutinized her face for signs of femininity.

Luckily he was one of those quite feminine-looking youths himself, and his beard had not begun to grow.

"Pppht!" Ayisha made a scornful sound. "There are many in Egypt with light skin and eyes these days—Franks, Greeks, Albanians—and look at you—your eyes are almost gold." Ayisha gestured. "My mother told me my father came from Venice, but she said he was a big liar, too, so maybe he was English. But what does it matter?" She spat in the dirt. "He sailed away from us years ago, and your uncle's money with him."

They walked on in silence. Up ahead was the fork in the street where she would turn right to the river and Gadi would turn left to the marketplace. It couldn't come soon enough for Ayisha.

"I remember the first day I saw you on the streets," Gadi said. "You just appeared, from nowhere." Again his gaze dropped searchingly to her chest.

Ayisha snorted. "From Alexandria, you mean. It took me forever to get here. My feet nearly fell off."

His gaze dropped to her feet. "You walked from Alexandria? All that way?"

"How else? You think my rich English father bought me a camel that I might ride into Cairo like a lord?" She laughed. "I wish I did have a rich English father. Oh, the life I would live . . ."

The turnoff was almost upon them. Gadi made one last try. "Did you hear about the Englishman with the picture?"

"Of course, the whole marketplace is talking." She decided to take the bull by the horns. "Everyone tells he has a picture that looks a lot like me. In fact Ali says I should dress as a girl and see if I can get money from the Englishman."

Gadi frowned. "Hey, that was my idea!"

She snorted and said in a sarcastic voice, "Do you think the Englishman would be that stupid? I know I'm small. I might be able to pass for a woman from a distance, but up close? And the girl in the picture is supposed to be English. How am I supposed to speak to this man in English, eh?"

"Oh." Gadi hadn't thought of that.

She could almost see him deciding his uncle had made a big mistake: because if the Englishman was looking for her and if she really was a girl, why would she not go to him? The pickings were bound to be good.

Gadi's uncle hadn't told him everything, that was clear.

"Well, my uncle still wants to talk to you."

Ayisha turned toward the river, wondering how Gadi could have missed the pounding of her heart. It was almost deafening.

"Surely," she said over her shoulder. "But not today, Gadi. I have much work to do."

To her relief, he let go of her arm and turned away. Ayisha continued to saunter casually on, aware that Gadi turned and watched her with a frown.

She'd convinced him this time, but for how long? Gadi's uncle would not be so easily fooled. The net was closing in on her. Her options were narrowing, but she could still, perhaps, get something from the Englishman . . .

A short time later Ayisha stood by the gate of the Englishman's house, dithering. It was not like her, but something about this man undermined her resolve. Part of her kept insisting the only safe thing to do was to stay away. Another part of her said she should make a bid for what she wanted, that fortune favored the bold. Or was it the brave?

Or the brazen? That was the part that Ayisha was doing her

best to squash; the part that leapt with excitement the moment he stepped out the front door in those long, close-fitting buff breeches and his glossy high boots.

He saw her straightaway, of course, and that at least gave her a decision, for she would not let him see her run like the coward she suddenly felt like.

Get it over. He could only refuse. Nothing ventured and all that.

"Miss Cleeve, come in out of the heat and let me give you a nice cool drink," he said, with every evidence of pleasure—only he was secretly crowing with triumph, she could tell. He'd said she'd be back and she was.

She didn't want to accept, but Egyptian manners demanded she be polite and accept the offer of a drink, at least.

As Higgins set a glass of lemonade before her, she gave Rafe a narrow look. "You said you want to help me. That you don't like the way I live. And that my grandmother worries about me."

"Yes," he said cautiously.

"Then why not help me?"

"How?"

"Give me the money you say my grandmother will give me."

He raised a dark brow. "How much?"

She named a huge sum, a bold sum. Laila would have a fit at her asking for so much, but why not? She really was the old woman's granddaughter. It would solve all their problems. She and Laila and Ali could escape Cairo and start a new, good life, free of her past, and best of all, free of Omar.

"And what would you do with this sum?"

"Buy a house in Alexandria," she said without hesitation.

He steepled his fingers and eyed her over them. "I see. And who would live in this house?" His tone was noticeably cooler.

"Ali and me and Laila," she told him. His expression made her hesitate, but she should make a push for the money, she decided. It was the least Papa could do for her. "So will you give me the money for that?"

"No."

She scowled. He hadn't even bothered to consider it. "Why not?"

"Because Lady Cleeve didn't ask me to come all this way to set you up in a house with other people. She asked me to find you because she's damned well fretting herself to flinders worrying about you. She's an old lady who's all alone in the world, and her heart's desire is to bring you home so she can love you and ensure your future."

Ayisha looked away, trying to hide the way his words made her feel. He painted a very appealing picture, but those kind, warm, loving feelings were for another girl, a dead girl, not Ayisha.

She tried to harden her heart against the unknown old lady. She wouldn't want to love and care for her son's by-blow, his illegitimate daughter by a foreign woman. Ayisha would probably be a huge embarrassment for her. The old lady would want her gone. Out of sight.

"But if I had a house in Alexandria—"

"I made a promise," the Englishman told her. "And I keep my promises."

"I don't care, you cannot make a promise for *me*," she said fiercely. "And you can't make me go."

The Englishman tilted his head and gazed at her thoughtfully. It wasn't a challenging sort of look, she decided, it was as if he'd just noticed a smut on her nose. Which was ridiculous. There was more than a smut. She'd been lavish with the dirt today. Apart from it being her usual disguise, it was a message to him: she was not—and never would be—an English lady.

Still that cool blue regard continued.

"What?" she said defensively. "What is it?"

"I won't give you money for a house in Alexandria, but I will buy one for Laila and I'll find a job for Ali, too."

Relief filled her. "You would—"

"But only if you come with me to England," he finished.

She fell silent. He'd put her in an impossible position.

Without Ayisha, Laila would never have the courage to escape her brother. Not without help. And Ayisha had to get out of Cairo now that Gadi's uncle was sniffing around. A house in Alexandria was the solution to all their problems.

This cool, uncaring Englishman could idly offer her their dream on a plate—and all it would cost was her freedom.

He was as bad as Gadi and his uncle. Almost.

Ayisha wished she could just fling his offer back in his even white teeth, but it was too tempting. Far too tempting. And he knew it, the smug swine.

"I will consider it." She needed time, time to see if she could think her way around this, time to see if she could have what she wanted and still stay free.

"When will you give me your answer?"

She put her nose in the air and responded in his own cool, care-for-nobody manner. "Soon."

*B*axter, I need a house in Alexandria," Rafe said when he was ushered into the cool, dark inner room of Baxter's establishment. "Do you have connections there?"

"I have connections everywhere. What sort of house?" Baxter was seated cross-legged on a pile of cushions, smoking tobacco from a hookah, the very picture of an Oriental potentate.

"Small, just for two people, and with a yard big enough to build an oven. The woman bakes bread."

Baxter put the mouthpiece of the hookah aside. "You've decided to stay?"

"It's not for me, but a woman and a boy—Miss Cleeve has been living with them."

Baxter sat up at that. "You've found her then? The Cleeve girl?"

"I have."

"Where? How?"

"She, er, dropped in on me at her father's house." The fewer people who knew Miss Cleeve had been living on the streets of Cairo disguised as a street boy, the better.

"Just like that? From out of nowhere?"

"Mmm. More or less."

Baxter sat back. "Second cousin to an oyster, as the saying goes. I can arrange a house, five percent commission, and you can take possession by the end of the week." Baxter scribbled on a piece of paper, rang for a servant, explained in Arabic, and sat back as the man hurried off. He gave a faint grin. "I heard you caught a young street thief. Don't suppose that was Miss Cleeve?"

"Close," Rafe said. Baxter was not the sort of man to gossip. "The boy is her young foster brother. He tried to steal the picture, and she came to free him from my clutches."

"I see . . ." Baxter gave him a hooded glance.

"She was disguised as a boy," Rafe clarified. "And apparently not in anyone's evil clutches. This house is for the woman who has taken her in, and the boy, Ali, who she seems to have adopted as well."

"This house is to be their reward?"

Rafe nodded. "And because Miss Cleeve won't go with me unless they are well provided for."

Baxter raised his brows.

"Loyal to the backbone," Rafe confirmed.

A servant brought coffee and tiny sticky pastries. Rafe took a ginger sip of the coffee. It was as appalling as ever.

"That brings me to the next matter," Rafe said. "I have a proposition for you. You have a considerable business empire, do you not?"

Baxter gave a noncommittal shrug.

"Would you have a place in Alexandria to train up an intelligent young boy?"

Baxter sipped his coffee thoughtfully, then grimaced. "Burned again. My cook had to return to his village, and ever since . . ." He set down the tiny cup on a brass tray. "A boy, you say? Your little thief? Her foster brother?"

"Yes, he's a thief, but a damned inept one. Unpracticed is my guess." He gave Baxter a direct look and said, "I would prefer he gets no further practice. After eight years in the army, I know men and young boys. He's a promising lad."

"How old?"

"Ten or thereabouts, I'd guess."

Baxter gave him a shrewd look. "You want to rid her of her encumbrances and allow her to leave with a clear conscience."

"Bluntly put, yes. I'll pay for his education—I presume there is a decent school in Alexandria—if you'll train him to be part of your business and keep an eye on him."

Baxter thought for a moment, then leaned forward and held out his hand. "Very well. Bring me this boy and if I like him, I'll give him a trial."

"What am I to do, Laila?" Ayisha paced the tiny yard restlessly. "He has made it impossible for me to refuse."

Laila swept the cobbles. "There is always a choice," she said placidly. "A house, a job for Ali—these things do not matter. What matters is you."

Ayisha stared. "What do you mean, they don't matter? It's everything we wanted."

Laila stopped sweeping for a moment. "This is not about what we wanted. This is about what you will do with your life. Will you take your life in your own hands and try to make something of it, or will you go on hiding from the world as you have since you were a child?"

Ayisha blinked. "But you know why I hide."

"I know it," Laila agreed. "And there has been good reason for it, it is true. But you cannot live your whole life like this. It is time to stop, to face what you are, to risk yourself for the possibility of happiness."

Ayisha frowned. "Are you saying I have been a coward? But I take risks every day."

Laila patted her cheek. "I know you do, and nobody would call you a coward. But you guard your heart; you are afraid to love."

"That's not true. I love you and Ali—"

"I know you do, but you are a woman now, and it is time you let yourself love a man. I know, you want to hide, to pretend you do not care, but this is me, who has known you since you were a child. I do not know this man who stirs your anger and your fear; I do not know if he is a good man or not, if he is the one for you or just a messenger. That is up to you. But you must leave this place, Ayisha, though it grieves my heart to say so. This country is not for you. You cannot be whole here. And you know it in your heart."

Ayisha felt her face crumple. "This is my home."

Laila shook her head, sadly. "It has been so for your life until now, but look inside yourself, my dear, and tell me you did not know, in your heart of hearts, that one day you must go to your father's country."

It was true, Ayisha knew, but she did not want it to be. "One day I will go to England, but not . . . not like this. I don't want to go with him." He scared her . . . no, not scared . . . He intimidated . . . That was not right, either. But he was a threat to her, she felt it every time he looked at her and she shivered inside.

Laila smiled. "So you know, but you fight it. Decide, child, decide now; do you live your life in fear, or do you take it like an orange and wring every last sweet drop from it? That is your choice."

She patted Ayisha's cheek. "Now, while you decide what to do, the old spice seller wants some more labels written. He was very pleased with those others you did. And after that, why not go down to the river and pick me some nice sweet greens? The river is a good place for thinking."

*M*iss Cleeve had demanded a pathetically small sum, but she obviously didn't know it. It would barely keep a society beauty in knickknacks for a quarter. Rafe followed the interpreter through the streets, heading for Laila's house.

He was leading a horse. The streets in this part of town were too narrow and the upper stories of the houses too close together for a man to ride. He hadn't realized that when he hired the horse.

He needed exercise and had hired a horse with the intention of riding every inch of pent-up frustration out of himself. After he called on Laila, he planned a good, hard ride up along the river.

Laila lived in a cramped and dirty part of town. As they approached Ali came racing up, a brilliant grin splitting his thin brown face. He admired the horse extravagantly, so Rafe swung him up on its back, to the boy's huge delight. He rode proudly, grinning and calling out to all who saw him.

He pointed out Laila's house. It was small and mean but the street out the front was well swept and clean. Ali slipped down and, taking Rafe's arm, led him exuberantly down an even narrower alley and banged on a high wooden door set into the wall.

"The boy says Laila will be at the back of the house," the interpreter murmured, just as the door in the wall opened.

A small, plump woman looked up at Rafe and the horse in surprise and quickly pulled her veil over her face. Her eyes were beautiful: large, liquid, and dark, but they scrutinized him in an unflinchingly critical manner that put him forcibly in mind of his first officer's inspection, when he was a green recruit.

He bore the small woman's stringent examination with cool amusement. With her cooperation or without it, he would take Alicia Cleeve back to England.

Ali performed the introductions, and Rafe bowed to Laila, who gestured to them to tie the horse to the gate and then enter the tiny courtyard. The yard was neatly cobbled and swept clean, with herbs growing in pots and a bright red geranium spilling from a high place next to the roof. There was a dome-shaped fireplace, piles of wooden trays, and a lingering aroma of fresh baked bread.

An elderly, ragged tabby cat sat on top of the dome and glared balefully at Rafe, its tail flicking a warning.

"So," Laila said, "you are the one."

"Apparently," Rafe responded through the interpreter.

She gave a little nod, as if he'd passed muster. "Peace be with you. Please to come inside?" She gestured toward the back door, where several pairs of shabby shoes sat neatly, side by side.

Rafe, whose boots were designed to have a valet pull them off, sighed at this local custom and bent to pull them off. Ali ran to help, tugging at them with gusto.

Laila ushered them into the tiny house; two rooms, one with several low divans, the second room a tiny curtained-off alcove. Their poverty was obvious.

"Coffee?" she said.

"Thank you," he responded. The bitter, burned taste of Baxter's coffee was still in his mouth, but he'd learned that Egyptians were intensely hospitable, and he didn't want to cause offense. He didn't need this woman's cooperation, but it would be easier on Alicia if he had it. Laila wasn't going to make it easy on him, he could tell.

Her actions were hospitable, but those dark eyes snapped with suspicion.

She brought back a tray containing two tiny cups filled with an ominously dark brew and a plate of tiny round sticky balls. She presented them to Rafe and the interpreter, then knelt gracefully on folded knees and waited for them to drink. She did not drink herself, Rafe noted.

Rafe braced himself and took a cautious sip of the thick, dark coffee. "This is good," he said in surprise. He took another sip, then another. He could get used to this style of coffee.

"You know why I'm here," he said. There was no reason to beat about the bush.

Laila cast a glance at Ali, sitting cross-legged by Rafe's knees, and said something in Arabic.

"Sending him outside to sweep the yard," the interpreter explained. Ali started to go, with drooping shoulders and lagging feet, the very picture of a martyr.

"Here, lad, look after my horse, will you? Give it some water," Rafe told him. He'd watered his horse at Baxter's, but it would keep the boy occupied and make sure nobody bothered his horse.

Ali's face lit up when he understood, and he ran out happily.

"You can go, too," Laila said in English to the interpreter, surprising them both. She added, "My English not good, but enough."

Rafe nodded to the interpreter, who, looking slightly annoyed, left.

Laila explained. "This between you, me, and Ayisha. I not know her English name—Alissya Cli—?"

"Alicia Cleeve," Rafe explained. He ate one of the sticky dumplings. "This is delicious."

She gave a terse nod, uninterested in his compliments. "You come to take my Ayisha to England."

"Yes—"

"But yesterday you go to Zamil's slave market," she said. "Why?" She fixed him with a clear look.

It was a bold frontal attack, unexpected from a woman. Laila rose slightly in Rafe's estimation.

"To see if he had ever sold this girl. You will, I think, recognize her." He pulled out the picture of Alicia Cleeve. "It was suggested to me that she might have been kidnapped and sold as a slave. And that Zamil might know."

"Such evil has happened before," Laila admitted. She held out her hand for the picture.

"Ahh," she smiled at it. "So, this is how Ayisha look before she came to the streets." She gazed at the portrait. "So young and sweet, so innocent. Finish your coffee?"

"Yes, thank you, it was very good."

"Turn the cup."

Rafe frowned. "I beg your pardon?"

"Turn the cup. Like this." She demonstrated, upending her own cup on the saucer, letting the thick grounds at the bottom drain.

Bemused, Rafe did so. It was a custom he hadn't come across before. It seemed rather messy.

Laila handed him back the picture of Ayisha. "You married?"

"No," he said, surprised at the abrupt change of subject.

"Why not?"

It was on the tip of his tongue to blast her impudence, but he said stiffly, "I've been a soldier and away at the war for the last eight years."

"You hurt bad?" She glanced at his crotch.

His lips twitched. Nobody could accuse this woman of subtlety. "Nothing vital."

"How many years you have?"

"Eight and twenty." He folded his arms and sat back.

She gave a brisk nod. "Time you get marry."

"You and my brother, two voices with but one tune," he said blandly.

She gave him a thoughtful look, picked up his coffee cup, and stared into it a long moment. Various expressions flitted across her face. She murmured something in Arabic, glanced at him, looked back into the cup, and nodded again. Slowly her body relaxed. She sighed and put the coffee cup down.

There was a short silence, then Laila said, "You will take my Ayisha from me. Soon, I think?"

Capitulation? So soon? But he wasn't going to question it. "She will have a better life than anything you can give her."

Laila nodded. "I know, and it is good," she said, surprising him. "But she not want to go."

Was she going to try to touch him for money? "She will go," Rafe said in a grim voice, "whether she wants to or not. Whether you want her to or not. She does not know what is good for her."

"You force her to go to England?" Laila said.

"Kicking and screaming if necessary," he confirmed. "And neither you nor anyone else is going to stop me."

"Good." She pressed her hands together. "You must make her go. She is stubborn, you understand. I tell her this life is not right for her, that it is a prison for her to live as she does—but will she listen? She needs a man. I see in her cup."

Rafe blinked at the abrupt about-face. He'd expected opposition, a further grilling on his morals and character, or an attempt to solicit a bribe, not this almost motherly approval. And the suggestion Ayisha needed a man . . .

"You are under a misapprehension, madam," he told her crisply. "I have not come in search of a bride. I am simply here to escort Miss Cleeve to her grandmother."

Laila's brown eyes twinkled. "So you say."

Rafe said nothing. The matchmaking mamas of Almack's had a sister in spirit here.

"She is a woman, my Ayisha, not a young girl," Laila continued with all the subtlety of a sledgehammer. "Almost twenty summers. Beautiful. Time she marry, too."

Rafe resolutely steered the conversation in a different direction. "I am curious—how did you come to know Alici—Ayisha?"

"It was five, maybe six years ago. She young girl, then, starving—I don't like see any child be hungry. She follow me, follow the smell of my pies. I watch her from the corner of my eye. I feed her. I feed hungry children before, many times. But Ayisha, she is special. She repay me."

He frowned. This was the crux of the matter. "How?"

"She collect fuel for my fire." Laila spread her hands in a gesture of simplicity. "How can I turn away a child like that, starving, yet full of honor?" She gave a gusty sigh, remembering. "And so I let her sleep in the back." She indicated the backyard.

"In the back? You mean outside? In the open air?" Rafe was appalled.

"You think is bad, but it safer for her outside than in. My brother, he think she is worthless boy, but he tolerate her sleeping in the yard because she good worker and help me with the baking. If he know she is girl . . ." Her eyes dropped and she spread her hands in the fatalistic gesture so common in the east. Rafe was able to fill in the rest.

"She wants me to buy her a house in Alexandria," he told Laila, interested to see her reaction.

Laila's eyes widened. "She tell you about that?"

"Yes."

"But you not give it to her?" Laila asked anxiously. "She must go with you to England."

"I won't give her money. And she *will* go to England."

"Good."

"You won't miss her?"

Laila's eyes widened. "Of course I miss her. She is close to me like a daughter. My heart will ache without her." She touched her heart. "But I know she must be with her own blood. She must become herself."

Laila was nothing like he'd expected. He'd expected a conniving creature who would use Miss Cleeve as a bargaining chip. Not one who urged him to take the girl to England for her own good. Even though she clearly depended on her earning capacity.

"How did Ali come into the picture?" he asked.

Laila smiled fondly. "He another one like Ayisha. No family. She bring him home like a hungry puppy one day, and . . ." She shrugged. "It was a very small mouth to feed; there is not much to him, even now."

The boy ate like a horse. "What if there was a possibility of a job for Ali?"

Her eyes lit up. "An apprenticeship?"

He shook his head. "I can promise nothing, but an acquaintance of mine will consider him for a job."

"Who?"

"A man called Baxter."

She nodded thoughtfully. "The Englishman who dresses like an Arab. I have heard of him. He is rich and has many fingers in many pots." She eyed Rafe shrewdly. "Why you do this for Ali?"

"Ayisha will leave Egypt more easily knowing you are safe and the boy has future prospects."

She nodded. "Yes, this is true. She worry about everyone, that girl. This Baxter, is he a good man?"

"I believe so, but I've only met him twice. I know his cousin well."

She dismissed Baxter's cousin with a wave of a hand. "When Ali's mother died, his neighbor take the boy in, but he beat him too much and Ali run away. I not let Ali go to any man who is cruel."

Rafe nodded. "Then come with me now, and you and Ali can meet Baxter together."

She glanced at the door. "Not now, for my brother will soon be home, wanting his dinner," she said. "But come back tomorrow, mid-morning. He will be gone then and we can go to speak to this Baxter."

Rafe stood and bowed. He'd developed a real respect for this little woman. He understood now why Ayisha and Ali felt so responsible for her—loved her. She had asked nothing for herself. "Tomorrow, mid-morning then."

In the doorway he pulled his boots back on, then turned back to Laila, asking casually, "Where did you say Ayisha was again?" She hadn't actually said.

Laila shrugged. "The river, I think. Collecting greens."

Seven

"Azhar! Ho there, Azhar!"

Ayisha forced herself to turn casually. Gadi? For the second time in as many days? It was not a good sign. She was on the outskirts of town, almost at her favorite place for gathering greens. It was not one of Gadi's usual haunts.

"Going to the river again, I see." Gadi hooked his arm through hers." Maybe this time I will come with you." His hand closed around her upper arm.

"I need to go to the market, first, see what is available," she said casually and turned. Gadi's hold on her tightened.

He wasn't looking at her, he was looking up ahead. To where a couple of men stood, loitering unconvincingly.

She stiffened and tried to pull away. "What do you want, Gadi? I have no money on me."

Two more men stood on the way to the market, blocking her escape. One was thickset and stocky, and as he moved purposefully toward her Ayisha felt a sick certainty in her stomach. Gadi's uncle.

She'd made it her business years ago to discover the owner of the filthy feet with twisted, horny nails, last seen when she was thirteen years old and lying under her dying mother's bed, trying not to breathe.

It was Gadi's uncle who'd said, *Keep looking. She'll be somewhere—she has nowhere else to go. A white child-virgin will bring a fine sum at Zamil's.*

Gadi gripped her arm with both hands. "I told you my uncle wants to meet you."

She was no longer a child, but she was still white and a virgin. And trapped.

Without warning she twisted and kicked Gadi, aiming for his male parts. He doubled over with a howl. His uncle and the men behind her started to run. Ayisha drew her knife, looking desperately around her. The only way out was the river, but she could not swim. Still, it would be better than being taken as a slave. Maybe, she thought, thinking of crocodiles.

Gadi's uncle and his men formed a semicircle around her.

"I'll kill anyone who tries to touch me." She brandished her knife and backed away, wishing desperately she'd brought the other one as well.

Gadi's uncle grinned, showing broken yellow teeth. He said something and each man produced a knife.

"Don't be foolish," Gadi's uncle crooned. "We don't want to mark your pretty white hide, but we will if we have to. But I'll sell damaged goods just as easily. I've been after you a long time." He stepped forward. "I've never been able to work out where you got to that night."

Ayisha edged back, feeling the river's soft bank squishing underfoot. "Don't come any closer," she snarled. She was trapped. Her only alternative was to take on these men with her knife, or she could just turn and jump. The river would sweep her away. She might live . . . if she did not drown. If there were no crocodiles . . .

Gadi's uncle edged closer with an expression of smug triumph on his face.

The river had always been her friend. Ayisha murmured a swift prayer, took a deep, despairing breath, and braced herself to jump.

A shout and the thunder of hooves caused her to whirl, startled. She stared, stunned. It was the Englishman on a tall black stallion, roaring with fury, riding as if the devil himself was driving him.

He drove the animal straight at the group of men and in panic they scattered. In the same instant he leapt from the horse, landing on one of the men. The man was knocked flat and lay gasping, his breath knocked out of him. The Englishman rose.

"Behind!" she shrieked, as another man came at him with a knife. The Englishman ducked, the knife missed by a hairsbreadth, but in one swift movement the Englishman seized his attacker and flung him bodily into the river. He screamed and splashed frantically.

Ayisha was not the only one who couldn't swim.

The Englishman stood between her and the other three men. Only Gadi was out of his range. They came at him from three sides then, but Ayisha had no time to watch or help him, for Gadi came at her with a knife.

She twisted away and slashed him with her knife. He screamed and turned back on her. He slashed at her, once, twice, but she was more agile than he, and he missed both times.

She heard a terrible cracking of bone and from the corner of her eye saw another man go down under the Englishman's fists, howling in pain. But she could not take her eyes off Gadi.

Gadi kicked out at her suddenly and knocked her knife out of her hand. She bent, lightning fast, and scooped up a large river stone. Her years on the streets had trained her to use what came to hand; she might be unarmed, but she could still fight.

She flung the rock at him, hard. It bounced off his forehead. He reeled, blood trickling from a small cut, but still he kept coming.

"I'll get you for that," he snarled and raised his knife, a deadly crescent blade sharpened to a razor edge.

She didn't dare take her eyes off it, not for an instant. No time to grab another rock. He was too close. The best she could do was to dodge the blow, or at least minimize it.

There was another splash and a yell, and Gadi's eyes flickered sideways as another man was hurled bodily into the river.

And in an instant the Englishman was with her, leaping at Gadi with a ferocious roar. Gadi's knife flashed as he lunged, but the Englishman was too quick. He dodged the blow and followed it with a hard punch, then another. Gadi staggered, his knife flailing.

The Englishman landed a third punch hard in the side of

Gadi's head. Without a sound, Gadi dropped his knife and pitched face forward into the mud.

He didn't move.

The Englishman turned to Ayisha. "Are you all right?" He was only slightly breathless.

Ayisha nodded.

He gave her a swift, searching look, smiled, cupped her jaw in a brief caress, and turned back, standing between her and the last man left. Gadi's uncle.

He had a knife; the Englishman had nothing but his hands. But he'd already defeated four men with those hands. Gadi's uncle hesitated, his face working.

The Englishman's pale blue eyes blazed. "Just one piece of scum left now." He stalked toward Gadi's uncle with a strange, cold smile on his face. His big, bloodied fists were purposefully clenched.

With a yell, Gadi's uncle turned and fled.

At the same time, Gadi, spluttering, wrenched his face out of the mud and crawled away on all fours. The third man, the one whose bones had crunched as he fell, picked himself up and tottered drunkenly after them.

The Englishman took no notice. He turned to Ayisha, scanning her face intently, running his hands lightly over her body, checking for injuries. "Are you hurt?"

She shook her head, wondering at the abrupt switch from savage warrior to gentle protector.

She was shaking. She could hardly believe it was over. The thing she'd feared all these years had finally happened, and she'd survived. She shivered.

He immediately drew her against him, wrapping his strong, warm arms around her, holding her against his chest. She leaned against him, feeling cold, despite the warmth of the day, and as his arms tightened around her she felt safer than she had in . . . years.

W hat were they after?" he asked after a while.

Ayisha stiffened. "I don't know."

He said nothing for a moment, then tipped up her chin, the better to look into her eyes. "They must have said something.

Was it some dispute? Had they discovered you were a woman? It surely couldn't have been robbery."

She couldn't avoid those eyes. Something about the very blueness of them, their bright intensity under the sleepy-looking lids—if she looked into them, all her secrets could come pouring out.

And then where would she be?

Would he be looking at her with such tender concern then?

No. That concern was for Miss Alicia Cleeve, the legitimate daughter of an English lord and English lady. Not for Ayisha.

But a girl could dream. She closed her eyes and leaned her head against his chest. She could hear his heart beating.

He held her like that for a moment in silence. "Very well, I won't ask you again. Shall we go back, now?" His voice was a little cooler. He didn't like that she wouldn't tell him.

He would like it less if she told him.

She gathered herself together and stepped out of the circle of his arms. She gave him a bright smile. "Thank you for saving me. If you hadn't come along, so gallantly, like a knight from a storybook, galloping to save the maiden . . ." She glanced around. "I didn't know you could ride."

"There's a lot you don't know about me." He followed her gaze. His horse was standing a hundred feet or so away, cropping grass, its reins dangling. "I hired it for the day."

He walked toward it. It retreated a few steps away, looking wary. "Blast, I didn't think . . . My own horses come when I whistle. We're going to have to catch the brute."

It was nearly an hour later by the time they'd caught the animal—Ayisha had managed to coax it with a handful of succulent leaves—and by then the fright of her attack had passed.

She stroked the muzzle of the big black horse as she fed it a handful of leaves.

"You like horses?"

She nodded. He mounted with a lithe movement, then held out his hand. He took hers in a strong, sure grip and on a count of three, swung her effortlessly up behind him.

She snuggled close, wrapped her arms around his waist, and laid her cheek against his hard, broad back. She could smell him, the scent of fresh masculine sweat, cologne water, and horse.

She felt strangely light-headed and almost lighthearted. The thing she'd always feared had now come to pass; Gadi's uncle knew who she was.

She no longer had a choice. Her masquerade was at an end. She could not stay on in Cairo. Unmasked, too many people would know . . . Her only choice was to go to England.

With this beautiful, gentle, frightening warrior, a man she did not understand but could not resist.

*T*hey made me wash all over—again!" Ali greeted Rafe darkly when he arrived the next day.

"Yes, and what a fuss he made," Ayisha added after she explained to Rafe what he'd said. She was doing her best to pretend nothing had happened the day before, but there was a shy awareness in her lovely eyes that warmed him.

He was, in fact, hard put not to haul her into his arms and check again that she was all right. He'd woken several times in the night, reliving the sight of that handsome young thug slashing at her, hearing the sound of his knife as it slashed through her clothing.

Clothing, not flesh, thank God.

He should have fed that fellow to the crocodiles.

Her eyes scanned his body anxiously. "Are you all right? You were bleeding—"

"A couple of scratches, that's all," he said curtly. He wasn't used to being fussed over. "Cleaned up and forgotten."

"Good. I can't remember if I thanked you, but—"

"You thanked me. Several times." The best thanks had been that moment when she'd come to him willingly, shivering with reaction and seeking comfort, knowing she was safe. And afterward, when they'd ridden back, her arms wrapped around him, her slender body pressed against him.

"Oh, that's all right then," she murmured. She seemed about to say something else, then closed her mouth and turned back to the boy.

He watched her fussing over Ali, and his chest tightened. No wonder that in two years of balls and country house parties he hadn't found a woman to marry. He'd been looking in all the wrong places.

Rafe stared down at her, wanting to take her back in his arms, knowing it was too soon. Ali was not the only one looking unusually neat and clean, he saw, though she was still dressed as a boy. It was a tacit admission that her days of disguise were coming to an end.

As he'd imagined, her freshly washed complexion was very fine and clear. Like cream and roses. He itched to touch her skin, to feel whether it was as silky soft as it looked.

She caught him looking and a delicate flush stole over the tender skin. "It is for Ali, that's all," she said, as if needing to defend her cleanliness. "We all wish to make a good impression. A person's family is important."

Rafe inclined his head. *A person's family?* The daughter of an English baronet declaring she was family to a street orphan? And said with such dignity, such pride.

She was something special, all right. Most girls would be only too glad to drop shabby acquaintances in order to become elevated in the world. Not this one.

He'd seen more innate good breeding in this ragged little beauty than in a dozen dukes' daughters back home.

Still, it wasn't going to be easy for her in England. English society was a maze of fine nuances and traps for the unwary and ignorant, designed to sniff out and exclude those who didn't belong. Her birth would ensure her entree into the *ton*, but not necessarily her acceptance.

Ayisha had spent almost as many years living in the backstreets as she had in her father's house. When most English girls of her class were learning to play the pianoforte, embroider, paint watercolors, and dance, Ayisha had been learning the meaning of hunger and danger, learning to steal and fight, act the boy and survive.

No, it wouldn't be easy, but he'd be there, every step of the way to help her. She had the courage for anything.

He would carry in his mind forever the sight of her, her back to the river, armed with just a knife, with a pack of local thugs closing in on her. That desperate glance behind her, at a crocodile-filled swift-flowing river. He saw it in her eyes, the decision to jump or stand and fight. A slip of a girl against five armed men.

Eight years at war and he'd never been so frightened in his life. Frightened he wouldn't get there in time.

Finally Laila emerged from the house, veiled and dressed in an all-enveloping robe.

To Rafe's astonishment, she took his hand and kissed it.

"Ayisha tell me what you do," she said, her eyes moist. "Anything I can do for you, Englishman, I will do."

"It was nothing. Anyone would have done the same," he said gruffly.

She smiled and patted his chest. "Not anyone. Only a warrior."

They hurried through a maze of backstreets, Ayisha leading the way, until they reached Baxter's.

"I see you've brought a delegation," Baxter said with a wry expression as his servant ushered them all in. Rafe performed the introductions, introducing Ayisha in English as Miss Alicia Cleeve.

Baxter's eyes widened. "He said he had found you. Pleased to meet you, Miss Cleeve." He bowed.

"Please call me Ayisha," she said, adding with a glance at Rafe, "I prefer it."

Baxter bowed. "Miss Ayisha. And this is Ali."

Ali bowed and gazed around the room with bright-eyed curiosity.

"And this must be Laila." Baxter gave Laila a searching look, then bowed.

Laila murmured something to Ayisha in Arabic, but before Ayisha could respond, Baxter, with a mischievous look, responded in the same language.

Her eyes widened in surprise; she looked flustered and said something that made Baxter laugh.

"She is shocked to hear a foreigner speak such good Arabic," Baxter explained, adding to Rafe, "She told Miss Cleeve that although my blue eyes are pretty enough for a girl, I am nevertheless a fine figure of a man."

He winked at Ayisha and added, "I, however, prefer brown eyes, and you can tell Laila hers are the prettiest I've seen in a long time." The very small amount of Laila that was visible grew noticeably pink.

"She not need to tell me nothing," Laila retorted in English. With dignity she seated herself on the farthest cushion, not meeting anyone's gaze.

Baxter watched her with an amused expression, then he ordered coffee to be brought while he interviewed Ali.

Baxter took Ali into his office and they began to talk. The office was separated from the room the others were in by a heavy

woven curtain, which was only partly drawn, so the sound of
their voices was faint but perceptible.

The coffee was brought in along with a plate of small cakes.
The servant poured the coffee and handed it around, then left.

Rafe eyed the coffee and decided not to risk it. From the
corner of his eye he saw Laila sip, then put the cup down with a
grimace. She glanced at Rafe.

"These fellows make the worst coffee I've ever tasted," he
said quietly.

She leaned forward and peered closely at the cakes. "The
cakes are stale. See? There is mold on this one." She glanced at
the office where Baxter and Ali were in close conversation. "You
say the coffee is always bad?"

Rafe nodded.

Laila hesitated and glanced from the office, where Baxter
and Ali talked, to the doorway where the servants had gone.
"They shame their master," she said softly, then rose and slipped
from the room.

Ayisha, seated next to Rafe, had no interest in coffee. She
watched Ali's interview like a hawk, craning forward to hear.
The servants returned and collected the barely touched coffee
and stale cakes.

Ayisha, not taking her eyes off Ali, muttered something under
her breath and clenched her fists.

"What's the matter?" Rafe asked.

"I'm going to strangle that boy!"

Rafe glanced through the gap at Baxter, who didn't seem
displeased with Ali. If anything he looked amused. "Why?"

She rolled her eyes. "Baxter asked him, 'If a stall holder sold
oranges for five paras a dozen, how many oranges would you get
for half a piastre?' And what does the little monkey say? He
says—" She mimicked his voice. "'Five paras a dozen is too
much, I would go to Ahmed Four-toes, who has the stall behind
the mosque, and he would sell them to me for four paras a
dozen—maybe less!'" She clenched her fists. "He has this big
chance and he is ruining it!"

Rafe put a hand over her fist. "No, he's not. Look at Baxter's
face. He looks more amused than anything. What's he saying?"

She translated for him. "Who is Ahmed Four-toes and why
would he have them cheaper? And Ali is saying, 'He lives near
the mosque with the blue minaret, and he has two brothers and

four cousins who work the docks at Alexandria and they can always get things cheaper. Ahmed can always get you the best price.'"

Baxter laughed.

"Stop worrying," Rafe murmured. "I venture to suggest the boy is doing well. Is there such a person as Ahmed Four-toes?"

"Oh yes. He can get you anything you want, but although he is always the cheapest, he is not always the best. It pays to inspect the merchandise carefully with Ahmed Four-toes," she said absently.

Baxter continued presenting Ali with knotty problems, and Ali answered all without hesitation, adding in his own opinion quite often.

Ayisha watched and listened, oblivious of Rafe's proximity, forgetful of her hand resting in his. He made no move to draw her attention to it. It felt exactly right sitting tucked into his.

After about fifteen minutes, she turned to Rafe, puzzled. "What are they doing now? Backgammon? Why? Ali is here to work."

"You can judge a person from the way they play games. Is Ali any good at this?" He settled back against the cushions as Baxter and the small boy began a game of backgammon.

"Yes, but he's better at chess. I wish Baxter had asked him to play chess." She nodded toward a chess set sitting on a low table. "He beats me every time. He really is clever, you know."

"I suppose your father taught you chess," Rafe said quietly.

She nodded. "I was never very good. I do not plan ahead—" She stopped and looked at Rafe, looked down at their joined hands, and snatched her hand back, quite as if he'd stolen it.

They were sitting very close on the low divan. She glanced up at him and shifted to put more distance between them.

"Don't you think it's time you stopped pretending?"

"Pretending?" She eyed him warily.

"That you're not the daughter of Sir Henry Cleeve."

She looked down and bit her lip. Lord, but she was beautiful. He wanted to kiss her, and he would, he vowed, but not here, not in this room, with Baxter and the boy and whoever else watching.

"It's not that. I just don't feel comfortable being called Alicia Cleeve," she said finally.

"Then what am I to call you?"

"Ayisha," she said. "Just Ayisha."

"I will call you Ayisha in private," he agreed. "And you will call me Rafe. But in public I'm afraid it must still be Miss Cleeve."

"What public? We've hardly ever spoken in public."

"Yes, but on the ship, for instance, I must refer to you as Miss Cleeve."

"Ship?"

"Higgins is going ahead to book passage for us on a ship leaving Alexandria next week."

She gave him a trapped look. "I haven't agreed yet. You haven't got a house in Alexandria."

"The arrangements are being made. It should be available by the end of this week."

"So soon," she whispered.

"Yes, we can all go to Alexandria together and you can see them settled in and then we'll disembark."

She looked anything but happy. He hardened his heart. She would be happier in England than she'd ever been here, he vowed. He would make it so.

As the game of backgammon drew to a close, Laila returned to her original seat and a moment later the servant entered again with coffee and a dish of small pancakes.

"This boy almost beat me at backgammon," said Baxter emerging from the office. He seated himself among them again. He stared at the steam rising from the small cups, frowned, and then sniffed. His frown deepened, and he picked up a cup and tasted it.

"Hallelujah!" he said and drained the cup blissfully. "Nobody in my employ made this, I'll swear. This is better than the coffeehouses make." His gaze shot across to Laila. She looked away.

Baxter picked up a small pancake. "Still warm," he said and ate it.

Laila leaned forward and poured him a fresh cup of coffee.

"Are you responsible for this?" Baxter demanded. "The coffee?"

"Yes," Laila said in a low voice. "I am sorry, I know it was not my place to interfere—I meant no disrespect, sir."

Baxter waved away her apologies, but Laila continued. "I

hate to see good coffee wasted and the other was not fit to serve," she said. "I showed your servants how to make it."

"Did you now?" Baxter looked amused. "You made the pancakes, too?"

She nodded. "Yes, they are quick and easy to make. I showed the boys how."

"Let's hope they don't forget." Baxter gave her a thoughtful look. "I recently lost my cook, and he and his family provided all my needs. These lads are new. They're honest and willing enough, but they haven't exactly got the hang of coffee yet."

He ate another pancake, eyeing her thoughtfully. "You are widowed, I think. And Ali is your son?"

Laila raised her head and said with dignity. "Divorced. I have no children, but Ali is the son of my heart."

Baxter inclined his head. "Lucky boy." He turned to Ali. "Now, here are three paras. Go and buy me the best cakes you can find." The boy took the money and ran off eagerly.

Baxter said to Rafe and Ayisha. "Would you mind if I left you here for a few minutes? I need to speak to Laila about the boy, of course, agree on terms of employment, but if you don't mind, I'd like to speak to her in the kitchen. I would ask the advice of a knowledgeable woman."

Rafe nodded an assent and Baxter turned back to Laila. "Laila?"

She met his eyes, and for a long moment they just looked at each other. Then she gave a little nod.

Baxter held his hand out to assist her to rise. After twenty years in Egypt, it was a mistake he shouldn't have made, thought Ayisha.

Laila hesitated and regarded him a moment, her head tilted to one side. Then, to Ayisha's amazement, she placed her hand in Baxter's and rose gracefully from the cushions.

He smiled, then gestured for her to precede him.

Laila went, with something of a swish. Ayisha gaped. If she didn't know better she would think Laila was . . . flirting.

Eight

❦

"So, what do you think of my kitchen?" Baxter asked Laila when they reached the kitchen. It was a mix of European and traditional styles, and since Baxter was a wealthy man, it was very well equipped.

"My cook and his family had to return to his village to take up an inheritance," Baxter told her. "He was a married man, with a wife and two children. They lived in special quarters at the back of the house. May I show you these quarters?"

Laila gave him a searching look, then inclined her head in acquiescence. He took her out to the rear courtyard. It was quite spacious and contained a small patch of neglected herbs.

Laila cast a critical eye over it. "No oven?"

"My cook purchased all his bread from the local baker."

Laila sniffed. He showed her the cook's quarters: four rooms, minimally furnished. "The cook took his belongings with him, but if the right person applied for the job, I would, of course, supply anything that was needed," Baxter finished.

Laila turned and gave him a searching look.

"Why are you telling me this?"

Baxter hesitated, searching for the right words. "Ramsey asked me to buy a house in Alexandria on his behalf."

Laila frowned. "But I told him—she must go to Engl—"

Baxter interrupted. "A small house, he said, for one woman and one boy."

Laila gasped and her hand stole to her breast. "One woman and one boy? You mean . . . me and Ali?"

Baxter smiled. "I believe so. He said a house with a yard in which they could build an oven, for the woman is an excellent baker of bread and pies and wishes to start a business there."

"A house . . . In Alexandria . . . for Ali and me?" she repeated in a whisper.

"Yes. But I have another suggestion: become my cook, Laila. Become my cook, live here in these quarters with Ali, and I will build you an oven for your business."

Her eyes narrowed. "You would let me sell my bread and pies?"

"Yes, as long as it did not interfere with cooking for me and running my house. As you say, my servants take advantage. To be honest, the domestic side of things is something I have no interest in."

She gave him a long, searching look. "You mean this? You want me to work for you?"

"I do."

She examined the cook's quarters then, with a more critical eye, and then the courtyard and the kitchen. Finally she turned back to him. "And what will this cost me?"

Baxter's eyes twinkled. "The quarters come with the position—rent free."

"And for this, I must cook and clean—"

"Supervise the cleaning, supervise the servants. You wouldn't have to do it yourself."

"And I could still run my business."

"Yes. And there is a wage." He named a sum that made her eyebrows disappear under her veil.

"You will pay me, as well?"

"Of course."

She narrowed her eyes at him and braced her hands on her hips. "What else do you expect? I tell you now, I am a respectable woman."

Baxter smiled. "I know, and I admire that. The wage and conditions are exactly the same as I paid my previous cook. So, will you take the job?"

There was a long silence. "I want it," she said. "But I must ask my brother. He is the head of my family."

Baxter grinned. "Excellent. I will talk to your brother, but I believe we will come to an arrangement. So you and I have a deal." He held out his hand in the European manner, and though it was not her custom, Laila held out her hand to shake it.

He surprised her then by taking her hand in both of his. He lifted it slowly toward his mouth. She stared, fascinated, unsure of what to do. He pressed his firm, warm lips against the back of her hand in a slow kiss.

Laila shivered, feeling the heat of him against her skin. Flustered, she snatched her hand back.

He smiled. "You taste good, like fresh bread."

"Because I made bread this morning," she said in a brusque voice. "Do not do that again. It is not respectable." She straightened her veil with hands that shook a little.

He bowed, but said nothing. His smile didn't change.

She touched him lightly on the shoulder. "Go now," she said crossly. "We have wasted enough time. The others will be waiting."

Baxter's smile intensified. If she'd been truly angry, she would not have touched him at all.

*F*or several moments after Baxter and Laila had left and Ali had run off, Rafe and Ayisha sat side by side on the low cushioned divan, saying nothing.

Finally Rafe said, "You're very fond of Laila, aren't you?"

"Of course, she is my friend. More, she has been like a mother to me."

"She told me how you two first met," Rafe said. "How she gave you some food and you repaid her with fuel for her fire."

For a moment there was silence, then Ayisha said, "It was more than simply giving me food. I had been fed before. Stall holders at the market will sometimes toss a street child a piece of damaged fruit, or stale or broken bread. They toss it in the dust, and watch as the hungry ones pick it up and cram it in their mouths. Like rats."

He looked sharply at her. "I hope you were never so desperate."

"I was. Often. The day I met Laila, I had not eaten for four days," she said in a flat voice.

His hand tightened, his knuckles whitening.

Ayisha looked at him. He still thought to make an English lady of her. He needed to know this about her.

"I was nearly fourteen. I'd lived nine months on the streets," she said. "Mainly by stealing. But four days before, I saw a thief punished. I heard him howl like an animal as they sliced off his hand."

She'd stared in horror at the man's stump, spurting with blood; at the hand lying in the dust, the fingers twitching, as if still alive.

Someone scooped the hand up—she didn't know if it had been given back to the moaning thief or thrown to the dogs to eat. She was frozen, unable to think past the horror that it could have been her hand lying in the dust, twitching.

Each bright droplet of blood had collected dust and sat on the earth before slowly seeping in. "They say blood is thicker than water," she said. "It's true."

"I know," Rafe said grimly, and a note in his voice made her look at him and remember he had spent eight years at war.

She stared at him, appalled. She'd only seen this happen to one man and had never forgotten it. But he—he must have seen horrors like that over and over. He'd probably even chopped hands off and killed men. "If you were a soldier, you must have seen it happen many time—"

"Yes," he cut her off abruptly. "But it's your story I want to hear."

What did it do to a young man, she wondered, to live that over and over, to spend years of his life, fighting, living a hard, rough life, trying to kill, hoping not to be killed.

Until yesterday, no sign of it showed; he was always clean and elegant and self-possessed. Too self-possessed, maybe, she thought. His cleanliness, his shiny boots and immaculate linen— was it a kind of armor, like her rags and her dirt?

At the river she'd seen a different side of him, a raw, rough, gritty side: the warrior. The fighter. The protector.

She would never forget the sight of those blue eyes blazing, the strange smile he wore as he attacked those men with his bare hands. His fists were bloodied, his knuckles scraped raw, but after it was over, his big calloused hand, when he'd cupped her cheek so briefly, had carried a tenderness that was almost shocking in such a scene of violence.

"So you saw a thief punished and after that you were afraid to steal," he prompted her.

"Yes, and after four days I was very hungry." Her empty belly had been gnawing at her for days. She was living like a rat, picking up scraps wherever she could.

"Then I smelled the most glorious smell." She smiled. "You have never eaten one of Laila's pies, but believe me, if you ever had . . ." She sighed. "Laila, though I did not know her name then, was carrying a covered tray through the streets, selling them, hot from the oven. I followed, inhaling the scent as if it were food. I hoped maybe she would toss me a piece of broken pie or a crust. But she didn't."

He nodded her to go on.

"I followed her home, but still nothing. She opened the gate and waved to me to come in."

"And you followed—"

She snorted. "No. After nine months on the streets I trusted no one. So she went inside and closed the door." She gave a rueful smile. "But still I couldn't leave that smell."

"Go on." His expression was grim.

"A moment later she came out again. She put a pie on the step; a whole, untouched—" Her voice broke, and she pressed her lips together, remembering, trying to gather her composure.

He touched her hand, and she drew it away. Sympathy at this point would make her cry. Lord, why was she so emotional? She'd told Ali this story a dozen times.

She swallowed and forced herself to continue. "She put a pie on the step; a whole, perfect pie sitting on a beautiful, clean plate. A *plate*."

The scent of the pie had made her mouth water, but the plate had brought tears to her eyes—as it did, even now, just remembering. She looked at him through swimming eyes and could see he hadn't understood.

In a shaking voice she explained, "I hadn't eaten off a plate in months, you see. The pie was wonderful, but the plate—the plate said I was—I was human, not a—not a—"

"Not a rat," he finished quietly, and drew her against him. She nodded and let herself lean against his big, solid shoulder, smelling the clean, masculine scent of him, wiping her eyes as she remembered.

Her belly had screamed at her to cram the pie in as fast as she could and run; instead, she'd taken the plate to a safe place and eaten the pie slowly, with relish, like a person, not a rat. Because the plate had reminded her of who she was.

He handed her a handkerchief. His knuckles were scabbed and ugly, his handkerchief pristine. She wiped her eyes.

"The pie was still warm and delicious. It was the best meal I ever had," she finished and she blew into the handkerchief, feeling a little foolish. All that fuss over a plate.

"Laila told me that afterward, you collected fuel for her oven."

"Of course," Ayisha said, sitting up straight, and handing his handkerchief back. "She gave me something priceless. I had to give something back, even if it was nothing special." She had washed the plate and dried it as best she could, then collected a bundle of sticks and dry grass and dried camel dung.

She added, "Laila didn't just give me a pie, that night, she gave me back myself."

He nodded. "I understand."

"I still owe her," Ayisha said with meaning.

He gave her a straight look. "I know. And I will see her right, I promise you. Baxter's men are even now negotiating to buy a house in Alexandria. It will be in Laila and Ali's names. No one can take it from them, ever."

She said nothing for a long time. She picked up the cushion again and fiddled with the fringe. Her fingers shook.

"Very well," she said in a voice that caught a little. "When Laila has a safe home to live in and Ali has a job, I will go with you to England." Her chin was firm and resolute, but her wonderful eyes betrayed how torn she was.

It was a huge step. He saw now that he'd been arrogant being so sure her life was so dreadful. It was, but he hadn't looked past the obvious. In the past few days he'd learned that beyond the poverty and hardship of her life, there was love, strong love.

He knew the power of that. He would never use the word love to describe how he felt about his friends—not out loud—

but that's what it was, he acknowledged. Gabe and Harry and Luke were closer to him than his own brother. Their friendship and unquestioning support had got them through the worst times of the war.

He wouldn't give up that friendship for anything.

He looked at Ayisha. She was giving up everything she knew for the sake of her friends. And she was going to . . . what?

To a society that could pick her to bits if it got a chance. Politely, viciously, bloodlessly.

Could he protect her from that? Could he be enough?

"I know it's hard to think of leaving your friends," he said awkwardly. "But you'll have your grandmother, and you'll make new friends. You will like England, I promise you."

She said nothing, just hugged the cushion to her.

Rafe clenched his fists. Triumph was always a mixed blessing, but it had never left such a sour taste in his mouth.

She would be happy, he swore it. He would make it so.

A s Baxter and Laila reentered the sitting room, the curtains parted and Ali appeared with a wrapped parcel, grinning in triumph. "Open sesameeee," he said in English and unwrapped a dozen sesame and honey cakes.

"I've offered Laila a job," Baxter said.

Ali looked surprised and then crestfallen.

"And you, too, Ali. I want you both living here. Laila will cook, and you will work for me and learn."

Ali managed to bow, salute, and thank Baxter effusively, while at the same time bouncing up and down on excited toes.

"I have to see what Omar says first," Laila said in a dampening voice. "He might say no."

"He will," Ali said with certainty. "But I can still come. Omar cares nothing for me."

Ayisha silently agreed. If Laila left, Omar would have to support himself, as well as cook and clean for himself, and she couldn't see him doing that. That's why they'd planned to run away; they knew Omar would never let Laila go.

"We'll cross the Omar bridge when we come to it," Baxter said firmly. "In the meantime, Ali, I will expect you tomorrow morning, first thing."

Ali's face split in a grin. "Yes, sir," he said in English, and saluted smartly.

Baxter looked slightly taken aback.

"I perceive the hand of my valet, Higgins," Rafe said dryly. "He was a batman in the army and seems to have taken it on himself to begin training young Ali in what Higgins calls 'civilized ways.'"

"Well, don't salute me again," Baxter told Ali. "I left all that behind me years ago."

"No, sir," Ali said, and bowed in an uncanny imitation of Baxter's earlier bow to Laila.

Rafe chuckled. "You've got your hands full there, Baxter. Send him to England when you get sick of him."

As they were walking home later, Ayisha said to Rafe, "If Omar will not allow Laila to work for Baxter, will you still buy the house in Alexandria?"

"Yes. She can use it or rent it out. I promised you that house, and I don't break my word."

She nodded. "And you truly would send Ali to England?"

"Why not, when he's older? Only if he wants to, of course, but travel will do him good. I'll send him the fare."

She walked on, trying to keep her steps in time with his, but his stride was so much longer it was impossible. "You act as if it is not the other side of the world."

"It isn't," he said. "It's a fair trip, I admit, but travel is getting easier all the time." He glanced down at her. "I can see you've been fretting about going to a strange country with strange people—I do understand how you would be anxious about that—so I'll make you this promise. If after a year in England, you really hate it and want to come back here, I will give you the money to return. In fact I'll escort you."

She gasped and stopped dead in the street to stare up at him. "You would do that for me?"

"If you were desperately unhappy, yes," he assured her. He took her hand in his. "I know you resent the way I've left you no option, but believe me, Ayisha, my only desire is for your welfare and happiness."

His voice was deep and sincere. This time she knew what was coming when he took her hand in his, and she made no attempt to stop him. She couldn't. She knew exactly what to expect when he lifted her hand and pressed his lips against the back of her fingers.

Only this time Ayisha felt the imprint of his mouth clear through to the soles of her feet. She shivered, and without quite knowing why, pulled her hand free. She could feel her cheeks burning. They resumed walking.

"Why did you do that?" she muttered after a moment.

"I couldn't help myself. It's what a man does when he wants . . ."

"Wants what?"

"To . . . take care of a woman," he finished.

"Oh." He'd promised her grandmother he'd take care of her, she remembered. She was a responsibility.

She looked down at the hand he had kissed. She'd never had her hand kissed before, except for him. And now, twice, he'd kissed her hand. It didn't feel like a responsibility. It made her feel . . . strange, special.

As if she were a . . . a princess, and not . . . what she was. She closed her eyes briefly and wished she was that princess, wished she could be . . . how he made her feel.

But all that was for a dead girl. Not Ayisha.

Still . . . She recalled Laila's words. She might not be a princess, but a poor girl could eat an orange as well. She could still partake of that sweet orange of life, and she would, she decided. She would suck it dry.

She would make her own happiness.

They reached the corner next to Laila's house, where Laila and Ali were waiting. Rafe said a crisp good-bye—he was looking a little hot, from the sun, no doubt—and marched up the narrow street.

Ayisha watched him striding away up the lane. *My only desire is for your welfare and happiness.* His long black boots gleamed in the bright sun.

"English clothes are very . . . revealing," Laila commented, watching him go. "A fine figure of a man, that Englishman."

Ayisha jumped and realized that she had, indeed, been staring at the smooth flex and pull of his powerful muscles as he walked, and at his firm masculine backside in the tight buff pants.

Her cheeks warmed. She turned to Laila and noticed her cupping one hand in the other. "What's the matter with your hand? Did you burn it?"

Laila flushed and looked down to where her hand was cradled just under her breasts. She gave Ayisha a rueful look. "No, and I think maybe you have the same problem as me."

Ayisha looked down and saw she was holding her own hand similarly. She dropped it immediately. "There's nothing wrong. It was just—" She broke off, flushing.

"I know; these Englishmen," Laila supplied. She gestured with her chin. "It is a very unsettling custom, this kissing of hands."

"Yes," Ayisha agreed fervently.

"And maybe," Laila added thoughtfully, "it is something to do with their blue eyes. They make women think of rumpled beds and long, hot nights . . ."

She caught Ayisha staring at her and added hastily, "Other women, not respectable ones like you and me . . ."

A yisha lay on her bed mat in the courtyard, wrapped in a rug, her cat curled against her, kneading her arm, purring like a rusty coffee grinder. The night was cool, a breeze, moist from the river, stirred the air. Far above her the stars glittered cold and bright.

Were they the same stars that looked down on England, she wondered? She couldn't be sure. But the moon . . . the moon was the same all over the world.

On his pallet under the bench, Ali stirred in his sleep.

When she was in England she'd be able to come out and look at the moon and think of this place, these people.

When she was in England . . . No longer if.

Laila was secure: she would either work for Baxter and live there in the cook's house with Ali, or she would have a house in Alexandria. Either way she would be safe.

And so would Ali. Already he was beginning each sentence with "Baxter says . . ."

The cost was worth it, even though Ayisha's future was less secure. No future was secure, she reminded herself. Illness could strike at any moment, accidents happened; all she could do was try.

England was a green land, Papa had told her, and very beautiful. A cold land, where it rained nearly every day, and whole days where you could see only a few yards ahead because of mist.

Mist was beautiful, Papa said, but it made him cough. Papa's lungs were bad. Born in the heat of India, he could not take the cold.

Could she take the cold? She wasn't sure. She'd never been really cold, not for long. In winter she and Ali slept bundled up in thick rugs, and on clear, cold nights they slept beside the oven.

In England it snowed. Snow was wonderful according to Papa: you built snowmen and rode on sleds and threw snowballs.

But Mama told stories of long snowbound winters in the mountains of Georgia. Snow could freeze your fingers and toes so that they fell right off, Mama said. Ayisha wasn't sure if that was true or not. You never could tell, with Mama.

Soon, maybe, she would see snow for herself.

Tom butted her hand, a gentle reminder that she'd stopped patting him. She smiled and cuddled him to her. "You won't like the snow in England, Tom," she whispered to the cat. "But we will keep each other warm." With her cat, she would not feel so alone in cold, green England.

No matter what, she was sure there would be no long, hot nights.

O mar says no," Ali announced as a servant admitted him to Baxter's presence. He'd knocked so hard on the door, he'd woken the entire household.

Ali continued, "He said, 'No sister of mine will work for a foreigner.' But really it's because without Laila he will need to work himself, or starve. He is a lazy slug, that Omar."

Baxter, yawning, waved him to sit down. "Good God, boy, who told you to come at such a ridiculous hour?"

"You said first thing," said Ali indignantly. "This is first thing."

Baxter peered at the early morning sky. The sun was barely up. He shuddered. "From now on first thing means eight o'clock." He yawned again. "Do you know how to make coffee?" Ali nodded. "Then make me some coffee while I get dressed. I will have a coffee and then I will talk to Omar."

"No, you must not," Ali said immediately. He grasped Baxter's sleeve earnestly. "If you go there, it will be . . . trouble."

For Laila, was the implication.

"The only way to deal with bullies is to confront them," Baxter told him.

Ali snorted. "This I learned on the streets. But if I stand up to Omar, it will not be me who suffers. When I am older, it will be different." He clenched his fists. "And when I am a man I will take Laila away from that place."

Baxter looked at Laila's ten-year-old champion and rubbed a hand over his bristly jaw. Did he want to talk to Omar or not? He didn't take on a fight unnecessarily. And when he did, he liked to win.

He'd taken a shine to Laila right off, but was that reason enough to take her brother on? After one meeting? These things had implications . . . especially in the Orient. Especially when a woman was involved.

"I need a shave and a coffee, in that order," he told Ali. "Then I will think about it."

The tension drained out of Ali's skinny frame. "So you're not going to talk to Omar?" He looked relieved but sounded disappointed.

Baxter looked at the boy and thought about the woman he'd met only the day before. He'd liked her on the spot. He'd made an instant decision to employ her. His instincts had never let him down. He made a decision. "Did I not ask you to make coffee?"

"But—" Ali began.

Baxter pointed at the kitchen. "Go! And wake Jamil and tell him to come here to me."

But when Jamil came, it was not to shave Baxter, but to deliver a message to a woman in the poorest part of town . . .

A few hours later, Jamil murmured something in Baxter's ear, and Baxter sent Ali on an errand to buy some fruit at the market. The moment Ali had run off, Jamil brought a woman through the back entrance, her identity swathed and hidden.

"So, Laila, your brother says no," Baxter said when she had seated herself. "You now have a choice—if you still wish to come and work for me."

"A choice?" She dropped her veil. Her liquid dark eyes examined him.

Baxter caught his breath. She was lovely. Her skin was smooth and creamy. Her full, rosy lips were a little puffy at one corner.

Not a young woman and, he thought, eyeing that bruised and swollen lip, not one to whom trust would come easily.

But there was a certainty about her steady gaze, as if she'd come to terms with who she was. He liked that in a woman.

"There is a way, but you will have to trust me," he said.

She gave him a clear look. "I have had few reasons to trust men in my life. But tell me your plan."

He told her and her eyes narrowed. "Why would you do this? You do not even know me."

He shrugged. "Simple. I like my comforts, and I like you. And I trust my instincts about people. But it's up to you. Think about it and let me know your decision."

"Take this and go shopping," Rafe told Ayisha when he called on her next morning. He handed her a purse. "Buy whatever you will need for the journey." He glanced at her clothing. "It might be easier if you wore those clothes on the journey to Alexandria—we will go by horse and then take a boat down the river. But you will need to board the ship as a woman."

Her eyes flashed—he'd been pushing her hard, he knew—but all she said was, "Is there anything special I should buy?"

"I don't know—dresses, stockings, underwear, shoes, shawls, hats—that sort of thing." What did he know of what women needed? "Don't pinch pennies, buy whatever you think you might need. Take Laila with you."

"Laila is busy," she told him.

"You'd better get going," Rafe told her. "There is much to do. We leave for Alexandria in a few days."

She took the purse. For a woman who'd been given carte blanche to purchase whatever she wanted, she looked downright miserable, but he couldn't help that.

Shortly afterward Baxter knocked on Omar's door. He'd looked in on his place of business on the way and called to a thin young man, bent over a pile of documents. "Ben," he called. "I want you to come with me. Bring paper and pen and ink."

He had to knock twice on Omar's door. As they waited Baxter sniffed the air. "Smell that? There is a bakery near here. Get us some fresh bread, Ali. We will make a proper breakfast after this." He tossed him a coin.

Ali looked at the coin doubtfully. "But it is Laila's bread," he said. "You do not need to pay."

"Laila's bread? Of course. I'd forgotten she's a baker."

"It is very good bread," Ali told him. "It sells very quickly."

"Then run and buy some for me before it all runs out," Baxter told him. "I could do with some very good bread." Ali shrugged and went around the corner.

The door was finally opened by Omar himself. He was around Baxter's age, a plump man with thick lips, a paunch, and thinning hair. He peered blearily at the visitors and scratched his stomach. "What is it?" His clothing was rumpled, as if he had slept in it.

Baxter introduced himself, stepped inside, and repeated his offer of employment for Laila. He carefully outlined the conditions of employment.

Omar sniggered when he finished. "That's what you call it, is it? Keeping a woman in the house? I found out all about you. A widower, aren't you? Think I don't know what you want my sister for?"

"You are mistaken," Baxter said coldly. "It is a fair and honorable offer I make; your sister is a respectable woman."

"She is," Omar said. "Which is why I say no. Laila's duty is to her family."

"Your family being you?" Baxter asked.

"I am head of the family. I decide what my sister does."

Omar's gaze slid over Baxter like oil, taking in the rich fabric of his robes, pausing at the gold signet ring on his finger.

Sizing him up, Baxter thought. He waited for the offer he knew would come.

Omar glanced at Ben, standing meek and silent by the door. "Who is that?"

Baxter shrugged. "Just one of my clerks."

Omar looked conspiratorially around, leaned forward, and murmured, "For a price, I might reconsider." His breath stank.

"Let me get this clear," Baxter said. "For the right price, you will allow me to debauch your sister?"

Omar shrugged. "If the price is right."

At that moment, Laila came in from the rear of the house. Her eyes flew to Baxter, then to Omar, and then back to Baxter.

"What is going on here?" she asked. As if she didn't know.

"Outside, woman, this is men's business," Omar snapped.

She left with quiet dignity.

"Can you read?" Baxter asked Omar.

"Of course," Omar said with a certain bravado.

Baxter pulled out a notepad and pencil, sat down cross-legged at the low table in the middle of the room, and swiftly filled the page with fluent Arabic. When he'd finished, he handed the page to his assistant, Ben. "Tidy that up. Two copies," he said. "And hand me the pouch."

Ben sat, pulled a leather pouch, ink, and paper from a satchel he'd been carrying, handed the pouch to Baxter, and began to copy rapidly.

As Ben's pen flew, Baxter began to count out money. He did it slowly, deliberately, watching Omar out of the corner of his eye.

Omar, who'd watched Ben's swift, neat writing with a bemused air, was instantly distracted. His eyes bulged as the pile grew. He sat, his mouth wet, watching avidly. His hands twitched.

Baxter finished counting and set the pile in the center of the table. "Is that sufficient?"

Omar nodded eagerly. He reached for it, but Baxter's hand shot out and grabbed him by the wrist, so hard Omar winced.

"Not yet," Baxter said in a hard voice. "You must first sign the agreement that you will give your sister to me in exchange for this sum of money."

Omar snatched the pen and scribbled his name on it, barely glancing at the paper.

His hand crept toward the money.

"Sign the other copy," Baxter ordered.

Omar signed. Baxter countersigned each document and handed it to Ben, who also signed, then sealed each document with red sealing wax.

He handed one copy to Baxter and the other to Omar. "Take it."

Omar seized the money, stuffed it into a shabby cloth bag, and bundled it into his shirt before Baxter had a chance to change his mind.

Baxter rose and went to the back door. "Laila," he said. "Pack your things, you're coming with me."

She didn't move. "Omar said yes?"

Baxter nodded. "He did."

She glanced at Omar, standing behind him, and her eyes narrowed. "How much did he ask for?" she asked Baxter in a low voice. "And what did he promise?"

"Not at all what he imagined," Baxter said softly, and she stared at her brother.

Omar was reading the document, silently, his lips moving slowly. He looked up, a shocked expression on his face. "*Bride price?* This is a contract for marriage?"

"*Marriage?*" gasped Laila.

Baxter glanced down at Laila and shrugged. "He was prepared to sell you, but I don't buy people. A marriage contract, on the other hand, is a legal promise, and an exchange of money is quite acceptable. However, it's entirely up to you. It's a practical alternative, that's all."

Laila stared back at him, stunned. "But this is not what we agreed. You don't even know me," she whispered.

Again he shrugged. "I've trusted my instincts all my life. And your message said you would trust me to do what was needed." He smiled. "Trust begets trust."

"Beget?" Omar sneered. "She is barren."

"It is true." She gave Baxter a long, searching look. "Are you sure of this, sir?"

He smiled. "You can call me Johnny. Or Jamil if you prefer."

"I like Johnny," she said. Her eyes were shining.

"It would just be a practical arrangement," he reminded her carefully. "No hearts and flowers."

"Hearts and flowers?" She looked puzzled, and he recalled that she probably had no concept of romantic love. Here they understood practical arrangements.

"It's practical," he repeated. "A solution to both our needs."

"Practical." She nodded. "Yes, I will come."

"But I did not agree to marriage," Omar blustered.

"You did, and in writing, signed, witnessed, and sealed." Baxter patted the inside pocket where his copy rested. "Laila will come with me now. The rest is up to her."

"Now? But who will make me breakfast?" Omar grumbled.

"Pay someone." Baxter told him. "And if you ever lay a finger on Laila again, or even come near her without her invitation . . ." He paused to let the message sink in. "I'll thrash you to within an inch of your life."

*B*axter has taken Laila!" Ali burst in on Ayisha and Rafe. Ayisha had gone to his house to return the change from her shopping expedition.

"What do you mean, Baxter has taken Laila?" she demanded. Ali excitedly explained.

Ayisha could not believe her ears. "He has offered her *marriage*?"

"Yes, he says it is practical, and I think so, too, for if they are married, Omar cannot touch Laila. But Baxter made him sign a document in writing with a red wax on it, so maybe that will be enough. Laila has taken everything of hers and yours and mine to Baxter's house."

"What about my cat?"

"The cat, too. Baxter likes cats. Laila has forgotten nothing. She even took a little bag that clinked from behind a brick in the oven."

Ayisha was stunned. "We are to live at Baxter's house now? No more Omar?"

"Yes, it is very good, is it not?" Ali hurried on, "Laila has gone with Baxter, but she has not yet said she will marry him. I don't know why. I like Baxter. And he is rich. If she marries Baxter, will that make us rich? It would be nice to be rich. Do you think she will marry Baxter? And if she does, what will that make me? If she is my foster mother, will that make him my foster father? He says we will all live with him. He told Laila to bring everything she wanted, so we packed everything and now we live at Baxter's—Laila, me, and you. Do you think that means I will sleep inside tonight? In a bed, a real bed?"

Ayisha laughed at the eager torrent of questions. "I don't know what will happen, but yes, I think tonight you will sleep inside in a real bed. And so will I."

And, she thought, that was Laila and Ali settled safely. Which meant . . .

"What's all this?" a deep voice said from the doorway. "I heard Baxter and Laila's names mentioned."

Ayisha explained what had happened. The excitement slowly drained from her as the consequence of Laila's move became clear. In Rafe's blue, implacable gaze she saw he knew it, too.

She had no more excuses to delay. Her time in Egypt was at an end.

Nine

⁓

*H*e has sent Higgins on to Alexandria to book passage on a ship and says we will leave here in two days. Two days, Laila. What will I do?"

Laila hugged her. "You will follow your destiny, child, as I follow mine." They were sitting cross-legged, facing each other on a low, wide bed in the previous cook's quarters. Compared to Laila's house, it was luxury.

"Will you really marry Baxter?" Ayisha asked her. The room smelled of soap and sunshine; Laila had scrubbed the place from top to bottom, washed all the bedclothes, and dried them in the sun.

"Of course." Laila smiled. "But not just yet"

"Because he is rich?"

Laila shook her head. "Rich is very nice, but a rich woman can be as happy or as unhappy as a poor woman. Money brings comfort, that's all." She looked around the room and patted the rich bedcover. "I have comfort here already. And if your Englishman gives me a house—"

"He will," Ayisha said with certainty.

Laila smiled. "Then I am no longer a poor woman, and I can choose."

"Why marry Baxter, then? You don't even know him."

Laila shrugged. "I married my husband without even meeting him."

"So is that why you will wait? To know Baxter better?"

Laila shook her head and gave a rueful smile. "Marriage is always a gamble. You don't know until you're in it what it will bring. You just have to close your eyes, pray, and jump—then do your best to make yourself happy."

Ayisha sighed. A leap of faith. It was exactly how she felt about going off with a tall, dark stranger with blue, blue eyes. If she wasn't careful, she would be . . . lost.

"If that is true, why wait?"

A slow, feminine smile grew on Laila's face. "The waiting is for Baxter, not me," she said softly.

"I don't understand. You know he wants you. He asked you."

"Yes, and he talks of 'practical arrangements' and 'convenience.'" Laila snorted.

"Is it not?"

"Oh yes, but that is not all it is." She smiled to herself. "A woman knows when a man wants her."

"How does she know?" Ayisha burst out. "How?"

Laila's face softened. "Ah, you are thinking of your Englishman, little one. I cannot tell you the answer; it is something every woman must learn for herself."

"Is it?" Ayisha said in a flat voice.

Laila laughed. "Ah, that is what frightens you, eh? You fear that you will give him your heart, and that he will break it, eh?"

She took Ayisha's hand. "That is our fate, as women. We cannot help but love, and sometimes it hurts . . . it hurts so much." Her eyes got that faraway look, and Ayisha knew Laila was thinking of her former husband. How it must have pained Laila, to be divorced by a husband she loved, for something she could not help. Adding salt to the wound of barrenness.

"But," Laila brightened and said briskly, "just when you think you will live out your life as a dried-up old woman, along comes a man who with one look from his wicked blue eyes causes your heart to beat faster."

Ayisha couldn't help but smile at the frank relish in Laila's voice. "So when will you marry him?"

Laila smiled a deep, womanly smile. "As soon as Mr. Johnny Baxter understands why he asked for me."

Ayisha frowned. "What if you are wrong? What if it is just for a practical arrangement?"

Laila gave her a woman-to-woman look. "A rich man can have any woman he wants. Or any cook, for that matter. And Johnny knows where I stand. I made it very clear to him on that first day that I am a virtuous woman and will put up with no nonsense."

Laila pulled a face. "So his only solution is to bring a clerk to my brother's house? Give Omar a large sum of money and trick him into signing a marriage contract? I don't think so." Her eyes gleamed with feminine power.

"That first day, from the moment our eyes met, I felt something. He did, too, I could tell. And when he touched my hand . . . ooooh!" She waved her hand like a fan to cool her face.

"So, when Mr. Johnny Baxter understands why he did what he did, I will marry him. Until then, it will do him no harm to wait. Waiting makes a man more . . . appreciative." And she smiled in a way that recalled Ayisha's mind to what she thought of as "the stallion conversation."

Laila's words that day and the images they'd conjured up had burned deep into Ayisha's consciousness.

She hadn't been able to rid herself of the image of Rafe Ramsey, riding hard between her thighs . . . She could still feel his body lying on top of hers, her hips braced between his hard thighs, smelling the clean, manly smell of him.

And then riding back from the river with him, hot and sweaty and with blood on his hands, her arms around his waist, listening to his heart beat through his shirt.

Ayisha shivered, thinking about it.

Laila smiled and patted her hand. "I know, there's something about these blue-eyed men." She was silent for a long moment, then she said, "Do you think my Englishman has tight breeches and long boots like your Englishman has? I would give something to see my Johnny in such clothes."

*T*he night before their departure, Rafe sought Laila out in her new domain and found her cooking up a storm in preparation for Ayisha's farewell dinner. A small army of minions meekly minced, pounded, and peeled vegetables under her supervision.

After an exchange of pleasantries and the obligatory coffee and something to eat, he broached the subject on his mind.

"You are to marry Baxter, I believe. Congratulations."

"Maybe I marry him." She pursed her lips mischievously. "I have not yet decided."

Her insouciance surprised him. Baxter was a good catch. Still, it was none of his business. He said, "You will be lonely, I think, without Ayisha."

"She is the daughter of my heart," Laila confirmed, "and I will miss her sorely. But it is good she go to her grandmother. That girl need family." She eyed him sharply. "Her grandmother maybe find her a good man to marry?"

"Quite possibly," Rafe said repressively. "I have come to tell you the house in Alexandria is now yours." He gave her the deed. "In your name and in Ali's."

She wiped her hands carefully and took the rolled document as though it was something fragile and not quite real. Her eyes were moist. "Thank you, Rameses; you are a man of honor and I will pray for you every day of my life." She winked and added, "And for your wife, too."

Rafe's lips twitched. She never gave up.

He went to tell Baxter they would leave at first light. He paused, then said, "I understand there's a wedding in the offing?"

Baxter's mouth twisted in a sardonic smile. "There's a marriage contract. Laila hasn't actually accepted me . . . yet."

"I'm surprised," Rafe said frankly. "I would have thought she'd jump at it. Most women would."

"That's the interesting part," Baxter said. "She hasn't. I think she's angling for more."

"More? Good God."

"Outrageous I know," Baxter said dryly. "But it's not about money. I think she's angling for a courtship."

For a man who'd made an amazing offer, and been not quite turned down, Baxter was taking it amazingly well, Rafe thought. He seemed almost proud of Laila's reluctance to accept him.

And so he should be, Rafe suddenly realized; if she married Baxter eventually, he'd know it wasn't for money or position.

And even though Baxter had openly reiterated it was just a practical arrangement, still, it would be pleasant to feel that one was desired for oneself, not just for one's money.

Or one's relationship to an earl. And one's presumed ability to breed an heir, he thought.

He brought his thoughts back to Baxter. "Rather a quick decision on your part, wasn't it?"

Baxter shrugged. "I've made most of the important choices in my life quickly and on instinct. Hasn't let me down—most of the time." He grinned at Rafe. "Have to say, Ramsey, I thought you'd be a damned nuisance when you first came here."

Rafe quirked an eyebrow. "Damn, and I thought I was doing my best to turn your life upside down. Tell me, where did I go wrong?"

Baxter chuckled. "Well, you did bring a certain amount of turmoil, but I like it. When you came here first, this place was like a mausoleum. When my cook left, all his family left, too, his two wives and a horde of children and assorted relatives. I found I missed them. Now, with Laila and Ali—and I have no doubt Laila will drag in more orphans off the street—there'll be a bit of life in the place again."

Rafe gave a twisted grin. "You're a good man, Baxter, and I'm glad to have met you. If you ever visit England again, come and stay. You'll be most welcome." He held out his hand and the two men shook hands.

S hortly after dawn, Rafe arrived at Baxter's house on horseback, leading a mare for Ayisha to ride. Behind him came two local men also on horseback and a mule laden with luggage.

"Horses?" said Ayisha in surprise as she left the house.

"We will ride to Boulac," he told her. "It's not far, and from there we'll take a boat down the Nile."

The others had followed her out to bid her a final good-bye: Laila, Ali, Baxter, and the servants. Even the cat.

Everyone was a little heavy-eyed from the feast the previous night; Laila had given Ayisha a wonderful send-off, with mounds of delicious food. Afterward they sat around a fire in the courtyard, under the stars, recalling times past and telling stories, singing, and playing music, and in Laila's case, dancing. It had been a night of laughter and of tears.

This morning Ayisha was all bright, determined cheerfulness. Faking it gallantly, thought Rafe, noting the red-rimmed eyes.

She was still dressed as a boy, but had donned clothing especially for the journey: Bedouin robes and a head cloth, fastened with a knotted rope around the crown instead of a turban. Perfect for riding, as it happened.

"Have you got your things?" Rafe asked Ayisha. The contrast between her jaunty manner and her slightly puffy eyes ate at him.

She brought forward a small bundle and he handed it to one of the guides, who added it to the baggage.

"Well," she said in a voice that shook only a little. "I suppose this is good-bye."

She hugged and kissed first Baxter, then Ali who'd dropped his boyish air of bravado and was choking back sobs.

"Be good, little brother, and come to me in England when you are a man," she said in a husky voice. "And practice your writing and send letters to me often, for I will miss you."

"I will," he promised.

Laila was last; the two women hugged in a long, convulsive embrace. Laila openly wept.

Ayisha was the first to pull away. "Fear not for me, Laila. I seek my destiny, remember? I will suck dry the sweet orange of life. And thank you, thank you for everything." Her voice broke, and she pressed her lips together, unable to go on.

Laila wiped away a tear with a corner of her robe. "Remember always that you are the daughter of my heart, and much— very much—beloved."

Ayisha nodded, unable to speak. She bent and picked up the cat, buried her face in his fur, and then slipped him into her robes. Closing the robe around him, she walked toward the horse.

"What are you doing?" Rafe said. "You can't take that cat."

She stared at him in blind bewilderment. "Why not?" Her arms tightened defensively around the cat. "He's my cat."

Rafe glanced at the others. "It is a long and difficult journey."

"Tom is tough. He can survive anything."

"Can he travel in a cage?" he asked. "Could he stand being locked up?" The animal had always looked half wild to him.

Silence. Her head was bent over her cat.

"Because the ship will demand he be kept in a cage a lot of the time. And also when we are traveling in a carriage." He glanced at the horses. "We will spend hours on these horses today and then we will be in a boat on the river. Will he stay all that time in your robes?"

They all knew the answer. Her lower lip was trembling. She bit down on it, hard enough to make Rafe wince. The cat climbed out of her robe and set its paws on her shoulder, butting her chin with its head. Rafe could hear its rusty purring.

"He's an old cat, Ayisha," Rafe said gently. "Old cats don't like change."

She buried her face in its fur so he could not see her expression. The cat kneaded her shoulder, staring at Rafe with a baleful expression, as if it knew he was taking its mistress away. Its tail, with the missing tip, twitched.

"He is right, my daughter," Laila said softly. "The cat is too old to change his ways."

"Give it to Ali," Rafe told her. He nodded to Ali.

Ali ran forward and held his hands up for the cat. "I will take good care of him, Ayisha, I promise."

Ayisha lifted her head. "Of course I knew he couldn't come with me," she said with a hollow attempt at brightness. "I just . . . wanted to say good-bye to him. He is—he was my oldest friend." With lips clamped together in a wobbly smile, Ayisha handed her cat over, and without a further word, turned and mounted her horse lithely, needing no leg up.

Rafe mounted his own horse. "Ready?" he asked her.

She nodded, unable to speak.

"Good-bye, good-bye," the others called.

She waved back, smiling, her eyes blind with tears. Ali ran alongside the horses, the cat having jumped from his arms to the top of the wall. It sat, as his mistress disappeared, watching her with slitted golden eyes.

Two minutes away from home, just as Ayisha managed to get her tears under control, they passed a dusty-looking black-clad man, his face bruised from a recent beating. He stared up at Ayisha, his jaw dropping, and his eyes narrowed with dark fury.

"By God, it's that villain from the river." Rafe started forward.

She held up a hand to stop him. "No, leave it. I will handle this." In Arabic, Ayisha called out to him. "Uncle of Gadi, greetings. I hope your aches and pains are terrible indeed. May they get worse! As you see, I am leaving with the Englishman. He has much gold. You will get none. My mother cursed you with her dying breath. It is all you deserve."

He cursed her and raised a fist, then glanced fearfully at the Englishman.

She laughed. "Still a coward, eh? You asked me once how I escaped you that night." She paused until they had almost passed him. "I was under the bed all the time, right under your nose, just this far from your feet." She held her hands six inches apart. "And you know what, uncle of Gadi? Your feet stink!"

Her tears disappeared. She kicked her horse into a gallop, shouting back to Rafe, "Race you to Boulac, Englishman!"

The winds were fair and they made good time to Rosetta. They didn't disembark there, as many did, to make the short trip to Alexandria overland, via the lakes, but took the longer route by sea. Rafe had spoken to the captain, who told him it wasn't a good time to pass through Alexandria, better to go direct to the port. As they still had plenty of time to board the ship, Rafe agreed.

Ayisha had a mischievous look on her face when he told her of the change of plan. "Not a good time, my foot," she said. "You only agreed after you heard there were no horses for hire, and you'd have to ride a donkey from Rosetta to Etka and again from the Lake of Akoubir to Alexandria. I know!"

He grinned. "Well, but my legs are too long for riding a donkey. It would look ridiculous. And I would feel like a monster."

In the days since they'd left Cairo, she'd cheered up a great deal. She had seemed to enjoy the trip, pointing out things of interest and odd curiosities, and appearing cheerful and positive, but Rafe knew much of it was an act.

Whenever she thought herself unobserved, her bright expression faded, and several times he caught her watching the land slipping by with unseeing eyes. Something was worrying her, and it wasn't just going to a strange land—though God knew, that was intimidating enough.

"Your grandmother will be so delighted to see you," he told her once.

"Yes, I'm sure she will be," she said politely, sounding anything but certain. "And I, her."

"Higgins will endeavor to procure you a single cabin," he told her another time, thinking she might be apprehensive about the voyage. "It will depend on the other passengers," he explained. "You might have to share a cabin."

She looked at him with an odd expression.

"With another lady, possibly several ladies," he added hastily, and she'd laughed.

Finally, they approached the ancient city of Alexandria from the sea and sailed around to the western harbor, where their ship waited. Rafe, having been here a short time earlier, pointed out the local places of interest: the Isle of Pharos, where the ancient Pharos lighthouse, one of the seven wonders of the world, had once stood and which was now occupied by a massive fifteenth-century fortress. There were a number of Roman remains, including Pompey's Pillar, and between the buildings they saw the tip of Cleopatra's Needle pointing upward to the sky.

"And there is Higgins, awaiting our arrival," Rafe observed, seeing the figure of his valet frantically waving, standing with a small flock of porters.

"Excellent timing, sir," Higgins said, directing the porters to the baggage. He turned to Ayisha as he ushered them toward the ship. "Miss Cleeve, how have you enjoyed the journey?"

"It's been fascinating, thank you, Higgins," she said. "But please call me Ayisha."

"Miss Ayisha," Higgins agreed, with a quick glance at Rafe. Rafe nodded. Higgins would be the best one to teach Ayisha how to talk to servants. He was sure she wouldn't listen to him nearly as well.

"I wasn't able to get you a single cabin, I'm afraid, miss," he said as he guided them to the gangplank. "There were only three berths still available: two men's berths and one ladies'. I was able to obtain one of the staterooms for Mr. Rafe but only because—"

"Miss Ayisha will take the stateroom," Rafe told him. "I will take her berth."

"Mrs. Ferris won't like that, sir," Higgins said.

"Who the deuce is Mrs. Ferris?"

"The lady whose cabin Miss Ayisha will share. It was the only other berth available."

"It will be nice to have another lady to talk to," Ayisha said placidly. "Please, Higgins, could you show me the way?"

"Of course, miss, we're all on the same deck. There's only twenty passengers." He directed Ayisha toward the stairs.

"Higgins, when does the ship leave?" Rafe said, not moving.

"In two hours, sir," Higgins replied. "The tide will turn then, and the ship will depart."

"Excellent," Rafe said. "Two hours will be plenty, I'm sure."

"Plenty for what—" Higgins turned, but Rafe was halfway down the gangway. He shouted something after Rafe, but the wind was picking up and Rafe didn't catch it. Long strides took him toward the city. He knew exactly what he wanted, and he even knew the Arabic word for it.

"Sir, sir, the captain is dependent on the wind and tides," Higgins bellowed. "What if he leaves early?" He started to follow, but his master was already almost at the city entrance.

"He always does this." Higgins turned a gloomy face to Ayisha. "Some last-minute idea. And what if he misses the ship, eh? Then where will we be?"

"Tossing a coin over a stateroom?" Ayisha suggested with a smile.

Higgins looked appalled. "Oh no, miss, you'd have to take it. I couldn't possibly."

He eyed her garb and then said diffidently, "However, miss, since Mr. Ramsey has taken himself off for a while, may I suggest you use his cabin to change into your lady's clothes? It might be best if Mrs. Ferris didn't see you dressed as an Arab boy."

Ayisha glanced down at her attire. "I suppose so." She wasn't particularly looking forward to being turned into a lady.

"Excellent, here is the key to Mr. Ramsey's cabin. The number is on the tag. It's the best of the cabins—the owner's private quarters, and on the same level as yours. I'll fetch your baggage and meet you there, miss. Oh—and I'll get a bath sent up, too."

Ten

Ayisha didn't want to move. When Higgins said a bath, she'd expected a bucket of water—it was how she'd washed for the past six years, except for the days when they took the washing down to the river and went in and bathed in their robes.

This was a tin bath, large enough to sit down in—an unexpected treat. And the warm water, even better. But the soap . . . she sniffed again. Ali had said it smelled good enough to eat, but this wasn't the same smell. This smelled of . . . jasmine? And something else. She must ask Higgins.

But her fingertips were getting wrinkly, proof that she'd stayed in too long. She took a clean pitcher of water, stood up, and rinsed the soap off herself, hair and all. She stepped out of the bath feeling clean and—she sniffed her skin—delicious.

Higgins had thought of everything; there were even towels. She wrapped her hair in one and dried herself with the other.

The stateroom was a superior cabin and very ingeniously designed, with a bed big enough for two built into the corner of the ship, with drawers built in under it. The open side of the bed had a low enclosure of rails, like a child's cot, to prevent anyone in bed from falling out in rough weather, she supposed.

Everything was fixed to prevent it moving in case of storm; a small desk-cum-table was lowered from the wall and several chairs hung on hooks, to be taken down when necessary.

The cabin was quite luxurious and even had a separate, though tiny room for washing, and next to it a Bramah's water closet with a saltwater flush.

"Everything of the most modern and convenient," Higgins had declared proudly, obviously a little disappointed his master was not there to be impressed, too.

It was the best cabin on the ship, Higgins explained. It had been fitted out for the ship's owner and his wife when they traveled and was not normally available for passengers, Higgins told her, with a smug look. He'd done well to get it.

The timber lining of the cabin was painted white, and the brass hinges and handles, hanging oil lamp, and other fittings gleamed with a recent polish. Two windows over the bed, looking out the back of the ship, and a large porthole on the side wall let in plenty of light.

The ship had been a warship but was converted by the new owners, and though some of the cannon ports had been kept for guns in case of pirates, many now were fitted with windows— portholes—to let light and fresh air into passengers' cabins.

She shook out the dresses she'd bought. Rafe had been very clear that she was not to worry too much—just get some clothes to travel in. She'd be clothed in the latest fashions once they got to London. "Half a dozen dresses or so and the usual feminine folderol," he'd told her.

The trouble was she had no idea what "the usual feminine folderol" was. And six seemed an enormous number of dresses to her. Still, it had been such a long time since she'd had anything new, she was happy to take his purse and spend his money. She'd put on one of Laila's all-over robes, and veiled, she'd had a lovely time, choosing fabrics and haggling over prices to her heart's content.

She'd never done that sort of thing before, and it occurred to her she could have slipped into anonymous women's garb before this, but her concentration had been so wholly on not appearing female that she'd never done it.

The seamstress had boggled with amazement when she took off the outer robe and showed herself to be a boy, and then took off her outer boy's clothing and revealed herself to be a girl. She told the woman to say nothing, but she knew gossip would eventually spread.

It didn't matter anymore; she was going to England.

She looked at the dresses spread out on the cabin bed. In the short walk to Rafe's cabin she'd passed several Englishwomen, a Frenchwoman, and a few more whose nationality she hadn't been able to identify. None of them wore dresses quite like these. Hers, she decided, were prettier.

The Cairo markets were wonderful, and she'd bought shoes and scarves and shawls, but there were no European-style dresses to be had anywhere, so Ayisha had chosen the fabrics and taken them to a seamstress. She'd never made Frankish dresses before, the woman told her, but she was sure she could manage.

So Ayisha had drawn some pictures and described what she wanted—going on vague memories from six years ago and glimpses of Englishwomen in the street—and the seamstress had done her best.

They were very simple. Two days were not enough to make anything complicated, so they were all basically the same design: simply cut, with wide enough skirts to move easily, a plain, round neck, elbow-length sleeves, and tied under the breasts with a ribbon or a cord. But the seamstress had added extra little touches that made each dress special: a band of contrasting fabric, a fringe, some beads. Ayisha was thrilled with everything, even the underwear.

She wasn't at all sure what English ladies wore under their dresses. When she was a little girl she'd just worn a chemise, but she was sure ladies must wear more than a chemise. But there wasn't time, so she'd just bought short, cotton Turkish-style pantaloons that ended at the knee, and some simple cotton chemise-like garments.

It was getting late, so she donned a wheat-colored dress with a pretty pattern of green leaves and blackberries, and slipped her feet into the red leather Turkish slippers she'd bought. She loved these shoes with their contrasting black design and red tassels on the toes.

She opened the door to the washroom and peered at the

reflection in the small, round looking glass, but it was screwed into the wall at head height and she couldn't see much.

She combed her ragged hair and pulled a face at her reflection. She looked like a boy. She should have bought some sort of lady's hat, to hide how short her hair was. Would it grow to a respectable length before he met her grandmother? She hoped so. Maybe a scarf . . . Hadn't Rafe said in England ladies wore turbans?

She was looking through the half dozen scarves she'd bought when there was a knock at the door. "It's Higgins, miss."

She flew to open it. "What do you think of my new clothes, Higgins?" She twirled so he could see.

Higgins looked her over gravely, then nodded. "Very nice, miss." His gaze wandered to her hair and a crease formed between his brows. "Miss, if I could be so bold—"

"I know, it's my hair, isn't it? I didn't think to buy a hat, but Ra—Mr. Ramsey said that in England some ladies wear turbans, so I thought perhaps . . ."

"Only the older ladies wear turbans, miss," Higgins said. "Many of the younger ones are wearing the more fashionable short crop these days."

"Short crop? Does that mean . . . ?" She touched her hair tentatively. "Not like this, surely?"

"Not quite, miss, but . . ." He looked a little self-conscious. "I've never cut a lady's hair, miss, but I cut sir's, and all his friends when they come to visit."

"You cannot mean to make it shorter . . . can you?" She placed a protective hand over what hair she had left.

"Not so much shorter, miss, but giving it some shape. I venture to suggest with a little shaping, it could look quite pretty. It's good and thick and with a nice bit of curl to it."

Ayisha looked at Higgins's neat person and made up her mind. "Do it," she said. It couldn't look any worse, and if Higgins cut Rafe's hair, well, Rafe always looked so elegant.

"Right then, miss, if you would sit in this chair, please?" Higgins sat her on a chair and draped a sheet around her. From Rafe's shaving kit bag he took a pair of scissors and a comb. He combed her hair a few different ways, seemed to come to a decision, and began snipping.

Bits of damp hair fell all around her. The more hair fell, the more anxious Ayisha grew. He was a man's valet. He would be giving her a man's haircut. The best she could hope for was to look like a very elegant boy.

Snip, snip.

She forced herself to be philosophical. If it was as bad as she expected, she thought dolefully, she would simply wear a turban. Like an old woman. It would give her added maturity.

Snip, snip.

She had been a girl dressed as a boy. Now she would look like a boy dressed as a girl. She knew which one would look more ridiculous.

"There now, miss." Higgins carefully drew the sheet away from her so no hair fell on her new dress. There was an alarming amount of hair on the floor. "Have a look in the looking glass, miss."

Trying not to let her trepidation show, Ayisha looked in the glass. And looked.

"Higgins . . ." She turned her head this way and that.

"Higgins . . ." She stared at her reflection in disbelief, then whirled around. "I was so certain you'd made me look like a boy!"

Higgins grinned. "It's even more successful than I imagined, miss. You look very pretty."

She looked back at herself in the mirror. "I think I do, too. It's . . . amazing." She turned back to him, misty-eyed. "Thank you, Higgins, thank you!"

He frowned. "But, miss, you're—"

She blinked rapidly to clear her eyes. "Oh, don't mind that. It's silly I know, but it's so long since I've felt pretty. Oh, Higgins, you're probably going to hate this, but—" She hugged him, hard.

He emerged from the swift embrace looking embarrassed but pleased. "Don't mind at all, miss," he said gruffly. "Though you shouldn't make a habit of it. Anything I can do to help. It's difficult for you I know, without a maid."

"Maid?" She laughed. "I haven't had a maid since I was a little girl. I wouldn't know what to do with one."

"You'll learn, miss," Higgins assured her. "But in the meantime, if you need anything, you tell me. Now, miss, while I tidy up here and remove your things to your cabin, how about you go up on deck and see if Mr. Rafe is coming? It's getting mighty late."

"I'll take my things." Ayisha began to repack them in her bundle.

"It's my job, miss—" Higgins began.

"No, it's my maid's," said Ayisha happily. "The lazy creature! Now, let me do it—I'm not a fine lady yet."

Higgins hesitated. "You are, you know, miss. No matter where you've been living, or how, you're a lady born—in the best sense of the word."

His words took Ayisha's breath away. "Thank you, Higgins," she said. "Sometimes I wonder how I'm going to manage in England."

He began to sweep up her shorn locks. "You'll be all right, miss. Best country in the world. Just that you need to learn the rules, that's all. Every place has its odd little rules, don't they?"

"That's true," she said thoughtfully, folding her bundle up. Not just every place, but different groups in the same place. As a little girl there had been Mama's friends—ladies, none of them English—and then there were Papa's English friends and visitors from all over the world—men of affairs, mostly. And then the servants. And with each the rules had been different.

And on the streets there was a whole new set of rules. There, learning had been a matter of survival. This should be much easier. Higgins was right; it was just a matter of working out the rules.

Higgins finished tidying and started unpacking Rafe's things. "I had to learn how to get on in a big house myself, miss. Very different from how I grew up, and different again from the army. Servants in a big house, well, they can be just as snobby as the toffs—some more so." He winked. "But I'm flexible, on account of having been sir's batman when he was at war."

"I'm flexible, too," she said.

"So you are, miss. I expect you're a quick study, too. You're quality, miss, through and through. Now, here's the key to your cabin. Mrs. Ferris wasn't there before. Maybe she's up on deck. Most of 'em will be there, waiting for the ship to cast off." He pulled out his watch and shook his head. "Cutting it very fine, he is, this time."

* * *

Quality through and through? A lady born? Ayisha thought as she carried her things to her cabin. If he only knew. Still they were very heartening words.

She knocked, but there was no answer so she went in. It was smaller than Rafe's cabin, with one porthole instead of two. Two beds were screwed to the wall, one above the other. The lower bunk had a shawl and a book resting on it. Mrs. Ferris's, no doubt.

She looked at the title of the book. *The Mysteries of Udolpho*, by a Mrs. Radcliffe. She glanced inside and saw it was a story and wondered if Mrs. Ferris would lend it to her after she had finished. It had been such a long time since she'd read anything.

Ayisha was pleased. She rather liked the idea of sleeping on the top bunk. She could look out of the porthole. She glanced out and saw most of the activity on the wharf had stopped. There were just a few people standing around, waiting. The ship would be leaving soon. And where was Rafe?

She quickly stowed her things and hurried up on deck, grabbing a shawl at the last minute. Nearly a dozen people were gathered along the rail at one end of the ship—passengers, she assumed from their clothing. She felt a little too shy to join them just yet. And besides, there was no sign of Rafe.

The breeze picked up, snapping the fabric of the sails and Ayisha's clothes. Her short hair blew in the wind and after wearing a head covering for years, it felt lovely and free, but her skirts flapped around her legs in a disconcerting manner. The feeling of wind against her legs made her feel very exposed. English ladies' clothes were very thin. She was glad she had the shawl and not only because of the breeze.

She'd hardly noticed she had breasts while she was a boy—only that they were a danger and had to be kept invisible. The bindings kept everything flat. Now nothing was keeping anything flat and it felt most . . . peculiar.

She glanced down as she walked along the deck, keeping away from the other passengers. There wasn't much bounce, but still . . . She bounced on the balls of her feet, experimentally. The shawl bounced with her.

She would have to get a corset. She hadn't even thought of one before. Not that any were for sale in the market.

She leaned against the rail and gazed out to the city. The sun was appreciably lower in the sky. He'd been gone almost two hours. Where on earth was he?

*T*he captain had started snapping out orders, sailors were scurrying back and forth doing things to sails, winding ropes, and there was a loud grating sound that suggested they were hauling up the anchor, and yet there was still no sign of a tall Englishman in long black boots.

Ayisha paced restlessly back and forth on deck. Her new red leather Turkish slippers were beginning to pinch.

What on earth was so important that he must rush off like that and risk missing the ship?

And then she spotted him, striding along as if he had all the time in the world, carrying a large heavy-looking sack slung over his shoulder.

He came striding up the gangplank just as the men were about to raise it, making some sort of joke that made them laugh. An officer saluted, welcoming him aboard.

She waited for his explanation, but he almost passed her by, but then stopped and stared.

"Well now, look at you," he said softly. "You're a woman. And don't you look lovely. Who did your hair?"

A warm surge of pleasure at the compliment robbed her of the caustic speech she'd been about to deliver. "Higgins cut it for me," she mumbled.

"Very pretty." His gaze ran over her, taking in everything. She felt self-conscious enough before he'd looked at her. Now she felt exposed. Half naked.

She pulled the shawl tighter around her. "Are you cold?" he said.

"No," she said quickly. "But Higgins and I have been very worried."

"What about?"

Her mouth dropped open. "What about? You nearly missed the ship!"

"Higgins knows I never miss ships," he said. "Did you miss me?" He looked very pleased with himself.

She folded her arms. "No. But what made you go off like that? With no warning or explanation?"

He grinned. "You did miss me."

"Actually, Higgins and I had decided to toss a coin for your cabin."

He laughed. "Nonsense, Higgins would never have agreed to that. Now, aren't you interested in what I've brought you?" He held up the bag. "You'll never believe what's in this."

"I don't care what it is—"

"Sand," he said.

"Sand?"

"That's not all . . ."

"You nearly missed the ship for *sand*?" She glared at him. "How dare you drag me across Egypt, then almost abandon me on a strange ship with a bunch of strangers, for such a reason," she said grumpily. It was very hard to stay angry with him when he kept smiling down at her like that. It was a very annoying habit.

"I didn't abandon you at all," he said, his blue eyes dancing. "You had Higgins."

She thumped him on the arm. At the same instant his waistcoat gave a small yowl.

"What's that noise?" She stared as a small bulge in his waistcoat moved.

"Your bon-voyage present," he said triumphantly and pulled out a small, silvery white kitten covered in black spots. Its ears were large with tiny tufts of dark hair at the tips. It looked like a miniature silver and black snow leopard. It stared at Ayisha with big amber eyes and yowled plaintively.

"It's a kitten," she said. The snow leopard was a symbol of her mother's country.

"I know. I thought you'd like the company on the long trip." His voice was deep, faintly amused, and yet it conveyed his understanding of her grief at leaving Tom behind.

She stared at him wordlessly, her mouth working.

"Hey," he said in a coaxing voice. "I thought you liked cats."

She gave a ragged laugh and blinked the incipient tears away. "You know I do, and she's beautiful, thank you."

"That's better." He handed the kitten to her, and Ayisha snuggled it against her breast, stroking it and murmuring to it. At the same moment, the deck jerked beneath their feet and their ship pulled away from Egyptian shores.

Ayisha stood, looking out, stroking her kitten, until Egypt was just a smudge on the horizon.

"Shall we go below, get this young lady settled?" Rafe Ramsey said at last, and she nodded. Her throat had something stuck in it and she couldn't speak.

*T*hat is an animal!" a voice said as Ayisha entered the cabin. A thin, elegant, older woman was sitting on the lower bunk, legs outstretched, reading. She lifted a lorgnette and peered through it at the kitten.

"Yes, a kitten."

"I can see that, but what's it doing in my cabin?"

"This is my cabin, too," Ayisha said pleasantly. "I'm Ayisha . . . Cleeve," she added reluctantly, holding out her hand. It was the first time she'd used Cleeve. She didn't much want to, but she had to have a surname and it was her father's name, even if she wasn't entitled to it.

Mrs. Ferris looked her up and down through the lorgnette. "I agreed to share with a Miss Cleeve, but not an animal."

"I didn't know about the kitten, either; she was a last-minute gift," Ayisha explained, stroking the kitten. "She doesn't even have a name yet. Don't you think she's pretty?"

Mrs. Ferris sniffed. "Well, its markings are certainly unusual. I've never seen a spotted cat before. Has it got fleas?"

"I don't know," Ayisha said, "But I've ordered some warm water. I'm going to give her a bath, to make sure."

Mrs. Ferris sat up. "Give a cat a bath? I thought they hated water."

Ayisha smiled. "Not all cats. My cat, Tom, liked water. We shall see if this one does." As she spoke, there was a knock at the door.

It was Higgins, bringing a bucket of warm water, a deep basin, a tin mug, some soap, and a towel. He glanced behind her at Mrs. Ferris watching from her bunk, lorgnette raised. "Here you go, miss. I'll return in a short time to fetch it all away. I'm just arranging a sandbox and something to eat."

"Thank you, Higgins." Ayisha gave him a warm smile and took the water.

"Who is that man?" Mrs. Ferris demanded as the door closed.

"Higgins? He is Mr. Ramsey's manservant."

"And who is Mr. Ramsey?"

Ayisha busied herself pouring water into the bowl and wondered briefly how to explain. "He's a friend of my grandmother," she said in the end. "He's escorting me to her home in Hampshire."

"I see. I don't much like this Higgins fellow coming and going in my cabin. Where is your own maid?"

Ayisha seated herself on the floor, draped a towel over her front, and picked up the kitten. "I don't have a maid."

"Don't have a maid?"

"No." Ayisha lowered the kitten into the water.

"Why not?"

Ayisha pretended not to hear. It wasn't hard. The kitten objected vociferously, yowling and wiggling and trying to climb up her arm to get away from the water. She had very sharp little claws.

Ayisha soothed her with words and hands and finally, unhappily, she settled, chin deep in the water, staring up at her with big, reproachful eyes.

"See, it's not so bad, is it?" Ayisha told her.

The kitten seemed to consider her words, then bit Ayisha on the finger.

"Ow, little imp," Ayisha chuckled, not blaming her in the least. She lathered some soap in one hand—smelling faintly medicinal this time, Higgins must have a soap manufactory, she decided—and gently massaged it through the kitten's fur. She rinsed it thoroughly, put the towel on her lap, then lifted the miserable clump of wet fur out and began to gently rub it dry.

The kitten sneezed twice, and shook itself indignantly, but soon started to enjoy the toweling. She purred and began to knead the towel, catching the fabric in her claws, then decided the corner of the towel was its enemy and started batting at it with her paws and biting it.

Ayisha put the kitten on the floor and tidied everything up. The kitten looked curiously around, then, as if she hadn't just had a bath, proceeded to wash itself all over.

Mrs. Ferris observed the whole operation curiously. "I always heard cats were clean and this one certainly seems to be," she commented at last. "Funny little creature."

"She's lovely," Ayisha agreed, though it wasn't quite what

Mrs. Ferris meant. "I'll have to think up a name for her."

The kitten began to explore the cabin, sniffing and eyeing everything with caution. Ayisha tried to think of names. The kitten pounced on an imaginary enemy. Pounce? For some reason that conjured up a fatter cat to mind, and this one was slender and elegant. Ayisha eyed the scratches on her forearms. Sharp little claws. Claudette?

"What's it sniffing there for?" Mrs. Ferris asked. The kitten was sniffing in a corner.

It suddenly occurred to Ayisha that she might be sniffing for a specific purpose. Ayisha scooped her up in one hand. She opened the cabin door and picked up the bucket of dirty water with the other.

"I'll take her with me while I get rid of this," she explained to Mrs. Ferris hurriedly. "I'll be back in a short while."

Luckily Higgins was outside and well prepared. A few doors down was a small storeroom and with a little judicial bribery, he'd made arrangements for a sand tray, spare sand, and various other kitten needs to be stored there. There was also a basket, with a lid fastening, so that the kitten could be safely locked up when necessary.

Ayisha placed the cat in the sand, and with a little encouragement, the kitten sniffed at the sand, scratched a hole, and made a deposit. She covered the hole, stepped out of the tray, shaking sand off her paws fastidiously, and looked up at Ayisha in clear expectation of being picked up. Her tail rippled and her black-tipped ears twitched. *Mrroww?*

"I'll call her Cleo," Ayisha said, lifting her up. "She's bossy, regal, beautiful, and Egyptian. And," she added as the kitten gave a plaintive mew, "hungry."

"Yes, miss," Higgins agreed. "I got her a bit of fish from the galley."

D id you travel to Egypt with this Mr. Ramsey?" Mrs. Ferris asked her next morning.

"No, I met him for the first time in Cairo."

"How did you get there, then—to Egypt, I mean?"

"I was born in Egypt."

"You don't look Egyptian. And despite that outlandish first name of yours, Cleeve is not an Egyptian name." Mrs. Ferris was determined to work out exactly who Ayisha was, to pigeonhole her, and work out exactly how much respect she needed to give—or not give.

"No." Ayisha slid her feet into slippers and picked Cleo up. "My father was born in India." That would puzzle the nosey old creature. She didn't look Indian, either.

But Mrs. Ferris was not so easily fooled. "John Company? He worked for John Company?" She meant the British East India Company; it was the name insiders used.

"No, but his father did. Please excuse me," Ayisha said as she slipped out of the cabin. "The kitten needs to go."

But Mrs. Ferris was waiting with more questions when they returned.

"Who did you know in Egypt—it was Cairo, you came from, wasn't it?"

"Yes, Cairo, but there are too many people to name." Ayisha put Cleo on her bunk and climbed up herself, hoping Mrs. Ferris would take the hint.

But the interrogation went on. "Who of importance did you know?"

Ayisha rolled her eyes. "Well, there was Mr. Salt, of course," she began, naming the consul general. "Papa knew him quite well." She didn't though. Mr. Salt had come to their house once when she was a little girl, with an English traveler, Viscount something, who called his employee simply Salt. Salt was a young painter then and had shown Papa some of his pictures. She'd watched them between the railings of the stairs, but she only remembered him because of his name. It seemed so funny to her to call someone Salt.

Years later Salt had come back to Cairo, all important now, as Mr. Salt, the British consul general. She'd seen him up close several times, but by that time she was living as a boy. And even if she'd been dressed as she was now, he still wouldn't have known her unless she'd explained who her father was.

But people said Mr. Salt had slaves, so she wouldn't have told him anything.

"Pooh, everyone knows Mr. Salt," Mrs. Ferris said. "Who did you visit? What about—" She listed a string of names, to each one of which, Ayisha said, "No, no, no," and played with her cat.

"Where did your father live?"

"In the old part of Cairo, overlooking the river."

"Describe where, exactly."

Ayisha gave a vague description.

Not vague enough. "I believe you mean that old house that has a shifting population of clerks," Mrs. Ferris sniffed. "Well, if that's where you lived . . ." Clearly Ayisha was a person of no account.

"I don't know who lives there now," Ayisha said, annoyed. "Since my parents died, I've been living with an Egyptian lady."

"An *Egyptian*?" Mrs. Ferris said, scorn dripping from the word.

"Yes, a very kind and respectable lady who is shortly to be married to an Englishman."

"Who?"

"To Mr. Johnny Baxter," Ayisha told her, thinking that would silence the woman. Mr. Baxter was kind, handsome, and rich, as well as being English; nobody could disparage him.

She was wrong. Mrs. Ferris could disparage anyone. "That fellow who's gone native?" She pronounced it "gorn native." "A disgrace to his country!"

"He's not! He's a war hero," Ayisha declared hotly. "He was badly wounded in the Battle of the Nile."

"Then it's a pity he went native, isn't it?"

Ayisha jumped off her bunk and scooped Cleo up. "The kitten has to go," she declared and stormed from the room.

"Again?" Mrs. Ferris's voice floated out as Ayisha shut the door. "I hope that animal isn't sickening with something. I won't share a cabin with a sick cat."

Eleven

Do I look all right?" Ayisha asked Mrs. Ferris that evening. "I'll be eating at the captain's table tonight." The *Flavia* was a merchantman that plied the Mediterranean trade routes on a regular basis, carrying goods and a few passengers between England and the Orient. It was owned by an Englishman who lived in Italy, and its captain was a half Italian Irishman.

Mrs. Ferris paused in her preparations to say, "Captain Gallagher has a reputation as a sociable man with regrettably . . . democratic views." She said the word as though it left a nasty taste in her mouth. "So at some stage he will have each passenger—of any standing, that is; not of course, servants—join him at his table. But I doubt very much you will be in his company tonight."

She adjusted the pearls at her throat and added, "To be asked to dine with him the first night out is a signal of honor. I myself will be at the captain's table. I sailed from England with him, and we are quite old friends. So you need not worry about that dress." She cast Ayisha's dress a faintly disparaging look.

"I like this dress," Ayisha told her. She actually loved the dress. The color matched her eyes, and the seamstress had added a border of contrasting fabric around the hem. The border was a black geometrical design on a green watery background, and was interspersed with cream and pink lotuses and tiny crocodiles. Wearing it was like bringing a little piece of the river with her. She wore it with a creamy, fringed silk shawl.

She was quite certain she was invited to the captain's table; Higgins had brought her the message from Rafe earlier, saying he'd pick her up at six and adding that it was an honor to be invited for the first night, and to wear her best clothes. But there was no point in arguing with Mrs. Ferris.

She glanced at Mrs. Ferris's maid. "Is my hair all right?" She'd twisted a spangled greeny scarf and knotted it around her head.

"Yes, miss," the maid said. "That scarf looks quite à la mode."

"Woods," Mrs. Ferris said repressively.

"Yes, ma'am," the maid said and, with a quick half smile at Ayisha, turned back to her mistress.

There was a knock on the door and Ayisha stood to answer it, but Mrs. Ferris said, "The door, Woods," and her maid hurried to open it.

"Mr. Ramsey to collect Miss Cleeve," a deep voice said.

A thrill ran through Ayisha as she looked at him. She'd only ever seen him in buff breeches and boots, but dressed formally, in an elegant black coat, a brilliant white shirt, and a pale gray waistcoat, freshly shaved and with a faint smile directed at her, he took her breath away.

"You look lovely," he said. "That dress almost exactly matches your eyes. Nothing could, of course—they are unique—but it comes very close." His gaze dropped to her hem. "I see you've brought your beloved river with you. Another unique touch. Now, are you ready for dinner?"

Ayisha nodded and stepped forward. The smile in his eyes made her feel a little shy. And the dress was all right, he'd said so. And he understood about the river.

Behind her, Mrs. Ferris cleared her throat in a meaningful way and Rafe looked past Ayisha.

"Mrs. Ferris, I presume," he said with a smile. "Rafe Ramsey at your service."

Mrs. Ferris held out her hand and Rafe bowed over it.

"You are here to escort this girl?" she said in faint disbelief.

Ayisha bridled at her tone.

"I am," Rafe confirmed, holding his arm out for Ayisha to

take. She stepped forward and placed her hand on his arm. He covered it with his own.

Mrs. Ferris's lips thinned. "She said you were her grandmother's friend."

"That is correct."

"But I was expecting a much older man."

He raised one dark brow. "Were you, ma'am?" he said in a manner that suggested, ever so politely, that it was none of her business. "Life is full of disappointments, isn't it?" And he led Ayisha away.

She maintained a dignified walk until they reached the end of the corridor, then she gave a gleeful little skip. "I am so glad you were rude to that woman. She is such a—a—"

"I wasn't the least bit rude," he said. "I was extremely polite."

"Yes, politely rude." She tried to think of how to describe what he'd done. "Like a very polite wasp."

"Is she rude to you?" he asked seriously. "Do you want me to have her shifted?"

"You can't," she said. "All the cabins are full."

"If she's unkind to you, I'll get her moved," he said in a voice that convinced her he both could and would.

His concern touched her. Nobody had ever worried about people being unkind to her before. She'd faced much worse things than rudeness or unkindness; she could handle the likes of Mrs. Ferris.

"No, don't worry. I don't have to see much of her anyway. She's traveling with two other ladies—they're all widows, and she spends a lot of her time with them. And do you know, they all have maids, but the maids are sharing a cabin several decks down. Woods told me there are six girls in one cabin that's no bigger than mine, and they all sleep in hammocks. She doesn't like it, but I wouldn't mind sleeping in a hammock. I've never done so."

"You are not sleeping in a hammock!"

She gave him an odd look. "Only a short time ago I was sleeping outside on the ground."

"Yes, but I promise you, you never will again."

"You can't know that."

"I can. I will ensure it."

It was an odd thing to say when he was just delivering her to her grandmother's. How could he possibly ensure such a thing? But he had an implacable, angry look around his mouth, so she decided not to pursue it.

She returned to the subject of Mrs. Ferris. "Don't you think it's strange that Mrs. Ferris doesn't have her maid in her room? Wouldn't you rather share a room with your maid than a stranger? What if I was a bad person? Or snored?"

"Yes, but she wouldn't want to pay the same for her maid as for herself. The price of the cabin ensured you'd at least be of the moneyed class, which is much more important to women of that ilk."

She laughed. "Poor Mrs. Ferris. She's been cheated, hasn't she?"

He gave her a quizzical look. "Why?"

"Someone from the moneyed class?" She laughed again. "I haven't a bean to my name. Though I do have a royal cat, so that will have to do. Mrs. Ferris isn't fond of cats, but she's been all right about me keeping Cleo in the cabin."

"And does Cleo—excellent name, by the way—does she mind having Mrs. Ferris in the cabin? She struck me as a cat of very decided opinions."

"Who, Mrs. Ferris or Cleo?" Ayisha joked. "You're right, she is a kitten of strong feelings. You should have seen the fuss she made about being bathed." She told him all about it.

"And where is Miss Cleo now?" he asked. They reached the dining room and he opened the door for her.

"In her basket on my bed," she said as she passed through. "Glowering through the bars and yowling every now and then to make her disapproval known. But she'll get used to it. She's young. You can get used to anything when you're young."

R afe didn't say much at dinner. He was watching Ayisha enchant Captain Gallagher and two young officers, Lieutenants Green and Dickinson. There were seven others at the captain's table: Mrs. Ferris and her two friends, Mrs. Wiggs and Mrs. Grenville; a young vicar, Reverend Payne, and his wife— newlyweds who'd visited Jerusalem on their honeymoon.

Her enchanting the two officers wasn't a surprise; apart from being beautiful, she was the only unmarried female under fifty at the table.

But the captain was in his fifties, too, a happily married man and a proud grandfather. Rafe had discovered all this since he sat down. Ayisha had asked the captain all about his family and soon elicited the information that after siring seven sons himself, his pride and joy was his third grandchild, the first girl to be born to his family in three generations, his little *principessa*.

Rafe sipped his wine, sat back, and watched Ayisha, fascinated. It must have been years since she'd sat at an English-style dinner table, but nobody would have guessed. She ate with unself-conscious good manners and seemed totally relaxed. And her conversation was fresh, not practiced or limited to banal mundanities.

"What surprised you most about Jerusalem when you got there?" she asked Reverend Payne and his bride. They surprised themselves with their answers, and a conversation about travel and expectations and nice and nasty surprises developed in which everyone could join.

She had a knack for getting on with people. How much of that had been developed in the streets? Was it a form of defense? Disarm people so they would not attack you. Or offer you odd jobs.

Mrs. Ferris was less impressed, he noticed. Having comported herself as "most honored guest," she grew increasingly lemon-lipped as the conversation flourished, yet not around her. Finally irritation got the better of her. She leaned forward and said in a cool voice that cut across the conversation, "Miss Cleeve, my friends and I have been wondering where you got that extraordinary dress? The color is unexceptional enough, but the cut, and that border, with crocodiles—it's . . . extraordinary!"

Ayisha looked up, and from the look in her eye, she was ready to do battle, captain's table or not. "I like this dress," she declared.

Rafe decided it was time he contributed to the conversation. "So do I, it's unusual and elegant. And Mrs. Ferris, I think the color *is* exceptional. To find a fabric that matches Miss Cleeve's eyes so beautifully—that's the extraordinary thing, don't you think?"

At that, everyone naturally looked at Ayisha's eyes. The two soldiers joined in, enthusiastically agreeing that Miss Cleeve's eyes were indeed beautiful.

Mrs. Ferris got more lemon-lipped.

Miss Cleeve took a sip of wine and from over the top of her glass the beautiful eyes gave Rafe such a look of mischief that he was hard put to keep a straight face.

"Nonsense," Mrs. Ferris's friend joined the fray. "The fabric is a perfectly ordinary *eau de Nil* color."

"*Eau de Nil*," Ayisha repeated, clearly delighted. "Water of the Nile—my eyes are *eau de Nil*. Thank you, Mrs. Grenville. What a lovely compliment."

Mrs. Grenville gave a half-genuine smile, then glanced at her friend guiltily.

Rafe spoke again. "Miss Cleeve's luggage was lost in an accident, so she was obliged to purchase everything locally and at short notice. I think she's done remarkably well, don't you? I shouldn't wonder if clever accents like that border start a new fashion in London." He sat back, knowing his own fashionable appearance gave such an opinion credibility.

"She lost her maid in the same accident, presumably," Mrs. Ferris said tartly.

"No, of course not," Ayisha told her. "My maid took up another position with the wife of a wealthy merchant." Her eyes dared Rafe to correct the lie.

As if he would. Rafe said in a cool drawl, "The girl did quite well for herself, but of course it was on the eve of our departure, and she quite left Miss Cleeve in the lurch." He swirled his wine around in the glass and added, as an afterthought, "I understand you ladies each have personal maids traveling with you . . ." He smiled gently at Mrs. Ferris's friends, each of whom immediately offered poor Miss Cleeve the use of their maid whenever she should need her.

Mrs. Ferris had no option but to join in or appear ungenerous. "My maid, Woods, shall assist you in her spare time," she said, through lips that had almost disappeared.

After dinner Ayisha and Rafe walked on the upper deck. It was dark, the breeze was warm and balmy, and they strolled in silence. The only sound, apart from the constant splash of waves, was the creak of timber, the snap of the sails in the breeze, and the rattle of ropes.

Ayisha held her arms out wide, leaned into the breeze, and inhaled extravagantly. "This air is so fresh. I don't think I've ever smelled anything so deliciously clean."

Rafe smiled but said nothing. With her hands holding on to the ends of the shawl, it looked like she had wings and was braced to fly out over the sea. The wind plastered the fabric of her dress to her body, and the faint light of the crescent moon caressed each hollow and curve.

Lithe, slender, unfettered femininity.

His mouth dried.

Small, but definite breasts, nipples upthrust in the cool air. Strapped down for so many years, now set free.

He stepped away and looked into the darkness, at the dark, silky waves, at the stars and slender, crescent moon.

For the duration of this trip she was—she had to be—like that sliver of moon, out of his reach. He was honor-bound not to touch her. Lady Cleeve had entrusted her granddaughter's safety and welfare to him. Compromising her on the journey home was not part of their agreement.

Nor was it his desire; though she was all of his desire.

Causing speculation about them traveling together would only cause her harm.

He wanted to win her for himself, wanted her to choose him freely, for himself alone, not be forced to wed him for the sake of propriety.

She knew nothing of his background; the earldom meant nothing to her. Perhaps she thought him rich. Once she got to England she would see that while he was comfortably off, there were many men much richer.

He didn't think she'd care; at least he hoped she wouldn't. But she ought to have the choice.

"I shouldn't have provoked Mrs. Ferris," he said. "She's the sort who would spread malicious gossip."

She shrugged. "You can't stop women like that talking. And if they don't know anything, they'll just make it up. Besides, she started it—or rather the captain did. She as good as told me I was too shabby and obscure to merit an invitation to the captain's table on the first night, and so her nose was out of joint from the start."

She yawned. "Don't let's ruin this beautiful night talking about her. Tell me about the first time you went on a ship—a proper ship, not on a river or a lake—like this one, going to sea, to another country."

"That would be when we shipped off to Portugal."

"We?" she asked, moving closer.

"All of us: Gabe, Harry, Luke, Michael, and me. My friends," he explained. "My closest friends. The finest friends a man could have."

"Will I meet them in England?" The wind blew the skirt of her dress against his leg. It wrapped around his thigh, softly.

"You'll meet Harry and Luke. Not Gabe. Gabe married the Princess of Zindaria, so he lives there." He would take her to Zindaria one day, he thought. And then caught himself up on the notion. His insides lurched as he realized where his thoughts, his desires, were taking him.

He'd come to Egypt to escape a bride, not to catch one. He looked at her and swallowed.

There was a small pause. "And Michael?" she prompted.

"Michael was killed. It happens in war. Good men dying unnecessarily . . ."

She slipped a hand through his arm and pressed against him lightly, not in any flirtatious sense, he was certain, just in a comforting way. Still, his body leapt to attention.

"How old were you, then? On that ship to Portugal?"

"Eighteen."

She sighed. "Just a boy."

He said ruefully, "We didn't think so at the time. We thought we were men, heading for a glorious adventure."

It wasn't completely true. He'd had a coil of anxiety down deep in his gut that he did his best to keep hidden, wondering if he had "the right stuff," whether he'd turn out to be brave or a coward. He hoped he would be brave, but until you'd faced fire, they'd all agreed, you couldn't be sure what you were made of.

God, how young he'd been then. As if anything was ever that simple. A drift of cigar smoke and a deep murmur of voices told him they had company on deck. He withdrew his arm and stepped away. She gave him an odd look.

"I think it's best if we didn't spend very much time together on this voyage," he found himself saying.

"Why?"

"Because you are unchaperoned and I don't want people to gossip."

She was silent a moment. "What would it matter if they did gossip?"

He recalled her view of gossips: that they would anyway.

He cleared his throat, searching for the right words to explain. "In England, if a man—a gentleman, that is, an unmarried gentleman—is said to have compromised a young woman, he is considered to be under an obligation to marry her."

"What if she didn't want to marry him?" she said after a moment.

"She would come under the same pressure."

"And if they didn't marry?"

"She would lose her reputation as a virtuous woman, and he would lose his as a man of honor."

"That's not very fair, is it?"

"No."

"But I suppose it is the rule in England."

"Yes." And then, because the answer seemed thin, he added, "It is."

There was another short silence, broken only by the sounds of the sea and the sails. "Then it is no different than Egypt. I thought it would be different. Very well," she said briskly. "We shall see as little as possible of each other. Occasional polite chats in passing, but only if someone else is present—that's the sort of thing you mean, isn't it? Should it be with a man present or a woman?"

"A woman is best," Rafe said. She was taking it very well. It was a little disconcerting how well she'd taken it, in fact. Almost . . . enthusiastically. "Will you be all right?"

"Of course," she said, sounding surprised that he could ask such a thing. "I'll still have everything I need."

"You won't be lonely?"

"Of course not. There are plenty of interesting people on this ship to talk to. And I have Cleo, who will always be my friend. Don't worry, I will obey the rule. It would be terrible indeed if we were forced to marry."

The murmur of masculine voices grew louder and she glanced behind her. "Those soldiers are getting closer, so I'd better go. We wouldn't want them to see us together, alone up here in the dark together, would we? They might oblige us to marry, and that would be unthinkable. Good night." And she vanished.

Rafe blinked. That had been very abrupt. Almost as if she was angry.

He thought about it, going over the explanation he'd given her. There was nothing to offend her in what he'd said, he decided. It had been clear and reasonable, and he'd made it obvious he was only protecting her from the unwanted consequences of a little thoughtless friendliness. She'd grown up in a different culture, a culture where men and women didn't mix socially. She needed to be given a hint.

In any case, he'd seen her temper in action; it was hot and direct and sometimes physical. He bore the scars to prove it, he thought, touching the place on his neck where her scratches had long since faded.

No, if Ayisha was displeased, she made it clear. She was a bit like her cat in that way.

There must be some other reason why he felt uneasy about the way she'd walked off so abruptly.

He was tempted to join the young officers, blow a cloud with them, and enjoy some purely masculine company for a change. But he wasn't in the mood, he decided. Perhaps tomorrow.

*F*or the next three days he hardly saw Ayisha at all. The likelihood of that on such a small ship—it was almost as if she were avoiding him. She certainly took rules seriously. He supposed you would, given the rules she'd grown up with. The pasha's rules were serious indeed.

As were those of England, he reflected. Perhaps they didn't cut people's hands off, but they did hang them, or transport them to the other side of the world. She'd just confused the difference between the rules of polite society and the laws of the land, that's all. And he'd explain that to her, if she ever let him get close enough.

She seemed to have glued herself to the young vicar and his wife. And when she wasn't with them, she was with the three witches. Who were actually being quite friendly to her, he admitted when he saw one of them sitting with her on deck, teaching her to knit.

Even the sailors had taken to her. Normally they wouldn't have anything to do with passengers, but the kitten broke down barriers.

Ayisha took Cleo on deck each morning and afternoon to give the kitten some fresh air, and soon sailors and passengers found reasons to be in the vicinity as the tiny creature explored and played.

First she'd simply sniffed her way around, staying close to Ayisha, hiding under her skirts when anyone approached . . . only to leap out and attack their shoes and ankles. But slowly, as Cleo became accustomed to the place, she got bolder.

One day she tried to climb the mast and got stuck six feet up it, and wailed in fury to be rescued. Another time she had a fight almost to the death with the hanging end of a coil of rope.

At first it was funny, but as the kitten grew bolder and more adventurous, Ayisha became anxious. The kitten would disappear down any hole she found, wriggle into any dark corner, leap up onto any looming surface.

The day Ayisha had turned to see Cleo, her head sticking out through one of the drainage holes in the gunwales, peering down into the sea, was the day she stopped the deck excursions forever. "She's got no sense," she explained the next day when people asked her where the kitten was. "I wouldn't put it past her not to try to pounce on a wave or a passing dolphin."

The next day one of the sailors presented her with a kitten-sized rope harness attached to a long thin lead. "That'll stop 'er falling overboard, miss," the sailor said.

For the rest of the day the entertainment was in watching Cleo fight her harness. She fought it, rolling and growling and getting mightily tangled. She tried to run away from it and turned around, spitting furiously when it followed. She resisted it, planting paws and bottom firmly on the deck and refusing to budge when Ayisha tried to lead her. "It's like taking a loaf of bread for a walk." Ayisha laughed.

So she talked to everyone, and everyone talked to her. Except Rafe. Each time she'd seen him coming, she'd picked up the kitten and hurried away.

When the kitten first appeared with the harness, he'd seized the excuse to talk to her for the first time in days—it was unexceptional, being under the eyes of a dozen impartial witnesses—and yet she'd scooped up the kitten and disappeared back to her cabin.

She had got the wrong end of the blasted stick, as he'd

thought; it wasn't that they weren't allowed to talk at all, just be . . . discreet. Dammit, he missed her.

But she was as slippery as an eel, using all the other passengers to keep him at bay.

The two young officers, Green and Dickinson, gallantly squired her around the deck several times a day, and even escorted her and Mrs. Ferris to meals. Several times Rafe had knocked on the door of her cabin, only to be told by Woods that Lieutenants Green and Dickinson had already called for the ladies.

Tonight it had happened for the third night in a row.

No wonder Mrs. Ferris was being nice to her, Rafe thought sourly. It must be years since she'd had a handsome young officer escorting her to dinner—if ever. He decided not to go to dinner; he was feeling a little off-color anyway, as if something he'd eaten had disagreed with him.

R afe slept in late next morning, and when Higgins came with hot water for his ablutions, he stared at Rafe with a concerned expression. "Sir, I don't think you should get up. You look terrible, and you're still sick."

"Nonsense, Higgins, it's just a touch of dysentery. Army can't stop for a bit of dysentery." Rafe struggled out of bed and dashed cold water over his face. He rinsed his mouth out and spat. He'd thrown up a couple of times in the night, but he was determined not to give in to whatever it was. As soon as it had passed through his system he would be all right.

"You're not in the army any longer, sir," Higgins argued. "And you'd be better off resting in bed for a day or two. These tropical fevers, sir, you can't be too careful."

"Nonsense. Just shave me, will you? Blasted hand's shaking for some reason."

He sat on the bunk and, for once, let Higgins shave him. His head felt thick and achy. He did feel a bit feverish and unwell, he admitted to himself, but lying around in a stuffy little cabin would not do him any good. Better to go up on deck and get a bit of fresh air into him.

Besides, he was damned if he was going to let her avoid him another day. He'd drag her off by main force if he had to and explain that she'd got the rule wrong. She was allowed to talk to him—dammit, he needed her to talk to him.

With Higgins's help he got dressed and staggered to the door.

"You shouldn't be up, sir," Higgins said.

"Nonsense, ship's rolling, that's all." He started up the corridor and espied the object of his desire standing in the companionway, about to ascend the stairs. "Ayisha!" he called.

She stopped and whirled around.

"Need to speak to you," he told her, hurrying toward her, but the rolling ship kept tipping him off balance and he kept having to grab the walls.

She came running toward him. "What is it? What's the matter?" She caught him around the waist and put her shoulder under his.

"He's ill, miss," Higgins told her, "He was ill in the night, and I told him he shouldn't get up, but would he listen?"

She pressed a hand to his forehead. Rafe closed his eyes as he felt it. Lovely cool, soft hand. Cool.

"He's burning up," she said.

"Aaarrggh!" a scream came from behind her.

Rafe clapped his hands over his ears. "Shockin' noise," he said, glaring at her. "Mrs. . . ." He couldn't remember the name. Woman with no lips. "Should be shot, making noise like tha . . ." And he started sliding down the wall.

"He's got the plague!" the woman screeched. "He's brought it on board with him! Oh my God, we'll all die if we don't get rid of him!" And she ran up the corridor screaming, "Plague! Plague! Plague!"

Twelve

Ayisha struggled to get Rafe standing again. Higgins helped. "What's she talking about, miss? It can't be plague, surely?"

"Of course it can. In Egypt, plague is always with us." She steered Rafe toward his cabin. "Come on, help me—walk," she urged him. He staggered a few steps, mumbling. He was burning up and shivering at the same time.

Higgins stared at her. "You mean plague? *The* plague. The bubonic plague?"

"Yes, it's nearly always around, but it's worst in summer. Help me to get him through the door. You go first, and I'll try to hold him up."

"But the plague's a killer, miss. A terrible killer."

"Oh, I know, Higgins," she said soberly. "My mother and father both died of it. Let us hope and pray that this is some other fever."

Rafe straightened and shoved her away. He swayed in the doorway, using the doorjamb to keep himself upright. "Plague?" he slurred, peering woozily at her. "I got th' plague?"

"We don't know for certain," she told him soothingly. A

positive attitude helped, she'd heard an Italian doctor say when Mama was dying. But Papa was already dead, and Mama had no one to live for. Only Ayisha. Without Papa, Mama had given up.

Ayisha looked at Rafe, shivering, his skin tight and hot and shiny. He was not going to give up. She wouldn't allow it!

She tried to catch his arm, but he recoiled from her. "Go 'way," he ordered. "Don't come near me. Not get sick, not you. Not you." He held out his hand to ward her off. "You, too, Higgins, out."

"Now, see here, sir—"

"Out!" Rafe snarled. Years of army service did the trick. Higgins stepped out of the cabin. Rafe, looking exhausted by the effort of asserting his will, started to close the door, clinging to it for support as much as closing it.

"Look aft'r her, Higg'ns," he ordered. "Your life on it."

"I will, sir," Higgins said, almost weeping.

"What do you think you are doing?" Ayisha demanded. "You're not going in there to die, you stupid man. I won't allow it."

He smiled. "Bossy," he said. "Li'l bossy cat." Then he turned, grabbed a bowl, and threw up. "Bowls everywhere," he mumbled. "Good man, Higg'ns."

"It's plague, I tell you!" a voice shrilled from the corridor. "He must be got rid of!"

Ayisha whirled and saw Mrs. Ferris urging the captain, several ship's officers ahead of her. A gaggle of frightened-looking passengers peered from a distance.

"It's plague! You must get him off the boat, Captain," Mrs. Ferris reiterated.

"What do you think you're doing?" Ayisha demanded.

"Is it plague, miss?" the captain asked, his face grim.

"It's fever, but I'm not certain it's plague."

The captain shook his head gravely. "I can't afford to take the risk. I'm sorry, miss."

"What do you mean, sorry? What are you going to do?"

"He'll have to be set ashore, miss. Otherwise it'll spread—"

"And we'll all be dead!" shrieked Mrs. Ferris from the other end of the corridor. The other passengers murmured worriedly.

"He's not going anywhere," Ayisha snapped. "He's staying here. I'll look after him."

The captain shook his head. "I can't allow that, I'm sorry. I have the welfare of all my passengers to consider. He'll be put in a boat and towed to the nearest shore."

"To die, or be pushed out to sea by others frightened of infection, I suppose," Ayisha said.

"No, you can go with him if you like and arrange for locals to take care of him."

"How do you know there are any locals willing—or able?" she argued. She would *not* let them take him. Who knew what awaited them onshore? There could be wreckers, or pirates, or even hostile natives.

The captain snapped his fingers and his men wound rags around their mouths and noses. They donned gloves and moved purposefully toward the cabin.

"Stop them, Higgins!" Ayisha ordered.

Higgins gave her a helpless look. "There's six of them, miss, and the captain as well."

"*He* wouldn't let those odds stop him!" She was almost weeping with rage.

"Give 't up, sweeth'rt," Rafe mumbled. "Cap'n's right. Bes' thing t' do. Lose one man, save th' rest." He swayed toward the captain.

"Stop that, you fool," she yelled and shoved him hard backward. He reeled and staggered back inside the cabin. Before anyone could say a word she'd followed him in, slammed the door, and shot the bolt.

"Miss Cleeve, open up. This doesn't make sense," the captain yelled, pounding on the door.

"I will lock myself in here with him and look after him. I know what to do. He is *not* going to die," she yelled back.

"My men can kick down the door in seconds," the captain warned.

Ayisha glanced desperately around, and her gaze lighted on a box containing the dueling pistols. She flipped open the box and took out the pistols. "I have a pair of loaded dueling pistols in here," she called through the door. She had no idea if they were loaded or not. "The first man who steps through the door dies a certain death. The first two, actually."

"She's bluffing," she heard the captain say.

"She's not, sir," Higgins said. "I know those pistols and they're loaded, all right. Major Ramsey always keeps them primed and loaded."

"Perhaps, but that sweet child wouldn't hurt a fly," the captain scoffed.

"She would and all, sir. Behind those pretty ways, she's a born fighter," Higgins assured him. "She's lived a dangerous life, Miss Ayisha. Carries a knife and knows how to use those guns." He paused. Ayisha listened. She'd never touched a gun in her life.

Obviously the captain wasn't convinced, because Higgins went on, "She's done for several men that I know of—right villains they were, of course, and deserving of it—but if she's set on staying in there with Mr. Ramsey, Captain, I reckon you've got no option."

Thank you, Higgins, Ayisha said silently, and forgave him his feet of clay. Would the captain believe it? she wondered.

There was a pause and she pressed her ear up against the door, wondering what they were saying.

"I promise you the infection will not spread outside this cabin," she called out. "Higgins will bring me whatever I need and leave it at the door. I will take care of everything."

"It's madness, child," the captain said. "You're saying that you'll stay in there until you are both well—or dead!"

"It's not madness," she assured him. "If it's not plague, there's no reason to put anyone ashore. But if it is plague, I can help. Both my parents died of it, but I didn't, Captain—*I didn't*. There must be a reason for that, and I believe this is it. I've lived in Cairo all my life and I've *never* fallen ill."

She heard another lot of low murmuring.

"I promise you," she reiterated, "if you break into this cabin, the first two men in here will die."

"Very well, have it your own way," the captain said heavily. "You're either the stupidest young woman I have ever met . . . or the bravest."

There was a pause, then she heard their footsteps receding down the corridor. Dimly she heard Mrs. Ferris complaining and some other passengers joining in. The sound receded.

With shaking hands Ayisha put the pistols down. They were loaded?

She turned to find Rafe watching her. He was shivering desperately, but his skin looked tight and hot. "Wha' th' devil d'y' think you're doing?" he grated in a hoarse whisper. "Get out of here." His blue eyes blazed with fever and with rage.

"Don't be silly, you need looking after," she told him.

"I order you to leave!"

"Save your breath, I'm not a soldier, and I don't obey orders," she told him. "Higgins, are you still there?" she called through the door.

"Yes, miss."

"Bring me sheets, towels, extra blankets, hot water, and hot ginger tea, lemons or limes, honey. The most important thing is to see if anyone on board has any willow bark or Peruvian bark. Or anything that would be useful for a fever—if they will give it to us, that is."

"Peruvian bark will stop it?"

"I don't know, but it can't hurt. Nobody knows what cures plague or causes it. Some say it's in the air, some say it's a judgment by God, others say you get it from touching someone or eating certain foods. Everyone just has to guess, that's the trouble. But I know Peruvian bark and willow bark are good for fever, so . . ."

"There's a box of medical supplies—it's the black one in the bottom of the trunk. It's got Peruvian bark and willow bark. Can't remember what else. I got it freshly stocked by the apothecary before we left London. As for the rest, I'll do my best, miss."

"Good." She heard his footsteps retreating and turned back to Rafe. "Now we'll have to get you up on that bed. You can't stay on the floor." She tugged at his arm, but he made no attempt to move. "You'll have to help me, Rafe—I can't lift you by myself."

"Want . . . you . . . out," he managed.

"No. Now I can do this with your help or without it, but it will be much harder for me if you don't help."

He pointed to the door, his hand shaking with fever. "Go! Geddout."

Stubborn man. "I'm going to do this anyway and nothing you can say will make me leave," she told him. "So if you could just help me to get you onto that bed . . ."

He struggled to his feet, fending her off and using the furniture to drag himself briefly upright before collapsing on the unmade bed. He tried to drag the covers up over himself.

"Not yet you don't." She grabbed the covers. "First we have to get those clothes off you."

He tried to push her away, but the struggle to get to the bed had exhausted him. He'd stopped shivering. She felt his forehead. His skin was hot and dry and he was burning up.

She dragged his boots off, then his stockings. She unbuttoned and unlaced everything she could, then turned him on first one side, then the other, to drag his coat and waistcoat off. She decided to leave the shirt on, for the moment. She could easily lift it to check his armpits.

If it was plague, there would be swellings under his armpits or in his groin. She closed her eyes and prayed, then lifted the shirt and his arm.

"Wha' you doin'?"

"Examining your armpit." She felt it gently. No sign of a swelling there. Yet. Thank God.

Now for the groin.

She unfastened the front fall of his breeches and started to drag them down his legs, along with the cotton drawers he wore underneath. "Stop. What'ch doing?" he muttered.

"I have to examine your groin," she told him. "See if there is any swelling there."

He choked with what seemed like a laugh. "Not now. Maybe t'morr'w."

She shrugged and dragged the breeches and drawers down his long, hard legs. He pulled the sheet over himself.

"This is no time for false modesty," she told him. "I have to look."

He gave her a baleful, fever-ridden, stubborn look and held the sheet in position.

"I've seen the male shape before," she assured him. She'd seen Ali naked several times when he was a little boy. "And I need to check your groin!"

She yanked the sheet off and froze. The resemblance between what she beheld now and what she'd seen while bathing Ali was . . . vague at the very least.

This was a . . . a man. She felt a bit breathless.

A very sick man; she castigated herself for being distracted. She touched him gingerly, and slid her hand into the crease where his inner leg joined his body, avoiding his male parts as best she could, and felt carefully.

"Nothing," she breathed.

"Wha'?"

"No swellings," she assured him.

He opened one eye. "Course not. Too sick," he mumbled, gave a convulsive jerk, and started shivering again. She quickly felt to check the other side, and again, thank God, there was no swelling.

"I'll check again in an hour," she told him.

"Cold," he said, shuddering violently. She pulled the covers up and tucked him in. Still he shivered. She fetched more clothes and tucked them around him. He huddled into them, his eyes closed.

She found the small medicine chest and examined its contents. There were at least a dozen stoppered jars containing various substances, but although they were all clearly labeled, she wasn't sure what most of them would be used for. Two she did know and gave thanks for: Peruvian bark and willow bark.

A quiet knock at the door startled her. She jumped up and snatched the pistols. "Who's there?"

"Higgins. No one else, I promise, miss."

She wasn't sure whether to believe him. If the captain held a gun on him . . . "Put everything down outside the door, then move back," she ordered.

She waited until she heard his footsteps retreating, then cautiously opened the door, just a crack. She peered out but could see no one, so she poked her head around the door, the pistol primed and ready, just in case—oh God, she hoped she wouldn't have to shoot. But there was nobody there, just Higgins, waiting ten feet away.

"Thank you, Higgins," she called. "I've examined him and there are no swellings. That means there's no sign of plague. Tell the captain." It might still be plague—and she wouldn't lie to them if it was—but it would help if the captain and passengers were reassured.

She quickly moved everything into the cabin. Bolting it securely, she checked to see what he'd brought. Extra towels, blankets, bowls, a large pot of hot ginger tea—thank goodness. And an invalid cup with a spout—praise be. With fever, he should drink plenty of fluids, and this would make it so much easier.

She poured some of the tea into the cup and sprinkled Peruvian bark powder into it. She wasn't sure which of the barks would be most efficacious, but both were reputed to be good for fever, so she would alternate.

She waited five minutes, stirring to let the goodness of the bark steep, then carefully lifted Rafe's head and set the spout to his lips.

"You must drink this," she told him soothingly when he groaned and moved his head fretfully at the taste. "It's ginger tea with honey and Peruvian bark. It will help bring your fever down." He seemed to understand and obediently drank, swallowing each mouthful as if it were painful.

He managed half a cup, then lay back, exhausted.

She tucked the covers around him and returned to the examination of the supplies Higgins had brought. There was a medical manual—the captain's, no doubt.

She searched for advice. Sprinkle the sickroom with vinegar, she read, so she sprinkled vinegar everywhere.

Unlike many physicians, this one recommended fresh air. Ayisha agreed; she already had the two portholes open. The air was warm, salty fresh, and clean; it had to be good.

The physician recommended bleeding in the early stages of certain fevers, but only under certain conditions. She grimaced. She hated bleeding—the doctor had bled Papa copiously, and she had bad memories of it.

But if she had to, if it would save him, she would . . . Thankfully these were not the stated conditions. Yet.

She read that in some cases of plague a roasted onion soaked in olive oil had been used to soften the buboes—that was the medical term for the swellings in the groin, neck, and armpits—which were then lanced to release the putridity. The book didn't say if it worked, just that it had been done by others. Did they live or not? Still, if it was in the book the physician must have thought it was worth saying . . .

She swallowed. Very well then, if buboes formed, she would do that. Rafe's razor would be sharp enough to lance anything.

They hadn't tried that with Mama and Papa—perhaps if they had . . .

A positive attitude, she reminded herself. There were no buboes yet. In the meantime she would try to bring his fever down.

He stopped shivering after the first hour and threw all his bedclothes off, tossing and turning weakly. "Hot . . . hot . . ." he gasped. "Water . . ."

Gently she sponged his body with water and vinegar, smoothing the cool, astringent dampness over the broad planes of his chest and stomach and down his arms and legs.

She tried not to stare at his body, but she could not help herself. His chest was broad and firm, rising and falling now in jerky, uneven breaths. She stroked his damp skin, willing his strength to return. Thick bands of muscles, relaxed now in his unconscious state, twitched under her palm as she smoothed the sponge over him.

He was a rich man, and yet there was not an ounce of fat on him. A man of bone and muscle. Was that good or not? she wondered. She had some idea that a fatter man might fight a wasting fever better.

She lifted his arms and bathed him with vinegar and water, feeling again for swellings, but there were none.

She sponged down his body, following the wedge of hair that narrowed to his belly button, bisected his stomach, and merged with the thick tangle at his groin. His male parts were soft, and she drizzled cool water over them, and felt cautiously on either side for buboes. Nothing.

She glanced at his face and saw his eyes were open, watching her. She felt a leap of hope.

"Nothing there, no swellings," she told him. "There's nothing to worry about. You'll get well soon. Just sleep."

He made no sound, no sign that he understood, and she realized he was staring at her with blank, fever-ridden, unseeing eyes.

She sponged down his long, hard-muscled legs, lightly covered with hair. He moved them restlessly under her hands, and started tossing his head back and forth. His big fists clenched and unclenched.

She fed him some willow bark tea and he quietened again.

If she'd never met this man before, she'd still know he was a warrior, she thought as she sponged the big, hot, restless body. He was covered with nicks and scars.

He'd had several nasty, life-threatening wounds. A long silvery gash with puckered edges stretched from just under his arm to right across his ribs; a deep slash from a sword, she guessed. A miracle he'd survived that one.

He had a small, round hole in his shoulder and a matching one on his back: a bullet that had, seemingly, passed right through him. Another miracle.

There were scars on his jaw and one high up near his temple, she discovered when she was smoothing back his damp hair. Several small scars were recent: Gadi's uncle and friends, she thought guiltily.

She finished sponging him and stood back. So many scars should look ugly; instead he looked beautiful.

But right now he was weaker than her kitten.

Her eyes filled with tears. She dashed them away. Think positive, she told herself fiercely. Think *positive*!

He was staring at her again, his blue, blue eyes burning through her.

She knelt down beside the bed and smoothed his hair back, murmuring soft words of comfort.

Through the day she bathed him repeatedly, smoothing positive thoughts and strength into him with every touch. She fed him willow bark tea and Peruvian tea and barley water containing something called spirit of nitre, which the book had mentioned and was in the medical box.

He tossed and turned and muttered and mumbled, and all the time his fever rose and rose. She'd sponge him with vinegar and water, or cover him with cool, wet cloths, and they seemed to give him comfort, but then suddenly he'd be shivering, his body racked with spasms and she would reach for the covers again and tuck him in.

And all the time she prayed.

Several times in the day Higgins returned, asking after the patient, bringing with him hot water and checking to see if there was anything Ayisha needed.

He brought her meals, which she didn't want, but he stood outside, insisting she ate to keep up her strength—and he was right, she knew, so she ate. Tasting nothing.

In the late afternoon Higgins brought all Ayisha's belongings. Mrs. Ferris was worried about infection, he told her, and had refused to have them—or her kitten—in the cabin any longer.

The Reverend and Mrs. Payne were looking after the kitten. And praying for Mr. Ramsey. And for Ayisha.

Night fell, but the fever did not subside. Instead he felt hotter, despite everything she could think of to do.

Through the porthole she could see the curve of the moon hanging low in the sky. It shone on Cairo, too, she reminded herself. How were they getting on there? She missed Laila, missed her wisdom and experience. Laila would know if Ayisha was doing the right things or not.

Ayisha didn't. All day she'd poured medicine into him, but he seemed only to be getting worse. She felt so helpless, so frightened. What if she couldn't keep him alive?

How would she bear it if he died? She'd only just found him . . .

He shivered desperately. "Cold . . . cold . . ." he muttered.

She had every possible covering over him. The portholes were open, but the air outside was warm and balmy. She couldn't think of a single thing she could do to make him warmer. Except one.

She stripped down to her chemise and climbed into bed, slipping under the covers until she was touching him. Lord, but he was hot, his body was like a furnace, yet he shivered and muttered, "Cold, cold."

She spooned her body around his, holding him protectively, willing her health, her strength into him. She placed her palm against his naked chest, over his heart. She needed it there to feel any change in the night.

She lay curled against him, feeling the thud-thud-thud of his heartbeat, willing it to stay steady and strong. She would *not* let him die, she would not. She repeated it over and over in her mind. She wasn't sure if she was praying or not.

Exhausted, frightened, woken by any movement or change in him, she drifted in and out of sleep.

The second day was worse. He was hotter, weaker, more distressed, more restless. Three times a day she fed him boiled water with willow bark, and Peruvian bark three times a day in between times. At other times she gave him barley water with honey and sponged him or packed him with blankets, depending on whether he was complaining of cold or heat.

A dozen times a day she felt for buboes and each time she breathed a sigh of relief. Whatever it was, at least it wasn't plague. Yet.

All day she listened to him talking.

It went almost nonstop: shouting, or a constant mumbling delirium. It only stopped for short periods when he was asleep. Or unconscious.

But she came to dread those silent periods. They terrified her.

At least when he was talking he was alive, even if he didn't make sense.

In the silences she hovered over him, watching each breath, ready to pounce on him if he should die. She had no idea what she would do if he did—force him to live, somehow—she wasn't sure how.

"You'd better be only sleeping," she'd tell him in the silences. "Dying is not an option."

Or, "You promised my grandmother you'd take me to her; you said you *never* break a promise, dammit, so don't break this one!"

But most of the time she was quietly saying, "Breathe . . . Breathe . . . Breathe." And breathing each breath with him, for him.

Sometimes when he talked she learned things about him. Many didn't make sense. Some did.

He relived parts of his life. She could tell when he thought he was back in the war, she could hear him muttering disjointed orders, interspersed with thoughts, interrupted with shouted warnings. Sometimes his arms flailed around, or his fists bunched, as if he were fighting.

She curled up beside him on the bed, smoothing his forehead and making soothing, calming sounds. And again, she slept the night spooned around him, her palm pressed over his heart.

The third day was worse still.

As she changed the sheets, she stared at his naked body spread-eagled on the bed. Muscles she'd caressed on the first day now looked somehow . . . stringier. Had they shrunk? She couldn't tell, but she thought they had.

Could a big, tough body become wasted like that? In just two days? Or was she imagining it?

She felt for buboes; still nothing.

He lay quiet, still, hot, his breath rasping irregularly in and out like a rusty bellows.

He said not a word. Now she missed the demented ramblings that had so distressed her before.

She talked to him, ordering him to live, assuring him he was getting better, berating him for not fighting it harder.

"You will not die, Rafe, do you hear me? I forbid it!

"You will get well." Angrily dashing an unwary tear from her cheeks. "A positive attitude!"

She sent her meals back untouched, ignoring Higgins's reproaches. She couldn't eat with him lying so still and wasted. She would be sick.

She fed him medicinal tea, with barley water for strength, and he swallowed it, but barely. His lassitude frightened her.

As she fed him his last dose of willow bark for the night and slipped in beside him, she prayed fiercely for his life to be spared. She lay holding him against her, her hand pressed against his heart, feeling each breath rasp in and out, in and out. She was too frightened to sleep.

But in the wee small hours of the night his heartbeat and the rhythm of his breathing lulled her briefly to sleep against her will.

And in the faint light of dawn, she woke up cold.

She sat up with a jerk and a shout, "Noooo."

And beside her, he stirred.

She blinked. Her chemise was wet.

She was cold because her chemise was wet and the breeze from the porthole was chilling her.

Her chemise was wet because he was wet. He was sweating. She felt his forehead. It was cooling under her fingers.

Oh God, he was sleeping normally, his breathing deep and even. She pressed her palm to his heart and felt the strong and steady beat.

The fever had broken. Tears ran down her cheeks unchecked. He was going to live. His fever had broken.

Thirteen

❧

*H*e slept for most of the day, and in the late afternoon she glanced up to find him watching her. His blue eyes were as clear as the sky now, no sign of fever. And ever so slightly . . . annoyed?

"What are you doing here?" he asked.

"It's all right, you've been sick." She hurried over to the bed and felt his forehead. Blissfully cool and normal.

He looked up at her and caught her hand in his, frowning. "What are you doing?"

"Checking for fever. But there's none. You're going to be well again."

He tried to sit up and fell back against the pillows. "Good God, I'm weak as a kitten."

"Yes, you'll need to rest for some time yet and regain your strength. You've been very sick. I . . . I thought you were going to die," she said mistily.

"Nonsense, I'm as tough as old boots," he said and tried to sit up again, succeeding this time, though at a visible cost.

"No, you're as stubborn as old boots," she corrected him. "Now stay put, please. I need to wash you."

"Wash me?" The black brows snapped together. "You'll do nothing of the sort!"

"Don't be silly, you desperately need a wash. In case you haven't noticed, you stink. When the fever broke, you sweated like a pig, and now I need to get you clean so you can recover in comfort."

Black brows lowered as he peered under the sheet. His eyes widened briefly as he saw he was naked. He glanced at her, then cautiously sniffed himself. His head jerked back. "Faugh!"

She laughed. "Told you so. All the evil humors have been sweated out of you. So now will you let me bathe you?"

He drew the sheet up to his chin. "Even less so now that I've seen—deuce take it, Ayisha, you shouldn't even *be* here, with me in this state." He tucked the sheet around him. "Where's Higgins?"

"Outside."

"Then send for him. He can assist me."

"No, he can't," she said calmly. "Not for ten more days."

"What do you mean, ten more days? I thought you said he was outside? Has he gone somewhere?"

"No, he's still on the boat," she told him. "But I might be infectious, so the captain has put me in quarantine for another ten days, just to be sure."

"If you're in quarantine, then what are you doing in my cabin?"

"This is quarantine," she told him. "I told you, you were sick. We thought it might be the plague."

"Plague?"

"But it wasn't, and now you're recovering from whatever it was. But I might have caught it from you, and so we have to stay in here for a little while longer."

"A little—" He slumped back against the pillows. "I don't understand half of what you've said to me. No—" He held up his hand. "Don't explain it all again. I think I'll just have a sleep first and hope that it all makes sense when I wake up."

"Well, don't sleep too long," she told him. "I'll need to bathe you and change those sheets before night."

He shook his head. "No, you're not touching me, blast it. I can put up with it."

"Well, I can't," she told him. "If you think I'm going to sleep in dirty sheets with a man who stinks of evil humors, you've got another thing coming."

"Nobody's asking you to sleep in dirty sheets with any kind of man at all!" he retorted. "Go away. Sleep in your own bed."

She said nothing.

His brows knotted as he caught the implications of what she'd said, and his gaze swept the room. No other bed.

"You mean that blasted captain shut you in here without so much as a bed?" he said with gathering wrath.

"No," she said wearily. "I shut myself in here with you, and I've slept here—" She pointed at his bed. "There for the last three nights."

"With me?"

She shrugged. "You were sick and unconscious. And there was plenty of room; it's a big bed."

He stared at her for a long moment, then groaned. "My head aches. I can't think straight. Let me lie here for a bit while I work it all out." He lay down and closed his eyes.

She instantly fetched the invalid cup and put the spout to his lips.

"Wha—what the—" he spluttered, pushing it away. "What's this? I don't need you fussing over me."

"It's willow bark tea," she told him crossly. Fuss over him indeed. She was tempted to tip the tea over his big, thick head! "It will help with your headache. It tastes nasty, I know—and serve you right. As for fussing, you've taken it three times a day for the last three days, and it's done you a great deal of good."

He groaned and pulled the sheet over his head. It came out a few seconds later. "I really do stink, don't I?"

She nodded. "Like a pig. And you need a purge as well as a bath."

"A purge? There's nothing left in me to purge. I'm not taking any blasted purge!" he growled. Then he looked at her. "Why a purge?"

"If the evil humors can be sweated out of you, I'm hoping a purge will rid you of the evil humor you've woken up in," she told him sweetly. "I'm not putting up with that for another ten days, either!" It was the sort of thing you said before you swept magnificently out of the door, she reflected, but she was locked in, so all she could do was to turn her back on him.

She was shaking with fury—and maybe a little weak with relief that he really was all right. And possibly on the verge of tears for the same reason—but she was not going to cry in front of him. Stinking beast.

How could you fight day and night to save a man's life and then when you had, want to strangle him?

She was tired, that's all. She'd hardly had any sleep in the last few nights. She stomped over to the bed, not looking at him, and picked up two of the blankets he'd kicked off at some stage.

She folded one lengthwise in three, then in half, and laid it on the floor farthest from the bed. It would do nicely as a sleeping mat. She took a pillow from the bed, and placed it at the end of the oblong.

"What are you doing?" he demanded.

She ignored him. She wrapped herself in the other blanket and lay down on the mat.

"You can't sleep on the floor. Here, take the bed, I'll sleep on the floor."

"The bed stinks of sweat and sickness and so do you. I've slept on cobblestones in the open air for the last six years. I can sleep anywhere." She closed her eyes.

"It's too early to go to sleep."

She sat up and glared at him. "Look, I've had very little sleep for the past few nights, so I'm going to catch up on it now. With any luck I'll sleep for ten days and then I won't have to talk to you at all. And you won't have to put up with my *fussing*." She lay down again.

There was a short silence, then he said, "I'm sorry. I was rude and I've upset you. I just don't kn— I'm a bit confused, that's all. I seem to have lost days of my life, and I don't understand how."

"You've been ill and now you're better, and you've woken up bad-tempered and you stink," she told him tiredly, adding, "And I'm bad-tempered, too, but at least I had a wash and changed, so I feel better. I'll explain everything later, but first, I need some sleep." And she closed her eyes and slept.

R afe sat back against the pillows and watched her. She really had fallen right to sleep, then and there. He'd thought for a moment she was just trying to make some point. Some point he couldn't work out.

But now that his brain was beginning to work, he realized she looked pale and drawn and somehow, frail. She really was exhausted.

He closed his eyes and tried to think. The last thing he could remember was . . . a woman screaming? A woman . . . but not Ayisha. But the reason eluded him. Whatever the memory was, it slipped away like dreams so often did. Or nightmares.

But he really did stink.

If what she said was right and they were locked in, he'd better clean himself up while she was asleep. Again he struggled to sit up.

He must have been very sick. There were only a few times in his life he'd found himself so weak. He hated it. Hated being dependent on others.

He'd rather shoot himself than let her bathe him while he was helpless as a baby.

He struggled to sit up and swung his legs out of bed. He sat on the edge of the bed, breathing heavily, and surveyed the cabin. Beneath the far porthole sat a row of covered buckets, a pile of folded cloths, and some empty bowls and a chamber pot. On the chest of drawers screwed into the wall sat his medicine chest, a teapot, and that blasted spouted cup. Beside them lay his razor. Excellent. He ran his hand over his jaw; he could use a shave.

He wobbled to his feet and, naked, staggered over and found himself clutching the porthole for balance. His head spun. He stood for a moment, hanging on and gulping in sea air. It seemed to help.

He investigated the buckets next. Two were empty, two contained water. He dipped a finger in and tasted gingerly. One was fresh water, the other, seawater.

He took a washcloth, soaped it up with some medicinal-smelling soap he found, then scrubbed himself all over, using the seawater. He scrubbed every inch of himself from head to toe, contorting to get his back clean, scrubbing hard. He stood carefully over one of the empty buckets and used his tin shaving mug to ladle seawater all over him, sluicing himself down.

Instead of into the bucket, the scummy gray water went all over the floor. He stared at it, dismayed.

He glanced at Ayisha, sleeping the sleep of the just on the

other side of the room. Her breathing was deep and even. Dark lashes lay in delicate crescents on her pale cheeks. Her hair clustered prettily around her temples and ears, curling in that just-washed look.

She'd bathed. And somehow left everything neat and tidy and dry, like a little cat.

He stared down at the spreading pool of soap-scummy salt water, staggered back to his bed, ripped the top sheet off, and flung it on the puddle.

God, he was exhausted—again. He hated being so weak. He clutched the side of the porthole and breathed until the chill on his wet, naked body revived him.

He went to shave himself and got a severe shock when he saw himself in the looking glass. Under the rough beard, he looked . . . scrawny and his eyes were bruised-looking and sunken. Oh well, he'd look better with a shave.

His razor was out and opened. The pouch with the rest of his toiletries was back with his baggage. What had she wanted with his razor?

He shaved in cold water. He'd done it many a time before, but for some reason this time he kept nicking himself, and by the time he'd finished, there were flecks of blood on the sheet at his feet.

He scrubbed himself all over again with his own soap and this time rinsed off with freshwater. He glanced at himself in the looking glass. He was a sorry-looking creature all right, but he felt a million times better.

But Lord, what a mess he'd made.

The sheet was sopping. What to do with it? Solution obvious. He pushed it around the floor with his feet, mopping up all the water, then bundled it up and shoved it through the porthole. Problem solved.

He toweled himself and his hair dry, and tossed the used towel out of the porthole. Damned useful things, portholes.

Ayisha muttered something in her sleep, and he glanced across. Better cover himself before she woke.

He grabbed a pair of drawers from his travel chest and tried to put them on. Damn. He needed to sit down. He sat on the bed, pulled the drawers on, then exhausted, fell back on the bed. Faugh. It still stank.

He pulled off the bottom sheet, sniffed, and pulled off the blanket underneath it and bundled them through the porthole. The pillows went the same way. He sniffed the mattress. Still a faint sour, unpleasant odor about it.

It was stuffed with wool. Wool carried infection, he'd heard. He tried to roll the mattress up, but though it was thin, it wasn't thin enough to go through the porthole.

Damn. He sat down to think the problem through. And saw his portmanteau sitting there. He'd bought an Arabian sword of Damascus steel while he was in Cairo. Damascus steel was famous. Swords of Damascus could cut through anything—they'd shattered the crusaders' swords in the old days, so a mattress made of wool and ticking should be no trouble.

With renewed determination, he pulled the sword from his portmanteau and began to methodically cut the mattress in pieces, flinging each one from the porthole. It was as sharp as— maybe even sharper than—his razor, and it sliced through the fabric and wool without a sound.

She slept right through it.

Marvelous weapon, he thought as he sheathed it. He wished he'd had a sword like this in the army. He should have bought four, one for each of the lads. Five—one for Ethan. Maybe he'd write to Baxter.

He sat on the bed. It wasn't very comfortable with just a sheet of canvas over the woven ropes. Still, better than having a mattress harboring infection. He glanced at the sleeping girl. Why the devil had she slept in the same bed with a sick man? If she got sick because of him . . .

They could get a new mattress at the next port. Where were they anyway? He peered out of the porthole, but could see nothing, just a smudge of far distant land.

He pulled on his breeches and a shirt and felt halfway to being civilized again. There was a soft knock on the door.

"Miss? Are you all right, miss?" It was Higgins.

Rafe went to the door. What the devil? It was bolted—from the inside. But she'd said they were locked in. He unbolted it and flung open the door.

Higgins's face lit up. "God be praised, sir, it's true—you're well again." The older man's face crumpled and he worked to control his emotion. "I thought—I was sure—" He cleared his throat. "Miss Ayisha said you were better, but I . . . I wasn't sure . . . And seeing you—" He did an abrupt about-face, pulled out a handkerchief, blew into it loudly, then, after a moment, turned back to Rafe, his customary wooden expression in place.

"My apologies, sir, but I truly thought you were done for. The plague is a killer."

"Plague?" Rafe repeated. And suddenly he recalled what that woman had been screaming. *Plague.* He frowned. "But it wasn't plague, was it?"

"No, sir, but everybody thought it was. Some of the other passengers were panicking."

Rafe nodded. "So that's why they locked me in. But what I can't understand is why they've put Miss Ayisha in with me. She wasn't sick, was she?"

Higgins brow furrowed. "No, sir, she locked herself in with you. To stop them dumping you." At Rafe's mystified expression, he added, "Didn't she explain, sir?"

Rafe shook his head. "No, she didn't. She's asleep at the moment. See?" He stood back and gestured for Higgins to come in, but the man didn't move.

"Beg pardon, sir, but Captain's orders are that no one is to go into or out of this cabin for another ten days." He gave Rafe an uneasy look and said, "It was a direct order, sir, but if you insis—"

Rafe waved his explanation away. "No, superior officer in this instance. You did right. But fill me in."

Higgins did and by the end of his tale, Rafe was frowning. "You all believed I had plague? And yet nobody tried to stop her?"

"Everyone did, sir, including yourself. Everyone else wanted rid of you; the plan was to tow you to some godforsaken part of the African coastline and leave you there, to live or die in the hands of God. And you, sir, you were all for it—bent on being the noble hero you were."

He grinned, half tearfully. "But Miss Ayisha wouldn't have a bar of it. You should have seen her, sir! Like a young tigress she was, protecting her cub. She pushed you back into the cabin, followed you in, and shut the bolt. She even threatened to shoot the first two men who came in—they were going to break the door down and haul you out. But she stopped them."

Rafe stared at the slender young thing curled up on the floor and swallowed. "How long ago was this?"

"Four days—three nights, sir. She's tended you night and day for all that time, sponging you down, pouring Peruvian bark tea and God knows what into you. A real little heroine she is."

"A bloody little fool," Rafe muttered. What he'd heard shook him to the depths of his being. It was one thing to risk yourself for a friend in the heat of battle; it was another to shut yourself in with a man you thought had plague. Risking certain death. For a man she barely knew.

He sighed. "I'm starving, Higgins. Can you get me some food?"

"Of course, sir, and Miss Ayisha, too, I expect; she hasn't eaten eat a thing since before yesterday."

"Yes, Miss Ayisha, too. Oh, and see if you can rustle up a new mattress, some pillows, and some blankets. I've got plenty of sheets."

Higgins looked confused. "Yes, Miss Ayisha changed your sheets every day, but what happened to the other—"

"They went out of the porthole, Higgins," Rafe told him. "They stank."

"Out of the—" Higgins's face went blank. He straightened. "Of course, sir. I'll see what I can do, sir."

As the door closed behind Higgins, Ayisha stirred.

"Higgins is fetching us some food," he told her, "Did you sleep well?"

"Yes, thank y—what happened to your face?" She stood up, shaking herself from her blanket, and peered worriedly at his jaw. "It's all cut about."

"I shaved," he said with dignity. "In cold water."

"Oh." She bit back a smile. "I see. You could have asked Higgins to fetch some hot water. He comes back every hour in the daytime."

He took the blanket from her and made a rough bundle of it.

"Here, I'll fold it," she began and bent to pick up the other blanket. She frowned. "What's all this stuff drifting around the floor? It looks like—" She bent and picked something up. "It's wool."

"From the mattress, I expect." He bent and picked up her pillow, took the second blanket from her, walked to the porthole, and thrust them through.

"Hey, what are you—"

"They were dirty, too."

She looked at the bed and her jaw dropped. "What happened to the bed? There's no mattress."

"It's gone. It's better that way. Wool harbors infections." He took the shred of wool from her hand and dropped it out of the porthole. "Higgins is getting us a new one. Come and sit down. I'm worn out."

There was a knock at the door. "Ah, the food."

But it was Higgins, with a mattress, pillows, and blankets. "They didn't have a big mattress, sir, but one of the seamen sewed two ordinary mattresses together. Like wizards they are with a needle. Comes of mending sails, I suppose." He pushed the mattress through the doorway.

"And Higgins, could you get me a hammock, please?" Ayisha asked him. "And a length of rope so we can rig up a corner for privacy."

"Certainly, m—" He broke off, as Rafe caught his eye.

No hammock, Rafe mouthed silently from behind her.

"Certainly, miss," Higgins finished, his expression unchanged. "I'll see what I can do."

Rafe nodded. Good man.

They spent the next few minutes reassembling the bed. By the end of it Rafe was almost at the end of his tether. He collapsed across it.

Five minutes later a knock at the door revived him. "The food, at last," he said and staggered to the door.

But it was the captain. He looked Rafe up and down very carefully. "My felicitations, sir, on your recovery."

"Thank you, Captain," Rafe said.

The captain glanced at Ayisha hovering at Rafe's elbow, steadying him. "Miss Cleeve, you did a remarkably brave—and foolish—thing."

She smiled. "I told you, Captain, it wasn't such a risk—"

Rafe cut her off. "We'll discuss that later!" It drove him wild to hear her dismissing it so lightly. "Captain, now you've seen I'm not plague-ridden, perhaps you could lift this quaranti—"

"Sorry, but no, I have rules and they must be obeyed. However, I'd hate to be confined to a cabin for so long, and I see no harm in allowing you a short time on deck to take in some fresh air, sunshine, and get a bit of exercise—as long as you don't come into contact with my passengers or crew, that is."

He looked a query at Rafe, who nodded. "Agreed."

"Good. I suggest you come up on deck during mealtimes, when the other passengers are eating. I shall inform the crew. You will dine later, in your cabin, after the others have finished."

Rafe nodded. "A good compromise. Thank you."

The captain took his leave, then he turned back with another thought. "Will you be wanting me to perform a service, sir?" He glanced at Ayisha.

"No," Rafe told him. "I'll organize it once I get Miss Cleeve to her grandmother's home."

"Service?" Ayisha asked. "What are you talking about?"

"A wedding service, miss," the captain said.

"But—" Ayisha began.

"Thank you, Captain, but there's no need for this just now." Rafe shut the door.

"What was he talking about?" Ayisha asked with misgiving.

"Not at all good *ton*, weddings aboard a ship," Rafe told her. "We'll do the deed at your grandmother's."

"Do what deed?"

"Get married, of course." He caught her look of amazement. "Well, it can't come as a surprise. I explained it to you only a few days—or maybe it was a week ago, I don't know. But I'm very sure that you understood me at the time. Why, you didn't come near me for days."

She stared at him, as if stricken to silence.

"Come now, Ayisha, surely you can see that after having spent three nights alone with me in my room—in my bed—we would have to marry." All that time alone with him unconscious, and her with nothing to do, she must have considered the consequences, he thought, trying to squash the coils of guilt inside him.

He'd realized it the moment he knew she'd slept in his bed. Realized it and been delighted. For Rafe, it resolved everything. He would have her exactly where he wanted—in his arms, in his life, and in his bed. And all without him having to make flowery speeches or make embarrassing admissions.

And risk her tossing them back in his face.

Now he wouldn't have to do a thing—except do the right thing and marry Ayisha. It couldn't be better.

"But you were sick, unconscious," she argued. "You didn't even know I was there."

"Yes, but everyone else on this ship did. Come, my dear, there's no need to look so upset; the damage is done now, so let's make the best of it." Why could she not see the advantages? Marriage would solve her problems and his. It would even solve the question of the succession—not that he cared about that.

She looked at him. "The damage is done?" she echoed, an odd note in her voice. "The *damage*?"

He gave her a reassuring smile. "It's not so bad. We'll rub along together quite well, I suspect." And as his wife, he could truly protect her and take care of her.

"Oh, do you?"

He frowned. She sounded a little . . . annoyed? "Yes, there's nothing either of us can do about it except accept the fact."

"What fact is that?" she demanded. "That because I saved your life and a pack of complete strangers know about it, we must now spend the rest of our lived married to each other?"

He shrugged. "It's the way of the world."

"It's not the way of my world."

"Perhaps not, but in England—" he began, then changed his mind. "Well, actually it is. You cannot deny that marriages are arranged all the time in Egypt."

"Yes, but as you say, this is England." She glanced out at the blue water of the Mediterranean. "Not yet, perhaps, but it will be."

"And marriages are arranged in England all the time, too. Both of my friends made arranged marriages—in fact Harry's was made for the very same reason. And my own brother was arranging mine to Lavinia Fettiplace before I left—" He broke off. It was perhaps not the wisest admission he'd made.

"Oh, wonderful." She threw up her arms. "And I suppose she's rich and beautiful."

"Well, yes, but—"

"Of course," she raged. "So he'll be just *thrilled* when you toss her over for some girl you found in the gutters of Cairo."

"Not at first, he won't—and you weren't in the gutter, precisely—not that it matters. My brother will just have to put up with the change of plans."

The change of plans couldn't have suited Rafe better. He had no desire to marry Lady Lavinia. He'd fled the country to avoid it, in fact.

"Put up with it, will we?" Her voice throbbed with fury.

"Well, not me, Mr. Ramsey. Because I'm refusing your so-gallant offer to make a decent woman of me. I'm perfectly decent as I am, thank you!"

"Of course you are—nobody is suggesting otherwise," Rafe soothed. "There's no need to get upset." He put a hand out to her but she gave him such a look that he changed his mind. She had a right to be upset, he knew. Women wanted the flowery speeches, courtship, things like that. But it was too late for that—they were well and truly compromised and there was no other alternative but marriage.

"Only Mrs. Ferris and others like her, I expect. They'll be saying that I created a situation to get myself a rich and hand-some husband." She glared at him. "And you think so, too, don't you?"

"Now that's not true. I don't think that at all. I know very well I've been very sick. You meant well, I'm sure—I know," he said hastily, seeing her expression.

He took a deep breath and said in a calming voice, "Of course I know you meant nothing but the best. But life doesn't always have the outcome one expects, and though this may not be what we both . . . expected, still it's not so very bad, is it?" He gave her an encouraging smile.

"Not so very bad?" She clenched her fists, rolled her eyes upward, and emitted a furious growl.

Rafe frowned. Clearly he was a less desirable catch than he'd imagined, though at least she thought him handsome. He thought about telling her about the heir. A lot of woman might like the idea that their son would one day become an earl. But dammit, no, he wouldn't bribe her into it. That would be too undignified.

He came back to the recurring thread in her argument. "If it's Mrs. Ferris you're worried about, well, don't. She's quite beneath your touch. Just ignore her," Rafe recommended loftily.

"Ignore her?" she almost shouted. "How can I ignore her when I'm supposed to marry you because of what she and others like her think?"

"It's what the whole world will think," Rafe said irritably. It made perfect sense to him. What the devil was she getting so hot under the collar for? They'd got on perfectly well until now, and once she calmed down, they'd get on perfectly well again, he was sure.

"No, what the whole world will think—if I marry you, which

I won't—is something like"—she put on an overly genteel voice—" 'Oh, look, there goes Ayisha Ramsey. She was no one until she pretended Rafe Ramsey had plague. Of course he didn't, it was just a minor fever, but she locked herself in with him for three whole nights—such melodrama, my dear! And when he recovered, the poor man was forced to marry her. Sooo tragic.' " She stormed to the door, flung it open, and found Higgins standing there with a tray of food.

"Stand back, Higgins," she snapped. "I'm going up on deck, and I'd hate to brush up against you by accident—"

"Miss?" Higgins stood back.

"Because then I'd probably have to marry you—" she finished.

"Oh, now you're just being silly," Rafe began.

"Which would suit me a—a *damn* sight better!" she concluded in a throbbing voice and ran off.

She left in her wake a shocked silence.

"Sorry to interrupt, sir," Higgins said ruefully after a moment. "Just came to bring you some food and to let you know everyone's gone in to dinner, if you wanted to go above decks."

"Thank God, I'm starving," Rafe declared. He lifted the cloth from the tray and stared at the contents. "Clear soup? Poached eggs? I said I was starving, man. I'm weak as a kitten. I need meat. And some good red wine."

"Sorry, sir, but your constitution needs slow building up. It couldn't cope with meat and red wine—and you know it, sir. Remember when you had that wound and the fever came on after the surgeon had stitched you up? I moved heaven and earth to get you a good plate of meat when you felt up to it."

"And I threw it all up a minute after I ate it, I know. Terrible waste. But soup and poached eggs?" He looked at the pallid liquid, the runny blobs on a piece of dry toast.

"It's good chicken soup," Higgins coaxed. "If Miss Ayisha had her way, it'd be gruel."

Rafe glanced the way she'd run. "Are you sure you don't mean hemlock?"

Higgins smiled. "She's in a passion to be sure, but she'll calm down. You know she thinks the world of you."

"Does she? Doesn't look like it to me." Rafe took the tray and sat down. He peered under the cover of the second plate. Eggs, as well.

"Females don't always say what they think, sir, you know that."

Rafe snorted. "I know. They get emotional about things that are perfectly straightforward."

"That's true, sir."

He took a mouthful of soup. Not bad. He drank some more. "I mean, she knew the consequences. That first night out of port I warned her about us being seen together too often, unchaperoned; the danger of being compromised." He shook his head. "I should have got her a maid."

"It would have made no difference, sir."

"No, I suppose not."

"She was hell-bent on saving your life, sir, not thinking about being compromised."

"I know that, Higgins," Rafe said impatiently. "Headstrong little fool throws herself into danger all the time. Doesn't think about the consequences. That's why it will work, this marriage. She needs to be steered by a cooler, more rational head." He finished the soup and ate a mouthful of egg and toast.

"Yes, sir."

"Admittedly, the captain was a little premature, but how could it possibly be the shock she seems to think it is? She's acting as if it's an insult." He glanced at Higgins. "I mean, I'm a reasonable catch, aren't I?"

"An excellent catch, sir."

"No, not excellent," Rafe said seriously. "My birth is good, but the fortune is only average." He took another bite.

"I don't think Miss Ayisha cares two pins about your fortune, sir."

"Well, I didn't think so, either, but she's clearly got her sights on something—or someone—better."

Higgins hesitated. "How—exactly—did you propose, sir?"

"Propose? I didn't. No need to. Captain broached the subject first, and I went on from there." He pushed the plate aside. Halfway through a piece of toast and an egg, and he was full.

"Women like to be proposed to, sir," Higgins suggested diffidently. "Like to know they can say yea or nay."

"Well, you heard her, she said nay. Loud and clear. I imagine the whole ship heard her."

"Everyone's at dinner, sir," Higgins assured him. "They wouldn't have heard a thing."

"Well, you get off and have your dinner." Rafe waved him away. "And if you value your skin, don't tell me if it's roast beef."

Rafe lay down on the bed. Why did women have to complicate everything? It had been the perfect resolution, what he'd intended all along, almost from the moment he'd set eyes on her.

She seemed so alone. He was alone, too. She had one close relative, her grandmother, but she could very easily die, soon. Grandmothers did in his experience. And Rafe only had one brother and he wasn't the slightest bit interested in anything other than Rafe's ability to produce an heir.

It seemed like a natural partnership. She would be alone in a strange country, needing protection, needing to be cared for and looked after. And he was good at that. It was one of his few skills.

They'd started out their acquaintance at daggers drawn, but he thought things had settled down nicely between them since. The trip to Alexandria had been quite pleasant; they'd admired the sights and chatted about all sorts of things.

He'd left her friends in a secure position. She'd liked his little gift—he hoped it made up for his insisting she left the old cat behind. And that little chat up on the deck that first night, when she'd stood beside him and talked about things he hadn't thought about in years . . . with her hand tucked into his arm.

As for saving his life. He could not get over that. Pulling his pistols out to stop them from sending him ashore.

And what followed after that. Fever was damned unpleasant to deal with, he knew. But she'd done it, taken care of him like a little Trojan. He still hadn't quite come to terms with how he felt about that. Grateful certainly, but also . . .

He couldn't explain it, even to himself.

So offering her marriage was the right thing to do on all levels.

Her vehement rejection had shocked him.

But he wasn't going to give in. He'd lay siege to her, wear her down, talk her around to his way of thinking. It worked in war, it would work in . . . life.

He'd take her to her grandmother's, explain the situation, and ask for her grandmother's permission to wed her. The old lady would back him up, he knew. Allow her precious newfound granddaughter to be disgraced? Not in a million years.

So he'd sort things out at Cleeveden, and then head off to straighten things with George and Lady Lavinia. Not that he'd ever made any promises to her, thank God. But she'd known of the intention, and he didn't want to embarrass her.

He'd explain the situation. She'd understand. She wasn't a bad sort. Just not his sort.

George would come around in the end. Breeding was what counted most with George. The Cleeves might not be nobility, but it was an old and venerable line, and on her mother's side she was related to half the noble families in the land. George cared about an heir more than anything; he'd end up grateful that Rafe was even getting married.

And though she had no fortune, she would inherit something from her grandmother, he imagined, and in any case he was perfectly content with what he had.

But was she? Her reaction had shocked him, shown him he didn't understand her at all.

Since his grandmother died, he hadn't been close to many women. Apart from Gabe and Harry's aunts and Luke's mother and sisters, the transactions with women he'd had up till now were either distant, polite, and formal—he was very good at balls and dinner parties, for instance—or convenient, lusty, and with no strings attached. Those connections began and ended at the bedroom door.

The kind of connection Gabe and Harry had with their wives—even his brother George seemed to have it with his wife Lucy—that was foreign territory to Rafe. He was the outsider looking in.

But they'd all made marriages of convenience—even George—especially George. Their father had selected George's bride with the same attention to detail and bloodlines that George had chosen Lady Lavinia.

So Rafe was sure he was on the right track. All he had to do was get her to the altar, and then into his bed. In time, she would come to care for him. She had to.

She found love easy. She loved half of Cairo, it seemed: ragged little street thieves, pie makers, ancient, beaten-up cats, sleek little kittens. She would learn to love him eventually, he was sure of it.

How did you make someone love you?

The only person in the world who'd cared about Rafe was his

grandmother, but that's what grandmothers did, it seemed. Look at Lady Cleeve. She hadn't even met Ayisha, but she loved her already.

But that was Ayisha, he thought sleepily. Everyone loved her. Look at the way those young officers followed her around. A honeymooning vicar and his wife, the captain of the ship, two out of three harpies—even sailors made harnesses for her cat. She was like that. He was just one of many.

But he could protect her.

And dammit, she needed protection the way she rushed into things, an angel rushing in where fools didn't dare . . .

Yes, he thought sleepily, that's what he'd do; marry her, be kind to her, and protect her. And once he got her into his bed, he'd make love to her until she was boneless with pleasure. It was the other thing he could do well.

She'd have to care for him then, he thought. He closed his eyes, partly to sleep, partly to shut out the thought of the other women he'd pleasured and parted from, without a pang on either side.

Ayisha was different. He'd make her want him . . . and want to stay. Somehow.

Fourteen

Ayisha marched to the rail and thumped it hard. Stupid, thickheaded, idiot man—why couldn't he understand? She glared around the empty deck. She wanted to kick something—somebody, only he was still in the cabin.

The damage is done—indeed!

You meant well. Meant well? It made her sound like an interfering busybody. Didn't he know, the great cloth-head, that for the last three days she'd fought day and night to keep him alive?

The last thing on her mind had been propriety. And he should thank her for it instead of telling her she *meant well.*

All those hours hovering over him, making him breathe, breathe, breathe. The sleepless nights, the fear, worrying, fretting over him, feeding him Peruvian bark and willow bark and sponging him down, keeping him cool, keeping him warm, keeping him *alive.*

She stared out to sea with eyes that were awash.

What sort of person did he think she was? Could he not see why she'd done what she did? Why did he think she'd fought so desperately to save him—threatening to shoot two perfectly innocent men, so they wouldn't set him ashore. Men with wives, probably, who they loved, and children. Why did he think she would do such a thing? To trap herself a husband?

You meant well.

How could he not see how desperately she loved him? The blockhead.

She couldn't even begin to explain how his words wounded her. The words every girl dreams of, having her marriage described by the prospective groom; *the damage is done* but it's *not so very bad.*

We'll rub along together quite well, I suspect.

She should have let them dump him overboard, she thought furiously. It would have saved her—everyone—a great deal of trouble.

She paced along the rail, back and forth. She should have shoved him out the porthole. She could go down and do it now, see how he liked that.

She would *not* be married to prevent gossip.

She would not *rub along.*

She had come to suck the sweet orange of life, not the dry bean of compromise and convention. For Ayisha, it was all or nothing, and if he was too stupid and thickheaded and blind to know what she was offering, she would choose nothing.

No, that was wrong; she wasn't choosing nothing.

He had offered her nothing, and she had refused to accept it. And that was that.

Now, how to survive another ten days in a cabin with a man she wanted to strangle? Or shove out a porthole.

*A*n hour later Higgins came to let her know it was time to return to the cabin.

"Are you all right, miss?" he asked, his kind face worried.

"Yes, Higgins," she said quietly. She'd made her decision and she was calm and resolved. "I'm a little tired, that's all. Did you find me a hammock?"

His gaze shifted. "No, miss," he said.

"A spare mattress, then?"

"I'm sorry, miss."

She shrugged. "No matter, I'll just sleep on the floor. Could you ask Reverend and Mrs. Payne if I could have my kitten back in the morning, please?"

"Of course, miss, I'll speak to them." He bowed and hurried off. Ayisha returned to the cabin and quietly let herself in.

To her great relief Rafe was sound asleep in bed. Of course he must be tired. He would do a lot of sleeping over the next few days, she knew. That would help.

She slipped off her shoes and stockings and tiptoed over to the bed. He looked peaceful and handsome, but she felt his forehead, just to make sure.

Cool, dry, normal. His breathing was deep and even, too.

There was a tray with a cloth on the sea chest. Investigating, she found cold soup and a poached egg. She was very hungry, so she ate them anyway. It was no longer in her to waste food.

He slept on, the rhythm of his breathing unchanged.

She poured some clean, cold water into a bowl and washed her face, then looked around for spare blankets. None. She sighed. The floor was going to be very hard. It was amazing how quickly you got used to sleeping in a bed with a soft woolen mattress. But if you were tired enough, you could sleep anywhere, and she was very tired.

She took off her dress and hung it on a hook, then spread out her shawl on the floor and lay down.

"Get into bed, Ayisha," a deep voice growled, making her jump.

"I am in bed," she responded. "Good night."

"I said, get into bed. You're not sleeping on the floor."

"I will sleep where I please." She closed her eyes.

"This bed is big enough for both of us."

"This cabin isn't big enough for both of us." She screwed her eyes shut and concentrated on deep and even breathing. Impossible man. Just when she'd achieved calm, he must argue and stir things up.

He sighed. "Very well, if you're going to be stubborn . . ." There was a swishing of bedclothes and she heard bare feet padding across toward her.

"What are you doing?"

"I can't let a woman sleep on the floor."

"Don't be stupid. I'm used to it, you're not."

"I'm a soldier. I've slept on the ground hundreds of times."

"You're not a soldier anymore, the ground is a great deal softer than any wooden floor, and you've been sick. Go back to bed."

He knelt down beside her.

"Go away, I'm not moving," she hissed.

He lay down beside her on the floor. "Good night, little cat."

She lay there fuming. "This is ridiculous. I'm not sleeping beside you."

"Then use the bed," he said and snuggled up close to her.

She wriggled away. He wriggled close again.

"Stop doing that."

"It's cold."

"Then get in the bed." He didn't move, so she pushed him. "Go on. You've been sick. You need to take care of yourself."

"Can't leave a lady on the floor."

"Oh, for heaven's sake!" She rose and grabbed a blanket from the bed and threw it over him. She stood looking down at him and caught the faint glint of white teeth in the moonlight. Ridiculous, impossible man. If she stayed on the floor, he'd just keep annoying her and neither of them would get any sleep.

"Very well, since you're determined to be completely impossible, I'll sleep in the bed."

"Well, do it then, and stop keeping me awake."

She gritted her teeth and got into the bed. It was very soft and warm and comfortable. She waited, but he didn't say anything and after a few minutes she relaxed. It was really very comfortable and she was so tired . . .

A big, warm body slid in beside her.

She stiffened and her eyes flew open. "What do you think you're doing?"

"Getting into bed. You told me to, remember? At least twice. Hate to disoblige a lady."

"Then let me out."

"No. We'll both sleep better here."

"I can't sleep in the same bed with you."

"Why not? You did it the last three nights."

"That was different. You were unconscious then."

"So, it'll be more fun now. Ooof!" There was a short silence. "I'd forgotten about your elbows."

She examined the remark suspiciously. "What about my elbows?"

"Just that you have them. Lots of them."

"That's ridiculous, I only have two. Now let me out."

She felt slightly desperate. She didn't want to sleep here, so close to him. She was angry with him. She wanted nothing to do with him.

But he'd trapped her between the wall and himself. The only way she could get out was to climb over him, and she was fairly certain he'd enjoy stopping her.

"Now stop arguing; there's a good girl. We're both tired, so let's just declare a truce and agree you're sleeping here, with me."

She considered it. The bed was very comfortable. She would sleep better here. And it wasn't as if he'd left her any choice. "Very well," she said. "There are two mattresses sewn together, so you stay on yours and I'll stay on mine, agreed?"

"Whatever you say, my dear."

She tried to relax and was succeeding quite well until from out of the darkness he added, "Not that it matters. We're going to get married anyway. Ooof!"

Something woke Rafe in the middle of the night. He'd always been a light sleeper. He tried to work out what it was. And then he realized.

Her body was curled along his side, shaping herself to the contours of his body, on his half of the bed, holding him, one hand cupping the side of his face, the other with the palm pressed, skin against skin, inside his shirt, directly over his heart.

He turned his head cautiously to look at her. She was sound asleep, but was whispering something, the same word, over and over, her breath warming his skin. He leaned closer to hear what it was.

"Breathe . . . Breathe . . . Breathe."

For a moment he couldn't breathe, couldn't think, as slowly it dawned on him what she was doing. Protecting him, caring for him, keeping him alive, even as she slept.

"Breathe . . . Breathe . . . Breathe."

A tight ball formed in his chest. His hand came up and covered hers, where it lay over his heart.

He didn't care how much she argued and denied it; she was his.

* * *

*T*he next morning, Higgins woke them with a knock on the
door. Ayisha sat up, yawning. She glanced at the porthole.
The day was bright.

"We slept in," she said, sounding surprised.

Rafe pulled on his breeches. "We were both very tired." He
padded to the door in shirt and breeches.

"Morning, sir, Miss Ayisha. How do you feel, sir?"

"Better, thank you, Higgins," Rafe told him. "Much more the
thing. What's this?"

Higgins handed a can and a neat bundle over. "Can of hot
water for your ablutions, sir. And a bit of old sailcloth and some
rope. Figured you could rig up a private corner."

Higgins went off, promising to return with breakfast in about
half an hour. Rafe rigged up the sail to make a private corner,
then sat down and pulled on his boots.

He turned to Ayisha, who was still in bed, her bedclothes
clutched up around her neck as if he was about to pounce on her.
He smiled to himself. If she only knew how she'd held him in her
sleep. He'd woken first and moved away from her reluctantly,
knowing she'd be upset if she woke to find them practically in-
tertwined.

He'd woken with renewed hope. She'd embraced him in her
sleep; that had to mean something.

He gestured to the hot water and the private alcove. "Ladies
first. I'll go up on deck for a quick stroll. Fifteen minutes?" And
pulling on his coat, he left.

On his return, she headed above deck while he shaved carefully. It was disconcerting how much the short stroll on deck had
tired him out, he thought, stripping to wash the rest of his body.
He had to get his strength back.

When she came back, Higgins was waiting with their breakfast. At his feet was a basket containing one slightly aggrieved
kitten. Ayisha pounced on the kitten with delight and released
her, crooning and cuddling the tiny thing.

As they broke their fast on hot tea, porridge, new-baked
bread, and honey—no ham or bacon, much to Rafe's disgust—
Cleo prowled around the cabin, sniffing everything, learning her
new territory.

Rafe only managed a few spoonsful of porridge and a little

bread and honey, but Ayisha was busily working her way through everything there was. She was obviously ravenous. He felt a pang as he recalled she'd missed her dinner because of him.

He put his porridge bowl down for the kitten, who examined the bowl from all angles before lapping contentedly. Rafe sprawled sideways across the bed, his head propped in his hand, and watched Ayisha.

She gave him a look as if to say, what are you doing, but went on with her breakfast in silence.

"I like to watch you eat," he told her.

"Why?" She frowned and lowered the piece of crusty bread and honey. "Do I do it wrong? For England, that is? Should I cut this into small pieces or something?"

"No, no, don't worry. It's just that you really enjoy your food."

She shrugged. "Why not? I was hungry and this bread and honey is delicious. I had forgotten how delicious fresh Frankish bread was." She finished the last piece and licked her fingers. "And I love this Greek honey, mmm."

"You'll get no objection from me," Rafe said, watching her tongue curl around her sticky fingers. His manhood stirred at the sight. He gently rolled over and lay on his stomach.

"You can have honey every day once we're married."

"Don't start that again," she ordered. "I refuse to spend the next ten days locked in with you arguing about such a piece of nonsense. You've said your piece. I've given you my answer, and that's my last word on it."

"Very well, I won't browbeat you about it," he said, "but I'm still going to marry you." He held up his hand to stop her speaking. "And that's *my* last word on it. For today."

She snorted and picked up the damp washcloth to wipe her hands.

He moved into a more comfortable position on the bed and his eye caught the pistol case, still open near the door. He knew why she'd wanted the pistols—though it still dazed him—but he recalled that his razor had been out and open, too. Why?

"I noticed you had my razor out when I was sick."

"Mmm." She was cross-legged on the floor now, playing with the kitten.

"How did you plan to use it? I presume you weren't planning to shave me. Or cut my throat."

She gave a wry smile. "Not then I wasn't. You weren't talking such nonsense then. Just a bit of delirious rambling."

She said it as if it was nothing, but dealing with a delirious man was no joke. "The razor?"

She shrugged and glanced at the medical text next to the bed. "If it was the plague, I might have had to lance the buboes."

He closed his eyes, imagining it. He could never make it up to her, never. And now, as a reward for her heroism, she was trapped with him. In more ways than one. "You're not sorry you did it, are you—looked after me, I mean?"

"Of course not. How could I be?" She sighed. "I just wish people's reactions to it weren't so stupidly complicated." She meant marriage.

"Because the world is complicated."

"It's not. It's quite simple. I was simply taking care of a sick man. And you're simply giving in to the gossips."

"No, I'm protecting you."

She snorted. "I don't need protecting from the likes of Mrs. Ferris. I told you about people like her—if they don't have anything real to talk about, they'll make something up."

"But this is real."

"No, that's just it—it's not! You were sick. Nothing happened. Any compromising happened only in their minds—it wasn't real at all. And I refuse to give in to it, so please, let us not argue."

"I have no intention of arguing," he assured her. No argument at all; he was simply going to marry her.

She played with the kitten for a while, then said, "Tell me about this Lavinia person."

He smiled. "She's simply a young woman who my brother was negotiating for me to marry."

She frowned as she twirled a stray tuft of mattress wool into a kitten plaything. "He's your older brother, yes? Is it normal for older brothers to arrange marriages for their younger brothers?"

"Not really, but in this case he needs an heir."

"Then why does he not marry and beget one?"

"He's been married for ten years. His wife is barren."

"Oh. Poor thing. I'm sorry." She picked up the kitten and cuddled it.

"So it's up to me to beget the next Ramsey son, and since he's very concerned with breeding and bloodlines—his wife was selected by my father for her excellent family connections and her fortune, so he's doing the same for me—he did a great deal of research and came up with Lad—Lavinia."

"Don't you have any say in it?"

"Yes, but I was dragging my feet in finding a wife, and so he stepped in."

"Is she nice, this Lavinia?"

"I only met her once, but yes, she seemed nice enough."

The kitten pounced and skittered after the wool. "Pretty?"

"Very."

She nodded. "And rich?"

"Apparently. And she'd already agreed to let my brother and his wife raise the firstborn son."

She looked up, shocked. "What? But why?"

He shrugged. "He would be heir to the—the family business, eventually. George wanted to train him up to do a proper job of it."

Her brow furrowed. "You sound as if you don't care."

He said tightly, "It was nothing to do with me. They'd planned it all out. I was just the . . . instrument." It sounded better than stallion. And he was still unable to voice the rage he'd felt on learning of the plan. As if he wouldn't care what would happen to his child.

George had told him of Lavinia's agreement, presenting it as if Rafe should be delighted not to have a son cluttering up his life. He'd sounded just like their father.

Rafe might resent the action, but he couldn't quarrel with the end result—his wild-goose chase into Egypt. He smiled as Ayisha tussled playfully with the kitten. His little wild goose.

She said slowly, looking for ways to excuse him, "I suppose you knew you could trust your brother's choice. He must know you very well."

He snorted. "He hardly knows me at all. We were brought up separately."

"Why was that?"

"My mother died when I was small—it's all right," he said quickly, seeing her expression of sympathy. "My memories of her are very vague. But after that my father didn't want me underfoot; George was the heir and Father spent all his time training him for his future position."

"But that's terrible."

He shook his head. "If you want to know the truth, George got the worst part of the deal. My father was a frightful bore—always droning on about the family and its importance. So George grew up under the old man's thumb—and turned out just like him—while I got to live with Granny, my mother's mother."

She picked up the kitten and, stroking it, said softly, "You liked it at Granny's, didn't you? I can tell. Was she my grandmother's friend?"

"She was. And yes, the happiest times of my life were at Granny's." He lay back on the bed, remembering . . . and drifted off to sleep.

It was good that he slept, Ayisha reflected. Sleep, good food, exercise, and fresh air would soon restore him to normal.

She thought about the story he'd told. So . . . cold-blooded. People said the English were a cold-blooded race, but she'd never seen any evidence of it before now.

Growing up hardly knowing his father or brother? What had he said about his father? *My father didn't want me underfoot.* What kind of a father would send a fine young son like Rafe off to be raised by his wife's mother? He didn't need to; he was clearly rich. He just wasn't . . . interested.

She looked at Rafe, sleeping on the bed and impossibly handsome. What kind of man would let his brother choose his bride without bothering to find anything about her? And then fight to marry another woman, merely to stop gossip?

And what kind of woman would happily hand over her child to be brought up by others? Only the direst necessity would force Ayisha to give up her child.

What kind of people was she going to?

He slept on and off for most of the day, recovering his strength. Ayisha passed the time playing with her kitten, practicing the knitting she'd started with Mrs. Grenville—she'd sent it along with Higgins—or reading. Rafe had several books in his trunk and she found it such a joy to be able to read again.

In the evening they'd walked on deck together, enjoying the evening breeze and the sight of the stars coming out. After dinner Ayisha asked Higgins whether he'd been able to find a spare mattress or hammock.

"Sorry, miss," he told her, not meeting her eyes. "I'm unable to find any."

"Because you've instructed him not to be able to find any, haven't you?" she accused Rafe after Higgins had left.

"Would I do that?" A smile lurked in his eyes that showed her she was right, and he didn't care that she knew it.

"You should be ashamed of yourself," she told him.

"Oh, I am," he said. The smile moved to his mouth and took on a distinctly wolfishly tone.

But he hadn't been able to stop Higgins from finding her some extra blankets, not when she told Higgins how cold she'd been the previous night. He had too soft a heart to obey his master in that instance.

So when it came to bedtime, Ayisha put Cleo in her basket—they'd agreed it was a good idea to get the kitten used to sleeping in there; it would make traveling easier—and then made up a bed for herself on the floor beside the cat basket.

"What are you doing?" Rafe demanded as she rolled herself in the blanket.

"Isn't it obvious?" She lay down.

"No, it's extremely tedious." He got off the bed with a long-suffering expression.

"I don't care if you lie beside me on the floor," she told him. "I won't be tricked a second time, and you won't be able to stand it on the floor for long." She closed her eyes.

"I have no intention of lying on the floor beside you. It's much nicer on the bed," he said. "See?" And taking the corners of her blanket he lifted her straight onto the bed. One flip and she rolled right out of her blanket.

He slid into bed beside her. "That's better," he said, and when she opened her mouth to complain he simply leaned forward and kissed her.

She recoiled instinctively, but he cupped the back of her head with his hand and tenderly, implacably, took possession of her lips, her mouth. She lifted a hand to push him away, but somehow, somewhere between one heartbeat and the next, the impulse just . . . dissolved.

His mouth invaded hers, seeking, demanding, swamping her senses.

The sound of the waves, the creaking of the ship, the sound the wind made in the sails—it all faded away to nothing. There was only him, only her, only the moment. Awash on a sea of sensation.

The sharp masculine taste of him, intimate, deeply familiar. The scent of his skin, all man—Rafe and clean linen and hunger.

A slow rush of heat spread across her skin.

Hunger.

He moved slowly, sensuously against her and she shuddered at the press of his flesh against hers, the abrasion of his stubbled jaw, the insistence of the hot, demanding mouth.

And then, as suddenly as it had started, he released her and moved back.

She blinked, staring at him, dazed, oddly bereft. What had just happened there?

"If you keep looking at me like that, I won't be able to stop," he said, his voice rough as the bristles on his chin and just as appealing.

She shivered.

And then he smiled, ruefully. "Actually, I'm not sure it would make much difference. I'm still damnably weak from that blasted fever." And with a sigh, he lay back on his pillow and closed his eyes.

The world slowly crept back around her, revolving around one thought that battered at her dazed stupidity like waves against the ship's hull.

She'd almost let him seduce her. If he wasn't still weak from the fever, she wouldn't have lifted a finger to stop him.

That's what seduced meant, she told herself furiously. Making you do something you didn't want to do.

Only she had.

She'd wanted it, wanted him. She stared at his mouth, his perfectly ordinary, perfectly beautiful, devilishly seductive mouth and shivered again.

At her narrow escape, she told herself. While she'd been under the spell of his kiss, she would have allowed him anything.

Allowed? And who was it who'd run her fingers through that thick, dark hair and pulled him closer? Who'd reacted to the first touch of his tongue inside her mouth with a thrill of excitement and touched her own tongue to his?

And wanted more.

She pressed her palms against her still-hot cheeks and breathed deeply. Even recumbent on a pillow with his eyes closed, he drew her to him.

She'd known from the first day she'd seen him that he was

dangerous. What she hadn't realized was how addictive danger could be. She was playing with fire, and it could only end in tears. Her tears.

She started to climb over him.

A brawny arm rose up to bar her. "Where do you think you're going?" His eyes were still closed.

She pushed against him. She felt no sign of the weakness he'd mentioned. "I can't sleep here, knowing that any minute you might pounce on me."

He opened one eye and raised a brow. "Pounce?" he said in a pained voice, implying he'd never be so vulgar.

"Yes, pounce! Like you pounced just now."

He opened both eyes. They gleamed. "Is that what you call it in Egypt? In England we call it a kiss, in this case a good-night kiss. A delightful custom, don't you think?"

"I won't have it. Now let me out." She wasn't going to stay here and . . . banter with him. From the look of him his strength was increasing by the minute.

He didn't move a muscle. "I thought you enjoyed it nearly as much as I did."

She had no intention of admitting any such dangerous thing. "Move your arm. Let me out."

"I could understand if you didn't want to, but you do, so what's the harm? We're going to marry anyway, so why put ourselves through the strain of unnecessary celibacy?" He seemed genuinely puzzled by her refusal.

He took her hand, and caressed it. "Come now, sweetheart, why not alleviate the tedi—" He broke off.

She snatched her hand away and thought about punching him. She knew what he'd been going to say. *Alleviate the tedium of their quarantine.* He wanted to seduce her as a way of keeping boredom at bay.

"It's a pity it's so dark in here," she told him.

There was a short pause. "Why?" he said cautiously.

"Because if you could see my expression, you'd be only too happy to let me out, for fear I'd murder you in your bed."

He laughed. "Not when you worked so hard to save my life—"

"We all make mistakes."

"You're cross," he said. "Perhaps I could have phrased that last suggestion more felicitously, but—"

"I'm not going to argue. You know my decision."

"Yes, but it's not entrapment when I'm perfectly aware of the situation and happy to go along with it—"

She glared at him. *Happy to go along with it?*

"More than happy," he assured her hastily, seeming to realize his error. "Delighted, really, I promise you."

She fumed silently. Boneheaded, idiot man! "Either give me your promise—on your honor!—not to try to seduce me, or I'll ask the captain to put me ashore at Malta."

His brows snapped together. "But they'll put you into quarantine in Malta."

She shrugged. "I'm in quarantine here."

"Yes, but it's much more comfortable here."

"At least nobody will be trying to seduce me there."

He snorted. "Don't count on it." He thought for a moment, then sighed and said, "Very well, I promise to do nothing you don't want."

She shook her head. "Not good enough." The trouble was, she wanted his kiss, and once caught up in it, there was no saying what else she might want. Everything, she suspected.

She had to force a promise from him that would protect her from herself as well as him.

She wanted him, but she didn't want to live the rest of her life as someone who'd tricked him into marriage, and until he knew the whole truth about who she was, she couldn't even think about accepting him.

Besides, who wanted to marry a man who spoke of *alleviating tedium*? She glared at him. The big bonehead!

"I must have your promise—on your honor as a gentleman— that you will not try to seduce me. Otherwise I leave the ship at Malta."

"Does that include kissing?"

"No kissing." She felt a pang as she said it, but she knew what kissing was, now: something that dissolved all her common sense.

"If I promise, will you remain in this bed? I won't have you sleeping on the floor."

"It's quite comfortable if you're used to—oh, very well. But one wrong move—"

"I promise, on my honor as a gentleman, to make no attempt to seduce you."

She should have felt relief—and she did. But not as much as she should have. And there was a definite pang of regret.

But it was the right thing to do, she told herself, as she lay down next to him in the dark. Despite his thickheadedness, she wanted him: to marry him would be a dream.

But who founded a dream on a lie?

It would be like building a home over a snake's hole. Sooner or later the snake would come out to bite you, and it would poison everything you'd built.

She would gladly marry him, free and clear, though not for the sake of propriety. And not to alleviate tedium.

She couldn't even consider him seriously until he knew who she truly was and who her parents were. She would marry him without hesitation then—if he still wanted her, that is.

She was far from certain about that. He might still want her, but not necessarily as a wife. Who knew that reality better than the daughter of a mistress?

She closed her eyes and tried not to think about the man in the bed beside her. She could smell him, that delicious clean-linen, soap, and man smell of him. She inhaled deeply.

"Can I just explain what I meant about alleviating tediu—ooof! No, all right, we'll leave it at—ooof!"

"No talking," she said sternly.

"Very well, good night. And may I just say, what a pleasure it is, sharing a bed with—ooof!"

Rafe lay in the dark, smiling. He still had her where he wanted her. Maybe not quite as close as he wanted her. He rubbed his ribs reflectively. Even her anger pleased him.

He didn't blame her a bit. Whatever had possessed him to speak of alleviating tedium? He could have phrased that a lot more felicitously.

What the hell was the matter with him? He used to be famed for his dry and witty way with words. Now, every time he opened his mouth to her, he seemed to put his foot in it.

It was the fever.

No, he thought, it was her. He was deeply frustrated and it was scrambling his brain.

He hadn't meant "alleviate the tedium" in the way it had sounded. He'd been having visions of it all day, ever since quarantine and the possibility of marriage had arisen: a blissful ten days of enforced isolation, free of the irritations of the outside world, sailing peacefully along, making love, kissing, talking, kissing, getting to know each other, making love.

His idea of the perfect honeymoon.

Too late to explain that now.

Now it was going to be ten days of torture, having her and not having her, sleeping with her and not sleeping with her.

What the hell was the matter with him? It was only going to get worse.

Fifteen

W ould you really give your firstborn son to your brother to raise?" Ayisha asked him as they were taking their last promenade of the day. Ahead of them Cleo, now accustomed to her lead, stalked a shadow.

"What?" he asked. He'd been miles away. These promenades, three times a day in the open air, were his lifeline—and he didn't mean the cat's safety harness. Being locked up in a cabin with Ayisha was the punishment of Tantalus; he could see, hear, smell, but was unable to touch or taste.

She climbed into bed each night, a stiff little prickle of propriety, insisting on sleeping on the outer edge of the bed, threatening to sleep on the floor if he so much as moved an inch toward her.

But in sleep, her body sang another song. In sleep her body sought him, snuggling closer until she was curled against his length, her hand resting over his heart, her cheek nestled against his shoulder, her limbs twined around his. In sleep, she was warm and soft, separated from him only by a promise—and it was driving him mad. He slept badly, and woke each morning rock hard with desire.

"I beg your pardon, I was woolgathering," he said. "What did you ask me?"

"You said you were going to give your firstborn son to your brother to raise."

"I said Lavinia and my brother had agreed on it. I was never even consulted."

"Well, would you?"

"Give away my child?" He stared out to sea a long time. "Never," he said quietly. "Not while there was breath in my body to protect him."

She slipped her arm through his. "Then why did they think you'd agree to such a thing?"

He shook his head. "I think they—well, George, thought he'd be doing me a favor. Perhaps he thought because I'd never settled, a son would get in my way." George's exact words.

She frowned. "What do you mean?"

"He thought a son would slow me down, stop me having fun." After eight years at war, Rafe and the others had indeed broken out and kicked up their heels a little. But in the last year the "fun" had palled and become something almost . . . desperate.

Eight years as an officer got a man used to responsibilities, to having a purpose in life, and being cut loose from that was . . . difficult. Rafe hadn't thought a great deal about the future—in the army he'd been almost superstitious about it. Many soldiers believed that if you planned for the future, you'd be sure to be killed, so he'd lived in the here and now.

But when the fighting was all over and he'd decided to sell out—he couldn't stand the endless drilling of a Hyde Park soldier—he'd thought he'd take up some sort of position on one of the family estates. When he was a boy, several of his uncles had run various family businesses, and he rather thought he'd be good at that.

Learning that all that your family wanted of you—for the rest of your life—was a brief period of stud service, that was a slap in the face.

And if it had been done with the least bit of hostility or scorn, Rafe would have slapped back—hard. But George had thought he was doing Rafe a favor. George had worked hard to find what he considered the perfect bride for Rafe: one who wouldn't trouble him in the slightest.

The trouble was, Rafe liked trouble.

And pathetic as it was, Rafe couldn't rebuff the first friendly overture from his brother since their father had died. So he'd cut and run—to Egypt.

"I didn't mean about the son," Ayisha interrupted his thoughts. "I meant what did he mean, you'd never settled?"

"It's true. I haven't had a permanent home since . . . I don't know when actually. Not since I was a small boy." He frowned, only just realizing it. Had it really been so long?

"When your father sent you away." She said it in such a way that showed she understood why he'd never, ever send a child of his away. It wasn't that he'd minded living with Granny—he'd loved living at Foxcotte and he loved her. But to know how little he'd mattered to his own father. . . .

No child of his would ever be in doubt that they mattered.

"No, I lived with my grandmother, and that was my home then. It was after she died . . ." Good God, had it really been so long since he'd had anywhere permanent?

She gaped at him. "But your family is rich," she said, sounding quite distressed. "How could you not have a home?"

She was imagining he'd had to live on the streets, like she had, he realized. He laughed and slipped an arm around her waist. "No, you're imagining something dreadful. I've had a delightful time, I assure you. After Granny died, I never went to Axebridge—my father's home, now George's—if I could help it. On school holidays I stayed with Gabe and Harry, or Luke. And then the army was my home. And since then, well, I stay with friends, and when in London, I have lodgings."

"Can't you buy a house?"

He shrugged. "What for? Besides, I do own a house—my grandmother left me hers when she died." He hadn't found that out until he was one and twenty and the family solicitor had written to him in Spain. His father had appointed an estate manager and the house was rented out. Rafe wasn't needed.

"So you have a home."

"No, I own a house. There's a difference."

"If you own a house, you can have a home," she insisted. "Getting the house is the hard part. Making it into a home is easy."

"Is it?" he said. "Good, when we're married, you will enjoy making us a home."

She pulled herself away. "They say we'll be in Malta tomorrow." It was a warning. "I'll go down first," she said briskly and moved toward the companionway.

Malta was beautiful, a small jewel of an island set in brilliant azure waters, and like a jewel, it was tough at heart, with enormous fortifications rising from the sea.

Of course, being in quarantine, they were not allowed ashore, but in exchange for gold and several fine large turtles caught by the seamen, fresh provisions came aboard, including several large baskets full of fresh fruit.

Ayisha and Rafe strolled on deck while below, the ship's passengers were treated to turtle soup, various roasted game meats, and fresh vegetables and fruit, with local cheeses to follow. The smells that floated up from the galley were enticing, and Rafe was hungry, but they had to be patient. They received their dinner after the others, but Higgins would ensure they didn't just get leftovers.

On the shore they could hear music playing. Some kind of festival or celebration. Ayisha leaned over the gunwales, listening avidly, one foot raised.

"You'll fall overboard if you're not careful," Rafe told her. She was all grace and lissome beauty.

She laughed. "Isn't the music wonderful?" She closed her eyes the better to concentrate on the sounds floating across the smooth water of the harbor. "Oh—oh! I know that song," she exclaimed in excitement. "It's 'Highland Laddie,' and I used to be able to play it on the pianoforte." And humming along with the tune, she played silent notes on the smooth surface of the gunwale.

Her open enjoyment of such a small pleasure touched him.

"So, you can play the pianoforte," he prompted, hoping to encourage her to open up a little. She so rarely talked about her past.

"No, I wish I could," she said, still earnestly fingering soundless notes, with a kind of delight over something she thought long forgotten. "I started lessons, and I loved it; it was the best thing . . ." And she sang a line and smiled. "So lovely to hear this song after so many years."

"You seem very proficient to me."

"Yes, but only on a ship's rail," she admitted. "I only attended lessons for a year and then . . ."

"Then what?"

"They stopped." Her fingering faltered, and she snatched them back self-consciously and, as if looking for something to do with them, brushed her hair back.

There was a moment of silence, broken only by the soft lapping of the waves and the sounds from the town drifting across the water.

"What happened? Did your teacher leave? Or die?"

"Mrs. Whittacker? No, as far as I know she's still living there and giving lessons." She shrugged. "She used to give lessons to many of the Fran—the English and other children living there, not for the money, but because she loved chil—" She broke off, frowning. "No, she *said* it was because she loved children, but now that I think back, I don't think that was true at all."

She glanced up at him. "She made such a fuss of me, and I felt so welcome and so wanted . . ." She sighed. "When you're a child you believe everything adults tell you," she said in a tired-sounding voice. "It's only much later you understand that there was something very different going on . . ."

"What was going on with Mrs. Whittacker?"

She shook her head. "It doesn't matter now."

"Indulge my curiosity. I want to know why the lessons you so enjoyed stopped."

She shrugged again. "I think now she had a *tendre* for Papa. Perhaps she hoped to marry him . . . I don't know."

"Your father didn't return her sentiments?"

"No, of cour—" She broke off. "No, he didn't. Can you hear what this one is?" She leaned out over the side, craning to hear the next song floating on the balmy night breeze, but he knew it was an excuse to change the subject. Something had happened about those lessons, not just the disappointment of a widow's hopes. Something more personal to Ayisha.

"You sound upset."

"I don't know this one, but it's pretty, isn't it?" She swayed to the music.

She was obviously determined not to discuss it further. But the music and her movements had given him an idea.

"It's Strauss," he said and held out a hand to her. "Do you waltz, Miss Cleeve?"

She looked at his hand and shook her head. "You mean dance? No, I've seen people dance—they were the other part of Mrs. Whittacker's lessons, but I never got to that part."

"Then I'll teach you." He took her hands in his.

She tried to pull back. "No, I don't know how." She looked around, embarrassed.

There were, as usual at the time they took their walks, no sailors on the main deck. He could see a couple of them at work in the riggings, dark silhouettes against the evening sky and several more going about their tasks on the fo'c's'le and the poop deck. The ship would sail on the evening tide and soon there would be sailors everywhere, but for now . . .

"There's nobody to see you," he assured her. "Now, like this—one-two-three, one-two-three, one-two-three . . ." She stumbled a little at first, but Rafe was an excellent dancer with many years of practice—he'd served on Wellington's staff and the Beau was known for his fondness for balls—and she soon picked up the steps.

She was very light on her feet and followed his guidance almost instinctively. He watched as slowly her expression changed from scowling concentration to an I-think-I-can-do-this expression, and finally she looked up and gave him a dazzling smile. "I'm dancing," she exclaimed. "I'm dancing and it's wonderf—oops!" She trod on his foot, and laughing, returned to intent concentration.

He didn't think he could ever tire of watching her. The guarded expression she'd worn when he first met her had mostly disappeared. It came back whenever they were talking about her past—there was something dark and disturbing that she was hiding—but the rest of the time . . . she was breathtaking.

They whirled around and around the deck until the song finished and they were both breathless.

He released her and bowed, panting. "I must be getting old," he joked. "I'm blowing like a fish. Time was I could ride all day, dance the night away, then ride all the next day."

"It's the fever," she told him seriously. "You're only just off your sickbed; you mustn't overdo things. Fever can come back."

He listened for the next tune. It was something he didn't recognize. "Then, shall we sit this one out, my lady?" They returned to the rail.

"When were you talking about?" she asked. "Riding all day and dancing all night."

"The army. Anyone on the Peer's staff is—or soon learns to be—an accomplished dancer."

"The Peer? Do you mean your father?"

The question surprised a crack of laughter out of him. "Good Lord, no, I wouldn't know what sort of a dancer my father is. I can't imagine him stooping to anything so human. The Peer is what we called Wellington when they made him a lord. That or the Beau. To his face, of course, we called him sir or my lord."

"You mean you danced in the war? When you were a soldier?"

He laughed at her expression. "You can't fight all the time, and you'd be surprised how much more can be achieved at a ball instead of in a meeting. Some of our most important supporters were first introduced to the Beau at a ball. Their wives dragged them—they would never have come to a meeting."

"I see. I knew you'd done a lot of fighting, I hadn't thought about anything else. I suppose the dancing is where diplomacy comes in."

"That's right. But Egypt was involved in the war as well. Were your parents much affected by Napoleon's occupation?"

She shook her head. "I don't know. I was too small, and Papa never talked about it."

"I'm surprised he stayed. With a wife and daughter . . ."

She shrugged. "Tell me about your own father. Would he really not dance?"

"I hardly knew him at all. He handed me a pair of colors the day I got home from school and—"

"Colors?"

"It means he'd purchased me a commission in the army."

"The day you got home from school?" She gave him a troubled look.

He shrugged. "It's common for younger sons to join the church, the diplomatic corps, or the army."

"And you chose the army?"

He hesitated. He hadn't actually been consulted. It had, in fact, come as quite a shock to be told to leave the very day he'd come home.

But as it turned out, he'd been happier in the army than he'd ever been at Axebridge. He'd liked being a soldier. He enjoyed having a clear purpose, a role that mattered, and he was good at it: good at fighting, good at organizing, and good at leading men, he'd been surprised to discover. The army had become his home.

And since his four closest friends had also followed him into the army, it had cemented his schoolboy friendships into a kind of family—one that would last a lifetime.

"Yes, the army suited me," he told her. "Now unless I'm mistaken, that's another waltz. I think we have time for just one more dance before you should go down to change."

"No," she said, sounding troubled. "I think we have danced enough."

*H*ow strange to be thinking about Mrs. Whittacker at a time, at a place, like this, Ayisha thought that night. She lay awake on her side of the bed, waiting for the deep, even breathing that told her Rafe had fallen asleep. After that she could sleep, too.

It wasn't as if she didn't trust him; he was a man of his word, and as he'd promised, he'd made no move to seduce her.

Not in bed, that was.

There was a small matter of a kiss. And a dance.

The waltz was a small kind of possession, letting her be taken where he willed, dominated by him and the music. A foretaste . . .

She closed her eyes, reliving the dance. Once she'd got the hang of the steps, she'd let herself go, and oh, the feeling of circling in his arms, twirling in dizzy pleasure, giving herself up to the music, to his strong arms, his powerful body . . .

It made her wonder about the ultimate possession between a man and a woman . . .

It wasn't him she didn't trust. She was entirely too attracted to the man.

The memory of Mrs. Whittacker had come at a good time.

Ayisha needed reminding. She'd been seduced by more than just a kiss and a dance. It was the whole vision of her and Rafe married. Being with him for the rest of her life. Sleeping in the same bed, able to touch him as she wanted and be touched . . . To kiss him whenever she wanted, as long and as deep as she dreamed . . . To be able to open her heart to him and have him open his to her, sharing hopes, dreams, and troubles. And maybe, if they were blessed, having children with him. Making a home together, and a family. A family of her own.

That was the real seduction.

Remembering Mrs. Whittacker was like getting a bucket of cold water thrown in her face.

His promise, his offer of marriage, was for Alicia Cleeve.

Mrs. Whittacker had taught Ayisha the lesson of her life when she was nine years old. And it wasn't music.

She'd been going to lessons with Mrs. Whittacker for a year. Papa would walk her there each week and pick her up afterward. Ayisha loved her lessons and loved those walks with him. They were almost the only time she ever had Papa to herself.

Mrs. Whittacker always offered her and Papa tea afterward. She always had delicious things to eat: tiny iced cakes, ratafia biscuits, macaroons, and proper English tea.

Mrs. Whittacker called her Alice, Alice dear, or sweet Alice—never Ayisha. Papa had said she wasn't to mind and to answer to whatever Mrs. Whittacker called her.

Each month, Mrs. Whittacker put on what she called a *soirée musicale*, only it was in the afternoon. Ayisha had never been to one, but she knew all about it. Her best pupils and their parents were invited, and the pupils put on a small concert. The most exciting part of the concert was the duet section.

Each month two specially chosen pupils were given a duet part to learn. It was only at the concert they heard how the final piece sounded, as they sat down at the keyboard with another pupil and each played their part.

Ayisha still remembered the excitement she felt when finally she was invited to attend the *soirée* and was given the honor of a part to learn. How she'd practiced, knowing at the end of the month she would perform—her first concert, and in a coveted duet.

And then the first blow, that Papa and Mama were going to Jerusalem, so Papa couldn't attend the concert. Mama never went to that sort of thing—she was shy in company, because of her scarred cheek. Ayisha had always accepted it—until now.

"There will be other concerts, my dear," Papa had said. He and Mama were very excited about their trip.

The second blow came when Papa said she wasn't to go to lessons at all while he was away.

In retrospect Ayisha realized Papa had known what he was doing. At the time she thought her life had been blighted, that she'd never again be invited to one of Mrs. Whittacker's *soirées musicales*, let alone perform a duet . . .

She was right, but not for the reasons her nine-year-old self had imagined.

Her parents left for Jerusalem, but when the time for her weekly music lesson came, Ayisha had persuaded one of the servants to escort her. Not Ratibe, who usually looked after her, nor Yiorgi, who was left in charge of the household—either of those might have known of her father's edict—but Minna, the youngest of the servants, who was silly and frivolous and fun.

Ayisha had never disobeyed her father before. Mrs. Whittacker was surprised at Papa's absence, but the lesson continued, though there was no tea afterward.

The following week Mrs. Whittacker had asked her about Mama, question after question. She'd never questioned Ayisha before about anything. Then she'd cut the lesson short, claiming headache. Ayisha hadn't thought anything of it at the time.

The day of the concert came and she'd dressed in her best clothes. She came in with a group of other people.

"Sit there and don't move," Mrs. Whittacker told her, pointing to a seat in the corner.

Ayisha had waited, excited, nervous . . . She watched as the other pupils and their parents arrived and smiled at the pupils, wondering who her partner in the duet would be. She didn't know many other children. She watched them from her chair, wondering if any of them would become a friend. She dearly wanted a friend of her own age.

The concert started. Ayisha listened, watched, and waited.

Intermission. Everyone drank tea or lemonade and ate cakes. Ayisha got up to get a drink—being nervous was thirsty business—but Mrs. Whittacker hissed at her, "I told you to sit down," and she sat.

Nobody came to speak to her. Nobody said a word to her. But

there was whispering, and people were sneaking glances at her as they talked. What had she done wrong?

The second part of the concert drew to a close; there was only one more item: the duet. A girl with long golden ringlets stood, smoothing her pink dress nervously. Ayisha stood.

"I'm sorry, Susan, dear, your partner in the duet isn't here," Mrs. Whittacker said. "The concert is over."

"But—" Ayisha began.

"Ayisha, go and wait in the kitchen," Mrs. Whittacker snapped. "You other children may adjourn to the dining room where the refreshments are being served."

Distressed and bewildered Ayisha went to the kitchen, where Minna was waiting. The other servants stared at her. Nobody spoke to her.

Sometime later a servant came in and said to Minna, "Mistress says you're to take that girl home, now."

"I just need to fetch my music bag," Ayisha said, battling tears, and ran back to the drawing room to fetch it.

There were several children in the hall, including the girl, Susan, who from the look of her eyes had been crying. Ayisha went up to her to comfort her—she, too, had been deprived of the moment of glory for which she'd practiced so hard.

"Oooh! Get away, you filthy thing!" Susan exclaimed. "Don't you dare touch me."

Ayisha recalled looking down at her dress, thinking she must have dirtied it unknowingly in the kitchen. But it was as crisp and pristine as when she'd put it on. She tried again.

"Go away!" Susan had shrilled. "We're not allowed to talk to you. You're not even supposed to *be* here!"

On the verge of tears, Ayisha pushed open the door of the drawing room and heard someone say, "Who did you say she was?"

And Mrs. Whittacker replied, "She's Henry Cleeve's bastard, his filthy little by-blow—and by a slave woman, no less. I was never so deceived in all my life."

Ayisha didn't even know what bastard and by-blow meant, but she knew from the way she spoke Mrs. Whittacker hated her. And so did everyone else.

Filthy little by-blow—it sounded like a blowfly, who laid eggs in rotting food and produced maggots.

Ayisha didn't even remember how she'd got home. She supposed Minna had found her and taken her away.

Much later she'd learned what it all meant, that they all thought she was her half sister, Alicia, who had died. Papa had known it but had thought his presence would prevent it coming out.

It was a lesson she'd never forgotten: the music, the concert, the friendship—even the cakes had been intended for Alicia Cleeve, not Ayisha. Nothing was for Ayisha.

The offer of marriage from the man lying next to her on the bed was also for Alicia Cleeve, the daughter of a baronet and a lady.

Oh, he wanted Ayisha, she knew that, and he might even come to love her. Papa had loved Mama—she was his whole world.

But in Rafe's world—the real world—the son of a gentleman would never marry the illegitimate daughter of a slave—not knowingly. Not unless she tricked him.

But if she stayed with him, if she gave in to him, he would make her his mistress—perhaps his beloved mistress. And her sons would be bastards.

But no child of hers was ever going to hear anyone say, "He's Rafe Ramsey's bastard, his filthy little by-blow . . ."

There was always the offer of the captain to marry them then and there. The Reverend Payne had also offered to marry them according to the rites of the Church of England.

But she would not trick him into marrying her. He would come to hate her for it, she was sure, and that would be unbearable. She would rather live without him than live with him, despised as a liar. Or as a millstone around his neck.

So she was going to have to tell him. And soon, or he'd be angry for having made a fool of himself over and over, offering to marry her, based on a false assumption.

She turned over in the bed and watched him sleeping, the broad chest rising and falling.

How was she going to share a bed with a man who knew she'd made a fool of him? What if he was furious? It was a very small cabin. She had no fear he'd hurt her physically, but it would be most uncomfortable to have to keep sharing a space so intimately with a man who despised you.

Or a man who was bent on making her his mistress.

She'd wait, she decided, until she was released from quarantine. Then she'd tell him the truth. And until then, she'd keep him at arm's length. No more waltzing on the deck in the moonlight.

*T*he following evening they were taking their customary evening stroll around the deck when a sailor shouted, "Sir, miss," running toward them. "Capt'n's orders, you're to go to your quarters immediately and lock yourselves in." Behind him the decks erupted with action, sailors racing everywhere, hoisting extra canvas—and rolling out the big guns.

"What's going on?" Rafe asked.

The man jerked his head to the south. "Pirates, sir, coming up fast behind us. Now please, get below and lock yourselves in. It's going to be nasty."

Ayisha scooped up Cleo. Rafe took her arm and they hurried below.

While Ayisha put the kitten in her basket, he checked his pistols quickly. He turned to Ayisha. "Have you ever used a pistol?"

"No, but I can learn." White-faced but outwardly calm, she held out her hand to take a pistol.

"Good. The pistols are loaded. You just cock the hammer—carefully—pull it all the way back—like this . . ." He demonstrated on one pistol and she imitated him on the other. "Yes, that's it. And then you point it at a man's chest and squeeze the trigger. And don't hesitate to kill; a wounded man can still fight on. Right?"

She nodded. She looked scared to death, but her jaw was set. She was magnificent.

"Good." He replaced his pistol in the case, threw open his trunk, and drew out the sword of Damascus steel. "Now, lock yourself in. I'm going up to fight pirates."

She caught his arm. "But you're too weak to fight with a sword—you're barely over the fever. Take the pistols."

"No, you keep them. I'll be fine—I'm a soldier, remember?"

"Then wait, I'll come, too!"

"No." He wrapped an arm around her and gave her a hard, possessive kiss. "It's too dangerous. Stay in the cabin." He went, slamming the door shut behind him. "Bolt it," he yelled and ran toward the companionway.

Sixteen

Ayisha stared at the closed door. Bolt the door? Hide in the cabin? Wait and see what happened?

She leaned out of the porthole. The big pirate vessel was bearing down on them fast. Pirates swarmed all over it, hanging from the riggings, lining the gunwales.

She shivered. But she couldn't, she wouldn't just *wait*. Not while Rafe was on deck fighting for his life—for both their lives—all their lives.

Once pirates took over the ship, she and everybody else on board were done for. Rape, slavery, or murder.

She hadn't spent the last six years fighting for survival on the streets of Cairo only to wait tamely for pirates to come and get her.

She looked at the two pistols. Two shots. She didn't know how many pirates there were, but two shots could surely make a difference.

Boom! An explosion reverberated through the ship. *Boom! Boom!* The captain was firing at the pirates. The ship shuddered and shook with each explosion.

The pirates came on, undaunted. *Boom!* They returned fire.

But in minutes they were too close for either ship to fire cannons. She heard shouts overhead. The pirates were boarding.

Terror momentarily froze her. She wanted to dive under the bed and hide from the danger, as she had when she was a child. But hiding was not an option.

She tied a shawl around her waist and jammed the two loaded pistols in the waistband. It would have been easier in her boy's clothes, but she didn't want to be mistaken for a pirate in them, so her dress had to stay. She fetched her knife from her luggage and jammed that in the shawl, too, then headed for the deck.

"Where are you going?" a voice shrilled. It was Mrs. Ferris, peering out of her door. "We're supposed to stay in our cabins."

"And wait until it's too late to do anything?" Ayisha told her as she hurried past. "Not me. I'd rather go down fighting."

Or would she? At the top of the steps the sight made her recoil in horror.

Pirates were swarming onto the ship, boiling onto the deck in a savage, screaming horde. The ship's crew, Rafe, Higgins, and the soldiers were fighting desperately, with pistols, guns, swords, knives, belaying pins, and long hooks. The air was thick with smoke, gunpowder, shooting, yelling, and the clashing of swords.

She froze, too frightened to move, horrified by the sight before her but terrified to look away.

Rafe was fighting a big, black-whiskered brute, his elegant sword clashing fearsomely against the huge curved blade of the pirate. The pirate swore and snarled, both hands slashing at Rafe, sword in left hand, long-bladed knife in the other.

Rafe looked cool and strangely calm, his sword flashing, his blue eyes blazing. She'd seen that cold blue blaze demolish a gang of thugs, but armed pirates? She winced as the pirate's knife slashed through Rafe's shirt. Was he hurt? The pirate shouted and suddenly another villain came at Rafe from behind.

Without thought, Ayisha pulled out a pistol, cocked it, aimed, and fired. The pirate lurched, staggered a few steps, and collapsed on the deck. A pool of bright red blood spread from beneath him, but she had no time to dwell on it; a third pirate was hurtling toward Rafe. She fired, and that one was down, too.

Her pistols were empty. She looked around desperately for another weapon, feeling sick and helpless and terrified. Rafe was hard-pressed, fighting with savage efficiency, Higgins a couple of yards away. It was every man for himself—and still the pirates kept coming.

From the corner of an eye she saw a pair of grimy knuckles appear on the gunwale. A pirate climbing aboard? She darted forward and, holding the pistol barrels, she smashed the pistol butts down on the knuckles, as hard as she could. There was a yell and a splash.

Thank God. The pistols were still a useful weapon. She could do this. No one seemed to be taking notice of her. She darted back and forth along the side of the ship, smashing pistol butts down hard on knuckles, hands, and heads whenever they appeared over the side of the ship.

"Ayisha, duck!" She ducked automatically as—*swish!*—a blade missed her by inches. The owner of the blade snarled something at her, grinning through blackened teeth—then stiffened and arched. Blood gurgled out of his mouth.

It was Rafe, hauling his sword from the man's side and shoving him away with his boot. "What the hell are you doing on deck?" he yelled at her. "Get back to the cabin!" He turned to parry another attack.

But there was another head rising over the gunwale, so she smashed down as hard as she could. The head dropped from sight. Judging from the yells that followed he'd landed on others.

"Get below, Ayisha, dammit!" Rafe shouted. "Go!"

"Behind you!" she shrieked, and he whirled as two pirates came at him in a rush. At the same time, a skinny bald man with a gold earring jumped on Rafe's back, locking an arm around Rafe's throat, choking him. The pirate's other arm rose and Ayisha saw the silhouette of a slender, curved blade about to descend.

"No!" Yelling like a banshee, she leapt up and stabbed Gold Earring in the neck. He screamed and the curved blade clattered onto the deck. Blood gushed all over her hands and soaked Rafe's shirt as she pulled the dying man off Rafe's back.

Rafe, free of the man's weight, slashed a cutting blow at one of his attackers and kicked the feet out from under the other. The man tried to rise groggily from the deck. Ayisha used her pistol's butt and whacked him over the head.

"Good work!" Rafe told her, panting as he parried a thrust from the other. "Now, get the hell below."

"When you do," Ayisha yelled back and returned to bashing pirates. She whacked heads with eye patches, head scarfs, ringlets, and skull caps, hands with five fingers and fewer, knuckles with an assortment of tattoos and rings.

Rafe positioned himself behind her protectively, yelling at her whenever he had a moment, "Get below, you little fool!"

She took no notice; her tactics were working. With him keeping her from attack from behind, she was able to whack any pirate trying to climb aboard.

"Take that, you beast!" she heard a genteel voice on her left shriek.

Ayisha almost dropped her pistols when she saw Mrs. Ferris thump a pirate over the head with a large mallet. She'd positioned herself a short distance from Ayisha and was imitating her, repelling the boarders by bashing at hands and heads.

Ayisha had no time to call out encouragement—pirates were everywhere and she barely had time to breathe. She bashed and smashed at hands and knuckles, thumped heads, and occasionally slashed at the more persistent holders-on with her knife.

It seemed to go on forever. Ayisha could hardly hear Rafe's voice, there was so much other yelling, screaming, gunfire, and clashing of swords all around her. But she could feel him there, and hear him fighting, and whenever she had a second, she turned to check he was still standing.

God knew what she would do if he fell. She would protect him somehow, she vowed. If only he weren't still weak from the fever.

Soon she could hardly see, her eyes watered so much from the smoke, but she focused determinedly on the side of the ship, defending her six feet with every shred of energy at her disposal, knowing that Rafe was at her back, still standing, and—amazingly—Mrs. Ferris was by her side.

The number of heads and hands appearing slowed, and then suddenly there was the sound of a horn coming from the pirate ship. What did it mean? She looked around, reeling with exhaustion, to see what the next horror was to be.

But instead of the new tactics she feared, the pirates scrambled to leave the ship. They jumped, they dived into the water, they swung from ropes and dropped onto their own decks.

Ayisha watched them go with a dazed feeling of disbelief. Was this some new tactic, or were they truly leaving?

Where was Rafe? Ayisha turned to look. Sailors were tossing any remaining pirates overboard to be picked up by their comrades, or left to sink—and there was Rafe, filthy and blood-soaked, but standing tall and strong as he seized a dazed pirate and hurled him effortlessly overboard. He grabbed another and another and tossed them in the sea.

Thank God! Relief and joy filled her. Despite his bloody shirt he was all right. The way he was tossing pirates, he'd come through it unscathed. They'd both survived, thank God.

"We did it—we beat them!" Mrs. Ferris exclaimed beside her. Ayisha turned and stared. Mrs. Ferris was filthy and blood-spattered—and beaming from ear to ear. "We beat them off! I've never been so terrified in my life!" And the woman embraced her, laughing and crying at the same time.

At that moment a ragged cheer went up from the ship's company. The pirate ship was sailing away. Sailors crowded along the gunwales, shouting and jeering, jubilant in victory. It was infectious; even Mrs. Ferris cheered, though in a genteel, hip-hip-hoorah manner.

Relief and exhilaration bubbled through Ayisha, and she joined in the chorus with that most eastern sound of female triumph and celebration: a high-pitched, trilling ululation.

"That's enough!" Rafe cut off the sound abruptly by slinging her over his shoulder and marching toward the hatch that led to the companionway.

"What's wrong? We beat them, we won!" She squirmed to get down. "We beat them off!" All along the gunwales people were hugging each other and shouting after the pirates. The noise was deafening.

"Did you see Mrs. Ferris? Isn't it amazing that she came up on deck and fought? I wonder what came over her?"

Rafe made a sort of growling sound. Keeping her clamped over his shoulder, he shoved his way through the mass of people crowding to the rail to watch the pirates retreating.

And then she saw the carnage, the bloody decks, the wounded men being carried below, and the joy drained out of her. Bodies were being laid neatly in a quiet corner of the deck. She tried to count them, but they'd reached the hatch and he was climbing down the stairs and she couldn't see anymore.

He opened the cabin door, which was unlocked, kicked it shut behind him, dumped her on her feet, slammed the bolt shut, and turned on her. His blood-smeared, smoke-begrimed face was grim, his blue eyes burning with icy fire.

"I told you to stay in here!" His voice was low, but it throbbed.

"But we won!" She stared at him in surprise.

"I *ordered* you!" he grated. "And you disobeyed."

She stared at him in disbelief. How could he carp about orders when they'd just survived a pirate attack? "I told you before, I don't take orders from you. I'm not in your army—and neither are you, anym—"

He grabbed her shoulders and gripped hard. "You little fool, you could have been killed!"

She pushed him away, annoyed by his tone. "So could you. And you—" She poked him in the chest. "You're barely off a sickbed and in no state to fight!"

"I did all right," he growled.

"And so did I. We just beat off a horde of vicious pirates." She couldn't help but smile. She hadn't stayed cowering in here—she'd been terrified, but she'd gone out there and fought. And she'd made a difference. And so had Mrs. Ferris.

His frown grew blacker. "Will you stop grinning!"

She considered it briefly. "I don't think I can," she told him. "I know people have been killed and I feel terrible about them, but when you think you're going to die—and you don't—doesn't that make you want to smile?"

"No." His fists clenched. "I'd rather spank you for disobeying instructions."

"Pooh!" she said. "If you tried, I would whack you over the head with my trusty pistols." She pulled them from her waistband and, holding them by the muzzles, held them up in a playfully threatening gesture.

He snatched them from her and flung them into the corner. "Don't be so bloody flippant! You were supposed to use them to defend yourself!"

"I'm not being flippant and I did defend myself—and you." She turned on him, suddenly blazingly angry. "It made no sense for me to stay down here, shaking in my shoes, a ready-made victim, waiting to see who came through that door next—you, or a bunch of pirates bent on rape and slavery, or murder!"

"But—"

"What was I supposed to do? Shoot two pirates, then fight off the rest bare-handed? Or shoot one pirate and use the other shot for me? No—if I'm going to be taken by pirates, I'll do it in the open air, fighting them to my last breath. And taking as many of them with me as I can." She was shaking by the time she finished speaking.

There was a short silence, then he said hoarsely, "Have you any idea what it did to me seeing you up there on a deck swarming with pirates?"

She met his gaze square on. "Probably much the same as it felt for me to see you beating off three or four men at a time—when only yesterday you were exhausted after only six circuits around the deck!"

He closed his eyes briefly, opened them, and through a clenched jaw said, "This is not about me! I'm a soldier! I can fight with my eyes closed. You're a woman!"

"You're not a soldier anymore, and you've been sick and in my charge for most of the last week. Now, that shirt is saturated with blood—is any of it yours?"

He fended her off with an angry gesture. "A couple of minor scratches. Dammit, woman, look to yourself! You're covered in blood!"

She shook her head. "Pirate blood, not mine."

"In the heat of battle, people don't always realize they've been hurt."

"Oh. Well then, let me check you—"

"I don't need a bloody nursemaid!" he roared.

"Don't be silly, I just want to check if you're hurt!" She moved closer.

He stepped back. "Don't come near me!" His voice vibrated with fury. "I'm in no fit state to be touched."

"I've seen you—I've *touched* you in far worse states than this!" She grabbed his shirt.

He wrenched himself away. There was a loud rip.

Through the rent she could see a thin red line. "You *have* been hurt."

He made an impatient gesture. "It's just a scratch. Look to yourself—are you injured in any way?"

She ignored him. "Even a scratch needs tending, and I need to see all of you to be sure."

He glared at her. "You're determined to fuss over me, aren't you?"

"Call it what you will," she said. "People have been trying to kill you for the last hour and you just told me people don't always know they've been hurt. So."

"I was talking about *you*, blast it!"

She didn't respond, just met his gaze evenly.

"God, you're a stubborn woman!" Without warning he ripped his shirt off, balled it up, and hurled it out of the porthole. "See?" he stormed. "Nothing serious. Now what about you? Are you nursing any wounds under that filthy, bloody, ruined rag that used to be your favorite dress?" He grabbed the bloodiest part of her dress and yanked. The whole top of the dress ripped open.

There was a sudden, shocked silence.

She stepped back. They stared at each other for a long moment, motionless, panting.

Slowly she turned away and let the remains of her dress and her torn, bloodstained chemise pool around her feet. She stepped out of the ruined garments, scooped them up, and stalked to the porthole in nothing but her baggy Turkish knee-length drawers. She flung the dress and chemise out and turned to face him, shaking, her arms folded across her breasts. "No wounds—satisfied?"

He swallowed, then wiped his hands across his face. "God, Ayisha, when I saw you step out onto that deck . . . I was never so frightened in all my life." His voice was hoarse.

"I thought we were both going to die," she told him in a voice that had taken on a distinct wobble. "And I couldn't bear the thought that we'd never done this!" And she launched herself at his chest.

She flung herself at him, twining her arms around his neck and wrapping her legs around his waist.

His arms caught her, snapping around her like bands of steel as he stumbled against the bed and fell backward onto it.

And then he was kissing her, blindly, desperately, and she was kissing him back in a mindless, wild frenzy.

Anger, passion, fear, and relief swamped her in huge contradictory waves. She couldn't get close enough, she wanted to climb inside his chest, to hold him, to block out the dazzling, terrifying sight of him surrounded by evil predators, his sword flashing, his eyes blazing ice blue and burning.

She plastered wild kisses all over him, on his face, his mouth, his eyelids, tasting the roughness of his jaw, the bunched muscles of his shoulder—anywhere she could. Kissing, tasting, healing. Making him safe, giving him everything she had to give: herself.

No matter what, no matter who.

She'd been a whisper away from death; she could still feel the wind of the sword slicing a hairsbreadth above the nape of her neck—but she was alive, alive and in the arms of a man who made her feel more alive than she'd ever felt in her life.

She brushed against his groin and felt the rampant, burning hardness of him beneath the buckskin breeches.

At her touch, a powerful shudder racked the big body beneath her. He groaned and the sound fed the wild exultation bubbling through her.

His big hands came over hers and stilled her fevered movements. His breath came hot and hard, his broad, strong chest heaved with exertion.

His blue eyes pierced her with intensity. "Are you sure of this, Ayisha? Because if you say yes, there's no going back."

"Yes!" She bent and kissed him. "I want you. I want this. And I want it now." She didn't know what "this" was, but a powerful force deep within her drove her on.

She was alive, *alive*, and she needed him, craved him. Her body knew it, was throbbing, aching, guided by an instinct as old as time. And she trusted her instincts.

"Then if you're sure . . ." he said, his voice deep and gravelly. Slowly his gaze dropped to her naked breasts, just inches above him.

She felt her cheeks flood with heat. She'd forgotten her nakedness while she was pressed against him. She'd never been bared to a man's gaze before, and his frank stare filled her with a mixture of shyness and pride.

"Beautiful," he breathed. "Like cream of moonlight. Such a crime to keep them bound all these years."

He lifted his face and kissed her on each breast and the feeling of his hot mouth on the cool, tender skin . . . If she died now . . .

But she wasn't going to die, and he was alive, and oh . . . his rough-textured jaw against the softness of her breasts . . .

He teased her halfway to madness, brushing his mouth over her breasts in fiery gossamer drifts, holding her above him so she could not move, could not plunge on top of him and taste him, touch him in return as she longed to.

His mouth, his tongue, his jaw caressed her until her every nerve was aflame.

Finally his hold shifted. He cupped her face in his hands and brought her mouth down to his, deliberately . . . so slowly she was shaking with anticipation by the time their lips touched.

She kissed him back, feverishly, desperately, clumsily, not knowing what to do, wanting to drive him to aching madness as he had driven her.

She knew what came next. Her hands shook as she reached the front flap of his breeches, but it was haste, not nervousness.

Well, just a bit of nervousness.

She knew his body intimately. After bathing it so many times in the last week, there could be no surprises.

But what he did with his mouth . . . scrambled every bit of . . . sense . . . but she wanted . . . needed . . .

He pressed his hand over hers, stopping her undoing the breeches, pressing her palm down over that heavy, hot thickness beneath. "Slow down, little cat," he groaned.

She stared at him, panting. "I don't want to slow down." He didn't move, so she bent and bit him lightly on the shoulder.

He laughed. "Little wildcat," he said and rolled over on the bed so she was beneath him.

"Trust me," he told her. "It will be better slow."

"Better for whom?" she growled in frustration.

"For you." He smiled and the gleam in his eye deepened. "And therefore for me."

He kissed her again, deeply, his tongue like hot velvet, mating with hers, stroking with insistent rhythm until she was weak with wanting, then trailing slow kisses along her jaw, down her neck, until he reached her breasts.

"Wild strawberries," he murmured, tasting her nipple. He bit lightly on it, caressing the tip with his tongue, sucking, biting softly, caressing the tip with teeth and tongue, and all the time she arched helplessly beneath him as spears of rhythmic pleasure pierced her.

His big, warm hands moved with rough-skinned tenderness all over her, cupping, squeezing, stroking. He seemed to know exactly what to do to bring her to the brink of ecstasy. Ayisha wanted to do the same to him, but she couldn't think, couldn't even move, except to shudder and writhe in helpless pleasure.

She shivered as he cupped the soft mound at the apex of her thighs, caressing her through the cotton of her Turkish drawers.

From a long way away she heard, "Do you care about these things?"

"Things?" Her eyes flew open and the world came back a little, rippling dreamily. She could hear herself panting. He was panting, too, his eyes glazed-looking and intense.

What had he just said?

He tugged at the drawstrings. "I can't get them undone."

She stared at his mouth and forgot to answer. His beautiful, masculine mouth . . . and what he did with it . . .

Then he muttered, "Don't worry, I'll rip 'em off."

"No, I'll do it," she said, her wits scrambling back. Her fingers flew to untie the drawstring. She started to push them down over her hips, but again his hands closed over hers and drew them away.

"My job," he said softly and kissed her long and slowly on the mouth, and she melted again.

As he kissed her, his hand caressed the softness of her stomach and slowly pushed the drawers down, over her stomach, over her hips, and then she was kicking her feet out of them, and his hand was cupping her, massaging her softly while his mouth tenderly ravaged her breasts.

The hands that could seize a pirate and fling him across the deck caressed her with such delicacy she felt like weeping.

He parted her and one long finger stroked her lightly, circling and circling. Her world closed to just that one point, where his finger joined with her and she pulsated around it. And then he pressed and she jerked almost off the bed as a shaft of pure lightning shot through her.

She lay panting as her shattered awareness slowly came back to her. Her eyes fluttered open. He lay beside her on the bed, his eyes scrunched closed, looking as if he was in pain.

She didn't know what he'd done, but she knew what he hadn't done. Now, finally she would have her way. In seconds she'd unfastened the flap of his breeches, loosened the drawstrings of his drawers, and was tugging them down over his long, hard thighs.

She stared. What had she thought? No surprises here? How wrong she'd been. How had it got so much bigger? And darker. And thicker. And longer.

But she'd handled his body so often during the fever she shouldn't feel shy about touching him. She hesitated. He'd been asleep then and the touching had been for medicinal purposes only.

She stared at his heavily aroused manhood and decided perhaps she was a little bit shy, after all. She glanced at him to see what he was thinking. He lay there, watching, his eyes gleaming, waiting for her to make the first move.

She reached out and touched him tentatively. It was hot, the skin like tight velvet. With one finger she stroked it slowly to the tip and back. It tightened and grew and a small bead of moisture appeared at the engorged tip.

He moaned and his body arched as if in pain. But it hadn't hurt, she could tell by the glint in his eyes. She was doing to him what he'd been doing to her.

She smiled and a ripple of feminine power flowed through her. Her big warrior had trembled at her lightest touch. He watched her, the burning eyes glittering under the sleepy-looking lids, like a lion getting ready to pounce.

She ran her fingers down the length of him again and he flung his head back, his teeth clenched, and moaned, his heels digging into the bed.

"Cats always play with their captives," he said through gritted teeth after the long shudder had passed.

She smiled. If he didn't like it, he had only to move away. Or tell her to stop. But he didn't. She touched the tip and his powerful body arched and shuddered under the light touch. His thigh muscles were braced and corded, his hard stomach tense, his fists clenching the bedclothes as if he was on a rack of torture.

Wondering what would happen if she grasped him with her whole hand, she gently closed her fingers. Then squeezed lightly.

"Enough," he groaned, suddenly surging up and over her. His weight bore her down on the bed, and he settled himself between her thighs. Without thought her thighs closed around him.

Yes, this was what she'd been craving. She hadn't realized it until now.

He kissed her fiercely, possessively, and she kissed him back frenziedly, feeling the heated bluntness pushing rhythmically at her entrance. She knew what to expect. She'd heard people talk. She shifted, trying to accommodate him, but it was pushing into her, stretching her, tight, tighter.

His hand slipped between them and he stroked her over and over as he had before, and she shivered and felt herself soften.

He pushed again and—

"Aghh!" She couldn't help the sudden, surprised yell—it had hurt more than she'd expected.

"What the d—"

"It's all right," she said, grabbing his head and kissing him hard, at the same time moving her lower body inexpertly, her body throbbing, moving in time with his.

He groaned and gathering her to him, ravaging her mouth tenderly. At the same time he began to move inside her, slowly at first and then faster and faster.

It was uncomfortable at first, but slowly her body adjusted and she moved with him, and she forgot the pain as the addictive tension built and built. A rhythm took over her body, pounding through her, the two of them moving as one, moving faster, faster, spiraling higher, higher, higher . . .

Her body moved of its own accord, she was lost, mindless, about to explode, to splinter apart . . . All she could do was give herself up to it, to let it take her, sweep her away like the flooding of the Nile. Embracing him with every part of her, shattering together . . .

Seventeen

*R*afe opened his eyes to the melancholy half-light that comes just before dawn. It was the time when hope ebbed its lowest, when dying men gave up the struggle and slipped away.

Rafe was immune to it. Yesterday, last night, his life had changed forever.

Ayisha lay curled against him, her limbs entwined with his, and as always, her palm resting over his heart.

It never failed to move him, the care she showed him, even in sleep.

If he lived to be a hundred, he'd never forget the sight of her stepping out on deck, stepping into mortal danger, raising his pistols and defending him.

Defending him.

A girl of nineteen defending a veteran soldier. It humbled him, utterly. He felt a thickness in his chest as he gazed at her. She was so brave, so . . . precious.

Carefully he moved, so as not to disturb her, raising himself on one elbow, the better to look at her. Her short dark hair clustered spikily around her face. His sleeping beauty.

It was a cool morning and one thin shoulder poked out from

beneath the covers. The urge to bend and kiss it rose up in him, the desire to wake her softly, with kisses, but there were faint lavender shadows beneath the dark crescents of her lashes. She was worn out, his little warrior, after all that had happened. He wouldn't disturb her. He gently tugged the blanket up to cover her.

In sleep she looked so small and defenseless, but Lord, the raw, practical courage of her. She'd killed three men yesterday and beaten off who knew how many.

He thought of the way she'd responded to him, affirming life with a passion that burned.

And yet she'd been a virgin.

So what was *Alicia Cleeve is dead; here, there is only Ayisha* about?

He'd thought it meant she'd been raped. It took some people that way; the only way they could survive some terrible event was to become someone different, leave that person behind, take a new name, make a new life.

It wasn't rape, thank God. But what?

It didn't matter. She was full of secrets, but he didn't care. She'd given herself to him last night, and she was his now to care for and protect, and he had every intention of changing her name again—to his. A new life was ahead of them both.

A plaintive yowling from the box told him that a certain kitten felt it had been neglected far too long. He slipped out of bed and let her out. A brief butt of the head against his hand and she stalked to her sand tray while Rafe slid back into bed, careful not to disturb Ayisha.

Cleo inspected her empty food dish with an air of disapproval, drank from her water dish, then clawed her way up the bedclothes and onto the bed—she was still too small to jump that high. There she proceeded to sit on his stomach and wash herself daintily from top to toe.

Once her toilette was complete, she moved to his chest, butted him on the chin, and eyed him expectantly. He didn't move, so she batted him on the chin with a soft paw and mrrrowed at him. Beside him Ayisha stirred.

Rafe narrowed his eyes at the kitten. "Hush, that's blackmail," he told her in a whisper.

She narrowed her eyes right back at him, but in a seductive manner, and mrrrowed again.

"Quiet, I said," he whispered. "Your mistress is sleeping."

He scratched Cleo behind the ears and was rewarded with a rattly little kitten purr. The purring continued. Rafe drifted slowly back to sleep, the kitten curled on his chest.

A yisha woke to a kitten purring in her ear. Her eyes fluttered open, and there was Cleo curled on Rafe's chest. She blinked. What was the kitten doing there? She always slept in her basket.

"I told you not to make such a racket," Rafe's deep voice rumbled softly.

Ayisha, confused, rubbed her eyes.

He continued, "See? You've woken her up and that means banishment for such a heinous crime. Off you go." He scooped the kitten up and set her gently on the floor.

She smiled sleepily at the sight of him talking so earnestly to the tiny creature.

"That smile's a sight for sore eyes," Rafe said. "Good morning, sweetheart." He leaned over and kissed her, a long, leisurely, possessive kiss that stirred all the sensations of last night up in her.

Still kissing her, he pulled her closer. She could feel him hot and hard against her stomach.

"No." She pressed her hands on his chest and pushed him back.

He released her instantly, with a rueful smile. "Sorry, sweetheart, twice is a bit much when it's your first time. You must be sore."

She felt herself blushing and pulled the blue coverlet around her. "No, it—it's not that. It's just—" She took a deep breath. "We can't do that again."

His brows snapped together. "Did I hurt you?"

"No, but—"

He relaxed. "Good, I thought not. You enjoyed it, didn't you? You seemed to." His gaze caressed her.

She felt her skin heating even more and glanced away. It was hard to say anything when his eyes burned with that particular cold blue heat. It felt so very . . . personal. "Whether I enjoyed it or not is immaterial," she said firmly.

"I thought it was very material," he murmured.

"It's not going to happen again."

He sat back against the paneling at the head of the bed, crossed his arms, and grinned at her, obviously feeling very pleased with himself. "Yes, it is." The sheets ended just below his waist, only just keeping him in any way decent. Not that she was looking. Much.

She averted her eyes, and her gaze fell on a small spot of blood on the bottom sheet. Her virgin's blood, she thought and inconspicuously pulled a corner of blanket over it. Somehow, from the stories she'd heard, she'd expected a lot more. Such a lot of fuss over something so small.

"It won't happen again," she insisted. "Not unless you force me."

"You know I'd never do that." He gave her that sleepy look and immediately she recalled Laila saying his eyes made her think of rumpled beds and long, hot nights. Ayisha knew what she meant, now . . .

She nodded, trying to keep her mind on the subject for discussion, not . . . rumpled beds. "That's right. So."

"What about when we're married?"

He was so sure their marriage was inevitable. She gave an exasperated sigh. "We've been over this before. How often do I have to say it—we're not getting married."

"It's no longer up for debate," he told her, his voice hardening. "You were a virgin. I don't ruin virgins and walk away."

"Ruined?" She glared at him. "I'm not the least bit ruined. It hardly hurt at all and there was only the tiniest bit of blood." She tried not to blush and added, "I've shed more blood peeling vegetables."

The hard expression faded. His eyes gleamed. *"Peeling vegetables?"*

"You know what I mean," she said, embarrassed. "I'm in perfectly good condition. Apart from a few minor twinges, I feel wonderful, so let us have no more talk of being ruined."

"I'm delighted to hear it, but you've misunderstood," he said, his voice, gentle, faintly amused, but implacable. "Ruined means I've taken an innocent girl's virginity. And in my book, that means we'll marry—whether you like it or not. This is no longer just a matter of gossip. There could be consequences from this night's work."

She knew that. It was the reason she'd been trying to keep

him at arm's length. Until all her resolve had dissolved in one explosive moment of rage and fear and passion and the exultation of defeating death and embracing life.

He continued, "I won't force you to bed me, my dear, but I'll have no compunction whatsoever about forcing you to the altar. And if you want to argue about it, I'll send for Reverend Payne and the captain and instruct them both to marry us now, on the spot, quarantine or no."

Ayisha stared at him. There was a grim set to his jaw that dared him to call his bluff. Because it was no bluff at all.

Last night's events had changed everything, and they both knew it. It was time to come clean.

"I'm not who you think I am," she told him.

"Not this again," he said wearily. "Who are you then?"

"My mother was not Lady Cleeve; her name was Kati, Kati Machabeli. She—she was my father's mistress."

There was a long silence as he digested what she'd said. She tried to read his face, but she couldn't.

"Kati Machabeli does not sound like an Arab name." His voice was calm and gave nothing away.

"No, she was born in Georgia."

"I see. Who was your father?"

"Sir Henry Cleeve, of course. I didn't lie, precisely—just didn't tell you the whole truth." She bit her lip and added, "My father b—met Mama when he was on a visit to Damascus once. She was asked to interpret for him because her m—the man he was doing business with—did not speak English or French."

"And your mother did." He recalled now that Ayisha claimed to speak a number of languages, too. "What business was this?"

"Papa collected art and precious documents."

"And women, too, presumably."

"No! He wasn't like that. Mama was his only mistress."

That she knew about, Rafe thought.

"They fell in love. Papa brought her back to Cairo and set her up in a small house near the market. He came to visit every day, but she owned it, she kept the keys. It was her home."

"If she owned it, why did you have to live on the streets when she died?"

"I didn't mean own as in legally own, and anyway, I think Papa sold it when we came to live with him in his house—the one you rented. But he did love her and Mama adored him. They were very happy together, until the very end."

"I see." He considered what she'd told him. "Where did Lady Cleeve come into this picture? Did she mind your father taking a beautiful mistress? She was beautiful, I assume."

She nodded. "He didn't bring us into the house until after Lady Cleeve died. She never knew about Mama or me.

He raised his brows. "How do you know?"

Her forehead puckered. "I don't . . . Nobody ever said . . ." She looked at him stricken. "I've only just thought about it. You don't think of such things when you're a child. Oh dear, I hope she never knew. That would be terrible, to know your husband did . . . that."

He was glad she didn't try to justify it. He was even glad of her dismay at the thought that her father's wife might know of his infidelity.

It was common practice for men of his class to take their marriage vows lightly. From the Prince Regent down, gentlemen commonly took a mistress as well as a wife. Some even boasted of it.

Not Rafe. He took his promises seriously—all his promises. He would be a faithful husband, and he expected the same in return.

"So Alicia Cleeve was your half sister. What happened to her?"

"She died at the same time as her mother, of the plague, when I was six."

"How old was she?"

"Six. We were one month apart in age. I was the younger."

"Did you know her?"

"No, I didn't really understand any of it until we came to live with Papa. And even then I didn't fully understand—I was just a child. I knew Papa's previous wife and daughter had died, that's all."

"After that your father moved you both from the house near the market into his principal residence?"

"Yes."

Rafe raised his brows. Keeping a mistress he could understand; a lot of men did it, married as well as unmarried. But to move a mistress and illegitimate child into your home, as bold as brass—that was the sort of thing that could cause scandal. And scandal caused gossip. And gossip traveled, yet Lady Cleeve senior had heard nothing of this.

"What did your father's friends make of that?"

She gave him a puzzled look. "What do you mean?"

"Was there no scandal, no gossip?"

She shook her head. "I don't know. We didn't have many visitors."

"How did people—I mean your father's friends, not shopkeepers—treat your mother when she went out?"

"Oh, Mama never went into company. She was very shy and Papa never pressed her."

I bet he didn't, Rafe thought.

"It wasn't like you think. Mama had a scarred cheek," she explained. "She'd been atta—in an accident. She didn't like people to see it. Papa took me out with him, sometimes. He took me to music lessons with an English lady for a while." She looked away and added quietly, "But if people called me Alicia, he never corrected them. And he told me not to as well."

She met his gaze and added, "I won't do that anymore. I won't live in a dead girl's shadow, won't take what belongs to Alicia."

Rafe nodded. He believed her. He thought of the number of times she'd told him she was Ayisha and that Alicia was dead. Not her fault he didn't believe the literal truth when he heard it. She'd been as honest as she could; she'd lied to protect herself, not for gain. Nobody had forced this confession from her today, only her own sense of honor and self-worth.

Another question occurred to him. "When your parents died, why didn't you go to the British consulate?"

"I didn't know where to go." Her gaze slid sideways and he knew at once there was something she wasn't telling him.

"But—"

"They wouldn't have helped."

"Why not?"

She got up and walked to the window and stood staring out for a long time. For a moment, Rafe thought she wasn't going to tell him, but she returned to the table, sat down, and continued. "Evil men broke into the house as my mother lay dying. Papa was dead by then."

"And the servants?"

"They all fled when they first saw it was the plague."

"So you were alone with both your parents dying."

She gave a short nod.

"I'd heard the house was robbed."

She traced intricate, invisible patterns on the table as she spoke. "They smashed their way in and took everything of value. And then they looked for me . . . They were looking for the white child-virgin." She glanced up from the table. "I knew they meant me."

Rafe's jaw tightened. She'd been just thirteen—a little girl. How the hell had her father left her in such circumstances? A decent man would have ensured his daughter was protected, provided for. "How did you escape?" he asked her quietly.

A hint of mischief gleamed in her eyes. "You'll never believe it."

"Try me."

"I hid under my mother's bed."

"What?"

"Yes, it was so obvious a hiding place, it was amazing that they didn't find me. But Mama was dying of plague, and she saved me. She opened her eyes and cursed them—up to that point they thought she was dead so they got a terrible shock. The curse of a dead white woman . . ." She smiled ruefully. "They were not inclined to search her room very thoroughly."

From the open window the sounds of a somber tune, played on fiddle, flute, and squeezebox, drifted in.

"What's that music?" she asked, turning her head.

With difficulty Rafe concentrated on the moment. What she'd told him had knocked him endways. "The funeral ceremony, I imagine."

"So soon?"

He shrugged. "Best to get it over with before the heat sets in."

"I want to listen," she said, and with the sheet wrapped around her naked body she shuffled to the porthole.

Rafe wanted to know more; he had a raft of questions to ask her, but they could wait. He swung his legs out of the bed, dragged on his buckskin breeches, buttoned them, and followed.

The prayers were just a snatch of sound, swept away by the breeze. A hymn rose in a deep chorus: strong, male voices ringing across the waves. *Oh God, our help in ages past.*

The names of the dead were read out, one by one. They could hear the splash as each body slipped into the sea. "And therefore we commit this body to the deep."

"Keith Carter, Gianni Astuto, Zaid ElMazri, Antonio Palermo."

Rafe had never heard of any of them—but Ayisha had and wept for them.

The vicar's voice droned on. "Sergio Candeloro."

"He was only married six months ago. His poor wife," Ayisha whispered.

"Tommy Price, Vince Cafari, George Zaloumis."

"Oh, George." She sighed. "Remember? The young Greek boy, with the heartbreaking attempt at a mustache?"

"No." He'd been looking at her, not at boys with straggly mustaches.

"The others used to tease him about it, and he would blush and turn his fists on them. Now he'll never—" She stopped on a sob.

Rafe slid his arms around her. He'd known many young boys trying to grow their first mustache. Too many had died in a foreign land . . .

The trick was not to think about it.

"Jem Blythe."

"The boy who made Cleo's harness," she told him brokenly.

He tightened his hold on her.

He'd seen her with those boys on deck, laughing and talking with them, as if common sailors weren't beneath her notice. Of course she was used to hobnobbing with the riffraff of the streets . . .

There'd been no sign of flirtation—not from her, at least. The sailors had clustered around her like bees to a honey pot, but she'd seemed unaware of the sexual undercurrents. Given her years of acting the boy, she'd probably never tested her feminine powers.

And after last night, her innocence was unquestioned.

The last prayer was said, then came the singing of the twenty-third Psalm. "The Lord is my shepherd, I shall not want . . ."

Ayisha sang, her voice true and a little husky, cracking with emotion. She knew all the words by heart. Tears poured down her cheeks, and she sang with an intensity that made him wonder.

"Did you attend your parents' funeral?" he asked softly.

She shook her head and her voice wobbled and cracked, but she sang on.

Rafe held her tight against him. There was a lump in his throat, but not for the sailors killed by pirates. They'd died a clean and honorable death.

But Ayisha . . . She was so full of life, so full of emotion it was frightening. How could she open herself to grief like this when she'd already suffered so much?

The dead sailors were little more than chance-met strangers, but she wept for them, grieved for them and their families. And Laila and Ali, left behind in Cairo—and even that moth-eaten old cat—he'd witnessed the pain she'd felt at leaving them.

She loved too easily, that was her problem. Love was the hostage to pain. The more you loved, the more pain you felt . . .

She needed to learn to protect herself better, as he had.

*A*yisha stepped out of the washroom, dressed and feeling clean and fresher. The funeral had tired her out, but the weeping had loosened some of the knots inside her.

She crossed the cabin and started stripping the bed. There was a certain stain on the bottom sheet she needed to get out.

"Leave that," he ordered. "Come and sit down. We did not finish our discussion."

His interrogation, he meant. Ayisha tried not to sigh. She was exhausted. Too much had happened in too short a time. What she really wanted to do was curl up in that bed and sleep for a week—but she couldn't, not after what had happened, not with him there, watching her with those eyes, full of questions.

And echoes of heat from last night.

He dressed swiftly, pulled on his boots, stepped into the washroom, and emerged a moment later looking as neat and elegant as if his valet had attended him. How did he do it? Ayisha wondered.

The only thing that was the slightest bit out of place was his unshaven jaw, and privately she thought it looked even more attractive covered in dark stubble.

Her skin prickled deliciously with the memory of how it felt against her skin; the abrasive caress of it against the soft skin of her breasts had made her want to purr like a cat.

It won't happen again, she reminded herself.

She sat on the chair, folded her hands, and waited. Despite the cold water she'd splashed on them, her eyes still ached from all the weeping. She felt clean, but crumpled.

He sat and regarded her a long time in silence. She willed herself not to fidget. She had no idea what he was thinking, what he was feeling. But, oh, she could guess.

Anger, betrayal, contempt. She'd made a fool of him. She hadn't meant to, but circumstances had given her no choice.

None of those emotions showed in his voice when he asked her, "You said from the first that Alicia Cleeve was dead. You knew I didn't believe you, so why did you wait until now to tell me the full story? Why not tell me at the time?"

She gave him an incredulous look. "Confess my illegitimacy? Would you have taken me to England if I had?"

He frowned. "You didn't want to go to England."

She shook her head. "Papa told me so much about England, I've always wanted to go."

His eyes narrowed. "Then why did you refuse to come with me from the very beginning? I distinctly remember threatening to roll you in a carpet—kicking and screaming—and cart you onto a ship, if necessary. Not that you screamed," he said with ironic emphasis.

She blushed, remembering where she'd tried to kick him.

He continued, "And why tell me then, that first night, that Alicia was dead and here there was only Ayisha?"

"Because I didn't want to go to England under false pretenses, as Alicia."

"You did anyway."

"Only because you forced me."

"I did not. You came aboard of your own free will, no carpet required."

"You didn't force me intentionally, but you showed that picture to so many people, some people noticed the resemblance. Someone made a joke that they should dress me as a girl and sell me to you. And once that joke started to spread . . . well, the men who'd pursued me as a child put two and two together and came after me. Again."

He gave her an intense look. "Those men at the riverbank?"

She nodded. "The leader, Gadi's uncle, was one of the ones my mother cursed." She gave a wry, mirthless smile. "I couldn't stay in Egypt any longer."

"You could have told me the truth then. I wouldn't have blamed you."

"And would you have taken me to my grandmother's?"

"Of course. Why not?"

He hadn't had as much time as she had to think things through, Ayisha saw. "Because she sent you to fetch her beloved granddaughter, Alicia Cleeve, not some illegitimate brat her son sired on his foreign mistress."

She waited, but he remained silent, his face graven in its stillness.

"Forgive me if I'm wrong," she said, "but aristocratic grandmothers don't generally scour the world looking for any stray bastards their son has sired—or has the England of my father changed?"

There was a long silence. She wished she could tell what he was thinking but his eyes had gone that unreadable, opaque, ice blue.

"No," he said slowly. "England hasn't changed that much."

*T*he knock on the cabin door startled them both, mercifully breaking the silence. It was Higgins with breakfast.

Rafe carried in the tray and uncovered it. Bacon and eggs, toast with marmalade or honey, and a large pot of fresh, hot Italian coffee. There was even a fish head for Cleo, who showed her approval of the treat by dragging it behind her basket and growling over it.

Ayisha felt hollow. He'd just confirmed all her fears. The illegitimate daughter of Sir Henry Cleeve would be of no interest to her grandmother. Or to him.

She took a deep breath. So be it. She had started a new life as a child on the streets. She could do it again in England.

"What would you like first?" Rafe asked her, "Food or coffee?" Gallant to the end. As if she hadn't just confessed she'd deceived him.

The scent of the coffee teased Ayisha's senses and suddenly she was starving. "Coffee to start with, please."

He poured her a cup of steaming dark coffee, stirred in two lumps of sugar and some milk, and placed the cup in her hands. He knew exactly how she liked it. How did he know that?

She inhaled, then sipped it slowly. Ambrosial. The hot liquid flowed into her and she felt steadier. And hungrier.

He passed her a plate of bacon and eggs. "Eat up," he told her. "You need food after all you've been through in the last twenty-four hours."

He was right. Her mind, her heart felt bruised all over, so much had happened in the last day—and night. Pirates, death, her first experience with a man—probably the last with this one—funerals, and exposure of her deception.

And she hadn't eaten since midday yesterday. No wonder she was starving.

She hoped to God she wasn't with child.

"Bacon, at long last," he said approvingly. He ate with a neat energy, tidily but with gusto. Throughout the meal, he politely ensured she had everything she needed: salt, more coffee. He even buttered her toast, then passed her the honey.

"Malta is famous for its honey," he told her. "Its bees are black and fierce, but the honey is tangy and sweet. Try it."

She spread some of the golden honey on the toast. It was indeed delicious. Wild thyme and citrus and something spicy.

It was good she'd told him now, she decided, as she ate the last of her toast. It would have been better if she'd told him before they made love. Better still if they'd never made love at all.

No. She couldn't honestly regret that. To leave him, never having known what it was like to lie with him, feel him deep within her, part of her . . . Her body still throbbed with faint echoes of the night.

Magnificent, just as Laila had said.

She watched him as he crunched his way through the last piece of toast with strong, white, even teeth, and she knew that even though she was grieving deep inside for what might have been, even though sharp arrows of regret pierced her at odd moments, telling him the truth had been the right thing to do.

He was clean and straight and honorable.

If she hadn't told him, the secret would slowly, inevitably have poisoned their marriage. Some people could bury their guilt and go on. Not Ayisha.

It would have been like an ax poised over her head the whole time, waiting to drop. Better a swift, clean amputation than a slow death by poison, she told herself.

It was the right thing to do: it didn't make her feel any better.

She loved him. She'd lost him. But at least she'd had him for one night.

"Finished?" he asked.

She glanced at the table, puzzled. There was nothing left.

He gently pried the empty coffee cup from her hand. She'd been clutching it to her breast like a child.

He packed the tray up, ready for when Higgins came back. Were all soldiers so neat? she wondered.

"I always knew there was something you weren't telling me," he said, almost conversationally. "I'm glad to know it at last— and before we get to England."

It confirmed her worst fears. "What will you do when we get there?" she asked him.

"To England? It'll depend on the weather. I'll probably hire a carriage and postilion."

A postilion was a man who rode carriage horses and steered the carriage, she knew. "I'll travel alone then?"

"Alone? Of course not." He frowned. "Why would you imagine I'd let you travel all that way alone?"

She just looked at him. "I wasn't certain you'd even want to take me to Cleeveden."

"Good God, what do you take me for? Did you think I'd just dump you at Southampton and let you fend for yourself?" His voice was cool.

She made an embarrassed gesture. "It wouldn't surprise me."

"Well, I won't." He looked down his long nose at her and as always she wished she knew what he was thinking. "Are you worrying about how your grandmother is going to react when you tell her you're not Alicia?"

"Of course I am, what do you think?"

He frowned. "I don't know your grandmother very well, so I can't give you any guarantees about how she will receive you, but she struck me as a warmhearted woman."

"Is she?" she said politely. Meaning she didn't believe it."

"Yes, and if you want my opinion, I think she'll love you on sight."

She blinked at that. "You do?"

"I do. In any case, there's no use worrying about something before it happens. All you can do is prepare yourself for the worst and get on with living in the present. Old soldier's trick. Don't look forward, don't look back. Just live."

"And wait until you're shot," she muttered under her breath.

"No, make alternative plans, just in case," he said. "The thing is not to dwell on what you can't change and to concentrate on what you can."

His calm rationality was beginning to get on her nerves. What did he think she could change about this situation?

"Now, are there any more things you need to tell me, any other secrets you might want to dredge up as a reason not to marry me? We might as well deal with them all in one hit."

Ayisha's jaw dropped. "You mean . . . ?"

He raised an elegant brow. "Did you expect me to stagger back, yapping on about being betrayed, like a bad stage play?"

She blinked at him.

"You did," he said, "I can see it in your eyes. What a fellow you must think me. But I made a promise to you and I keep my promises."

"You still intend to marry me?"

His voice hardened. "Did I not make myself clear, earlier?"

"Yes," she said seriously. "But at the time you thought you were asking Alicia Cleeve."

He shook his head. "I don't know Alicia Cleeve. I know you."

He put a slight emphasis on the word *know*, and she was reminded of the biblical use of the word. Of course, he'd *known* her last night, and like the true gentleman he was, he was going to accept the consequences, no matter who she was.

Because she might be with child.

And because she'd locked herself in a cabin with him to save his life, and it caused gossip.

She'd deceived him, but despite that, and knowing that by marrying the illegitimate daughter of Sir Henry Cleeve he would be making a dreadful mésalliance, he was going to marry her anyway.

Because he was a gentleman of honor and he'd given her a promise.

The silence stretched. "You truly wish to marry me?"

"No 'wish' about it—I *will* marry you." His tone brooked no argument.

"Because of the gossip and me being . . . ruined?"

"The peeled vegetables are only part of it," he said solemnly.

"Peeled veg—" she began, then saw the faint gleam of humor in his eyes.

He sobered. "We may have started a baby last night, and I want our children to be born in wedlock. I assume you do, too."

"Of course, it's just . . ."

"We've spent more than ten days locked in a small cabin together, and we've got on remarkably well, considering the circumstances. It augurs well for the future."

It was hardly a declaration of love. She sighed. What did she expect?

He frowned at her continuing silence. "There will be compensations," he said abruptly. "You did not dislike making love with me last night, did you?"

She found herself blushing and shook her head.

"It will be better tonight," he vowed. "The first time is not always pleasant, for women."

There was a short silence, one she felt compelled to fill.

"It was . . . pleasant," she told him in a whisper. It had been more than pleasant. She couldn't imagine it being any better.

"Well then, you have no reason to hesitate." His eyes burned silver blue, steady and opaque.

Ayisha chewed her lip. She should refuse him. If she had the slightest bit of gallantry in her, she would. It was the decent thing to do.

But she loved him. And she didn't have it in her to say no to a lifetime of loving him.

She'd told him the truth about herself, and he was man enough to understand the consequences. Her grandmother would probably disown her, his brother would certainly despise her, and if word got out, society might whisper. It would not be easy.

"I am asking you now, Ayisha," he said in a tight voice. "But it is a formality, not a question. The outcome is already decided. You *will* marry me."

She'd made a clean breast of everything—almost. If he regretted this fit of gallantry later, that was his concern.

She'd do everything in her power to make sure he didn't regret marrying her. And she was going to love him more than he'd ever been loved in his life.

"I would be honored to marry you, Mr. Ramsey," she said softly. "Thank you."

There was a short silence.

"Excellent. For a moment there I thought you weren't going to be sensible. Not that I would have accepted any other response," he said in a brisk, businesslike voice. He rose to his feet. "We shall be married either at your grandmother's or at Axebridge. We shall decide when we get there." Meaning when they saw how her grandmother would react.

"Whatever you s—mmphh!" Ayisha forgot whatever it was she'd been going to say, because he'd hauled her to her feet and was kissing her. In a very unbusinesslike way.

Eighteen

*I*t wasn't an I'm-glad-you've-decided-to-be-sensible kiss at all. It was a possession, a dizzying, triumphant claim. Or at least that's how it felt to Ayisha.

He pulled her hard against him and lavished her with kisses, kissing her mouth, her eyelids, the soft skin behind her ear, her mouth, her throat, her mouth, her mouth . . .

"You won't regret it," he murmured between kisses.

Ayisha didn't try to answer. He might be marrying her out of gallantry, but this part—this at least was real. He wanted her. And she wanted him.

The swell of the sea was growing and the ship moved from side to side. Taking her with him, and without breaking their embrace, he moved until his back rested against the cabin wall.

"Better?" he said, and without waiting for her reply, he deepened the kiss. The taste of him in her mouth excited her. She knew now what to expect, and she wanted it, wanted him.

His body pressed against the whole length of hers, his hard chest crushing her breasts, his groin pushing against her belly, one long, hard horseman's thigh pressing between her quivering thighs.

She ran her palms over the warm planes of his body, kissing him feverishly, drowning in the waves of velvet fire that surged through her. His tongue caressed hers, sending fiery trails wherever it touched: teasing, igniting, inflaming.

He ran one hand slowly down her back, tucking her lower body between thighs parted and braced against the movement of the ship. Her body ached for the hardness of his arousal, writhing sinuously against him, loving the friction, aroused by it, driven by the need for a deeper intimacy. Aching, burning, frustrated.

His chest rose and fell as if he'd been running, his eyes, heavy-lidded and sleepy-looking, gleamed silver blue, the pupils dark, dilated, and rich with promise. *Rumpled beds and long, hot nights . . .*

He stopped on a sudden intake of breath and set her gently to one side. Why? Her legs trembled as if her bones had dissolved and she staggered.

He steadied her, one hand on her waist. And then she heard it, the knocking, and the voice calling, "It's Higgins, sir."

He straightened his cravat and opened the door. "What is it?" His voice was faintly ragged.

"The captain's compliments, sir. A bottle of wine for you and a small something for Miss Ayisha. There's a note with it." Higgins held out a tray with a bottle of wine, a small box, and a folded note.

Rafe took them and Higgins left.

"Wine from Italy, very nice," Rafe commented, looking at the bottle. He passed the note and the box to Ayisha. "Read it, it's for both of us."

She broke the seal on the note and read it. "It's in thanks for us helping to fight off the pirates yesterday. Isn't that nice?"

"What's in the box?"

She opened it and gasped with pleasure. "Oooh, Turkish delight." She popped a piece in her mouth at once and, feeling the burst of sweetness in her mouth, made an ecstatic sound. "It's delicious. I love Turkish delight—will you have some?"

He shook his head with a faint smile. "No, thank you."

"But you must taste it, it's the most delicious sweet."

"Very well, if you insist," he murmured, but instead of reaching for the box, he bent and kissed her thoroughly.

"Delicious indeed," he said when he lifted his head, and she felt herself blushing. He lifted her to her feet and drew her closer, but again they were interrupted by a knock.

"Me again, sir," Higgins called through the door.

Rafe yanked open the door. "Forgotten something?"

"No, sir," Higgins said apologetically. "The ladies sent this to Miss Ayisha. With thanks and in admiration of her bravery." He handed over a small tin and four books. "And one of the sailors, a lad called Jammo, gave me this for Miss Ayisha's cat." It was a piece of string, with one end tied in an intricate knot.

"What—" Rafe began.

"It's called a monkey's fist," Ayisha told him. "Some of the boys showed me the different knots they tied—some are very pretty. And how clever, this looks exactly like a fat little mouse. Here, Cleo!" She bent and waggled the string until the kitten was twitching with anticipation. She tossed it a few feet away, the kitten bounded after it, pounced, and a battle to the death commenced.

Ayisha laughed. "Thank Jammo for me and Cleo, will you, Higgins?"

"Of course, miss."

She took the books eagerly. "*The Mysteries of Udolpho*, in four volumes," she exclaimed, examining them. "It belongs to Mrs. Ferris—I saw volume one in her cabin. She must have seen me looking at it. How extraordinary of her to send me a gift."

She opened the first volume. "Oh, listen to this:

'Fate sits on these dark battlements, and frowns, / And, as the portals open to receive me, / Her voice, in sullen echoes through the courts, / Tells of a nameless deed.'

"How wonderfully thrilling it sounds, I cannot wait to read it."

She opened the tin. "Biscuits of some sort. They must have bought them in Malta. How kind."

She hugged the gifts to her and said, "Higgins, why is everyone being so kind to me today? I don't understand."

Higgins smiled. "They reckon you helped save the ship yesterday, miss. Everyone's talking about your courage. Major Ramsey's, too, of course," he added. "But they expect a war hero to be brave. Nobody expected a lady to fight. Mrs. Ferris is quite the heroine, too, I might add, having followed your example. You two ladies stopped quite a few villains getting aboard. So enjoy them, miss; you deserve much more." Higgins gave Rafe a look as he said it.

"Go away, Higgins," Rafe said calmly. "And don't come back. Miss Ayisha has finally agreed to marry me, so there are things we need to . . . discuss."

Higgins's eyes lit up. "Congratulations, sir, miss." He beamed. "Don't worry, sir, you won't be disturbed again." He bowed and left.

She offered the tin to Rafe, but he shook his head. He wasn't hungry. Or at least he was, but not for food.

She looked up at Rafe with eager, shining eyes. "I must thank Mrs. Ferris and the other ladies. And the captain, too, for the Turkish delight. And Jammo. It's so kind of them. It's like a birthday. Do we have a pen and paper?"

Realizing there would be no kissing until the letters were written, he sighed inwardly and searched in his baggage for some writing paper and a pen. Her unaffected delight in such simple gifts touched him; she probably hadn't had many gifts in her life. Or much appreciation.

He found his writing case and passed her several sheets of writing paper. "Pen and ink or porte-crayon?" he asked.

His body ached, unfulfilled. It was probably just as well they'd been interrupted. It wasn't decent to be seducing her again, so soon after a funeral, so soon after her first time. At this hour of the morning. When she was already dressed.

Tomorrow. Or perhaps tonight.

"It might be easier to use the porte-crayon with the movement of the ship," she said thoughtfully.

He took out a silver porte-crayon, shaved the lead to a fine point with his penknife, and gave it to her.

"Pretty," she said, examining it. "Papa had one very similar." She looked from one to the other. "But this traveling pen and ink holder is so ingenious I can't resist using it. Besides, it is more polite to respond in ink, is it not?"

"True." There was something very endearing in the way she was fussing over a few simple thank-you notes. He pulled the quill from the container, trimmed the nib, and handed it to her.

She thought for a moment, dipped the pen carefully in the inkwell, and began to write with a firm, clear hand. He smiled, recalling how she'd once pretended she couldn't read.

He glanced at her, frowning with concentration as she penned her thank-you notes, smiling to herself and glancing across at him with such a pleased and happy expression it moved him deeply.

If he hadn't fallen ill, he might never have known her, not as he did now. Extraordinary to be grateful for a fever that had nearly killed him. Without that he might not have even thought of marriage.

But he had, and he'd proposed and now she'd—finally!—accepted, he wanted it done. The knot firmly tied.

He moved to the window and stared out at the sea with its gleaming, white-capped waves. He wanted this journey over, he wanted this business settled, once and for all. This business. His marriage.

He wanted it settled and tidy and clear.

He seriously considered getting the captain or that parson to marry them here and now—the day the quarantine was up. But there would be scandal and gossip and people would whisper behind her back that she'd trapped him into marriage.

He wouldn't allow that, wouldn't allow anyone cause to speak about her like that. If anyone had trapped anyone, it was he. He'd trapped from the very outset, using Ali as bait. And any number of times since. He'd used her friends, her loyalty, even threats; he had given her no choice but to come with him.

And if he had his time over, he'd do it all again. Looking back, all he could see was a job well done. She needed to be rescued from her appalling situation.

What would Lady Cleeve make of the tale? Of Ayisha? He wished he knew her better, but he had no idea.

People turned a blind eye to children born in wedlock but sired by someone else. Those children were invariably the result of an aristocratic affair, a baron slipping a cuckoo into the nest of a duke. Some, like the Devonshire brood, were an open secret. But legally they were not bastards, and in any case they were of equal blood.

Let a lady give birth to a stable boy's brat, however, and the child would be discreetly got rid of, raised in obscurity, never knowing who his mother was. And as for a lord siring a child on a lowborn mistress, that was as common as dirt. As long as the fellow was a gentleman and ensured the child was provided for, nobody thought twice about it.

He could only think of one *ton* family where a bastard of low blood was acknowledged, and that was Harry Morant and the

Renfrews. But it had taken years. And if Harry hadn't been picked out of the gutter and raised to be a gentleman by his eccentric great-aunt, it would have been a different story. Harry would still be in the gutter now.

Even so, had he not been raised with his half brother, Gabriel Renfrew, who stood up beside him, demanding everyone treat Harry with respect, Harry would still be an outsider, unacknowledged by his closest relatives.

Harry's aunt, Lady Gosforth, adored him now, but it had taken a long time for her to accept him.

Harry's mother was a maidservant. Ayisha's had been a foreign mistress.

It wouldn't be as socially damning now that he'd got Ayisha's promise to marry him. Being married to the heir of Axebridge counted for something in society. Once they were married he could fix everything. He'd be able to look after her properly then.

He turned and watched her penning her thank-you notes. His wife-to-be. He'd never thought of marriage as anything except a duty.

But now, looking at her, he felt . . . as if a heavy stone was lodged in his chest, aching, and yet somehow . . . proud.

He must have made some sort of sound because she turned her head and glanced at him, then smiled, a swift, fleeting smile that dazzled him all the same. The weight in his chest thickened.

*T*hat evening when they went up on deck for their usual walk while the other passengers were at dinner, Ayisha hesitated at the foot of the companionway.

"What's the matter?" Rafe asked. Usually she was eager to escape the cramped cabin and get into the fresh air.

"Nothing," she said brightly and moved forward. But when they reached the deck she hesitated again, then stepped out in a move that brought back to him the way she'd stepped onto a deck full of pirates and fighting, braced for something she dreaded.

"It's all clean," she exclaimed in astonishment as she looked around the deck. "No stains at all."

"No, they've been scrubbed and sanded away," Rafe told her, realizing she'd expected to be taking her evening walk on a bloodstained deck. "Captain Gallagher would have had the crew wielding holystones almost immediately. He runs a tight ship."

"What's a holystone?"

"A block of sandstone. They use it like a scrubbing brush and it sands as well as cleans. Sailors call it a holystone because they kneel to use it, and it's big and square and heavy enough to be a Bible," he explained. "Have you noticed what's ahead of us?"

The sun was setting and the ship was approaching two headlands, silhouetted starkly against the golden brilliance of the sun. The one on the right was a massive dark chunk of rock rising from the sea like a giant pyramid.

"Is it—is that the Rock of Gibraltar?" she breathed. "It's so much bigger than I'd imagined."

Rafe nodded. "Amazing, isn't it? On the other side is Morocco, and out there—" He pointed ahead. "Out there is the Atlantic Ocean. My guess is we'll get some rough weather then. It was very rough on the voyage from England." He'd been sick as a dog, in fact.

Just then they heard a shrill whistle from above. They glanced up and saw one of the sailors waving to them. He pointed to the port side of the ship, so they crossed over to look.

"Dolphins!" Ayisha exclaimed. "I've only ever seen a picture of one." There were a dozen of them, racing along beside the boat, arching out of the water and diving.

She watched entranced as they leapt and dived, racing the ship, weaving in and out. Rafe watched her as much as the dolphins. Her zest for life enthralled him, and today it was as if a bubble of joy was inside her. Those presents, no doubt.

She leaned over the gunwale, smiling, laughing, and exclaiming when she saw a little puff of water spurted from one of their heads, her hand held out as though she could touch a dolphin.

"My mother told me a story once about a young man who fell overboard and would have drowned," she told him. "But instead dolphins came and flipped him up to the air with their snouts. And they let him hold on to them and they took him back to the island where he lived. Isn't that amazing?"

"Amazing."

She turned a laughing face to him. "You don't believe it, do you? I didn't when Mama told me, but now, looking at these dolphins, seeing their smiling faces and their eyes . . . I think maybe it is true, after all."

"Smiling faces? They're fish," Rafe said.

"No, they're not. They're special," she said. "People say they're magical creatures and now that I've seen them, I believe it."

After a few minutes the dolphins suddenly veered off to the side and disappeared. "Oh, that was lovely," she said. "I suppose it is time to return to the cabin again."

Rafe pulled out his watch. "A moment or two more. We'll wait until the watch bells sound as usual." When the sailor's evening watch sounded two bells, a pause then one bell, they usually went belowdecks.

They stood on the starboard side of the boat, sailing into the sunset, watching the enormous Rock of Gibraltar slip by.

Ahead the Atlantic Ocean gleamed molten gold and rose as the sun dropped gently into it. They watched until the sun had disappeared completely. The ocean slowly silvered, then grew dark. Overhead, the sails snapped, and gulls wheeled and shrieked, their unearthly cries echoing into the falling night.

She shivered.

"Cold?" Rafe asked, and without waiting for her response he drew her closer, wrapping her in his coat, warming her with his body. "It will be colder in England," he said. They both knew he wasn't only talking about weather.

*D*inner that evening was something of a celebration, with fresh lobster, followed by a rabbit pie, a chicken fricassee with mushrooms, fresh fruit and a rum syllabub, and to go with the feast, a bottle of champagne.

"I took the liberty of tellin' the captain of your betrothal, sir," Higgins confessed. "And he sent this down with his congratulations, thinking Miss Ayisha might prefer it."

*T*hey were disturbed early the following morning by a knock on the door. Rafe, who was in the middle of making love to Ayisha with slow, devastating intensity, growled, "If that's Higgins, I'll kill him. I told him to go away."

From the other side of the door came, "It's me, sir, Higgins."

"You told him that yesterday," Ayisha said, laughing. She gave him a little push. "Go on, you know he won't go away."

He gave her a dark look. "As long as you don't go away, that's all that matters." He slid out of the bed, dragged on his breeches, fastened them, and flung open the door. "What?"

"I—I do beg pardon, sir." Higgins sounded a bit rattled by Rafe answering the door in nothing but a pair of buckskin breeches and a lot of bare skin. The open door shielded Ayisha from his sight, but Rafe's dishabille would reveal more to Higgins than just skin.

Ayisha didn't care. She'd never been so happy. She'd never known such happiness was possible. It bubbled through her veins like the champagne the captain had sent them, lapped against her consciousness like the waves lapping constantly at the ship, and filled her with a warm glow; sunshine from within.

She didn't care that no words of love had been spoken. He'd said nothing, and she'd been too shy to offer them herself. Her heart was so full of love for him, it threatened to boil over and scald them both. So she kept the words to herself, silent and precious in her breast, until he was ready to hear them.

What were words, anyway? During the last two warm, dark nights of lovemaking with Rafe Ramsey such a precious bond had been forged between them . . . At least she felt it, and if he didn't—no, he must. The way he looked at her, the way his eyes darkened in that come-to-bed expression . . .

It didn't matter, now, what faced them in England. She and Rafe would survive it. She believed it with all her heart.

She sat up in bed, the blue coverlet pulled up to her chin, and admired the lean, muscular physique of the man, his broad, powerful shoulders divided by the long furrow of his spine, the two shallow dimples angling into the base of his spine. His ribs were visible. He hadn't regained enough flesh since the fever, but he was a magnificent sight, hard and sleek and powerful.

The breeches hugged his body, curving tight against his backside and down his long, hard thighs.

Her eyes devoured him, her body remembered how he felt against her, around her, inside her, and without warning a shudder reverberated deep within her, passing through her body like a whiplash, causing her to arch and then subside.

He must have caught the movement from the corner of his eye, for he half turned, his eyes bored into her and darkened, knowingly.

Higgins went on, "Message from the captain, sir. Since the quarantine period is up today, he'd like you and Miss Ayisha to

take breakfast with him this morning. Eight o'clock, sir, is when
he'd like you there. That's about half an hour." He paused and
added, "You will want to shave, of course, so I've ordered hot
water for you and also for Miss Ayisha to bathe in. It'll be here
in a moment."

"Blast," Rafe muttered, glancing at Ayisha. She gave him a
rueful shrug. There was no way out of it without giving offense,
and neither of them would wish to do that.

"Very well," he told Higgins. "Thank the captain and bring
on your hot water. We'll be there at eight."

I congratulate you both on surviving your incarceration; I
know it must have been difficult," Captain Gallagher said.
Breakfast was a private affair, served in his quarters. "I must say
you look well on it. Miss Cleeve, you look positively radiant."

She smiled. "The time passed surprisingly fast."

"Mainly because she's a born cardsharp," Rafe interrupted.
"Captain, you see before you a man in debt to the tune of mil-
lions."

She laughed. "Don't believe a word of it, Captain, it's all nonsense. I did become quite skilled at a number of card games, but
it was self-defense, the way Mr. Ramsey plays. Still"—she gave
Rafe an airy look—"I must be grateful to him. If ever I need to
earn my living, I can always take to playing cards."

They all laughed.

She added, "It will be lovely, though, to be able to go anywhere I please and to talk to other people."

"Yes, the walks on deck made it much easier to bear," Rafe
said. "Thanks for allowing it."

The captain shook his head. "As long as you had no contact
with others, I could see no harm in it. My orders are to quarantine
possible infection, but the conditions are left to my discretion.
Though the medical fraternity cannot agree how the wretched
thing spreads, both contagionists and anti-contagionists seem to
agree that clean, fresh air is beneficial—or at least cannot hurt."

Ayisha said nothing. Left to his discretion, eh? She addressed
herself to her breakfast. She didn't mind being shut in a cabin
for ten days, but she would never forget that the captain had
planned to set Rafe ashore, not knowing or caring what became
of him.

The captain continued, "And I'm delighted you've agreed to make a match of it—not that you had much choice, but—"

"We are both well content with the outcome," Rafe interrupted, and to drive home his point he picked up Ayisha's hand and kissed it.

A ripple of pleasure passed through her. Her face warmed, and she could not help but smile at him.

The captain looked from one to the other and a broad smile spread across his face. "Like that, is it? Excellent, excellent. And do you want me to perform the ceremony, or perhaps Reverend Payne?"

Rafe shook his head. "Thank you, but no. Miss Cleeve wishes to be married in her grandmother's presence, and I must respect her wishes. We shall marry there, or in the church near my brother's home."

"Excellent," the captain nodded. "Mrs. Ferris's maid will see to your things, Miss Cleeve."

"My things?" she asked, puzzled.

"Since you are not married, you will, of course, be returning to share a cabin with Mrs. Ferris."

"There is no necessity—" Rafe began.

The captain simply looked at him. "Mr. Ramsey, among the passengers are three rather vocal and strong-minded Christian ladies, a parson, and a parson's wife. They might accept—reluctantly—the necessity of you two sharing a cabin while you were sick and under quarantine—Miss Cleeve's actions gave us no choice in that. But now the quarantine period is completed. You either marry this day, or Miss Cleeve must return to Mrs. Ferris's cabin."

"Miss Cleeve will not be married in haste on a ship to appease the sensitivities of a handful of impudent busybodies," Rafe snapped. "She'll be properly married in a church, as she wishes, with her grandmother present.

Ayisha pushed aside the remains of her breakfast. It was delicious, but she wasn't hungry anymore. She rose. "If you'll excuse me, gentlemen, I'll go and pack."

If she didn't know from Rafe that a shipboard marriage would be socially frowned upon, she wouldn't have minded being married by the captain. But a church wedding with her grandmother present was truly a lovely prospect, so a short separation was not too much to bear.

She would miss their lovely evening walks on a deserted deck, watching the sun go down, and the afternoons spent playing cards and talking or reading in quiet, companionable silence. Most of all she would miss the long nights of slow, blissful lovemaking.

But they would be in England soon. And then they would be married, and they'd spend the rest of their lives together. It would be all right once they got to England.

*T*hey sailed into Portsmouth with the ship's bell clanging, steered by a pilot who'd climbed aboard from a small boat as fog rolled in around them. Soon all Ayisha could see were the skeletal shapes of other ships riding slowly at anchor, a cluster of masts rocking gently, ghostly in the silken, swirling fog.

They were piped ashore—an honor indeed—with the ship's company lined up to farewell them.

"I'm sorry it's not better weather for your first day in England," Rafe said, taking her hand to steady her as she stepped into the jolly boat.

"But the fog is beautiful," Ayisha told him, looking around with wonder in her eyes. "I've never felt anything like it. It's so deliciously fresh against my skin." She held her face up to the caress of the moist air and inhaled deeply.

"Don't tell me the smell is as delicious," he said dryly.

She laughed. The port reeked of rotting fish, seaweed, and acrid mud. "It's odd that it smells more fishy and sea-like here than it does at sea. But it's interesting."

Two sailors rowed them toward the landing. Seabirds called from invisible locations and muffled sounds floated across the water. "Sounds echo so mysteriously in fog," she commented as they were rowed ashore. "It's like another world."

"It's also blasted inconvenient. Mind how you go," he said, helping her ashore. "The steps will be wet and slippery."

He walked them into town at a cracking pace. Ayisha had almost to run to keep up with him. She was given no time to explore Portsmouth, had barely enough time to get her land legs back before they were heading out of town in a carriage that he called a yellow bounder.

In a matter of minutes he'd arranged everything; hired the carriage and postilion, sent Higgins off to collect his curricle from Harry's place and meet them at Cleeveden, and collected English money from the bank.

The only thing that slowed him for a moment was the sight of Ayisha shivering in her cotton dress and shawl. He'd whirled her into a shop and five minutes later whirled her out, now wearing a soft woolen cloak in a deep rose color, lined with green silk, trimmed with white swansdown around the hood, and with a swansdown muff to match. Ayisha loved it.

"Your grandmother will no doubt enjoy buying you clothes more suitable for the climate," he told her as he helped her into the carriage.

Ayisha nodded. She was looking forward to it. There were so many beautiful things in that small shop.

"Is there some reason for your hurry?" she asked as they trotted out of Portsmouth. She could see no reason for haste; the ship had taken more than four weeks to sail from Alexandria, nobody could possibly be expecting them.

"I want to make it to Winchester tonight. If this fog extends far inland it'll slow us considerably."

"What's at Winchester?"

He gave her a slow-burning look. "A very good inn."

A very good inn. She felt her cheeks warming and could not help but smile. He'd missed her. Joy bubbled up in her. She'd missed him, too, missed sleeping beside him, entwined with him, breathing in the scent of his skin, feeling the warm, relaxed power of his big body. She missed waking up to be greeted with that quiet, deep, "Good morning, sweetheart" and the kiss that invariably followed. And the lovemaking that followed that.

She understood now why Laila missed being married so badly. In those last weeks on the ship, Ayisha had tossed and turned in the narrow bunk in Mrs. Ferris's cabin, warring with herself; her body warring with her mind. Her body ached for him. Just one thought or glimpse of him was enough to cause her body to tingle and clench deep inside. She lay awake for hours, thinking how easy it would be to slip down from her bunk and run the short distance to Rafe's cabin . . .

Now, in one terse phrase, with one burning look, he'd conveyed that he'd felt the same. He'd missed her.

The carriage hit a pothole and Ayisha bounced, nearly sliding off the seat. He steadied her, drawing her against him.

"That's why they call these things 'yellow bounders,'" he told her. "I would have preferred a larger vehicle, but there were none to be hired."

"I don't mind the bouncing," she said. "And I especially like this window." She gestured to the wide glass window that ran across the entire front of the carriage. "It lets me see where we are going and all the wonderful sights."

"What wonderful sights?" he asked. "There's nothing but fields."

She laughed. "English fields," she reminded him. "So tidy in green and brown and yellow—all in patchwork, with lovely hedges, and all so much greener than I expected—I cannot wait for spring and all the flowers. And the villages are so tidy and pretty and so very different—look at that house with its neat, black wig."

His lips twitched. "Thatched roof."

"It looks like a wig. It's all so English, you see, and fascinating to me."

"I'm more fascinated by what's inside the carriage," he said and brushed his lips over hers. But then they slowed to pass through a village and a number of people peered curiously in at them. "No privacy at all," he grumbled, straightening, but he kept his firm, possessive hold on her. The care he took of her warmed her almost as much as the feel of his magnificent body. She pressed closer.

They stayed like that for most of the journey, Rafe sprawled, relaxed, his long legs crossed in front of him, explaining the various things that caught her attention, and sneaking kisses when he could.

Ayisha snuggled against his side, encircled by his arm, marveling at the greenness and dampness of England and basked privately in the good fortune that had brought this beloved man to her and made him want her. She watched the lush green countryside of England flash past her and counted the hours to Winchester with the very good inn.

But twenty miles before Winchester, the carriage broke an axle and they were forced to put up instead in a small, wayside inn, where there was no private accommodation: only two rooms containing several beds, one for men, one for women.

* * *

*T*he axle was replaced overnight, enabling them to make a good start the next morning. It was a cold day and they traveled in companionable silence. Rafe stared out of the window with a grim expression; taciturn, no doubt because his plans for the previous evening had been ruined. Ayisha watched the passing countryside with Cleo on her lap, stroking the little creature absently. While also regretting the lost opportunity for making love, she was growing increasingly nervous about meeting her grandmother for the first time.

She wouldn't tell her grandmother the truth until tomorrow, she thought. Allow herself a day of being simply a granddaughter, without the complications.

Rafe was confident the circumstances of her birth would make little difference to her grandmother; he'd said so several times. He was sure her grandmother would love her. She hoped he was right.

He was so strong and self-sufficient himself that he couldn't understand how important it was to her that her grandmother liked her, how much Ayisha needed to belong. This country was very beautiful, and she'd grown up hearing stories and dreaming of England, but it was also very strange to a girl who'd grown up in heat and dust and bright, pitiless sunshine.

They reached the small town of Andover by mid-morning, where they stopped for a short time to change horses and refresh themselves.

Shortly after they left Andover, Ayisha saw a signpost flash by. "Foxcotte!" she exclaimed.

"What?"

"I just saw a sign to Foxcotte. Wasn't that where you used to live?"

"My grandmother's house, yes. The village of Foxcotte is close by," he said in a bored voice. "I haven't been there since I was a boy."

"But I thought you said—don't you own it?"

"Yes."

"Then why haven't you been back?"

He shrugged. "Not interested."

"Who lives there now?"

"Nobody."

"You didn't rent it out?"

He gave her a cool look. "No, why should I?"

"No reason," she said, amazed that anyone could own a house they didn't visit and didn't use. It seemed very wasteful to her, but it wasn't her business. "Will we live there after we're married?"

"No, we'll live in my London house," he said curtly.

She nodded, a little disappointed. She rather thought she'd enjoy living among all this lush green countryside, but of course, if he hated Foxcotte, there was nothing more to be said. It seemed very strange. She'd gained the impression he'd been very happy living with his grandmother. That he hadn't gone back there since he was fourteen augured strong feelings.

"We'll be at Penton Mewsey soon," he commented. "Cleeveden is just beyond it."

The two houses must be very close," she said, to cover the tumult of butterflies that had started leaping in her stomach at his words. "Cleeveden and Foxcotte, I mean."

"Yes, about five miles apart. That's how my grandmother and yours knew each other so well as girls." The carriage slowed, the postilion turned his head and made a gesture to Rafe, who nodded. The carriage turned into a gateway and bowled briskly up a smooth gravel drive.

"Welcome to Cleeveden," said Rafe. "Your family home."

Nineteen

Cleeveden was a large, elegant stone house with an impressive portico, flanked by a dozen or more Doric-style pillars. It was set on a smooth rise of lawn in the middle of an elegant park. It looked like a house from a painting, not one in which real people lived.

"It's a new house," Rafe told her. "They demolished the old one and built this one when they came back from India. Only the park remained, but even that was redesigned."

Ayisha barely took in what he was saying. It was much bigger and much grander than she'd expected. She'd imagined her grandmother in one of those pretty cottages they'd passed, not in a large, stone . . . temple. She bundled Cleo back into her basket with suddenly nerveless hands.

"Does my hair look all right?" she asked Rafe, brushing the short, dark locks with her fingers. "She'll think I'm a boy, some sort of uncivilized savage. I wish it had grown more." She straightened her clothes, trying to smooth the travel creases from her dress.

"Stop worrying, you look beautiful," he said and gave her a swift kiss. "She's going to love you."

He'd sent a note on ahead the night before, thinking an elderly lady might need time to adjust to the happy news of the imminent arrival of a long-lost granddaughter.

The carriage pulled up at an imposing stepped entrance. Gripping Rafe's arm for support, Ayisha took a deep breath and went forward to meet her grandmother. She pulled the bellpull and waited.

After what felt like an interminable wait, the door was opened by a butler. His gaze ran over them without a flicker of expression. He addressed himself to Rafe. "Good morning, Mr. Ramsey, miss. Please, enter. Lady Cleeve received your note yesterday, sir, and is expecting you."

Ayisha's grip on Rafe's arm tightened as they entered the house and she looked around her. It still looked more like a temple than a home. The entry hall was large and imposing, marble paved and lined with statues. A sweeping set of wide, marble stairs rose at the end of it, curving gracefully upward. Overhead a domed cupola let in light.

"The postilion will require refreshment and the horses need attending to. We also have baggage," Rafe said, and with a flick of a wrist the butler sent a couple of footmen out to attend to things.

"Miss, if you care to accompany this maidservant," the butler said, indicating a waiting maid. "Lady Cleeve has issued instructions that you be attended to. No doubt you also need refreshment," the butler said.

"Oh, but—" Ayisha began, ready to say she needed no refreshment, that indeed she couldn't swallow a thing.

But the butler continued, "Lady Cleeve wishes to speak to Mr. Ramsey in private first."

Ayisha glanced at Rafe, a hollow feeling in her stomach. This was not how she'd thought it would be. If Ayisha's grandchild arrived, she would have been in the hall to greet her—if not on the steps—not having private discussions with other people first.

"Miss Cleeve and I will see Lady Cleeve together," Rafe said firmly.

"Her ladyship was most insistent," the butler said.

"I said, we will both—"

"That's very thoughtful," Ayisha interrupted Rafe quickly, seeing he was about to make an issue of it. "Go on, Rafe. I need to make use of the conveniences. I'll join you shortly." She needed some time to think.

"Then I'll wait until you're ready," he said, folding his arms.

"No, go ahead, please," Ayisha said. "Don't keep my gr— Lady Cleeve waiting."

Rafe gave her a searching look. "Are you sure?"

"Very sure," Ayisha said, feeling anything but.

"Lady Cleeve awaits you in the drawing room, sir," the butler said, indicating the room. "I shall announce you."

With some reluctance, Rafe followed. Ayisha went with the maid, who led her to a small room off the entry hall.

"There's a necessary in here, miss," the girl told her, "and some warm water to wash with. After that, I'm to take you to the kitchen for a cup of tea and a bite to eat." She gave Ayisha an embarrassed, half-apologetic look.

Ayisha knew why. The kitchen was no place for a welcome guest. It was an insult and the girl knew it.

"Where is the kitchen?" Ayisha asked calmly, determined not to show any hint of distress. She hadn't asked to come here. She'd been brought here at Lady Cleeve's request. And she would *not* drink her tea in the kitchen.

The girl pointed. "Down there, miss, through that green baize door."

Ayisha looked. There were several doors. "Do any of those lead outside? It's just that I have my cat with me and I think she would appreciate a patch of dirt in which to do her business."

"Shall I take her out for you, miss?"

"No, thank you, she's unsettled enough. I'll take her myself."

"Very good, miss. If you turn right down that narrow passage at the back there, then turn left, it will lead you to a back entrance. Only staff use it, mind, but . . ." She trailed off uncomfortably.

"Thank you," Ayisha said. "There's no need to wait. I will join you in the kitchen when I'm ready."

The girl nodded and disappeared through the green baize door. Ayisha felt hollow and apprehensive. Why was Lady Cleeve behaving like this? She didn't even know Ayisha wasn't Alicia yet . . .

She stiffened her spine. If her grandmother had changed her mind, Ayisha could bear it. Even as a starving child in Cairo, she'd never once descended to begging in the streets, and now that she was in England she refused to beg for crumbs of affection.

A moment later the butler emerged from the drawing room and went through the green baize door to the kitchen area. Ayisha tiptoed back down the hall and listened at the drawing room door.

"—and when I found out the girl in the drawing was not Alicia, but Henry's bastard—well, it was too late to recall you. You'd already embarked for Egypt."

Ayisha froze. How could Lady Cleeve possibly have found that out already?

"She is, all the same, your only living granddaughter," said Rafe in a tight voice. "The circumstances of her birth are not of her making."

"She's an opportunist, come to get what she can." Her grandmother sounded so certain, so implacable.

Something inside Ayisha shriveled.

"Rubbish! Good God, madam, I had to practically threaten her to get her to come here."

Ayisha bit her lip.

"A pity you did—"

"And in any case, what if she did come to better her life? Why shouldn't she? She's your son's daughter, your flesh and blood—and she's been abandoned to earn her living in Cairo as best she could from the age of thirteen! It's a disgrace."

"Well, *exactly*," Lady Cleeve declared righteously. "And I beg you will not sully my ears by describing *how* she earned that living."

Ayisha leaned against the doorjamb, her eyes closed in pain as the harsh words washed over her. She didn't know how it was, but somehow, her grandmother's mind had been poisoned against her.

"Madam, you try my patience sorely." Rafe's voice was as cold as a whiplash. "From the day her parents died, Ayisha lived disguised as a boy! Why? To prevent male attention, not solicit it. She earned what little she did by working: running errands, selling pies and bread in the streets, and collecting firewood. Living always on the brink of starvation."

There was a short silence, then Rafe continued, "The disgrace was your son's. He should have made better provision for his only daughter, taken better care of her."

Ayisha heard a ladylike snort. "I saw her from the window when you arrived; she looks like no boy I ever saw. Depend on it, my dear Mr. Ramsey, women of this order know how to pull the wool over gentlem—"

"She is of no 'order,'" snapped Rafe. "Ayisha is unique, and she is my affianced wife."

"*What?* You can't possibly marry the girl! Good God, man, but her mother was a slave!"

The words hung in the air. The silence stretched. Aisha couldn't breathe. How did Lady Cleeve know? It was the one secret Ayisha had kept from Rafe.

She could tell from the quality of the silence that it mattered. Mattered a great deal. Trembling, with knuckles pressed against her teeth, Ayisha waited for Rafe's response.

"A slave? What evidence do you have of such an accusation?" For the first time since she'd met him he sounded less than certain.

"Ahh, I see you didn't know."

Why hadn't she told him? Ayisha lashed herself silently. She'd meant to when she was telling him the truth about herself, but he'd shocked her by renewing his marriage proposal and it had driven everything else out of her mind.

After that, there hadn't seemed to be an appropriate moment to say, "Oh, and by the way, my mother was a slave. Papa bought her from her former master."

She ran shaking hands over her face. She hadn't told him later because she was a coward. It wasn't Mama's fault she'd been taken by Cossacks as a girl.

Ayisha's illegitimacy hadn't mattered to him, and she'd convinced herself Mama's slave status wouldn't, either, not because she truly believed it, but because she was so happy and she didn't want anything to spoil it.

Because the daughter of a slave was a slave, too. No matter who her father was.

"It makes no difference to me who her mother was," Rafe said coldly.

Not true, she thought sadly. The length of that silence had

told her the news had shocked him. Deeply. Now he was just being stubborn, unwilling to admit he'd made a mistake. Papa had been just the same.

Through the crack in the door, she heard her grandmother say, "If she didn't tell you that, what else might she be hiding from you? She's convinced you she's led a life of virtue, but how do you know it's true? She could have been with dozens of men—"

"Ayisha was a virgin when I met her."

"How do you know?"

Rafe said nothing.

"Ahh, you've had her already. I understand now." Her grandmother sounded very tired, Ayisha thought, worn out and sad, as if it was all too much for her. She wished she could see her face . . .

The old lady went on, "In that case, I suppose you'll set her up in some house in St. John's Wood. It's where gentlemen keep their mistresses, I gather," she said bitterly.

"I'll do nothing of the sort!" Rafe snapped. "I've promised to wed her and I will."

Yes, thought Ayisha miserably, because he prided himself on keeping his promises. Even when those promises had been based on false information . . .

"*Wed her?* What about the succession?" Lady Cleeve asked.

Ayisha frowned. What succession? What did she mean? She pressed closer to the door.

"What does the Earl of Axebridge have to say about this proposed marriage?"

"My brother has no say in the matter."

His brother was *the Earl of Axebridge*? Ayisha was stunned.

Lady Cleeve said, "Once he learns his heir is proposing to marry the illegitimate daughter of a foreign slave I expect he'll have a great deal to say about it. Especially since it looks very much like the son of your marriage will, eventually, inherit the earldom."

The old lady's words fell on Ayisha like a crushing weight. She had no idea Rafe came from such an important family. She knew he was a gentleman, but his lack of title had deceived her into imagining a marriage between them might be possible. But he was *the heir to an earldom* . . .

Ayisha, Countess of Axebridge? It was unimaginable.

She heard Rafe say, "I marry who I choose. And I have chosen Ayisha."

Oh, how stubborn he was. And all because he felt honor-bound to marry her, because in saving his life she'd been compromised. And because he'd taken her virginity. And desired her. And because there might be a child . . .

There would be no child, she knew; her monthly time had come in the week before they'd arrived in England. So there was no actual necessity to marry.

Another thing she hadn't told him.

Gratitude and honor and desire were not enough, she thought in sick despair. Not when he would lose so much by marrying her.

Lady Cleeve continued, "And what of your *fiancée*, Lady Lavinia Fettiplace—what does she have—what does her family have to say about her being jilted in favor of the illegitimate daughter of a *slave*? A charming gel, from one of the finest families in England—and an heiress to a fortune, I believe." She snorted. "What a scandal that will make. Will your brother have nothing to say about that, either?"

A heavy coldness settled in the pit of her stomach as she heard the words. He was already betrothed to Lavinia? And she was *Lady* Lavinia, not Miss Fettiplace? Beautiful and rich, he'd said. He'd left off that she was titled as well.

And therefore the perfect consort for an earl-to-be.

It was the final straw. She could not let him do it. She loved him too much to let him ruin himself for the sake of gratitude and honor. And stubbornness. And kindness.

She heard footsteps coming from down the hall and stumbled into the next room. Her legs folded beneath her and she sank onto the thick, rich carpet, bent double in pain and misery. Tears blinded her.

Next door she heard the clink of china. They were serving tea. Her palms rested on the soft pile of the carpet. She glanced down and choked on a bitter half laugh. This was exactly the sort of rug he'd threatened to roll her in and carry her off.

The bittersweet humor calmed her. She sat up and wiped her face with the hem of her skirt. Weeping would mend nothing. There was nothing, in fact, to mend. It had all been a dream, based on half-truths and lies of omission and pathetic wishful thinking on her part.

As she'd learned as a child on the streets of Cairo, dreams filled no stomachs. They might give enough hope to carry you through the darkest nights, but they were no foundation for a life.

You needed something more solid for a foundation: honesty. And love.

There was a desk in the corner with writing paper and pens. She quickly penned a note. It was cowardly, she knew, but when Rafe was in one of his stubborn, gallant moods, there was no gainsaying him. If she argued, she knew full well he was just as likely to carry her off to the nearest church and marry her out of hand.

And she did not know if she would have the strength to resist him, face-to-face. Not when she wanted everything he was offering and more.

But she would not be the cause of his ruin.

She folded the note in three, addressed it to Rafe, and sealed it with red wax; she didn't want anyone else reading it.

When the servants had gone, she tiptoed back out into the hall and tucked the note into the handle of Rafe's valise. Then she picked up Cleo's basket and her own smaller valise and followed the maid's directions to the servant's rear exit.

Outside she saw two paths, one leading toward a walled kitchen garden, and the other leading away from the rear of the house toward what looked like a village. She hurried along it.

She had no idea where she was going. She had a little money—Rafe had given her some English money to spend in the shop where he'd bought her the cloak. It was more than she'd had when she'd left her father's house the night the slavers had hunted her.

She was a child then, and she'd managed. She was older now and much wiser. And she was in England, where she'd always wanted to be. A plaintive yowl interrupted her thoughts and she smiled at Cleo, whose paw was poking through the slats in the basket. And she had a small, imperious furry friend for company and to love. It would be—it would have to be— enough.

Rafe was furious. He wanted to strangle Lady Cleeve. How dare she speak of Ayisha like that. How dare she not come out to meet her—he knew how hurt Ayisha had been by that; she'd tried not to show it but he'd seen the pain in her eyes, the dignity with which she'd walked down the hall with the maidservant.

He looked at the tea things the butler had brought in. Two cups, not three. A curt order had sent the butler hurrying from the room to fetch another cup.

"When you meet Ayisha, you'll see how mistaken you are about her, Lady Cleeve," he said.

The old lady didn't respond. Her lower lip was trembling. She saw him notice and with dignity turned her head away to hide her distress. The gesture was pure Ayisha.

A little of his anger drained away. Ignoring the teapot, he rose and poured her a sherry from the decanter on the sideboard. He handed it to her saying, "Drink. It will make you feel better."

She took it with a trembling hand and drank it down in one gulp. She shuddered as it went down, then handed it to him with a whispered thanks.

"Does she—does she look like Henry?" she asked after a moment.

"You're worried you'll like her, aren't you?" Rafe said gently. "No, she doesn't look like Henry."

She sighed.

"She looks just like that painting," he finished.

Her eyes widened. "That's me, when I was a girl."

Rafe said, "It's Ayisha, now. Only the hair and clothes are different. She's your granddaughter; nobody could doubt it. And from everything I've learned, Sir Henry loved her—and her mother—very much."

"I've been told otherwise," Lady Cleeve said wearily.

Rafe frowned. "By whom?"

"A woman who knew Henry in Cairo—one of his friends."

Rafe poured them both another sherry. "Go on," he said. "How did you meet this woman?"

"A month ago one of my friends was taking a cure in Bath. In the Pump Room she met a lady who had lived in Cairo for some years. Naturally the story of my long-lost granddaughter came up—I suppose half of England knows the story by now—so when the lady, Mrs. Whittacker, told my friend she'd actually known Henry in Cairo, of course my friend put us in contact and we arranged to meet." She sighed and gave Rafe a rueful glance. "I almost wish I hadn't. If I'd been left in ignorance, this day would have been very different . . ."

"Tell me," Rafe prompted.

"Mrs. Whittacker told me all about Ayisha and her mother. She was a great friend of my son's, apparently. She told me how this slave woman got her claws into Henry and that Henry was entrapped and unhappy."

"I don't believe it," Rafe said bluntly. "It's obvious from the way Ayisha speaks of them that her mother and father were very much in love."

Lady Cleeve gave him a troubled look. "Is it not in her interest to say so?"

Rafe shook his head. "Ayisha believes it utterly, and I believe her." He leaned forward and touched Lady Cleeve on the knee. "You will believe it, too, when you see the way her eyes light when she talks of them."

Lady Cleeve looked uncertain. "Mrs. Whittacker told me Henry's affair with this woman was the scandal of Cairo. The girl was born a month after my granddaughter, Alicia, was born—and for that I cannot forgive Henry. If he only knew how humiliated his wife must have been—"

"Ayisha said he was very discreet. She doesn't believe Lady Cleeve knew anything about her or her mother. It was only after her death and Alicia's that Henry moved Ayisha and her mother into the house."

Lady Cleeve shook her head. "That's not the story I heard. Mrs. Whittacker said the woman and child simply arrived and foisted herself on Henry while he was still distraught with grief. She said it was common knowledge in Cairo that poor Henry had been taken advantage of, and that everyone believed the child was no more Henry's than she was."

"And yet Ayisha is the image of yourself as a girl," Rafe observed, indicating the portrait.

Lady Cleeve sighed and slumped in her chair, looking worn and crumpled. "I don't know what to think now."

"I never met your son, but the impression I have from Ayisha is that he was a very strong-minded, intelligent man who took little heed of what others thought, who was autocratic, self-centered, and somewhat selfish, but was very affectionate in private to Ayisha and her mother."

Lady Cleeve stared at him.

Rafe went on, "I should add that the self-centeredness and selfishness is my own interpretation of what she's told me. Ayisha adored her father and will not hear a word against him or her mother. Despite the mess he left her in."

There was a long silence. Lady Cleeve's expression was enough. She knew her son, and he was the man Rafe had described, not the one that this Mrs. Whittacker had portrayed.

"Ayisha did say she thought her father went a little peculiar immediately following the death of Lady Cleeve, for after he'd moved her and her mother into his home, he sometimes referred to her as Alicia in company."

"Yes, I can see that," the old lady said slowly. "The letter he sent saying Alicia and her mother had died was a little strange, too. Hence the confusion." Her fine papery skin wrinkled in bewilderment. "But why would Mrs. Whittacker try to blacken her name to me?" she asked. "What would she gain by doing such a thing?"

Rafe shrugged. "What do you think she wanted?"

Lady Cleeve shook her head. "Nothing. Only my friendship."

The friendship of a lonely old lady. A wealthy old lady, the widow of a baronet, Rafe thought, but he didn't say so. He would let Lady Cleeve work it out. "This woman, does she have a family?"

Lady Cleeve pursed her lips thoughtfully. "She's widowed and has been living with relatives. It isn't comfortable for her, poor woman, in fact, we discussed—" She broke off, as if she'd suddenly realized something.

"What?"

"We discussed the possibility of me hiring a companion—and yes, the thought had crossed my mind she might be suitable." She slumped back in her chair. "Oh dear. Oh dear me. To think I believed her—but she was so very convincing—and she really had lived in Cairo for years and did know Henry, I am convinced of it, though he never mentioned her in his letters. He never mentioned his mistress and daughter, either. But, oh dear me." She looked at Rafe in distress and he had a sudden glimpse of how Ayisha might look as a troubled old woman.

She pressed her soft, wrinkled old hands to her cheeks. "To think I might have sent my granddaughter away unseen. On a complete stranger's say-so."

Rafe leaned forward and patted her knee again. "Be assured Ayisha is not after your money. All she wants is a grandmother. She told me once that it was a terrible thing to be without family, to belong to no one."

Lady Cleeve swallowed.

"She was talking about you, not herself. I was trying to persuade her to come with me to England, and her resistance first started to crack when she realized you were all alone in the world." He added in a gruff voice, "It cost her some heartache to leave, you know. There are people in Cairo who love her very much. She is, you will discover, very lovable."

Lady Cleeve's eyes filled with tears.

Rafe handed her his handkerchief and as she applied it to her eyes, she said in a shamed voice, "I'm sorry for what I said about St. John's Wood. I am . . . I have a tendency to be bitter about mistresses and their offspring, you see. My husband . . . well, you don't need to hear about that."

Rafe had no interest in ancient history. He needed to get one thing clear: "I *will* marry Ayisha. Nobody—not you, not my brother, not the entire *ton*—not even Lord Wellington could stop me."

"But why didn't she tell you her mother was a slave?"

Rafe acknowledged the validity of the question, but it didn't worry him. "She will have her reasons," was all he said.

"You take it on trust?" she said incredulously. "You have that much faith in her?"

"I have complete faith in her," Rafe said softly. "And when you meet her, you will know why. You are quite right to be cautious about meeting her."

The thin, arched brows came together. "Why would you say such a thing?"

Rafe smiled. "Because you won't be able to help loving her. Everybody does." It was true. She'd charmed an entire shipload of people, even sour old Mrs. Ferris in the end.

"You love her very much, don't you?"

Rafe stilled. The question echoed in his mind. The answer echoed even louder, shaking him to his foundations.

He stood abruptly. "If you'll excuse me, I'll go and see what's keeping her."

"I told Adams to serve her tea in the kitchen," Lady Cleeve confessed. "I hoped she would understand from that that there was nothing for her here."

Rafe swore under his breath. "I'll find her." He yanked open the drawing room door.

The butler, Adams, stepped back, startled. Listening at doors, Rafe thought.

"Where is Miss Cleeve?" he snapped.

The butler looked puzzled. "I don't know, sir. I thought she might be in here." He glanced past Rafe to Lady Cleeve and said, "She was supposed to come to the kitchen, but she never did. We thought she might be in the garden with her cat, but she's not there, either."

Rafe whirled and looked at the pile of luggage still standing in the hall. The cat basket was gone. So was Ayisha's valise and her new warm cloak. Threaded through the handle of his own valise was a folded piece of paper. He snatched it, broke the seal, and read:

My dearest Rafe,

I am sorry to leave you like this, without saying good-bye in person, but I can do it no other way.

You never told me you were the heir to an earldom, never told me that there was any possibility I might become a countess. And you never said you were already betrothed to a titled, rich lady of distinguished family. You spoke on the ship of ruining me, but it's clear from what Lady Cleeve said just now that if you married me, I would be your ruin, and that I cannot do.

You are kind and gallant and noble of heart, but I love you too much—

Rafe stopped reading for a moment, his heart pounding, his breath frozen in his chest. She *loved* him? Yes, there it was, in dark blue ink on elegant white paper. She loved him. Too much.

I love you too much to let your feelings of obligation and gratitude bring you to social ruin.

Obligation and gratitude, Rafe thought. What rubbish! But he'd never told her what he felt. It was as much his fault as anyone's that she'd rushed off.

It is very difficult to leave you, but I must. I could not bear to live as a mistress in St. John's Wood.

Rafe swore as he read that. She must have heard everything.

Do not worry about me. I have the money you gave me in Portsmouth and I will be all right. I survived Cairo, and I will certainly manage in England. My father always said he would bring me to England, so in a way he has, and I am glad of it.
Do not worry about me, dear Rafe. Just take care of yourself and have a wonderful life.

With all my love, yours ever, Ayisha

PS. Please convey my best wishes to Lady Cleeve and explain to her that I never had any expectations of her. You know it's true. I would not want her to think ill of me.

Rafe felt the kind of hollowness that he used to feel before a battle. He couldn't lose her, not now. He crumpled the letter in his fist. "She's run off," he said. "I'm going after her."

"If she doesn't want to be here—" Lady Cleeve began.

"Not another word, madam," Rafe snapped. "Or I won't be responsible for my actions."

Shocked, Lady Cleeve took two steps back. "I only meant that she has chosen—"

Rafe silenced her with a look. "You!" He snapped his fingers at the butler. "She must have left by a back door, so show me how she would have got out. And I want every servant in this house out looking for her—now! Understand?"

The man gabbled something, Rafe didn't care what. He was racing down the hall toward the rear of the house, towing the butler with him.

The little fool. Where the devil did she think she was going? She knew not a soul besides himself in all of England. Still, on foot she couldn't have gone far. It shouldn't take too long to find her. And when he did . . .

He ran along the narrow path that ran from the rear of the property beside the wood and led to the village of Penton Mewsey, scanning the path ahead and the surrounding countryside.

But there was no sign of a small figure in a dark pink cloak.

He came to a road and saw in the distance a wagon going away from him. He narrowed his eyes. He could see a splotch of something reddish on it. Was it someone sitting on the back? Someone in a dark pink cloak? He couldn't be sure.

Dammit. He turned and ran back to Cleeveden. He passed some servants. "Keep looking," he ordered. "Follow this path as far as it goes."

"No sign of her?" Lady Cleeve greeted him anxiously when he returned.

"I think she might have got a lift on a cart," Rafe said. "I'm going to go after it." He yanked on the bellpull and told the servant who came running: "Tell the stables I require their fastest horse to be saddled and brought to me at once."

*H*e rode down the path and galloped along the road in the direction the wagon had gone, but when he caught up with it, he saw the splash of red he'd seen was a tattered old rug wrapped around a chest of drawers.

With a curse he wheeled his horse around and headed back the way he'd come.

At the junction of the path and the road, he headed down the path toward the village of Penton Mewsey. There was just a handful of shops and houses, and Lady Cleeve's servants had already investigated. There was no sign of a young lady in a dark pink cloak with a cat in a basket, they told him. Nobody had seen any young lady, not hereabouts, sir.

The original path continued past the village. Rafe followed along it. A light rain started. Rafe ignored it. From time to time another path branched to the right or the left, and at each fork he shouted her name and waited, wondering which path Ayisha would choose. She was a city girl, had lived most of her life in Cairo, and this countryside was foreign to her, with its fields and hedgerows, its tangled woods and rolling hills. She would take the path the most trodden, he decided.

But after following a dozen paths to each village, hamlet, or roadside within a five-mile radius without success, he began to wonder. He'd crossed a few larger roads. She hadn't ridden off in that first wagon, but maybe she'd been offered a lift, maybe she'd hailed a passing vehicle.

She had a little money—not much, he knew, but it might get her as far as Andover, or even Winchester.

If the driver was trustworthy.

She knew about villains, he tried to tell himself. She knew what life in the streets was like. She didn't trust easily. How long had it taken before she trusted him?

He groaned, thinking about it.

She still didn't trust him. Didn't trust him to know what he wanted, know what was good for him. Otherwise she would never have left him.

If you married me, I would be your ruin.

Not his ruin, his salvation. What did he care for the opinions of others?

He should have married her on the ship. They could have married again in a church. His worry then about protecting her from gossip meant nothing now that he'd lost her.

He should have told her about Axebridge and the succession. He hadn't thought it would matter.

Liar. Of course it mattered. Most women liked the idea of a title. Most women loved the idea. He'd been courted for that title . . .

Had he, deep down, feared she might be the same?

The chill deepened. Rain pelted down in icy streams. If he hadn't left in such a hurry, he would have brought his greatcoat. No matter. He pulled up his collar and continued the search. Where the hell was she? Had she found shelter? He had visions of her crouched in the mud, under a bush, wet and cold and miserable. The thought was unbearable.

His clothes were soon sodden, heavy with water and clinging clammily to him. He was shivering with cold, but he didn't stop. If he was cold, how much colder was Ayisha, daughter of a hot climate? And women's clothing was so much more inadequate than men's—men's! He stopped, started. She'd disguised herself in boy's clothing before. Had she done it again?

He galloped back to the village of Penton Mewsey and questioned everyone he could find, but nobody had seen a young man or boy with a suitcase and basket containing a black-and-white spotted cat.

By that time darkness was falling. The rain stopped. Rafe knew there was only the slimmest of chances, but he rode the paths again in the dark, calling out her name. But the sound echoed hollowly through the silent landscape. It was so cold his breath hung in smoky drifts. The clouds obscured the moon and he couldn't see a thing in the inky dark. All he could hear was the dripping of water and the squelch of mud beneath his horse's hooves.

He turned his weary horse toward Cleeveden. He'd resume the search in the morning.

He slept badly, rose early, and this time used a map of the local area to set out a coordinated search, military style. Higgins had arrived the previous night with Rafe's curricle and horses, so Rafe put the former soldier in charge of the search.

Rafe sent the servants out, each with strict instructions to search a particular area, looking for a young woman or a youth with a black-and-white spotted cat in a basket. She might leave her heavy valise behind, she might not care about her clothes, but she would never abandon that cat.

Rafe himself rode to Andover and questioned people there. A coach had passed through the previous afternoon, but whether there was a young lady on it, or a boy and a cat, nobody could say. He wasn't sure then where to go. To the east was London, to the south was the way they'd come; which way would Ayisha go?

He tried both. He took the London road first, and rode more than forty miles, as far as the second coach stop, but nobody at any of the inns had seen her. He then retraced his steps and rode south, but again, after several coach stops, gave up the chase. Nobody had seen her.

How did a young woman with a spotted cat and a valise disappear to completely from the face of the earth? She must have been offered a lift in some private vehicle, he decided. She could be anywhere.

Exhausted, dispirited, and sick at heart, Rafe rode back to Cleeveden. It didn't surprise him at all when the servants who'd been out hunting all day had nothing to report. He'd felt it in his gut all day.

He'd lost her.

Twenty

❧

"H ave the vicar of your local church call the banns," Rafe told Lady Cleeve a week after Ayisha had gone missing. He'd spent every day out searching, in vain.

Lady Cleeve's jaw dropped. "Call the banns for whom?"

"For Ayisha and me, of course."

"But she's gone. You don't know where—"

"I'll find her," Rafe said firmly. "And when I do I'll marry her. I've written off for a special license, of course, but it won't hurt to have the banns called." It was a slim chance, he knew, but if Ayisha was still in the district, she might attend church, and if she did, he wanted her to hear the banns for her wedding being called. That would make his determination to marry her quite clear.

"Her mother's name was Kati Machabeli. I've written it out here." He passed her a slip of paper. "I'm going to Axebridge to get my brother's vicar to do the same. And to inform my brother of my intentions." He gave Lady Cleeve a cool smile. "We shall be married in the chapel at Axebridge. I want the world to know this marriage has the Earl of Axebridge's approval."

Lady Cleeve frowned. "Does it?"

"It will," Rafe said. "He will have no choice." His brother owed him, and Rafe would force from him at least a facade of approval.

I am betrothed," Rafe told his brother and sister-in-law the next evening at dinner. He'd reached Axebridge at dusk.

"I see," George said cautiously. "And who is the bride-to-be?"

"Ayisha Cl—I suppose legally she is Ayisha Machabeli."

George's brow rose. "Who?" His tone was cold.

"Ayisha Machabeli. She is the natural daughter of Sir Henry Cleeve and a Georgian woman called Kati Machabeli," Rafe told his brother the next day.

His brother's mouth tightened. "*Natural* daughter?"

"Yes," Rafe said coldly. "Ayisha's mother was Sir Henry's mistress. He bought her as a slave." He was determined there would be nothing hidden, nothing kept back. George would know exactly who his brother was marrying.

"And you think this—this *female* is suited to be the mother of a future Earl of Axebridge?"

Rafe looked at him. "Call her 'this *female*' in that tone again, brother, and I'll shove your teeth so far down your throat you'll never find them."

What followed was the kind of silence you could cut with a knife. The two brothers stared at each other across the table.

"And yes, she's magnificently suited to be the mother of a future Earl of Axebridge," Rafe continued after a moment. "She would never countenance a devil's bargain such as your Lady Lavinia Fettiplace agreed to. Ayisha would fight tooth and nail—literally—to keep her children safe and in her arms."

Lucy, his sister-in-law, made a small sound, and Rafe glanced at her. Her plain, rather horsey face was filled with distress.

"You must not blame—" she began.

Her husband placed his hand over hers. "Silence, Lucy," he said. "We need explain nothing to him."

She shook her head. "Of course we must, George. It is his child we were plotting to take, after all."

Rafe blinked at such unexpected honesty.

"It's all my fault—" she began.

"It was my idea," George spoke over her. "So any blame must

go to me. I put the proposition to Lady Lavinia, you can hold me entirely respon—"

"But you did it for *me*, because of *me*, because I am such a hopeless failure as a wife!" Lucy, Rafe's sister-in-law, burst out harshly. Tears poured down her cheeks.

Rafe stared, stunned by the unexpected outburst.

To Rafe's surprise, George leapt from his chair and put his arms around his wife. "You're not a failure, Lucy," George said urgently. "And I forbid you to ever say so. You're a wonderful wife and I—I couldn't live without you," he added in a lower voice. He pulled out a handkerchief and began to dry her cheeks gently.

Rafe watched in amazement. He'd never seen his brother this . . . this human. And until this moment he had no idea that his brother even cared about his wife.

Rafe himself had always liked Lucy, had even felt a bit protective toward her. She was plain and gangly and a bit horse-faced, but was always kind and gentle and quietly perceptive. For Rafe as a boy, she had been the one good thing about visits to Axebridge.

George, he recalled, had been bitterly disappointed when he first met her—the Earl of Axebridge had selected a bride for his heir and Lucy's bloodlines and fortune were both excellent.

"Good breedin' stock," his father had declared. "Lackin' in looks of course, but that's all to the good. The plain ones tend to stay loyal, especially if they're wed to a handsome dog like yourself, George."

Not that it mattered what George thought. His father was not to be gainsaid. And he was proven right when shy, awkward Lucy had taken one look at her handsome fiancé and fallen desperately in love.

But it seemed, somewhere along the way, his brother had come to care for her. Care deeply, if Rafe was any judge.

"It was for me, Rafe," Lucy said once she'd composed herself. "George did it for me. I was so . . . so desperate for a child. And Lady Lavinia . . . Lady Lavinia had said . . ."

Her husband took over. "Lady Lavinia made it clear she disliked babies and children and talked of leaving the children to servants. And while there is nothing wrong with that . . . It's just that Lucy . . ." He gave his wife an anguished look.

"Oh, Rafe, I *ache* to hold a babe in my arms," Lucy said brokenly. "I ache so much I nearly stole a baby in the village. I only lifted it up for a moment—I did put it back, but . . . it worried George." Her face crumpled.

For a long moment there was no sound in the room but the crackling of the fire and the soft sobs of Rafe's gentle sister-in-law. Her husband held her helplessly.

After a time, Lucy's weeping stopped, and after pouring a drink for everyone, George took up the story. "I thought if Lady Lavinia didn't want to bring the children up . . . Lucy could. She'd make a wonderful mother . . ." He looked at Rafe. "I'm sorry, Rafe, I didn't consider your position; I was thinking of Lucy, only Lucy . . . I hope you'll forgive me one day."

Rafe was shattered by the admission. He'd seen the arrangement with Lady Lavinia as yet another sign that Rafe mattered nothing to his family, that his brother had no respect for Rafe and cared for nothing except the Earldom of Axebridge and the succession.

But it wasn't the future of Axebridge that had driven George to such a desperate measure, it was love for his wife.

And that Rafe could completely understand. And forgive.

"I didn't know. And now I do, there's nothing to forgive," Rafe said quietly.

"But—"

He shook his head. "I'm not marrying Lady Lavinia. I have Ayisha now, and there's nothing to forgive. It's all right, Lucy, I forgive you, both of you. I understand."

His words brought fresh tears to Lucy's eyes, and Rafe found he had to walk to the fireplace and stare into the fire; the sight of his brother comforting his wife brought such . . . feelings . . . welling up in him.

He ached for Ayisha, he wanted her in his arms. Here. Now.

The thought crossed his mind that like his sister-in-law he might ache, unfulfilled and empty, for the rest of his life.

When he returned to the table, George said, "So, you are serious about marrying this girl you found in Egypt?"

Rafe looked up, ready to defend Ayisha, but his brother looked earnest and sincere.

"Ayisha, yes, very serious."

George gave him a searching look. "You care for her," he said on a note of discovery.

"I do," Rafe admitted. He swallowed and added, "Very much." For some reason their confessions and the realization that his brother loved his wife had dissolved some of the distance between them.

George nodded. "Then we shall be delighted to welcome her into the family, won't we, Lucy?"

"Yes, of course," Lucy said. "Would you like to have the wedding here at Axebridge, Rafe?"

Rafe nodded. He was shaken by the simplicity of it all. He'd anticipated a fight, recriminations, acrimony, and bitterness. And in a way, that's what had happened. But he hadn't anticipated acceptance. And forgiveness.

"Lovely," Lucy exclaimed. "I've always wanted to organize a wedding. And where is Miss Machabeli at the moment?" Both George and Lucy looked at him in gentle inquiry.

The silence stretched.

"I have no idea," Rafe said eventually. "I seem—I seem to have lost her." His throat was suddenly too full to speak, and all he could do was to pull out Ayisha's letter to him, push it toward his sister-in-law, and go and stare into the fire while they read it.

So what do you intend to do?" said George later that evening over a brandy.

"Find her. Get her back. Marry her," Rafe said and sipped the mellow liquid. He could not quite get over the fact that here he was, talking to his brother like . . . a friend.

"I only came here to tell you I was marrying her and to tell the vicar to call the banns, even though I've written to the Archbishop of Canterbury for a special license, just in case."

Lucy squeezed his hand. "You'll find her."

Rafe hoped to hell she was right. The thought of life without Ayisha was . . . too unutterably bleak to contemplate. "I've also written to Bow Street and they'll make inquiries in London and Portsmouth. And I'll open up my London house and get it ready for Ayisha and me to live in."

"You won't live at Foxcotte?" Lucy asked.

He shook his head. "No, Ayisha's always lived in a city. I think she'd find the country too dull."

George nodded. "So what are you going to do with Foxcotte?"

"Do with it?" Rafe frowned. "What do you mean?"

"It's not good for a property to remain unoccupied for such a long time. It's your decision of course," his brother said, being careful not to step on toes, "but if it were mine, I'd be getting tenants in or selling it."

Ayisha had said much the same, Rafe recalled.

"I'm not selling it." Rafe was surprised by the vehemence with which that came out. He moderated his tone, "I might not have been there since I was fourteen, but I don't want to sell it."

"So you'll get tenants in?"

"I'll consider it," Rafe said. "I'm going back to Lady Cleeve's— she's Ayisha's grandmother, lives near Penton Mewsey, not far from Foxcotte—and I might drop in on Barry, my agent, on the way and see how things stand."

"You think Ayisha might still be in the area?" Lucy asked.

Rafe shrugged. "I have no idea. But I can't help thinking she'd go back there or write if she was in trouble. Lady Cleeve is her grandmother, after all."

"Do I have your permission to put a notice in the newspapers?" George asked.

"Notice? You mean like a missing notice?"

George smiled. "No, I meant a betrothal announcement from me, as the head of the family. If the girl—"

"Ayisha."

"Yes, if she sees it, it might help your case to make it obvious your family supports the match. I think a large notice with the family crest should do the trick."

"It would, George. Thank you," Rafe managed to say. He knew full well that the large notice and family crest was not for Ayisha to read—even if she read newspapers, she wouldn't recognize the family crest. It was a message for the *ton*.

His brother was making it clear to the world that this marriage had the full support of the Earl of Axebridge. And that the Earl of Axebridge expected the *ton* to fall into line and support it, too.

It was more family support than Rafe had experienced in a lifetime.

A t midafternoon Rafe passed through Andover. Ten days since he'd last seen Ayisha. Desperation gnawed at him increasingly, the fear that she might indeed be gone forever goading him on in his relentless search. He refused to give in to despair. He would find her. He had to. His entire future happiness depended on it.

He rode past the turnoff to Foxcotte when an idea struck him. What if she'd gone there? She knew it was his, knew it was close—she'd noticed the sign that first time.

What if Ayisha had gone to earth at Foxcotte?

He urged his horse faster, rode through the village at a smart clip, and stopped at the big, old wrought-iron gates, with the fox emblem so familiar and beloved from his boyhood.

Then the gates were black and gleaming and always stood open, waiting for his return. Now they were dull and closed, chained shut with a thick chain and an old padlock.

Beyond them the gravel drive was weedy and unkempt. No carriage had driven up there in a long time.

Rafe tied his horse to the gate and climbed the wall. Some of the stones had fallen away, he saw. Repairs were needed.

As he walked up the path, memories flooded him. The place was a mess, but oddly, his spirits lifted. He'd always loved this place, had been happy here.

But because he'd never really come to terms with his grandmother's death he felt somehow . . . guilty. She'd died alone, with nobody to hold her hand, comfort her. He should have been there. She'd taken him in when nobody had wanted him. He'd let her down.

Logic argued that it wasn't his fault, that nobody had told him, but he knew in his heart he hadn't written as often as he should have, and if he had, someone—one of the servants—would have told him. The guilt remained, so he'd never been back. He would not profit by her death.

It was a mistake, he realized. This place would have helped his guilt, not exacerbated it. He reached the front of the house. Of course it was locked. He peered in at the windows and all was stillness, dust, and holland coverings over the furniture.

Nobody had been here in a very long while.

He walked around the side, glancing in at each window he came to. It was the same: shadows, dust, undisturbed for years, and holland covers. The stables were silent and empty, also chained and padlocked shut. The high-walled kitchen garden was largely gone to weeds; only a corner patch next to the gardener's cottage was cleared and neat. A wisp of smoke twined from the chimney of the old gardener's cottage.

Rafe smiled, remembering. Old Nat's cottage, built into the wall. Nothing had changed. There was the sagging clothesline strung between the cottage and the old apple tree, and on it were pegged an apron, some dishcloths, and two of Mrs. Nat's enormous bright pink flowered flannel nightgowns, flapping like giant sails in the wind. He smiled at the familiar sight.

The old gardener would be ancient by now. Or maybe there was just Mrs. Nat still living there. Mrs. Nat who'd always produced a thick slice of cake or a handful of biscuits for a growing boy.

He didn't go over and knock on her door. If he did, she'd make a pot of tea and he wouldn't get away for an hour or more. He needed to keep searching.

He needed to get back to Cleeveden, see if there was any news there.

Nobody had been inside Foxcotte for years. Ayisha wasn't here, after all.

He trudged down the drive, climbed the fence, and rode back to the village. He'd get tenants in, he decided. He'd laid his ghosts. The place was starting to crumble, and he didn't want that to happen.

The agent, Mr. Barry, was very pleased to see him. "I'm just about to have my tea, Mr. Ramsey, and I'd be honored if you'd join me," the man said.

A hearty tea of bread, butter, honey, jam, cream, cheese, pickles, and several kinds of pastries was laid out on the table, along with a jug of cool local beer. Rafe had no interest in the spread, but he accepted. Best to get the property sorted as quickly as possible. He wanted everything in order once he found Ayisha.

They discussed the property—or rather Mr. Barry discussed, while Rafe listened and nodded while the man ate his tea. Rafe ate nothing. These days he had no appetite for food. He sipped a little of the sour local beer.

"I've had several offers to rent Foxcotte, sir. Try one of these." Barry passed him a plate and Rafe absently took one of the pies.

Barry continued, "I did write to you, if you recall. Please eat something, sir. You're looking a mite peaky if you don't mind me saying so. Have a bite of that little little pie there, why don't you?"

Rafe, sighing inwardly at the man's kindly concern, forced himself to take a bite, just to shut him up. "I did get your letters," he said "but now I'm thinking—" He broke off and looked at what he was eating. A flattish, triangular pie that looked and tasted very familiar. And not from his boyhood. His heart started thumping.

"Where did this pie come from?" he asked Barry in a voice that was strangely calm.

"The village bakery, sir. They're a bit different but very tasty—sir? Sir?"

But Rafe had shoved the rest of the pie in his pocket and was gone. In three steps he'd slammed out of the cottage, hurled himself onto his horse, and was galloping toward the village.

Oh God, he prayed. Let it be her. He didn't dare hope, but the pie . . . it was exactly like—

Please, God.

What if she was there, in the bakery itself? It had to be her, it had to.

He burst into the bakery and looked wildly around. No sign of Ayisha. Hollow desperation gripped him.

He pulled out the remains of the pie and brandished it fiercely. "Who made this pie?"

"Summat wrong with it?" The baker came forward, a big meaty-looking fellow, his chin jutted belligerently.

"No. But *who made it*?" Good God, he was shaking.

"A young lass brings 'em in."

Oh God, oh God. "Where does she live?" Rafe said, amazed to hear how calm his voice sounded.

The man gave him a long, suspicious look. "I don't rightly hold with telling toffs where a pretty young girl might live— she's a good lass, an' all—"

Rafe wanted to punch the man in his fat, smug face, and at the same time shake his hand for protecting Ayisha, for it must— it had to be her. Instead he fixed him with a cold look and said, "I must insist—"

"Oh, Thomas, don't you know who this is?" A plump, middle-aged woman came bustling forward. "It's young master Rafe from the old house, isn't it, sir?"

"Yes." Rafe stared at her and through the fog of desperation, his memory stirred. "Jenny—no, Janey Bray, isn't it?"

The woman beamed. "That's right, but I'm Mrs. Thomas Rowe now. Fancy you rememberin' me. I haven't seen you since you were a lad, but I remember you, sir. Always liked my curd cakes, you did."

"I remember. Now, the young woman who made these pies," Rafe reminded her.

"Old Nat's granddaughter? She bakes them pastries herself and brings 'em in every day. Something a bit different, aren't they, sir? Very tasty."

"Old Nat's granddaughter?" he echoed hollowly. "You're sure? Absolutely sure?" Damn, damn, damn. If she was known to these people, she couldn't be Ayisha. The bitterness of deflated hopes swamped him.

"That's right. Turned up, she did, nearly two weeks ago, gave Nat's place a good clean out—well, it needed it—been so long since Mrs. Nat passed on, and old Nat before her. I disremember who told us she was Nat's granddaughter—do you recall, Thomas? No, me neither, but that's who she is, right enough."

Hope stirred cautiously. Rafe said carefully. "She's at the old gardener's cottage?"

"That's right, sir, you remember—" But Rafe was gone.

The gardener's cottage was built into the high garden wall, and one of its charms that Rafe recalled from his boyhood was that you could walk into the cottage from the kitchen garden and go right through it and be outside the estate.

Rafe rode around the back way, his heart racing. To think he'd avoided going there earlier because he thought old Nat's wife would keep him talking.

With shaking hands he tied his horse to a tree, wiped his damp palms, and knocked at the door of the old gardener's cottage.

The door opened and she stood there dressed, village style, in some faded old dress of Mrs. Nat's and an apron. There was a smut of flour on her cheek, her hair was carelessly tied up with a bit of green cloth, her nose was red, her lips were chapped from the cold, and she was still the most beautiful woman he'd ever seen in his life.

His hungry gaze devoured her. She stared at him, shocked, unmoving, silent, her eyes as wary as they had been when he first knew her.

He didn't care. He'd tamed her then and he'd do it again. Or die trying.

The kitten emerged and rubbed against his ankles, meowing plaintively to be picked up.

Rafe only had eyes for Ayisha.

"You're all thin again," he choked out. What a stupid thing to say. All the speeches he'd rehearsed in his mind, all the words he'd saved to bring her back to him and when it counted, that was all he could say. But it was true. She was pitifully thin. She must have starved all this time. He ached for her.

He stared at her, willing the words to come, but he could only stare. And stare. Devouring her with his eyes.

"You're thinner, too," she said softly.

"Perhaps, but if I am, it's not because I was starving," he said, his voice husky with emotion. "It's because I'd lost you."

She gave a wobbly smile and gestured behind her. "I had food, but I wasn't hungry for food. Only for you."

At her words his self-control cracked, and he stepped forward, seized her around the waist, and lifted her off her feet, holding her against him, never to let her run from him again. He held her tightly, exalting in the feel of her in his arms again, breathing in the beloved scent of her, burying his face in the softness of her neck.

Her arms came around him and she hugged him, kissing him on the crown of his head, on his ear, anywhere she could, caressing him with loving urgency. "Oh, Rafe, oh, Rafe," she murmured.

He slid her slowly down his body until their faces were level, and kissed her deeply. "Never leave me again," he ordered. His whole body was shaking.

She cupped his face in her hands and stared earnestly at him. "Are you sure about this, Rafe? I don't want to ruin your life."

"The only way you could ruin my life is to leave me," he said forcefully. "I need you. In my arms, in my life."

She gazed into his eyes a moment, then gave a tremulous little sigh. She tightened her grip on him and whispered, "Then take me now my love, for I need you, more than I can say."

He kicked the door shut behind him and carried her to where she'd dragged a mattress in front of the fire. He laid her on the mattress, sat down, and pulled off his boots.

She lay quietly, looking up at him. "I've missed you so much, Rafe." She ran her hand lightly up his spine.

He might as well have been naked, the way he could feel her lightest touch, even through several layers of clothing.

He stood to remove his coat. "Don't ever run away from me again," he told her, pulling off his shirt.

"It was worst at night."

"Yes, well, in England it gets cold at night." He began to unbutton his breeches.

"The temperature wasn't the problem. I found these wonderful thick, warm nightdresses."

He gave a choke of laughter as he realized she'd been wearing Mrs. Nat's enormous flannel nightgowns. "You've been wearing—"

She placed her hand around his thigh, and he forgot what he was going to say.

"Did you really miss me, Rafe?" she asked.

He turned, his breeches half undone, and gave her an incredulous look. "Miss you? *Miss you?*" The glow in her eyes completely unmanned him, and he groaned and sank to his knees in front of her. "I'd rather lose an arm or a leg or both my eyes than lose you again. I've never felt so . . ." He shook his head. "My heart is too full for words."

"Then show me," she said softly, pulling him down to her.

He showed her, loving every inch of her with a tender thoroughness that left her weak and gasping, helpless with love and on the verge of tears—why tears, she could not imagine.

She was his, to do with as he wanted, for now, at least. Nothing was resolved between them, only that she'd missed him desperately and he, apparently, felt the same. For now it was enough.

The flames danced, gilding his skin, caressing every glorious muscle, every masculine angle and plane, her man of gold and shadows. Outside the wind whistled through the trees.

The tiny cottage suited her perfectly, caught between two worlds. On one side was the grand house he owned, and on the other, the wild, wild woods. Was this where she belonged?

No, she belonged in his arms, she thought, as his hands and mouth slowly drove any coherent thought from her mind. No matter where in the world they were, as long as she was in . . . his . . . arms . . .

And then she heard them, the words he'd never spoken, so deep and soft that at first she wasn't sure she hadn't dreamed them. "I love you, Ayisha."

Her eyes flew open. His gaze locked with hers. Frantically she tried to scrape her wits together.

He said it again. "I love you, Ayisha." His body still moving within hers, scattering every thought but one.

"I love you, Ayisha."

She wanted to respond, but she had no words, no will. She shattered around him, his words ringing in her ears, as the rhythm pounded through them: "I love you, I love you, I love you."

Afterward she lay in his arms, watching the fire glow and dance. After a time she sighed and sat up. "I shouldn't have allowed that. I won't be your mistress, I—" she began.

"Hush," he said, kissing her. "I love you. I want you for my wife and always have."

Her eyes filled as she took in that he meant every word. "Oh, Rafe, and I love you, so very, very much. I always have," she confessed. "I think even in Cairo, though I tried hard not to. But if you are to be an earl . . . My grandm—Lady Cleeve said I would be your social ruin."

"Stop fretting. I don't care what anyone else thinks. You mean more to me than anyone or anything. I love you and I need you and I'm going to marry you."

"I won't give up my children," she warned.

"Neither will I, though it's not an issue." He told her what he'd learned, how his gentle, tragic sister-in-law had almost stolen a baby. And how it had driven his brother to make the bargain that had so enraged Rafe.

"The poor, poor lady," she whispered. "We must do something about that, Rafe. We must find her a baby to love."

He looked at her with an unreadable expression. "Ayisha Cleeve Machabeli, if I wasn't already head over heels in love with you, I would have fallen in love with you again, just now," he said in a husky voice.

Oh, how his words warmed her. She couldn't help but show it, and next thing she knew they were making love again.

"Why did you come to Foxcotte?" he asked much later.

"It was the only place I knew," she told him. "I almost didn't find it. It was late and pouring with rain, and I was lost and feeling my way in the dark, following the wall, thinking it must lead somewhere. And then I felt a window. And then a door. So I knocked, but nobody answered. And I tried the door and it opened, so . . ." She'd found wood and a tinderbox and soon she had a fire going. It was a heaven-sent refuge for her and Cleo.

"It was only when I went into the village that I learned this was Foxcotte after all. You said you hadn't been here since you were a boy, so I thought it was the last place you'd think of looking for me. You didn't come here looking for me, were you?"

"No, not to Foxcotte. I came to visit my agent and make arrangements to rent the place out. He was eating one of your pies . . ."

He kissed her again, then said, "It's time we dressed. I'd like to return to Cleeveden while there's still light."

"Must we?" Ayisha didn't want to go back to a grandmother who despised her.

"Stop fretting. I think you will find that much has changed since you ran off."

"What's changed? Tell me."

But Rafe wouldn't explain. He kissed the tip of her nose. "Trust me. Get dressed and come and find out."

Nothing she could say or do would budge him from that position, so she dressed and gathered her things together, ready to make the journey back to Cleeveden.

"I could have been happy here," she said, looking around the tiny cottage.

"Happy?"

"Lonely, but content," she corrected herself. "It's a dear little cottage. And the countryside is beautiful. And did you know? I started a garden."

He gave her a surprised look. "I thought you would dislike country life."

She shook her head. "No indeed. I've never lived in the country before, but it's lovely. I would love to live here." She laid her hand on his arm. "But if it's painful for you, we need not."

He smiled. "No, I've laid my ghosts. I couldn't bear to see this place without my grandmother here, knowing how she died alone. But I loved this place as a boy and I love it now, all the more since it brought you back to me. Grandma would be so happy to have us here. It's settled then; once we're married, we'll live at Foxcotte. And," he added, "we'll keep this cottage for our own private place."

* * *

My dear Ayisha," Lady Cleeve came down the stairs to greet them. "I must apologize—" she broke off. "Good heavens, it's like looking into a mirror fifty years ago."

Ayisha exchanged a glance with Rafe. "Are you all right, ma'am? You look a little pale," she said.

Lady Cleeve straightened. "I'm all right, my dear, thank you. Seeing you, seeing your face does me a great deal of good, even though it emphasizes how foolish I've been. Come with me." She led them to the sitting room and pointed to a painting hanging on the wall.

"There," she said. "Me, just before I married your grandfather. If ever I doubted you, doubted the wisdom of you coming here, this picture is the proof that you were meant to come to me. You are my own flesh and blood, and nothing else matters." She held out her arms to Ayisha, and Ayisha hugged her.

Later they spoke over tea and cakes.

"I saw your letter to Rafe, my dear—he did not mean me to read it," Lady Cleeve added with a rueful look, "but I did, and it showed me how badly I'd wronged you. But I cannot wholly blame Mrs. Whittacker; it was my own prejudice that made me cruel. I want to explain why I responded as I did—about St. John's Wood."

Ayisha stilled. That hurt was still very tender.

"I didn't really mean it. I am . . . bitter about mistresses, that's all." She twisted a handkerchief in her bony old fingers and began, "You see, my husband kept a mistress all the time we were in India—a local woman, far beneath my notice—but to my shame I was deeply jealous. Not only did she have my husband, you see, she was able to keep her children. There were four."

She added in a lower voice, "I lost five babies to the Indian climate. Henry was my only child to survive his infancy, but when he turned seven, my husband sent him off to England to school." Her face quivered. "Such a little boy he was, too. I begged my husband to let him stay with me another few years, or to let me go with him to England, but he said it was bad for a boy to be smothered by a doting mother, and my place was at my husband's side. And he sent my little boy away."

The old lady's face worked as she fought to keep her emotions under control. Ayisha slipped out of her chair and knelt beside her grandmother.

The bony fingers knotted hard around the handkerchief. "Every day I had to see that woman walking down the street past our house with all her healthy, glowing, happy children around her—the children my own husband had given her. While I was left alone. And bitter . . . When I saw my Henry again, he was all grown up and polite, like a stranger." Her voice cracked on the last word.

She wiped her eyes, took a few deep, shaky breaths, then looked down at Ayisha. "I took out that hurt and anger on you, my dear, and I cannot express my regret deeply enough—"

"Hush, it does not matter," Ayisha said, stroking the gnarled old hand. "Papa wronged his wife, there's no denying it, just as his father wronged you."

She hesitated, then added, "My friend Laila says we should leave the past in the past, because if we take it with us, it will only poison the future."

"Your friend is a wise woman."

Just then there was a knock at the door and the butler entered. "Mr. Pilkington, the lawyer, my lady."

Lady Cleeve brightened. "Send him in, Adams."

Rafe and Ayisha stood. "We'll leave you alone," Rafe said.

Lady Cleeve waved them back with an imperious gesture. "No, stay. I sent for Pilkington last week to have him change my will." She tossed Rafe a mildly challenging look. "Removing the name of Alicia Cleeve and replacing it with that of Ayisha Machabeli, only daughter of Kati Machabeli and Sir Henry Cleeve, baronet, my granddaughter."

The lawyer entered. Lady Cleeve performed the introductions but when she came to Ayisha, introducing her as "My granddaughter, Ayisha Machabeli," the lawyer corrected her. "Ayisha Cleeve, I believe," he said, with a smile.

He explained, "Last week when your ladyship gave me the instructions for the new will, I was struck by the name Kati Machabeli. It rang a bell, so to speak. So I went through your late son's papers and sure enough, I found this and this." He laid a flimsy document on the table.

Lady Cleeve picked it up and glanced at it, stared at the lawyer, and examined the document more carefully. "Is this genuine?" she demanded.

"I believe so," the lawyer said.

"Would you care to enlighten us of the contents of the document?" Rafe said dryly.

The lawyer started, "Oh, of course, of course, sir." He passed it to Rafe. "It's a wedding certificate recording the marriage of Sir Henry Cleeve to Kati Machabeli—it took place a month before Sir Henry's recorded death."

"They got married?" Ayisha exclaimed. "When was this?"

The lawyer gave her the date. "I must apologize for not bringing it to anyone's attention sooner, but I did not realize. My late grandfather dealt with all of this and—" The lawyer hesitated. "There's no denying it, Grandad was getting rather muddled in his old age. The files were in a shocking mess, and although I managed to get them into rough order after he died, I didn't read them closely, since all concerned had been dead several years."

Ayisha looked at Rafe. "Their last trip to Jerusalem. I was to go with them, but I came down with measles the day before they left and couldn't go. I knew Mama was very excited about the trip, but . . . I had no idea this was planned . . . And when they returned they were dying . . ." She frowned. "Do you know, I think Mama tried to tell me, only I didn't understand . . ." She sat back in her chair, stunned. "*Married.* How wonderful."

"Ahem," the lawyer cleared his throat uncomfortably. "I'm afraid this marriage does not, er, as it were, change the status of your, ahem, birth. You are still, ahem, as it were . . ." He trailed off.

"Illegitimate," Ayisha said. "Yes, I understand that. It doesn't matter. The marriage proves what I've said all along, that Papa truly did love my mother." She looked at Rafe, her eyes swimming. "And he tried to protect her. The marriage would free her, you see, make her her own person."

"I know." He smiled. "I think it also means you are entitled to be known as—for the next few weeks at least—as Miss Ayisha Cleeve."

"Yes, indeed," Lady Cleeve said.

"It also means you inherit all Sir Henry's property," the lawyer said.

"Really?" Ayisha exclaimed. "Does that include a house in Cairo?"

The lawyer blinked, but searched through his papers. "Yes, there is a house, currently leased to a—"

"Excellent," she said. "Can we give it to Ali?" she said to Rafe.

He laughed. "Give it to whoever you want. It's yours to do with what you like."

"Then I will give it to Ali." She beamed at the lawyer. "Thank you, Mr. Pilkington. You've made me very happy."

Rafe glanced across at Ayisha's grandmother. She was watching her granddaughter with a soft expression. Rafe leaned forward and tapped her on the arm.

"I did warn you to be cautious," he murmured with a smile.

She gave him a misty smile in return. "Too late, Mr. Ramsey, too late. My granddaughter is an extraordinary young woman. Thank you for bringing her to me."

"She's only on loan," Rafe said firmly. "The banns have been called. In four weeks she will be mine."

Ayisha heard him and laughed. "No," she said. "I'm yours already. And in four weeks there will be a wedding."

Twenty-one

❧

All week long carriages had been rolling up the graveled drive of Axebridge as people gathered for the wedding. The guest list contained two dukes, a marquess, several earls, a handful of barons, a clutch of baronets, and many more distinguished guests. Shy, plain, extremely well-connected Lucy, Countess of Axebridge, had asked, and everyone had come.

Lucy was determined her new sister-in-law would be launched in the best possible company. If people were going to gossip about this wedding, they would gossip for the right reasons, she vowed.

The beautiful sixteenth-century Axebridge chapel was filled with flowers; a lovely informal mixture of spring blossoms, wild narcissus, bluebells, and hyacinths mixed with hothouse orchids, sprays of pussy willow, and long-stemmed water irises. The fragrance of the flowers mingled with the scent of the beeswax that had been used to polish the ancient oak pews to a glowing shine. Every pane of stained glass sparkled, every inch of brass, silver, and gold in the church gleamed.

Ayisha gazed at her reflection in the looking glass and took a deep breath. "I hope you're watching, Mama," she whispered, "I hope your wedding was as beautiful as mine is going to be."

Her dress was of delicately embroidered white-on-white silk and was heavy, soft, and felt beautiful to wear, with a skirt that swirled as if made for dancing. Hundreds of tiny pearls were sewn in rows down the bodice—simple, but very elegant, Lucy had said when Ayisha had first shown her the design.

With it she wore her grandmother's magnificent pearl rope, and over the exquisite veil of Spanish lace that Lucy had lent her she wore a circlet of pearls. On her feet she wore a pair of white satin boots.

Ayisha loved boots, loved the slight extra height they gave her and the extra warmth they gave. And since the chapel was a five-minute walk from the house, and the English weather so chilly, she was not going to have frozen toes at her own wedding.

The rest of her was in no danger of freezing, either, for Rafe had given her a green velvet cloak, lined with white satin and fringed with white fur, to wear in case it was cold.

She glanced across at the bed, where Laila's parcel lay, and smiled. "For your wedding night," Laila had said at the time. Ayisha had left it until this morning, and when she'd unwrapped it . . . It was the naughtiest harem outfit, straight from the *Arabian Nights* stories, sheer silken pants, a tiny jeweled bodice, and some delicate veils. And as accessories, an ankle chain with bells and small finger cymbals.

An outfit to drive a man wild with desire.

Ayisha couldn't wait.

"Are we ready?" George, Earl of Axebridge, entered the room. He looked her up and down. "You look very beautiful, Ayisha. My brother is a lucky man." He turned to his wife and said, "And the matron of honor, my Lucy in blue, as lovely as the day we married."

"Oh, what nonsense," Lucy said gruffly, but her face glowed with pleasure.

She was plain, Ayisha thought, but with her face lit with love like that, Lucy became beautiful.

The three of them walked to the chapel arm in arm. It was extraordinary, Ayisha thought, how these two had welcomed her into the family. More, she thought, glancing at Lucy; they had taken her to their hearts.

A small crowd of people had gathered outside the chapel,

mostly local people come for the spectacle and for the coins that
the groom would throw afterward, but there were three ladies
Ayisha recognized.

"Mrs. Ferris, Mrs. Wiggs, Mrs. Grenville," she exclaimed.
"How—?"

"We were in the neighborhood and saw the notices in the paper
and we thought, why not come to see you wed," Mrs. Ferris said.
"I hope you don't mind."

"Mind?" Ayisha said. "I'm so pleased to see a familiar face.
Please, go into the church."

"Oh no, no—we didn't come to intrude," Mrs. Grenville said.
"It's such a grand affair and—"

"Please," Ayisha said. "You could sit on the bride's side of
the church. There will be plenty of room. I have only my grandmother."

The three ladies exchanged glances. "Well, if you put it like
that . . ." and they hurried ahead into the church.

Ayisha took a deep breath and, on George's arm, stepped into
the church, peeked around the corner. And gasped.

She'd expected to see the church looking half empty, with the
pews on her side of the church containing just her grandmother
and the three ladies. Instead they were almost as full as Rafe's
side.

Every one of Rafe's friends had chosen to sit on the bride's
side. At the front was her grandmother, looking stunning in gold
tissue and claret velvet, ready to give the bride away.

With her sat a distinguished-looking gray-haired man, her
grandmother's surprise guest, Alaric Stretton, the artist who'd
started everything with his picture of Ayisha at thirteen.

Behind her grandmother sat Harry Morant and his sweet-
faced wife, Nell, who'd arrived the day before with their tiny
daughter, Torie. Baby Torie had spent most of the time since in
Lucy's arms. She was a very happy baby, quite content to be
passed around.

Beside Harry and Nell sat big, brawny Ethan Delaney, sneaking an arm around his little, pregnant wife, Tibby. There was
Lady Gosforth, magnificent in purple, escorted by her flinty-eyed
nephew, Marcus, Earl of Alverleigh, and Nash Renfrew, his
brother.

Only Rafe's friend Gabe and his wife, the Princess of
Zindaria, were missing, but the princess was expecting a child,

and the trip was too arduous for a woman in advanced pregnancy. They'd sent a representative, a handsome young man wearing the uniform of the Royal Zindarian Guard. He sat beside Nash, chatting as if they were old friends, on the bride's side of the church.

There was Lady Ripton, Luke's mother, the warm, motherly woman who'd insisted her son bring his lonely young school friend, Rafe Ramsey, home for Christmases and Easters. With her sat Luke's pretty young sister, Molly, as well as his two older married sisters and their husbands. Luke was not sitting with them; he was Rafe's best man.

All of them on her side of the church, declaring themselves to be her family. Ayisha's eyes blurred.

George gave a signal and the opening chords of music played. Ayisha looked down the aisle to the front of the church and there, standing tall and grave and utterly beautiful, was the man she'd crossed the world for, the man she loved with all her heart. The moment he saw her his eyes lit with blue fire . . .

The music swelled and she slowly walked toward him. Her prince, her pasha, her love.

Epilogue

❧

Foxcotte
1818

"Can't believe the change in old Johnny," Bertie Baxter said. He'd arrived without warning, fresh off a ship from Alexandria, bringing a packet of letters and gifts from Baxter, Laila, and Ali.

"Thought the sun had finally fried his brains when I heard he'd stepped into the parson's mousetrap for a second time, but, have to say, he looks well on it—despite the chaos of the place."

"Chaos?" Ayisha said. "But Laila's a meticulous house-keeper."

"Oh, it's not her, no, she's a fine woman and seems to suit Johnny down to the ground. It's those brats of hers."

"What brats?" Ayisha asked, mystified.

Bertie Baxter gave her an odd look. "Thought she was a friend of yours, ma'am, but if she ain't—"

"She is, my very dearest friend," Ayisha exclaimed.

"Then how is it you don't know she's the mother of four children?" Bertie Baxter said bluntly.

"Four children?" Ayisha echoed.

"There's the oldest boy, Ali; he's a good lad, by and large.

Johnny's very proud of him. And there's no harm in the baby, Rafiq—named after you, Rafe, I gather, but the worst are those twins."

"Twins?" Ayisha gaped.

Bertie nodded. "The little girls. Three years old and pretty as you could want with big brown eyes and curly hair, like a pair of little dolls—but don't you believe it," he added darkly. "Little hellions, both of them. Got this habit of crawlin' all over a fellow—without so much as an invitation—pullin' at his clothes, ruinin' a neckcloth that took an hour to perfect, mussin' a chap's hair."

Ayisha exchanged an amused look with Rafe. Laila must be in seventh heaven with three adopted children. The details would be in the letters Baxter's cousin had brought; she hadn't read them yet, not wanting to be rude and read them in front of the guest who'd brought them. But already she knew the letters would be full of happy news.

Bertie Baxter went on, "All Johnny's fault, of course. He encourages them to think of people as furniture." He shuddered. "Never thought the day I'd see Johnny Baxter with a clutch of brats crawling all over him—and laughing about it."

He stood up. "Well, I'd best get going if I want to get home before dark. Good to see you again, Rafe, and delightful to meet you, Mrs. Ramsey, after hearin' so much about you. Thank you for the refreshments."

He started to leave, then swung back. "Oh, almost forgot, Laila gave me a message for you, Mrs. Ramsey. Said it was important. Now what was it?" He frowned in thought. "Oh yes, she said to tell you she has a very fine stallion now, and she hopes you have one, too."

Ayisha fought a blush and did her best to keep a straight face.

Baxter rattled on, oblivious, "All very well for her to *say* she has a stallion, think it a hum, myself. In all the time I was there, I never saw her with any sort of horse—stallion or not. And why a stallion? Why not an ass? That's what they usually ride there."

"Why not a stallion?" Ayisha managed with an innocent look.

"Take it from me, Mrs. Ramsey, a stallion is not a suitable

mount for a lady. Nasty, unpredictable brutes. A nice gelding or a mare would suit you much better."

"I don't agree," she said.

Baxter gave Ayisha an earnest look. "You don't have a stallion, do you, Mrs. Ramsey? Rafe wouldn't mount you on such a dangerous thing, surely?"

Rafe made a noncommittal sound. He was watching Ayisha with narrowed eyes.

"Oh, but a stallion makes for such an exciting ride," she said mischievously, giving Rafe a provocative look. "I wouldn't mount anything else."

Rafe's face took on a graven expression. Ayisha giggled. He'd worked it out.

Bertie Baxter shook his head. "Ladies tend to be foolishly romantic about stallions. I shall leave it to Rafe to convince you of the virtues of a nice gelding."

Ayisha smiled. "Yes, do, Rafe, convince me."

They bid farewell to Bertie Baxter and as the door closed behind them, Rafe said smoothly, "So I'm a stallion, eh?" His eyes gleamed at the thought.

She wrinkled her nose at him. "What makes you think I was talking about you?"

"Baggage," he said and tossed her over his shoulder. Ignoring her struggles, he took the stairs two at a time, heading for their bedroom.

"But I want to read my letters," she said between giggles.

"Yes, but we stallions are nasty, unpredictable brutes, and need to be mounted. Now."

She laughed. "Perhaps gelding might improve your temperament."

He didn't bother to answer. In minutes he had her flat on the bed, her skirts around her waist, and himself poised to enter her. "Still want to have me gelded?" he growled softly, his hands doing things to her that melted her insides.

"Mmm, no," she murmured happily as he slowly entered her. "I love you . . . just . . . the way . . . you are."

Later they lay exhausted, entwined and blissful.

"Thank you for bringing me out of Egypt," Ayisha murmured after a while. "Laila once told me I was living a half life there, and I didn't believe her. But now I know . . . You've given me so much—love, a home, and a family—more than I ever thought possible."

"And you, my love, have brought me home after years of being outside, and that I thought was impossible."

He stroked the silken skin of her stomach. "Little did I think, that night in your father's house, having set a trap for you with Ali and that picture, waiting to catch a thief, that I would catch instead—"

"A bride?"

He turned his head and gazed into her lovely eyes. "More than a bride. I caught the love of my life."

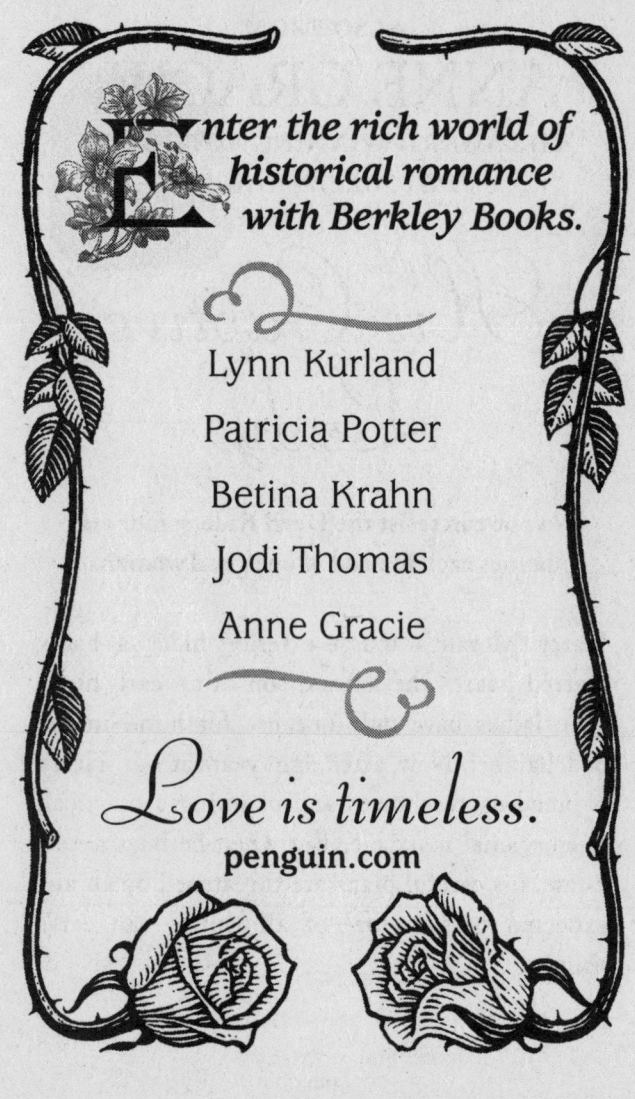

Enter the rich world of historical romance with Berkley Books.

Lynn Kurland

Patricia Potter

Betina Krahn

Jodi Thomas

Anne Gracie

Love is timeless.
penguin.com

M9G0907

Discover Romance

berkleyjoveauthors.com
See what's coming
up next from your
favorite romance
authors and
explore all
the latest
Berkley,
Jove, and
Sensation
selections.

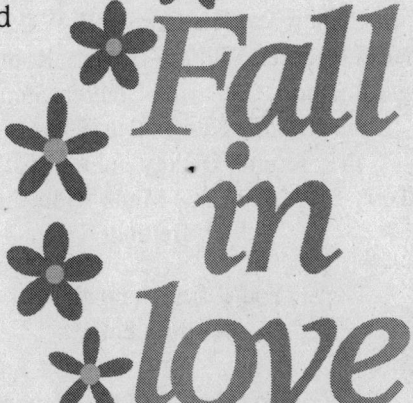

Fall in love

- See what's new
- Find author appearances
- Win fantastic prizes
- Get reading recommendations
- Chat with authors and other fans
- Read interviews with authors you love

berkleyjoveauthors.com

M1G0907